Dedication

*To my editor, Natalie, who consistently demonstrates her own passion
to get the story right, and in doing so gives freely of her
time and effort to make me look better.*

DANIEL ELLER

In The Heat of Passion

ISBN: 9780980108118

Printed in the United States of America.

Published by
Hollyhock Publishing, LLC
13865 Hollyhock Road
Cold Spring, MN 56320
www.hollyhockpublishing.com

"The ruling passion, be it what it will, the ruling passion conquers reason still."

-Alexander Pope (1688 - 1744)

PROLOGUE

October 7th, 1994
Hamlet Lake
Sherburne County, Minnesota

I bet I'm the only ten-year-old who has ever gotten to sit all alone on the front seat of a Chevy corvette. Grabbing the steering wheel with both hands, I pretend I'm at the race track. I hear the roar of the engine and see the car gliding around curves, responding to my slightest touch.

I have a hard time seeing over the steering wheel so I get up on my knees. It's starting to get dark. It's been misting and the windshield looks foggy to me. The lights from the houses across the lake sparkle off the water. They bounce off the hood of the shiny red corvette, through the raindrops on the window. It reminds me of a kaleidoscope, just like the one I saw at the Science Museum. I sit and stare, wrapped up in my imagination. This is the first time Vince has ever let me sit in his car by myself. This is as exciting as it gets.

The blast actually shakes the car. At least I thought I felt something. My hands freeze to the steering wheel; I turn my head trying to figure out what it was. I know the sound; it's the blast of a gun, a big gun, like the one Vince has in the house. I listen... nothing. Nothing but my heart. I see a movement out of the corner of my eye; I quickly turn. It's Vince, coming from the deck, running toward the car. He looks in the window. My gosh, I think to myself, what's wrong with him? He looks scared; he's bug-eyed. Then he disappears as fast as he came. I watch for my mom, she should be coming. I'm scared. I want to get out of here.

I sit staring at the edge of the garage waiting for my mom to come around the corner, my fingers still glued to the steering wheel. A light goes on. Now I can see part of the deck clearly, the outline of the edge of the garage. There's a shadow, just one, it's there and then disappears. I stare like that for the longest time. Afraid to move.

It seems at first like a whining noise from far away. I wonder what it is. Then it gets closer and I know. A siren. More than one siren. Only minutes later, through the rearview mirror, I see the lights coming down the long driveway, spinning, reds, whites, and blues. The lights shoot right past me to the edge of the deck. The first person out looks like a cop. He's in some kind of uniform, anyway. Right behind him come two guys wearing white. They come from a red and white ambulance. I know something terrible has happened.

My hands come off the steering wheel. I crawl over to the other seat to get a better look out the side window. Another police car pulls in. The cops stand on the edge of the deck, talking. The first cop who got there points toward the car, toward me. I crawl to the floor, put my head on the seat; I can't stop my hands from shaking. I feel warm tears running down my face onto the seat. I lift my head a little bit and wipe my eyes with my jacket sleeve. I close my eyes and put my hands over my ears, trying to shut out the world.

It doesn't work. I hear the footsteps across the driveway before the door opens. I don't know if they are coming for me or not. I don't look up. The door next to me opens and a deep voice says, "Young man, I'm Deputy Lentz. There's been a terrible accident. Your mother's been hurt. We've called your grandparents. If you could come with me, I'll take you to the neighbor's house until your grandfather gets here."

I don't know what he means. Terrible accident? Accidents happen in cars. How could there be an accident? I left my mother inside just a little while ago, talking to Vince. He told me to go wait in the car, he was going to drive us home. Where's she now? How could she have had an accident? I look at the cop. He holds out his hand. His voice is so calm, his look so safe, that I crawl out of the car and take his hand. He walks me up to the neighbor's house to wait for my grandpa.

chapter 1

CHIEF DEPUTY BOB Lentz was getting off duty after a long boring Saturday at the Sheriff's Office. As he opened the door to his squad car, he heard the dispatcher issuing directions to cars nine and twelve to go to the home of Vince Fischer on Hamlet Lake. There had been a shooting. Lentz had known Vince Fischer for twenty years or more. The dispatch caught him by surprise; Vince Fischer wasn't a name he would associate with a shooting. No thought of going home, he pulled out of the parking lot onto Highway 10, turned on the siren and floored it.

Minutes later, he turned onto the long driveway, past the lake homes, to the Fischer residence. Dark had just settled in. From a distance he could see the flashing lights of the patrol cars and the ambulance. As he neared the lights he slowed down, passed a red Corvette parked by the garage, and pulled beyond the ambulance and stopped. The deck light was on and he could see two paramedics working frantically on the body of a young woman lying flat on the deck. There was a deputy off to the side watching.

Lentz walked onto the deck, stood above the paramedics, and looked at the deputy. "What's the story?" he asked.

"I was the first one here," the deputy replied. "Charlie was right behind me. When we got here, this guy's leaning over the body, screaming, 'Donna, don't leave me, don't leave me!' We pulled him back...he said it was an accident."

Lentz's eyes settled on the young woman lying on the deck. She had long brown hair and big lifeless brown eyes. Both paramedics suddenly stopped working on her. They knelt, one on each side, motionless, staring at her face. One looked up at Lentz. "She's gone," he said. The other leaned over the body and put his hand over her face to close her eyes. Lentz froze, speechless for a moment.

A deputy broke the silence. "The guy's inside talking to Charlie. There's a young boy in the Corvette, the guy says it's her son. He gave us the number of the grandparents. We called and his grandpa's on his way. The neighbor's been over." The deputy motioned to the house up the hill. "He said we can bring the boy over there until somebody picks him up."

"Charlie's inside with Mr. Fischer?" asked Lentz.

"Yeah, they're in the kitchen."

Lentz walked through the breezeway, to the kitchen door, and looked in through the window. Vince Fischer was sitting at the kitchen table, his head in his hands, his body shaking with sobs. The deputy was standing close by. He noticed Lentz in the window and silently acknowledged him.

Lentz walked back to the red Corvette. He didn't see anybody in the car. He looked through the side window and saw a young boy on the floor, his head on the seat and his arms over his ears, as if he was trying to close out the world. Lentz opened the door and the boy jumped.

"Young man," Lentz said, "I'm Deputy Sheriff Lentz. There's been a terrible accident. Your mother's been hurt. We've called your grandparents. If you would come with me, I'll take you to the neighbor's house until your grandfather gets here."

The boy looked at him for a moment and then crawled out. He took Lentz's hand and they walked up the driveway.

As Deputy Lentz walked down the hill, back to Vince's house, he saw the coroner's car pull in. There was a fog settling in, touching the tree tops. The rays from the yard lights filtered through the branches, casting shadows into the sky. All of the lights from the patrol cars and the ambulance were still spinning, creating a carnival atmosphere.

Lentz had not been here since Vince had first built the

house. Its outline appeared in the flood of lights with alternating colors bouncing off the windows. It was a huge A-frame of logs and fieldstone, with wings off each end. The lights were on inside and he could see the vaulted ceiling of the main room, logs and knotty pine, with a balcony along one side.

By the time Lentz got back to the deck, the young woman's body was on a stretcher, covered with a white sheet.

"What happened to Olson?" he asked.

"He was looking at the body," replied one of the paramedics, "when the deputy came out and said that he thought the guy was having a heart attack, he was hyperventilating, so he's in with them. There's nothing he can do here. He told us to take the body to the hospital."

Lentz watched as the paramedics loaded the victim into the ambulance. The sheet had been strapped down and he was surprised at how small the body looked. He guessed maybe 5'2" or so. As they closed the door to the ambulance, he turned to go into the house. He saw the shotgun lying on the deck and quickly turned around. "Hey Pete, has anybody touched this shotgun?"

"I don't think so."

"Well make sure nobody does until everything's photographed!"

"You bet."

Lentz walked through the breezeway and went in the kitchen door. He was looking for the coroner, Dr. Olson, and as he entered the kitchen area he found him taking Vince's blood pressure. He stayed back, looking slowly around the home. It still had that new smell, all the stains and varnishes covering the logs and knotty pine. Except for a little mess on the table, the kitchen looked unused. He could see the main room, the great room, with a fieldstone fireplace that had to be twenty feet high and an exposed beam ceiling. He couldn't help but stare; then he shook his head as if awakening from a daydream.

Lentz felt a tug on his sleeve and Dr. Olson said, "I want to talk to you outside." The two walked through the breezeway, past the shotgun, past the standing deputy on guard, close to the red

Corvette.

"Her name is Donna Woods," said Olson. "A single twelve gauge shotgun wound to the back. From what I can see, it literally tore her apart inside. She died pretty quick. Looked like a pretty lady. While I was helping wrap the body, one of the deputies told me that Vince needed some help. He was hyperventilating and complaining of chest pains. That's why I was doing the blood pressure. The whole time he just kept saying it was an accident, the gun went off accidentally. He said he loved her, that they were going to get married. He just rambled on. He didn't make a whole lot of sense. The reason I wanted to talk to you out here, though, his physical signs don't correspond with the way he's acting. It's strange, there's something wrong."

Lentz said, "I've called the sheriff and the county attorney, they should be here shortly. Can you wait until they get here? They'll wanna talk this over."

"I can't. I have to get to the hospital. I'll send you my report."

When Lentz walked back into the kitchen, Vince looked up.

"Bob! Am I glad to see you! I can't believe this is happening, they're telling me she's dead. It was an accident. I was putting the gun away and it went off. I can't believe it…I can't believe it." He dropped his head and covered his face with his hands.

Lentz looked at Vince. He hadn't seen him for a number of years. When he had walked in earlier and Vince was talking to Dr. Olson, Bob simply hadn't paid much attention. Now he tried to make some assessment. Vince didn't look the same. His hairline had receded further, leaving just a ring over his ears. Sitting there, bent over as if in pain, he looked small. He looked like a little old man. For some reason Lentz thought of a monk.

"Just take it easy, Vince," Bob said. "The doctor said you have to take it easy. I called the sheriff and he said he's gonna get a hold of the county attorney; I expect them here any minute. We'll get a chance to talk as soon as they're here."

Bob surprised himself by his comment. Had a rookie said something like that, he would've jumped down his throat. First rule of investigation: when somebody wants to talk, you get the

4

statement. But this was different. Vince had already told everybody there what had happened. Things aren't going to change, he thought. It could've been an accident.

Vince sat with his face in his hands. Bob couldn't tell whether he was crying. He saw no tears. Looking around, he saw nothing out of the ordinary. Some empty beer cans on the counter. Suddenly something caught his eye. On a curio cabinet filled with expensive trinkets there was some money just lying there; crumbled up bills.

"Hey, Bob!"

Bob turned around and saw Scott Larson, the county attorney. The sheriff stood by his side.

"Sorry to have to bother you guys on a Saturday evening," said Bob, "but…" His words trailed off as he looked back at Vince.

The county attorney followed his gaze. Vince remained at the kitchen table, his hands over his face, crunched together, and his body shaking slightly. The county attorney motioned for Bob to follow him outside. As the three reached the breezeway, the sheriff said, "We've gotten notice from dispatch that the woman is dead. I talked to Dr. Olson by phone and because of the circumstances, he's recommending we have the body taken to the Hennepin County Medical Examiner's Office for an autopsy. What can ya tell me?"

"Vince wants to talk," Bob said. "He's been trying to tell me what happened. He told the ambulance drivers, the deputy who's with him. Under the circumstances, I thought I would wait until the two of you got here so we could talk to him together. From what I gather, this was a girlfriend of his, Donna Woods. He says the shooting was accidental. That's where I left it. When I got here, there was a young boy on the front seat of the Corvette in the driveway. Her son, probably ten or eleven. I took him over to the neighbors and they're waiting for his grandfather to arrive."

The county attorney looked at Bob and shrugged his shoulders. "I've known Vince for years. I know he had a rocky start, but as far as I know he turned all that around. Other than some minor traffic problems, I haven't seen his name on my desk

5

for anything. I guess we may as well go in and see what he has to say."

As they approached Vince, he raised his head. His face was flushed, his eyes red, but there were no tears. The sheriff led the questioning.

"I know this is difficult for you, Vince, but we have to know what happened."

"She was my fiancée—we were gonna get married. She had car problems; she brought her car out here. I was gonna have my mechanic fix it. We spent the day here, she and Troy, her son. Where is Troy?"

"He's with your neighbors waiting for his grandfather," Bob said.

"Does he know what happened?" asked Vince.

"No, I didn't tell him. I just told him his mother was hurt," Bob replied.

"This has to be terrible for him," Vince said. "He came with his mother. We had a good time, she was gonna take the Corvette, he was waiting for her. I let him go out and sit in it. He liked to do that. They came this morning. She brought her Ford, it had a puncture in the oil pan and she didn't know it, the engine was shot. We put it in the garage. The mechanic agreed to put in the new engine I picked up. We sat around, talked and had a good time. We had a few beers. She was gonna take the Corvette and we planned to meet in town for dinner at Anton's at 8:30. I've been having trouble with squirrels in my yard, on the birdfeeders. So this morning, before Donna and Troy arrived, I'd taken the shotgun out and I shot a couple of 'em. I leaned the shotgun against the garage by the breezeway so if I saw any more, I could grab it quick and shoot."

Vince had gained some composure. Now he was sitting up, his hands clasped tightly on the edges of his chair—white knuckled.

"As I said," he continued, "we had made plans to meet and as I was walking her to the car, it was misting, and I noticed the shotgun was getting wet. As I stopped to pick up the gun, Donna got a few steps ahead of me. I picked the gun up and the next thing I know, the gun just discharged. I didn't have my finger on the trigger or anything. I knew the shot hit her. God, it was an awful sound. I dropped the gun, I ran to her side, I could hear a gurgling sound, and I was just in a panic. I just hollered, 'Donna! Donna! Stay with me, stay with me.' I ran to see where Troy was, I could see his shadow in the car. I ran in the house and called 911. By the time I got back to Donna, her eyes were blank. I could tell she wasn't gonna make it. I didn't know what to do; I was in a state of shock. How could this be happening? We had such a good time. We were gonna get married. Then I heard the sirens; it seemed like hours but I'm sure it was just minutes. I told the paramedics what happened." His speech was racing. As he finished, he let out a deep sigh, allowing his body to sink back into the chair.

"Vince, I don't understand," said the sheriff. "Why would you leave a loaded gun leaning up against the house all day, especially when you had a young boy running around?"

Vince sat up. "I don't remember leaving it there loaded. I can't imagine how I did that. I can't imagine I would've been that dumb. I've had nothing but problems with squirrels chewing up my birdfeeders and digging up the flower beds, and I just wanted to get rid of 'em. I shot a couple this morning. I leaned the gun against the garage and forgot about it."

"Where did you shoot the squirrels, Vince?" asked the sheriff.

"Down by the shore, by the big oak trees."

"What did you do with them?"

"I threw 'em in the lake."

"What do you mean, you threw 'em in the lake?" asked the sheriff.

"Well—just that. I didn't know what to do with the carcasses so I just threw 'em out into the lake as far as I could."

"What time was that?"

"Early. Early this morning, probably around seven-thirty, eight o'clock."

"Was there anybody else here?"

"Yeah, John was here," said Vince. "He'd spent the night; he was on his way to pick up his girlfriend. I think they were going sightseeing up by Lake Superior. The colors were supposed to be the best this weekend."

"Did you talk to him before he left?"

"I believe I did," said Vince. "I believe I told him that I shot a couple of squirrels. I remember him asking me what all the shootin' was about."

"What did you and Donna do today?" asked Bob.

"Like I told you, we talked about her car, how I'd get it fixed. We had a few beers. I made Troy a peanut butter sandwich. We had been having some problems and we talked it out. We kissed and made up, that's why I sent Troy out to the car. The last time I kissed her, things got a little out of hand, if you know what I mean, and she didn't want Troy to witness something that may be a little embarrassing. So she told him that we were gonna talk for a while and then she would drive him home and we'd go for dinner. She was happy. We were both happy."

"Vince, I know it happened quickly," said the sheriff, "but do you remember whether your finger may have touched the trigger when you picked it up?"

"I don't see how it could've, I was just gonna take it with me and put it inside."

"Vince," asked the sheriff, "where was it exactly when it discharged? Had you picked the gun up to your shoulder or how were you carrying it?"

"It was loose at my side," Vince indicated, showing the sheriff where it would have been under his armpit. "I was carrying it right here."

"What happened to the gun after it fired?" asked Bob.

"I don't know," said Vince. "I think," and he paused, "I don't remember, but I think, I think I put it down by her side when I ran to help her. You know, guys, can't we do this some other time? I've just been through one hell of an experience, my mind isn't working right. I can't—I don't remember how it all happened, give me some time and let me think. All I can tell you, I would've never done this on purpose. I couldn't have. I loved her too much. We had too much going for us. It was just a terrible, terrible accident."

"Sheriff, Mr. Williams is here, he wants to pick up Troy," the deputy said from the door.

Vince jumped up. "I have to talk to him; I have to explain what happened."

"He said he doesn't wanna see you," the deputy replied. "He just wants to pick up Troy and, as he put it, 'Get the hell out of here'."

"Well, he can't believe I did this on purpose, he can't believe I would've harmed Donna. There's just no way in hell I would've done that."

"Relax, Vince," said the sheriff. "I'll talk to him."

"I don't understand; we've always gotten along. I can't believe he would think I could harm his daughter."

The sheriff walked out through the breezeway. Mr. Williams was leaning against the house, his head down. The sheriff knew him only by reputation. Mr. Williams acknowledged him with a nod.

"I'm really sorry, Mr. Williams," said the sheriff. "They've taken your daughter's body to the hospital. We've taken a statement from Vince; he said it was an accident. We don't know. At this point, we have no reason not to believe him."

"Accident! The deputy told me about the accident. What the Christ is a loaded shotgun doing on the damn deck in the first place? Accident, my ass. She wanted nothing more to do with him, his ego wouldn't take that."

"Well, I understand your feelings," said the sheriff. "The matter will be fully investigated. We'll have a deputy get in contact with you and if you have a statement to make, we'll need you to be as candid as possible."

"You bet your ass I will. Where's my grandson?"

The sheriff was a little taken a back. The language didn't seem to quite fit the persona. He brushed it off as grief.

The sheriff went back in the house. Vince was still mumbling about how it had been an accident. Deputy Lentz and the county attorney were doing a slow perusal of the house. As the sheriff walked up to the two of them, Deputy Lentz said, "I want to show you guys something. Let's go back into the kitchen." He quietly motioned to both of them to look at the curio cabinet. There on top, still undisturbed, were the crumpled up bills.

"Vince," said Deputy Lentz, "we're gonna have to take photographs and we want to make sure that the scene is undisturbed overnight. Is there somewhere you can go?"

"Sure, no problem," replied Vince. "I'll go stay at the Radisson."

"We would also like to have you come in tomorrow morning, Vince," said Bob, "and have you give us a recorded statement. Is there any problem with that?"

"I don't know why there should be," replied Vince. "I can call you at the Sheriff's Office in the morning and we can set up a time to get together. I would like to try and meet with the family…I hope they'll talk to me. I'll go pack a few things."

"Bring the clothes you're wearing back down," said the sheriff. "We'll need 'em."

The three of them stood quietly and watched Vince leave the room. Once he was out of sight, their eyes met, as if the same thought had crossed all of their minds—something's wrong.

For all the commotion earlier, Lentz thought it to be surprisingly quiet now. The fog had settled into the trees and with the yard lights the branches looked like gnarled fingers reaching for the sky.

Scott broke the silence. "There's a stink to the whole story. I don't understand how you leave a loaded gun sitting outside all day when you have a ten-year-old boy playing in the yard. I don't understand how a gun goes off accidentally, just happens to hit this lady five feet or so in front of you in the middle of the back. But you guys know Vince as well as I do. Why would a guy with all of this going for him kill a woman he was involved with? It just doesn't make sense. With his dough, he could probably have any woman he wants. I certainly would've never expected he was capable of doing anything like this."

"All of that may be true," said Bob. "But like you, I have a real uneasy feeling about this. I'll tell ya one thing that really bothers me—it's those crumpled up bills on the cabinet. If I was seeing right, they were hundred dollar bills. What are three one-hundred dollar bills doing on the cabinet in the kitchen, all crushed up? It just seems to me that it has some significance to what happened tonight."

"Bob, you were here when Chuck finished his examination of the body," said the sheriff. "What did he have to say?"

"Not much, really. Shotgun blast to the back, tore her up inside; she probably died instantly. He couldn't tell me any specifics—that will come from the Medical Examiner's Office."

"Well guys," said Scott, "there isn't much more we can do here tonight. We really won't be able to do anything until Dr. Michaels finishes his autopsy. Based on what I've seen here tonight, I'm certainly not ready to file any complaint, or try and convene a grand jury. If this was murder, this guy won't be any pushover. He's got money; he's got prestige, some standing in the community. I for one," he sighed, "don't intend to get my ass kicked by some big buck attorney out of the Twin Cities."

chapter 2

MATT COLLINS WAS sitting at his desk on a Monday morning, having his first cup of coffee. He looked without enthusiasm at all of the papers on his desk. He had gone through a terrible weekend and there was nothing in the piles of crap on his desk that was going to make him feel any better.

"God, you look terrible." His assistant, Kay, had walked in and he hadn't even noticed. "What happened to you over the weekend?"

"I had a big fight with Virginia Friday night. She wants to know where her payments are. She wants to start her own business. I told her things are slow, but she didn't believe me. By Saturday morning, I was so depressed I took my camera and sat in the woods all weekend, so I didn't have to talk to another human being. Pissed away two days—didn't even get any good pictures. Maybe you can call her—she'd probably believe you."

"No thanks," she replied as she turned to leave. "I'm not going to get in the middle of anything."

Matt had over twenty years experience as a trial lawyer. He did a little bit of everything. His expertise, when he was asked, was in criminal law. Over the years he had garnered a very respectable reputation in central Minnesota. He had handled some criminal cases with considerable notoriety and, much to his surprise, had experienced rather considerable success. It wasn't the type of law one could get rich on, however, not in rural Minnesota. Either he had been appointed by the court as a public defender or, when he was hired, it was by somebody who could scratch up a few bucks for his defense.

After twenty-three years of marriage, he and his wife had recently divorced. Nothing drastic happened, but when his son moved out to go to college two years earlier, he and Virginia just grew apart, quickly. When she finally asked for a divorce, he didn't want to fight over anything. After splitting the little they had acquired, he agreed to keep their son and daughter in college, pay their tuition, and pay her alimony until she could get on her feet. Sounded good at the time—he had struggled to make ends meet ever since.

As he pondered which pile on his desk to delve into, his receptionist, Melanie, broke the silence. "Matt, Peter Maxwell is on line two for you."

Matt sat up in his chair. What could Peter Maxwell want? Matt hadn't talked to him for years. He picked up the phone. "Hello?"

"Matt, Peter Maxwell. How ya doing?"

"Good, good," said Matt. "It's been a while."

"Too busy, I guess," replied Peter. "The reason I'm calling, did you read the paper over the weekend?"

"To tell you the truth, Peter, I didn't." Matt felt obligated to tell him why, but Peter never gave him the chance.

"Well, the Sherburne County Grand Jury has returned an indictment of first degree murder against my client, Vince Fischer."

"You're kidding," replied Matt, truly surprised. "That's on the death of that Woods girl; that happened close to a year ago. You mean they're just getting around to submitting that to a grand jury now? What happened?"

"That's what we're wondering," replied Peter. "Vince has been cooperative throughout the whole thing. He gave a statement to the police right after it occurred; he gave them another recorded statement within days. We thought the matter had been resolved and nothing further was going to happen. Then, several weeks ago, there were some rumors that the grand jury would be considering her death. I had Vince in the office and we concluded that maybe the county attorney was just trying to cover his ass, satisfy the family, you know. We certainly didn't expect any indictment."

"What can I do for you?" asked Matt.

"I was hoping you'd have a few minutes to run over to my office; there's something I'd like to discuss with you."

"Sure," said Matt. "If you have time, I can come right now."

It took several minutes to walk to the bank building where Peter had his office. On the way, Matt speculated about the purpose of the call. Undoubtedly, he thought, Peter wanted a recommendation on a criminal defense attorney out of the Twin Cities. Why hadn't he just asked that over the phone?

Peter Maxwell was the senior partner in the biggest law firm in St. Cloud; not senior in years, but senior in position: it was his firm. Maxwell, Dunin and Moore handled just civil matters, specializing in commercial and business law. The firm had twenty-two lawyers. Peter was known as the "deal maker," the one you'd call if you were trying to buy or sell a business. Peter and Matt came to town fresh from law school the same year, but they went different directions. Peter was still single. People assumed he was too busy building his clientele and law firm to worry about a family. Tall, with black wavy hair, he was quite handsome and was considered by many the most eligible bachelor in town. However, because he was seldom seen with a female companion, somebody, probably from one of the other firms, started the rumor that maybe he was gay.

The Maxwell firm was on the top floor of the tallest bank building in town. In St. Cloud that was only seven floors, but it still carried a little prestige to overlook everyone else in town. Another rumor was that when the building was being built, Peter required the bank to go one story more than the other bank building, also occupied by a law firm, so that no one could say they looked down at his office.

Matt stepped off the elevator into a plush lobby.

"I'm here to see Peter Maxwell," he said to the smiling receptionist.

"Is he expecting you?"

"I'm Matt Collins; I just spoke with him on the phone."

"Oh, of course! Please follow me, Mr. Collins."

As he followed her down the hall, he glanced to the side to see the attorneys, busy in their offices. No sloppy desks here—everything in its place. Lawyers, paralegals, secretaries on the move, the hum of activity. He was lead into the conference room and offered a seat at a large table. He sat down and stared at his reflection in the polished veneer.

The receptionist stopped at the door. "Would you care for a cup of coffee?" she asked.

"Yes, please."

While he waited, Matt took in the panoramic view of the city. He was always amazed at what had happened to the city in the twenty years since he came back from law school. The whole landscape had changed. A lot of the old landmarks were gone, replaced by new glass-fronted buildings. The one constant he could see was St. Mary's Cathedral, with its bell tower visible for miles. Within minutes, the door opened again. In walked Peter Maxwell with a tray filled with a coffee pot, a glass of orange juice, and several sweet rolls.

"We don't usually have all of this available," he said, "but we had a business meeting this morning and it's left over." As he poured Matt coffee, he glanced across the shiny table. "I want to talk to you about Mr. Fischer's case."

"Well, I'm not sure how much more I can tell you. I've dealt with Scott Larson, the Sherburne County Attorney, many times. You know as well as I do he has a tremendous reputation; he's been around forever, and he's a great trial attorney. He's not gonna be a pushover. If he's taking it this far, your man's in trouble."

"That's the point, Matt, he's not my man. Vince has been a business client of mine for over twenty years. To be honest, he's been one of my *best* clients. Vince has made a lot of money, and he's made *us* a lot of money. But we don't have any criminal attorneys and he wants me to find him a criminal attorney."

"That shouldn't be a problem," replied Matt. "He can

certainly afford to hire any criminal attorney he wants."

"But we want you," replied Peter.

Matt was so surprised he choked on his coffee before sinking back deeply into the plush chair. He couldn't believe what he was hearing. His first thought was that Peter was kidding. Why would the big shot in town ask him to represent one of his rich clients?

"Well, I wasn't expecting that," said Matt, regaining some composure. "Why me?"

"Several reasons," replied Peter. "I gather from your response you don't have the same impression of your lawyerly skills that is prevalent in the community. I'll tell you the truth. When we learned of the indictment on Saturday morning, I spent the rest of the weekend talking to every trial judge I know, asking them about criminal defense attorneys. Other than the crap I see in the paper, I don't come across criminal attorneys very often. I'm familiar enough with how reputations are gained that I don't believe everything I hear unless I trust the source. In talking to the judges your name kept popping up. I was told that based on their experience with you, they believe you are as good as any criminal defense attorney in the state. They say you come prepared, you know your case and how to try it. And, just as importantly, you can be a gentleman through the process. These are people I know and trust. So I take their comments seriously."

Peter stood up, walked to the window and paused, as if to gather his thoughts. Matt sat there, quietly, feeling a little warm under the collar.

"That's the first reason. Secondly, Vince is rather well known in this area. I don't believe he would've intentionally shot this young lady. I think most of the people who know him as well as I do believe the same thing. He needs a hometown attorney to defend him. He needs somebody who will handle this case like a gentleman. We don't want a hired gun, Matt. We don't want to bring in any Paladin from out of town and create the impression that he's trying to buy his way out of this. Remember Paladin, Matt? 'Have gun, will travel'?"

They both laughed.

"Then, I have a very selfish reason. Every big law firm in Minneapolis and St. Paul tries to hustle our clients. I know there've made overtures to Vince over the years. I don't want to lose him. If he ends up with one of the big name criminal defense attorneys from the cities, I risk losing Vince to one of the attorney's friends or associates. Anyway, you and I both know that this mentality that all of the good attorneys are in the Twin Cities is just bullshit."

Matt remained motionless. His reputation was for being quiet. Now, for the moment, he found himself speechless. Not a good posture for a trial attorney. But Peter's comments took a few minutes to sink in.

"Well, I certainly appreciate the consideration. What does Mr. Fischer say? How do you know he would be satisfied with me?"

"He'll listen to me," replied Peter. "I've already told him pretty much the same concerns. He agrees."

Matt considered this for just a moment before saying, "I'll take it."

"I also know," said Peter, nodding, "that some of your best work has gone unrewarded, financially that is. That wouldn't be the case here. You pretty much have a blank check for whatever you'd need."

"That'll be different," replied Matt, somewhat embarrassed. "What I would like to do is set up a time to meet with Vince. I can contact the prosecutor's office and tell 'em Vince is going to be my client and there's no need to send out a warrant. We'll appear voluntarily."

Peter looked at him, a smile crossed his face. "I've already done that."

"You mean you've told the prosecutor that I'll be representing Mr. Fischer?" asked Matt. "How'd you know I'd take it?"

Peter just widened his grin. "Vince is not scheduled to make a court appearance until next Friday. I'll have him at your office tomorrow morning at 10:00."

"Thanks for the recommendation," said Matt. "I'll do a good job."

"I know you will," replied Peter. "I told Vince I have complete confidence in you.

As Matt walked back to his office, Peter's words echoed in his head: *But we want you!* He was surprised. But he also knew it was common for St. Cloud attorneys, particularly the few bigger firms, to be paranoid about lawyers from Minneapolis and St. Paul. Being only sixty miles away, they had just recently started to hustle St. Cloud clients, especially the wealthy business clients and personal injury cases. Full page ads in the yellow pages were common, along with local T.V. and newspaper ads. Once in a while, the glitz paid off. Matt knew of local businessmen, including some of his clients, who once they were successful, decided they needed some prestigious law firm from the big city. What Peter told him made sense: *Don't risk losing your biggest client.*

Matt walked into his office with a little bit more bounce to his step than when he left. Kay noticed it immediately. "What's that smile for?" she asked.

"You'll never believe what just happened," he replied. "Are you familiar with the Vince Fischer case?"

"Sure," said Kay. "It's been in the paper and on every news broadcast over the weekend. He's been indicted for the murder of his girlfriend."

"Alleged murder," said Matt. "Alleged murder. They want me to represent him."

"You're kidding," she replied. "Are you gonna to do it?"

"What do you mean—am I going to do it? For twenty years I have been doing this stuff for practically nothing. I've got the first chance to make a few bucks on a case, damn right I'm gonna do it! This is a defense attorney's dream; it's got everything a good case should have. It'll probably have statewide coverage and, if my luck holds out, I could get this guy off."

"Luck?" she replied. "Luck has nothing to do with it!"

Matt smiled. "Where's Tim?" he asked.

"I don't know. I haven't seen him today."

"As soon as you see him, tell him I have to talk to him. I want him to go over to the law library and find all the newspaper articles he can from last year about the shooting. I'd like to be able

19

to read them tonight so when Vince comes in tomorrow I don't seem like a total idiot. Peter Maxwell had a hard time believing I hadn't heard about the indictment. I couldn't tell him I sat in the woods all weekend with my camera, and the last thing I needed to do was read a paper or turn on the news."

She grinned and said, "Very true." His office walls were covered with pictures of deer, ducks, loons, assorted wildlife. The product of all of those wasted hours in the woods.

chapter 3

MATT GOT TO work early the next morning. He had taken all of the newspaper articles home the night before, hoping to gain some insight into the case and Vince Fischer. He didn't learn much. It had happened on Saturday, October 7th, 1994, just about a year earlier. Donna was thirty-six years of age, twelve years younger than Vince. She was divorced and had custody of her two children, Troy, age ten, and Lisa, age fourteen. Troy was there when his mother was killed but apparently hadn't seen anything. Death was caused by a shotgun blast to the back. The balance of the articles generally talked about Vince and his company and his position in the community. Other than what he had read, Matt knew little about him. Matt grew apprehensive. What if Fischer didn't like him? What if he decided to get one of those Armani-suit attorneys from the Twin Cities? It would take a while for his ego to recover.

"Matt," Melanie said over the intercom, "Mr. Fischer is here."

"I'll be out in a second." Matt got up, walked back to the bathroom and looked in the mirror. Everything in order, tie straight, hair in place. He wondered if he looked like a big time defense attorney. There wasn't much he could do now. He closed the door and made the walk to the reception area. There sat Vince Fischer. Not a giant at all. Rather, a little man in jeans and a vest. Matt was surprised. This didn't look like a captain of industry. This didn't look like the kind of guy who would be having an affair with a 36-year-old woman who, from everything Matt had been able to learn, was a very attractive lady.

"Mr. Fischer. Hi. Matt Collins. I'm glad to meet you. I wish it could be under different circumstances," Matt said.

"*You* wish," Vince replied. "You can't imagine how much I wish I wasn't here."

"Come on back," Matt said.

After they had settled in, Matt looked at him and said, "Well, Peter Maxwell has pretty much filled me in on how you got to my office. To be honest with you, the only thing I know about this case is what I've read in the paper. It's my understanding that you gave the Sheriff's Office a complete taped statement. Do you have a copy of that?"

"I don't remember what I did with it," said Vince. "It was close to a year ago when I received it and because nothing happened for a long time, it may have been discarded. I just don't remember. In fact, I forgot all about it until you just mentioned it."

"I know you told 'em it was an accident, that the gun discharged accidentally. Maybe you can just go through that briefly. To be honest, Mr. Fischer, I view this meeting as just an opportunity for each of us to get to meet the other, to gauge whether we believe we can work together and then make some commitment for the future. We'll have a chance to go through everything more thoroughly later, after I get the police reports, the grand jury transcripts. Whatever the prosecutor might have."

"I understand," replied Vince. "I can give you a two minute summary."

"That'd be fine."

"I met Donna several years ago. The first time I saw her I couldn't believe it, what a knockout. I asked for a date, and honestly, I didn't expect she'd go out with me. I was thrilled when she said yes. That's how it started. I loved her children. Did you know she had two kids?"

"I read it in the newspaper."

"We did all kinds of things together. We went on trips. We had parties...picnics at the lake. Sometimes she would stay at the house for several days at a time. I even proposed to her on several occasions. She said she wasn't ready to make the commitment.

I loved her deeply. Then, several months before her death, something happened. She was busy, she couldn't come to see me, she couldn't stay for the weekend, or the kids had things to do. I knew something was happening. She told me she needed some space and I told her fine, we would separate for a while. So there was quite a while that I didn't talk to her, other than maybe an occasional phone call. But we didn't date; she didn't stay over at the house. We did not see each other at all. I was seeing other women at the time. I don't know if she had another boyfriend or not. But I certainly didn't get over her that quickly."

He paused for a moment, as if he wanted to gather his thoughts. Matt didn't feel compelled to interrupt. "And then in one of our conversations, she mentioned that she was having car trouble. I have to tell you, she didn't have much money. Even though her dad is well off, she didn't wanna ask him for anything. She had a very rocky marriage with somebody her father really didn't approve of. He was a drug dealer and an alcoholic and very abusive to Donna and the children. Her father had this 'I told you so' attitude, which didn't sit well with Donna. So she normally wouldn't ask him for any favors."

"Does her father live here in town?" asked Matt.

"Yeah, John Williams. You probably know him, he had an insurance agency."

"I've heard the name."

"In any event," Vince continued, "she told me she had car problems, that she'd hit a rock or something of that nature in the parking lot of a shopping center and it had apparently poked a hole in her oil pan. The oil had leaked out, she didn't know it, but that caused the motor to overheat and it had to be replaced. She had received an estimate of six, seven hundred dollars for the cost. I don't know if you know, Matt, but I'm sort of a car buff. I have a number of cars, including a 1969 Corvette that I am very proud of, and I consider myself a good mechanic. I also have a young man who works for me who can fix anything. So I told Donna that she should bring the car out to the lake, and that we would put it in the garage, I would buy her a new motor and I would have my mechanic fix it as soon as possible."

"Is that the reason she came to your house that Saturday morning?" asked Matt.

"Yes it is. She and Troy came out right before lunch and we had a chance to visit, and as the day progressed, we started to talk more seriously. There were times that we sent Troy out of the house to play in the yard so that she and I could talk about what had happened to our relationship and where we were going to go from there. I told her my feelings and I told her that I still wanted to get married. Quite frankly, she warmed up and we talked about our future and about the possibility of getting married. I had not been able to get her off of my mind. The thought was exciting. We kissed, old emotions were coming back, and I hadn't been close to her for months. I rubbed against her breasts, she had magnificent breasts."

Matt squirmed a little in his chair.

"Am I embarrassing you?" Vince asked.

"No. I'm not sure I really need to know all of this at this time," replied Matt, wondering why Vince felt compelled to tell him that part of the story. He felt like a voyeur.

Vince continued, "That's why I sent Troy out to the car, I could tell Donna was uneasy about what was happening in front of her son. I just told Troy to wait in the car and pretend he was a race track driver. After he left, we continued fooling around. I kinda had her up against the wall in the kitchen."

"Did you have intercourse?" Matt surprised himself by asking the question.

"No, not there, but that was our plan. She was getting a babysitter and we were going to Anton's for dinner and then she would spend the night with me at the lake. It was just about dark out. It had been misting. I was gonna walk her to the car; she was going to take the Corvette. After we left the breezeway, I noticed the shotgun leaning against the garage. I picked it up to take it with me and it just went off. The rest you know."

"This was all about a year ago, Mr. Fischer. You had no idea that the state was continuing in their investigation of this matter?"

"After I gave them the statement the day after Donna's death, I didn't hear back from anybody. It wasn't until March sometime that Bob Lentz contacted me at my office and said that he would like to come out to the home and do some videotaping. He said there were just a few things they had to finish up to close the case. I said, 'Fine, go ahead.' So he and half a dozen deputies came out on Good Friday, of all things. It was a beautiful warm day, the lake was still frozen. I remember Nikki was in the front yard with me. She was hitting golf balls out onto the lake and I would run out and retrieve them."

"Who's Nikki?" asked Matt.

"She's my wife," replied Vince.

"You've been married since this occurred?"

"Well, I got married just a couple of months ago but I had been going with Nikki since December. I met her at a business meeting in Montevideo. She was the bartender. I couldn't take my eyes off her. I had to spend a couple days in town, so the next day I asked her out for dinner, she accepted, and the rest is history. We got married this past August in Vegas."

The whole thing took Matt aback. He sat in his chair, no longer listening to Vince. It seems a little strange, he thought. How can you be involved in shooting your girlfriend in October, you know the matter is under investigation, but you meet another woman in December, she moves in and months later you marry her. The man doesn't waste time.

Vince continued to tell Matt what occurred when the deputies came to the house on Good Friday. "One of the deputies had a video camera and he videotaped the scene coming out of the breezeway to the deck where Donna's body had been. Then they asked me if I had a broom handle or some stick at least four or five feet long that they could use. I gave them one of the brooms from the garage. They had a female deputy stand where Donna had been standing and another deputy standing where the gun was located, then the deputy with the broomstick was putting it at different locations on his body: by his side, under the armpit, at his shoulder. The other deputy was videotaping the entire process. Bob and another deputy were just standing around. It probably took them about half an hour in all. They even took a couple video shots of Nikki hittin' golf balls."

"What do you mean?" asked Matt. "They were holding this broomstick like it may have been a gun?"

"That's how it appeared," said Vince.

"And one of the locations where a deputy placed it was on the shoulder where you would normally hold a gun to fire?" asked Matt.

"That's right."

"Didn't that seem to tell you something?"

"I told them what happened. I know where the gun was when it went off; I know it was accidental. If those jokers wanna come out and play around with broomsticks, that's up to them. I'm not gonna worry about it."

Matt needed time to think. "There's not much more we can accomplish now," he said. "I'll call the prosecutor and tell him that we'll be there next Friday morning and that I'll be representing you. I'll have Kay prepare our retainer agreement and get it over to Peter for his review."

"You don't have to send it to Peter. I'm a big boy. I can take care of myself. When you get it done and you want some money, just give me a call, I'll have my secretary pick it up." They shook hands and Vince left.

What a strange man, thought Matt. He knew this was going to be an interesting case and just hoped he'd be able to handle the client.

***

"Is he gonna hire you?" Kay asked when Matt got back to the office.

"Well, he said we should prepare a retainer agreement and he'll have his secretary pick it up and bring it back."

"What do you think we ought to fill in for the retainer?" she asked.

"I'm thinking twenty-five thousand. That should get us started. Maybe I can get Virginia off my back."

"Should help," said Kay. "A lot better than the fifteen hundred you're used to getting," she added with a sly grin.

"You really are a smartass," replied Matt.

Kay had been with Matt for fifteen years, right out of high school. When she first came to work for him, you couldn't ask her name without making her blush and look away. Now you couldn't get her to keep her mouth shut.

"Did I tell you that you look beautiful this morning?" Matt asked her.

Kay smiled. "Keep your mind on your business."

chapter 4

"WHAT DID YA think?" asked Nikki.

"I liked him. Peter was right, there's something about him that puts you at ease right away. Peter said jurors like him. That's why he's been successful. You know, Nikki, I am innocent. I didn't murder Donna and all I need is an attorney who can calmly and quietly convince a jury of that. I think Matt Collins is our man."

"Did you talk money?" asked Nikki.

"Well, Peter said it could cost up to a hundred thousand."

"Wow!" said Nikki. "A hundred thousand?"

"What do you expect?" asked Vince. "This is my goddamn life, you know. If I'm working, that's petty cash. Sitting in prison, I don't get squat. By the looks of it, that's probably the most money he's ever gonna make on one client. Compared to Peter's office, his was rather bleak. But I think he'll do fine."

"What does he look like?" Nikki asked.

"What's it to you?"

"Just curious. No big deal!"

"Well, he's tall, probably six one, six two, looks like he's in his early forties. Dressed nice. Looks like an attorney, I guess. According to Peter, he's got good credentials. Local boy, local college. Graduated from law school in D.C. He's been in town for over twenty years."

"I don't know," said Nikki. "I've never heard of him."

"Really, Nikki? How many St. Cloud attorneys are the subject of conversation in the bars of Montevideo?"

"That's a cheap shot," she replied. "I didn't deserve that."
"This is my life," Vince said. "I'll pick my attorney!"
She smiled.
"What's that for?" asked Vince.
"Oh, nothing."

chapter 5

"ALL RISE. THE District Court for the Tenth Judicial District is now in session, The Honorable Robert Thompson presiding," the bailiff shouted, "*The State of Minnesota v. Vince Fischer.*" Everybody knew this was the first case to be called. Matt and Vince had seated themselves at the counsel table. The prosecutor, Scott Larson, and his first assistant had done the same.

"Good morning, Your Honor," said Matt.

"Mr. Collins, you're here representing Mr. Fischer?"

"That's correct, Your Honor."

"And it's my understanding we're here on a first appearance on a grand jury indictment charging your client with first degree murder in the death of one Donna Woods. Is that correct?" Judge Thompson stared at Vince.

"That's correct," said the prosecutor.

"That's our understanding, Your Honor," said Matt. "We'll waive any reading of the rights, Your Honor, and I assume the prosecutor will provide me with copies of all the police reports so that we can waive the second appearance as well. The prosecutor and I have not had a chance to talk about this, but I would like to get a copy of the grand jury transcript and, unless he has some objection, I will prepare the necessary order."

"I have no objection, Your Honor," said Scott Larson.

"Well, then the only matter it seems we have to address," said the judge, "is the question of Mr. Fischer's release. Is there any request for bail?"

Daniel Eller

The prosecutor stood up in a laborious fashion, as if the weight of the world was on his shoulders. He was a huge man anyway and the way he lifted his body seemed to accent his size. He filled the counsel table. It seemed like Scott Larson had been the prosecutor in Sherburne County forever. Matt couldn't think of any other name ever associated with the position of county attorney. Larson was one of the few prosecutors in the state who was still allowed to have a private practice on the side. He had full-time assistants who handled the day-to-day court matters; he saved his time for important matters. Generally, that was on how the county was to run, attending board meetings, legislative sessions. But when any criminal case of notoriety came up, particularly one like this, possible murder, he was there. Based on a well-earned reputation as an excellent trial attorney, he was respected throughout the state. Moreover, he looked the part— large, stately, with a thick shock of gray hair. He also possessed a thunderous voice.

"As the court is aware," he began, "this is a case of first degree murder and even though Mr. Fischer is, as we know, a lifetime resident of this area and prominent business man, I believe the nature of the charges require that this court set some bail. I have no doubt that he will appear when necessary. But I think we set a bad precedent if we release him without any bail whatsoever."

Everything went as Matt expected. The judge set minimum bail at ten thousand dollars, in recognition of Vince's position and the fact that nothing had happened for over a year. The prosecution gave Matt a copy of the police reports, and the next court date was set. Matt and Vince stood in the hall for a short time. Matt had the entire file under his arm.

"Vince, I'll get you copies of this by tomorrow. I'll have Kay call. Now I'm gonna see if Deputy Lentz has a few minutes. I've known him a long time. Maybe I can pry something out of him."

***

Prior to joining the Sherburne County Sheriff's Office, Deputy Robert Lentz had been a detective with the police force in St. Cloud for twenty years or more. He was a big, likable guy

32

with an instant smile. He had earned a reputation as a good cop with a big heart. That had been easier to do twenty years ago when the most serious matters the police dealt with were minor consumption and truancy—maybe a theft here and there. The city had changed in twenty years. People blamed it on drugs, the disintegration of the family, the invasion of less desirables from bigger cities. Whatever the reason, twenty years ago, an armed robbery was a major event, now it was a common occurrence. Bob had survived the change. But the suspicion was that, given the number of serious crimes he had to handle on a weekly basis, he could no longer take the pressure of being a detective. He had left the city job to be with the Sherburne County Sheriff's Office, to be with the sheriff, an old friend, and what he believed to be a more relaxed atmosphere.

"Deputy Lentz, there's a Matt Collins here to see you," the receptionist called down the hall.

Bob heard the name and stood up with a big grin on his face. He liked Matt Collins. They'd been through many cases together and there was a mutual admiration and respect.

"Collins, you dipshit, how've you been?"

He grabbed Matt's hand and shook it vigorously as he motioned him into the cubbyhole he called his office.

"Between you and me, I was sure glad to see your name on this," he said. "We figured we'd see one of those pain in the ass guys from Minneapolis."

"Well," Matt replied, "I can be a pain in the ass too."

"Yeah, but at least you use Vaseline," Bob chuckled.

"I was hoping we could spend a little time talking about Vince's case," Matt said. "I assume you were the chief investigator."

"Actually I wasn't. I'm familiar with the case, but as far as doing most of the foot work—that was left to Deputy Kurt Weineke. I'm doing more administrative work these days. I had to get out of that shit. The doctor said it was killing me."

"It's killing us all," replied Matt.

"But I'd be glad to talk to you about Mr. Fischer," said Bob. "There's no deep secret here, you've got all the police reports, so

33

maybe we can get this resolved without a lot of hoopla. The short of it is we believe he murdered the lady. We don't know why, we don't know what happened that night to make him mad enough to do it, but we believe all of the evidence points to the fact that he took that gun and intentionally blew her away."

"How could you arrive at that?" asked Matt.

"I tell ya, we struggled with this for a long time. Everybody in the office knows Vince, or knows of him. Nobody wanted to believe it was murder. Even as things started to come in which tended to show otherwise, we had a tendency to discount them, or tended to give them some reasonable explanation. But, it got to the point where it was all sort of overwhelming and we decided we had to get in front of a grand jury."

"You got your indictment, now you have to prove it," said Matt.

"It's not gonna be as tough as you think," replied Bob. "Once you get a chance to go through that pile of discovery on your lap, you'll see what I mean. Let me tell ya, you've got your hands full. I can give you the case in a nutshell. First, let's look at the physical evidence. Dr. Michaels, the forensic pathologist, did a number of tests with that gun, the angle of entry. When you read the autopsy, you'll see what I mean. It's his opinion that the angle of entry of that shotgun blast into the body is approximately fifteen degrees. Given the height of your client and Ms. Woods, what that means is that the gun wasn't at his side as Vince claims, but at his shoulder where you would normally hold a gun to fire."

Matt thought back to his conversation with Vince. *If those jokers want to play around with broomsticks…*Matt knew it hadn't been an idle exercise.

"Secondly, the BCA did every test possible to try and get that gun to misfire, or to fire without having your finger on the trigger." Bob shrugged. "It just won't do it."

"Who did the tests?" asked Matt. "Bishop?"

"Yeah," replied Bob.

Eugene Bishop had been with the Bureau of Criminal Apprehension for many years. He had been a witness in several prior cases Matt had tried. Matt had always found him to be very competent and professional.

"And then you have motive," Bob continued. "It appears that Vince might've led two different lives. There's the one we're all familiar with, the business man, the civic figure. But were you aware that he had been married and divorced three times? And there were allegations of physical abuse in each of those marriages?"

"No, I wasn't," said Matt.

Bob nodded. "I didn't think so. Within days after Ms. Wood's death, this office received a letter from the third wife in which she outlines a history of being physically abused by Vince, including an incident shortly before their divorce when she was sure he was going to kill her. She gave us the name of his other wives. We've had a chance to talk to the second, but the first one is out of state and she won't respond to our letters. That's just the beginning. Vince claimed that he and Donna were talking about getting married shortly before she left that day and that as far as he was concerned, the relationship was back on. We've talked to her family. They all tell us there's no way in hell she was gonna marry him. They say that within the last months before her death, she had called on numerous occasions complaining about how he was constantly calling her and begging her to go out. He also called her girlfriends. It appears to us, Matt, that he was just obsessed with the young lady. So you put that all together and the grand jury obviously thought there was enough there for Vince to have to answer to the charges."

Lentz stopped for a second and looked through some papers on his desk. Locating a document, he held it up.

"When you read the autopsy, Matt, you're gonna find two interesting things. First, there was semen in her vagina and it had been there for more than a day, so it wasn't Vince's. And secondly, her blood alcohol concentration was .25, over twice the legal limit. Now Vince says they had only a couple of beers, but even if that lady was a pretty good drinker, at .25 she was bombed. There are a lot of things that have gone through my mind in this case,

Matt. When we have more time, we'll have to sit down and talk."

Matt had sat quietly, listening intently to Bob's recital. He knew him well enough to know he wasn't a bullshitter. He also knew there had to be more to this case than what Vince was saying, otherwise the prosecutor would've never brought it in front of a grand jury and a grand jury would have never indicted. I have a client, he thought, who is rich, a womanizer and an abuser. The question is whether that makes him a murderer. Not exactly what Matt expected.

chapter 6

MATT PULLED INTO his driveway. He was surprised to see his daughter Natalie's truck. She was in her last year of school at the University of Minnesota, and she hadn't called to say she was coming home. As he came around the garage, he saw her in the back yard, playing with the dog.

"This is a pleasant surprise," he said.

"Well, I had a long talk with Mom last night. She's a little pissed at you. About money."

She walked across the yard toward him, the dog jumping at her coat sleeve. She had cut her hair again, just above her ears. Blonde, blue eyed, he had forgotten how attractive she was. She gave him a big hug.

"My problems should be over," he said. "Since I talked to her I took on a big homicide case. I'll send money tomorrow."

"You know she's not like this, Dad. She's getting pressure to get the business started. I guess her landlord wants to be paid. So that should make her happy. I was about to take Brandy for a walk. Wanna come along?"

"Just what I need," he replied.

The two spent an hour in the woods, trying to pick out the prettiest maple tree in its fall colors. Every once in a while they could hear the honk of a Canada goose on the pond, or the whistle from the wings of a flock of mallards settling in for the evening. He told her about his big case. Her only comment was one of sympathy for Donna Woods and her children. She never did like the work he did—criminal law always seemed to be a sleazy way to make a living.

Later they ran into town for a quick pizza before Natalie had to get back to school. She had only come home to mend bridges. The divorce had been hard on her. She tried to keep both sides happy. So far she was doing a good job.

Matt went back into the empty house. Some nights it bothered him, but tonight it didn't. He had brought Vince's file home to read everything for the first time. He settled onto the couch with a stack of papers five inches thick in front of him, all the police reports generated by the investigation. He had purposely left them sit all day so he could review them at home without interruption. Matt paged through the papers, picking up a sentence here and there, looking for something out of the ordinary. He had done this hundreds of times before and he knew before it was over he would be going over each page, time and time again. At this point, he was trying to get the flavor of the case. In particular he was looking for two things: the report from the medical examiner and Bishop's report from the BCA.

His eye caught the coroner's name, Chuck Olson. Olson indicated that the paramedics reported they had found no pulse when they arrived, and that the victim had been lying on her back. The paramedics had opened the top buttons of her blouse as they were attempting to revive her and Olson had been able to see small contusions on her chest. He'd asked the paramedics to help him turn the body over. That was the first time he saw there was no blood on the deck. She had been wearing a leather jacket and there was a gaping hole in the back where the shot had entered. There had been obvious burn marks on the leather indicating that the shotgun had been quite close when fired. He had been able to see the hole it had made in her back. He'd helped put her on the stretcher.

After thumbing through several inches of paper, Matt spotted the heading, *Office of the Medical Examiner, Autopsy Report. Decedent, Donna Woods*. He had read many of these before. *The body was lying supine, fully clothed on the examination table*, the report stated. It went on to explain the clothing she was wearing and its condition. The leather jacket was removed. *One could appreciate,* the report said, *a defect in the back of the leather jacket approximately ten inches from the bottom. The defect measured three and a quarter inches in circumference. The edges were jagged and one could appreciate powder residue and burn marks measuring one and a half inches from the edge of the defect outward.* The report went on to talk about the removal of her sweater, which had a hole in it to correspond with the one in the jacket. It continued through the external exam which indicated small contusions or bruises at various locations across her chest and abdomen. Her sternum was shattered. The gunshot entry wound was circular in nature, under an inch in diameter. The doctor described the wound as somewhat eccentric in form, with a collar of abrasion around a portion, from approximately seven o'clock to two o'clock.

Matt's eyes swiftly followed the report until he got to the part where the medical examiner was describing the internal injuries caused by the shot as it entered her body. The doctor described how the force of the shell and the powder made a path through the internal organs and how the shot shell or pellets spread in every direction through the upper torso.

Matt leaned back in his chair and tried to recall exactly how Lentz had described Dr. Michaels' opinion regarding the angle of entry. He read the autopsy again, trying to picture in his own mind how it was being described. The angle definitely was from up to down, which meant that, unless something unusual happened, the gun was at a downward angle when fired. Matt remembered Deputy Lentz's description: fifteen degrees.

Matt once again flashed through the pages. He was now looking for the words *BCA* or *Bishop.* Another half an inch and he was there. The Bureau of Criminal Apprehension provides investigative, scientific and forensic expertise for all of the law enforcement agencies in the state. Rather than each local agency having to have its own ballistic expert, for example, the evidence can be transported to the BCA, the tests are conducted, and a report rendered. They are also required to testify in the event the matter goes to trial. The reports are rather succinct—the item received, the date tested, and the result. In this case, Eugene Bishop received a Winchester single action twelve gauge shotgun. The hammer had to be cocked to be fired. Lentz was right. Bishop had put the gun through all the tests the lab would normally use to see if the gun would fire without pulling the trigger. The gun wouldn't misfire for him.

He shuffled the papers looking for the report on the videotaping and found it within a couple of pages. This is interesting, he thought. This was something he must've missed. When Vince went in for his first interview with the Sheriff's Office the day after the death, they took his measurement. His height, and then from the floor to his armpit and from the floor to his shoulder. He wondered why Vince never told him.

The report went on to relate how they found a deputy sheriff the same height as Mr. Fischer, and a female officer from the Elk River Police Department who was the same height as Donna Woods. The videotaping was an attempt to recreate the version of events as related by Vince Fischer, and to test some of the assumptions of Dr. Michaels. They debated whether to take the gun along, decided that was too obvious, and came up with the idea of simply borrowing a broomstick and making sure it measured the same length.

Matt leaned back in his chair, truly intrigued. He knew he had to see that video tape. The cops had slowly and methodically built their case against Vince. Lentz was right—he had his work cut out for him and he was eager to get started.

chapter 7

MATT WAS HAVING a hard time staying awake. He'd just come from the Sherburne County Sheriff's Office where he'd been trying to locate a copy of the broomstick video. After making him wait for almost an hour, Deputy Weineke had finally told him the video player wasn't working and they'd have to get a copy made and mail it to him. Now he was driving back, on his way to Vince's home. The sun was streaming in, making him warm and tired. He was barely keeping himself from nodding off when he saw the Hamlet Lake public landing sign and realized he had just missed his turn. He snapped out of his lethargy and looked for a turnaround.

This was his first visit to Vince's house. He stopped the car at the end of the driveway as he surveyed the premises. It was a beautiful spot. The maples were turning bright orange; the sumac along the edge of the dark green grass was bright red against the pale blue sky. The contrast was stunning. The gardens were filled with the color of coreopsis and purple coneflowers, the last of some black-eyed Susans and every color of mum. The yard was huge and manicured, not a blade of grass out of place. The driveway was earth-toned paving stones leading up to a three-car attached garage. A huge deck led along the garage and the house to a breezeway which led to the back door. The fall sun sat on the horizon, glistening across the slight ripples on the lake. Matt slowly drove ahead.

He finally got a view of the front yard, running to the lake, then saw movement from the corner of his eye. Through the rays of sun he caught a glimpse of a woman in blue jeans and a sleeveless sweater leaning over the huge fieldstones that circled the flower garden. She was rather striking and he assumed it was Vince's wife. What was her name again? He stopped the vehicle for a second and watched. She slowly reached over and pulled some weeds from between the flowers and tossed them into the wheel barrow at her side. Suddenly she turned and looked. Matt quickly put his foot on the gas to get out of sight, embarrassed to be caught staring.

Approaching the deck he saw Vince Fischer waiting. He, too, was dressed in blue jeans, along with a t-shirt and a leather vest. They exchanged pleasantries. Matt had the file under his arm.

"It's too nice to be sitting in the house," Vince said. "Let's go sit out front." Matt quickly glanced at the deck and the spot where Donna must have fallen, where Vince said he had left the gun. As Vince escorted him around the house, the panorama of views continued until they came to an octagonal gazebo built off the master bedroom overlooking the lake.

"What a beautiful spot you have here," said Matt.

"Thank you," said Vince. "I ended up buying two smaller homes and tore them down to give me space to construct my dream home. I hired an architect out of Denver. I wanted it to have a mountain chalet quality. I could've built anywhere but my roots are in this area, my corporate office is here, and I wanted to stay local."

"It is certainly something to be proud of," said Matt.

They sat down around a wrought iron table.

"Care for a drink?" asked Vince.

"Maybe just a Coke or something," said Matt, as he glanced at the woman in the flower bed.

"That's Nikki," said Vince. "Makes pretty good viewing with that cute ass hanging over those rocks, don't you think?"

Matt didn't venture a response.

"She knows you're here. She thinks we're spending way too much money on you. If we're gonna spend that much, I think she would rather have some big named dick from the Cities. I think she's ignoring us on purpose."

"I'm sorry to hear that," said Matt. "I'm sure I can convince her otherwise."

Vince got up to get a drink. As he left the gazebo, Matt took the liberty of standing up and looking over the estate. What he really wanted to do was get a better view of Nikki. By then she was standing. Vince was right; she did have a nice butt. His first impression was right: she was striking. She had long blonde hair tied in a ponytail—to keep her hair out of her face while working in the flower garden, he thought. The sun, with its fall cast, highlighted the curls in her hair and the curvature of her body. He couldn't help but notice the shadow of her breasts under the loose-fitting sweater.

"Here's your Coke," said Vince. He'd only been gone seconds and had caught Matt staring at his wife. "I haven't had a chance to go over the police reports you dropped off. Been too busy with other things. Besides, that's what I figure I'm paying you for. Tell me what's all in there." As he finished his sentence he glanced at Matt. "You seem concerned."

"I *am* concerned," replied Matt. "I've read the reports; I spent some time talking to Bob Lentz. I've been thinking— any time a grand jury returns an indictment, I've learned from experience there's a possibility of a petite jury coming back with a guilty verdict. You know how this happened; you know it was an accident. What we have to do is get that to a jury." As he finished his sentence, Nikki walked up the steps into the gazebo.

"Matt," Vince said, "this is my wife, Nikki."

Matt stood up and put out his hand. Nikki ignored it, went around her husband, and sat down.

"He was just telling me," said Vince, "how we have to convince a jury that I'm innocent."

"Well, that's not exactly what I said," said Matt. "You claim you're innocent. All we have to do is convince a jury that the state hasn't proven you're guilty beyond a reasonable doubt. There's quite a difference."

Vince seemed a bit perturbed at being corrected.

"I was just about to explain to your husband, Mrs. Fischer, the information I have been able to gather as far as the state's case."

"Nikki." she replied.

"Pardon me?" asked Matt.

"My name is Nikki."

"I'm sorry."

"No reason to be sorry," she replied. "We don't have to stand on formalities. Vince certainly doesn't."

Matt sensed that this was some sort of jab at Vince. He let it pass.

"Let's get down to business," said Vince.

"Fine," said Matt.

"Let me tell you where we're at." He proceeded to go through all of the information he had gathered. The report of Dr. Michaels and his opinion as far as where the gun had to be held, the tests conducted by Bishop, and the importance of the broomstick video. It took him about fifteen minutes. Matt thought he had used a serious face, commensurate with the gravity of what he was telling them. It obviously hadn't worked. As he finished his summary, Vince looked at him and said, "That's all bullshit. Those fuckers know better than to think that I had any reason to shoot that bitch." Nikki lit a cigarette and turned away. Matt finally comprehended the task he had at hand.

"Well," Matt said, "I've had enough cases involving expert opinions to know you don't reach any conclusions until you've had a chance to have your own experts take a look at the evidence. What I have to do at this point is get a copy of the grand jury transcript. Both Michaels and Bishop testified, and I suspect there will be something more in there than their written report. And then there are several firearm experts I can contact and see who may be available to do their own testing on the gun. And, of course, we'll have to hire our own medical examiner to review the opinion of Dr. Michaels and see what he can tell us. In the past I've used the medical examiner from Milwaukee County, Dr. Evans. Everybody in Minnesota has been trained by Dr. Michaels or worked for him sometime in the past. They hate to dispute his conclusions." He looked at Vince. "Before I leave, Vince, there is one thing we have to do. Maybe Mrs. Fischer, I'm sorry, Nikki, could help us. I want to take your measurements. I happen to have a tape measure."

"What the hell is that about?" asked Vince.

"Well I saw in the reports that they took your measurements the day that you went in to give a statement. The measurements were used by Dr. Michaels in his conclusion. I'll show you." He stood up. "We'll pretend the wall is Donna and I'm you. What they're basically saying, Vince, is that if I pick up the shotgun and have it cradled in my armpit and it goes off, there is a certain trajectory or degree of angle from the muzzle of the gun to the target. To the extent that I raise the gun up to my shoulder, that degree changes. What Dr. Michaels is saying is that based on where the shot entered her body and its path once inside, if the parties are standing on the same surface, that should be able to tell you where the gun had to be. In this case, he says it had to be at your shoulder."

Vince watched quietly through the entire demonstration. When Matt was done, Vince turned his head toward Nikki and said, "Oh, fuck."

"What was that for?" asked Nikki.

"We're barely into this thing and I'm already tired of all this bullshit. They already took my measurements. You have it right there. I don't need any more of this shit. I didn't do it! A guy's word should be good for something."

Matt looked at Vince. "You may have just hit the nail on the head. This case may well boil down to whether your word is good for something. My suspicion is we should be able to find experts who will dispute, or at least question, what the state has presented. The best we can hope for is that we can neutralize Dr. Michaels and Bishop's testimony—meaning it could've happened the way they're saying and it could have happened the way you're saying. And if we get to that point, and notice I said *if* we get to that point, then the jury will have only one person who was there and who can tell what happened. And that's you. If they believe you, they can ignore all the circumstantial evidence to the contrary. If they don't believe you, they'll use all of that circumstantial evidence to put you in prison."

Nikki turned to look at Vince. "That's about as succinct as you can get it, huh Vince?" She grinned and stared at Matt.

Matt sensed she might be warming up a little.

chapter 8

MATT SAT AT his desk. Things were going more slowly than expected. He had made overtures to two ballistic experts and he was waiting for responses. The Milwaukee County Medical Examiner had agreed to look at the autopsy report; everything had been mailed to him. Matt pushed the button on the intercom. "Melanie, is Tim around? I have to talk to him."

"I'll tell 'em you want to see him," she replied.

Tim had been an investigator in Matt's office for a number of years. He was a graduate of an unaccredited law school and had never been admitted to practice in any state. What he lacked in accreditation, he made up for in tenacity. There was no job that was too grubby for Tim to complete. That's why he was an asset to Matt's office. Matt had realized years earlier it took a different kind of person to investigate cases of rape and incest and sexual abuse, to get statements from people who would rather knock your head off than give you the time of day. It wasn't always professional, but he always got you something.

Now Matt needed him to talk to some of Vince's girlfriends. Vince had told Matt that he was not obsessed with Donna. To the contrary, when Donna indicated she needed some space, Vince said he told her, "Fine. Let's stay friends and if your feelings change, I'm still here." He claimed that during that period of time, he dated half a dozen women and spent a lot of time with them at Anton's. He even suggested that Matt talk to the owners of Anton's, Tony and Lorraine. He said they would vouch for how often he was out there and the fact that he certainly wasn't broken hearted over Donna's decision.

"Have you finished reading those police reports on the Fischer case?" Matt asked as soon as Tim walked in the door.

"Yeah" replied Tim.

"Then you know what we're up against. Vince gave me the list of names of some women he was supposed to have been dating when he and Donna were separated. He said he was sure they would be glad to talk to us…could probably end up being character witnesses. It would be great to find some women that he was nice to, after some of the crap I've heard about him."

"So what do ya want me to do?" asked Tim.

Tim had an aggravating habit of always asking the obvious.

"I certainly wouldn't call you in, explain all of this shit to you, if I didn't want you to go out and simply get statements from these women. Quit doing that, damn it!"

"Doing what?" asked Tim.

"After I get done explaining to you exactly what I want you to do, you always ask the same stupid question: What do you want me to do? I want you to take them to dinner, what the hell do you think I want? Get the damn statements and get 'em back here."

Tim enjoyed getting him ruffled. He got up with a grin and left.

chapter 9

EVERYTHING WAS AT a standstill. Dr. Evans hadn't replied on the autopsy questions, neither ballistic expert had responded about whether they had time to take the case. Matt had gone through the police reports again, but nothing glaring or new stood out. He had received the broomstick video from Deputy Weineke and had viewed it a couple of times. It was pretty much what he expected. Maybe it was time for a little client control. He would call to see if Vince was available and offer to take the video tape out to the house for viewing.

It was six o'clock when he left his office. As he made the twenty-five minute drive to Vince's home, the video, or at least a small part of it, kept going through his mind. He could see Nikki in blue jeans and a sweater teeing up the golf ball on an open patch of turf where the sun had melted the snow. Matt had taken up golf several years ago. As with most things in his life, he had become obsessed with it. He had watched every video and read every golf magazine he could get his hands on. He could tell by the swing and the distance Vince had to run to retrieve the balls from the frozen lake that Nikki was a good golfer. But it wasn't the golf that really intrigued him. The sun was starting to set and fall had already turned slightly harsh. As he looked at the bare trees with the splash of color here and there, he couldn't help but remember his last encounter with Nikki, nor could he get the picture of her working in the flower garden out of his mind.

He again traversed the deck, the scene of the fatal shooting. He wanted to enter the breezeway and go into the house through the kitchen. As he approached the screen door in the breezeway, Nikki opened it and smiled, "You're a little early. Vince called and said you were going to be showing up but he's not home yet. This may give us an opportunity to talk. Come on in."

She seated him at the same kitchen table that Vince and Donna must have used that Saturday afternoon. Matt glanced into the great room. There was the gun cabinet that came up so often in the police reports.

"Can I get you a drink?" she asked. "I was about to open a bottle of Chardonnay, or if you care for something hard? I don't know if Vince told you, but I was a bartender when he met me."

"Yes he did," said Matt. "I don't need anything exotic, a glass of wine would be fine."

Matt watched how she carried herself across the room. It was a mystery to him that with all of her attributes, she had ended up tending bar in Montevideo. He pondered the incongruity.

"Thank you," said Matt, as she set the wine glass in front of him.

"I like good wine," she said. "I like fine things. That's why I'm here."

Matt thought it was said almost as an apology.

"Don't get me wrong, I love my husband," she said. "Not the way you love a person when you're twenty years old and passionately in love. He has his rough edges, it's his background. But other than a few smart comments, and a foul mouth, he treats me well and I love the security he provides. I love this place and I love what I can do at this place. The reason I am telling you this, Matt, is because I don't want this man to go to prison. He's told me about the relationship with Donna and he told me what happened the day she died. I can't believe he would've done it. I don't believe he murdered her."

"Have you read any of the police reports?" Matt asked.

"No," she said. "Vince brought them home but he locked them up somewhere and I haven't felt it my place to ask to read them yet."

The reason Matt asked was to know whether he dared bring

up the subject of the three prior wives. In the pile of police reports was a letter from Vince's third wife. The letter the sheriff had received several days after Donna's death. It outlined a history of physical and verbal abuse, including an episode where she felt that Vince was so angry he was going to kill her. From Nikki's comments, it was clear to Matt this had not been a topic of conversation between the two of them. He decided if it was going to come up, it would be at another time and under different circumstances.

"I can understand where you're coming from," said Matt. "To be honest, Vince told me you had some reservations about hiring me and I intend to prove those reservations wrong."

"I guess our first meeting did ease my concerns a little. The more I've been able to find out about you and your reputation, the easier it's becoming for me to abide by my husband's decision. But believe me, if at any time I become concerned as to whether you're the right person for this job, I'll have no problem telling Vince to cut the strings."

"Who's gonna cut strings?" asked Vince.

The conversation had gotten so intense neither Nikki nor Matt realized that Vince had walked in through the kitchen door.

"It's nothing important, we were just discussing your future," she said with a grin.

The three of them sat and relaxed over a glass of wine. They talked about everything except the case. It was a good diversion for all of them. Vince was proud to tell how he started his business, how he got rich. Actually, Matt had heard the story from Peter Maxwell, Vince's corporate attorney. It was more interesting hearing it from Vince. Vince had grown up on a farm outside of town. His dad was an alcoholic and physically abusive to his mother and all of the children. Vince had gotten out of there as soon as he could. Because he liked cars and he liked working on them, he found a job at a little gas station on the east side of St. Cloud. When the owner died of a heart attack, the widow asked him to take it over. He was twenty-two at the time. While managing the station, he noticed how many people came in to have their oil changed and were annoyed that they couldn't simply wait for the car but had to make arrangements for somebody to pick them up and bring them back later. Vince came up with the idea of doing quick oil changes, where you brought your car in, got your oil changed while you waited and watched television or read a magazine, and were on your way in ten or fifteen minutes. He started to advertise his "Super Lube" station and when it turned successful, he turned to Peter Maxwell, who helped him get it started right. Now, twenty some years later, he had over a thousand Super Lube stations throughout the Midwest and lived in his million-dollar estate with a knock-out wife. He still retained his rough edge from the days on the farm and the days of struggle. Like many of the *nouveau riche*, he had tried to fit in with the "artsy fartsy" crowd, as he called them, but it never appealed to him. And he didn't appeal to the "artsy fartsy" crowd either. So he performed some of the civic duties expected of a person of his financial stature, he did a little philanthropy, but he remained on the outside of the social scene. Somewhat with a sense of bitterness, Matt sensed.

As Vince talked on, Matt watched Nikki's face. It was obvious she loved to listen to the story. Matt realized, for the first time, how Nikki had gotten there. She fit his mold. She had all the looks he could handle and he could provide her with anything she needed. But Vince didn't have to worry about her dragging him off to every do-gooder benefit in town. They had their circle of friends, they both loved to travel and, as Matt was finding out, they both liked to get a little tipsy. By the time they got to the broomstick video, the wine had made Vince revert to the fashion of speech commonly found in the grease pits of the neighborhood gas station.

"Look at those fuckers running around with that video camera and broomstick. What the fuck do they think they're doing? Have you ever seen anything so fuckin' dumb in your life? I can't believe those fuckers are getting paid for this."

Matt looked at Nikki. She hadn't had as much wine and obviously didn't find it as funny. When it was all over, Vince turned to Matt.

"Well they certainly can't convict me on fuckin' bullshit stuff like that."

"Vince," said Matt, "I don't expect that they're even going to try and introduce that tape. I don't see how it would be admissible."

"Don't use that lawyer shit with me," said Vince. "Admissible, pissible. Who cares?"

With that, Nikki looked at Vince. "Vince, clean up your act. Matt isn't your enemy. He had the tape, he was nice enough to bring it out, he thought you should see it and at this point I think we should call it a night."

"She's right, Vince," said Matt. "And if it's any consolation, I agree with you. That tape isn't worth much but it's come up in several conversations and since I had it, I felt you oughta see it. If it's been upsetting, I'm sorry."

chapter 10

"COLLINS, YOU'RE not gonna believe this." Tim rushed in and broke the silence in Matt's office. Matt assumed he had completed the investigation of the women Vince had dated.

"I haven't met this guy," said Tim, "but Christ, I wanna be in his shoes. I've talked to these six ladies he gave as references, and I'll tell ya, one is prettier than the next. I mean, I've seen pictures of this guy. Where in the hell does he come off rounding up a bevy of beauties like that?"

"Well," said Matt, "money sometimes has a way of being seductive. The guy's got all the balls in the world. I think he probably has more money than he can spend. You put those two together, I'm sure he's not bashful with the ladies."

"Don't get me wrong," said Tim. "We're not talking about the socialites of the city. It appears that we may have a few bar flies in there. But I sure wouldn't kick any of them out of bed for eating crackers. The strange thing is that he was barely hittin' on 'em. They all said he was congenial, he was polite, and he was generous but not particularly horny. In fact, once the relationship got going, all he would talk about is Donna Woods. What a great lady she was. How beautiful she was. How he loved her kids. How he loved to spend time with her. How he would do anything for her. How he was hoping he could get her back. I got the conversations all on tape; I'll give them to Kay and have her give them to you when she's done transcribing them."

Daniel Eller

Matt leaned back in his chair. Everything Lentz had told him was coming true. What the hell had he expected? Those guys don't make a case by making things up. If Tim had been able to talk to those women, the deputies certainly had talked to them. There weren't any secrets anymore.

chapter 11

"COUNSELOR, HOW MANY murderers did you put back out on the street today?" asked Tony.

"None today, but I'm working on it," said Matt. "I'd be a little bit more careful how loud you say that," he continued. "I'm planning on meeting Vince Fischer here for dinner. I hope he's not here already."

"Oops," said Tony. "I'd better watch my big mouth. No, he's not."

"Maybe while we have a minute, I can ask you about Vince," said Matt.

"Sure. Vince and I go back a long ways. Back when he had a gas station on the East Side and I had a little used car lot on Main Street. He's always been good to me. I know he's been in and out of trouble with some women. Whenever he would have one too many at the bar, I'd hear part of the story—just his part. I tell ya, in the last couple of years he's had some real babes in here. I felt terrible about Donna, though. He brought her here a lot. Nice kid. I really liked her. I just can't believe he may have murdered her."

Matt took a few seconds to look around. It was early in the evening. Anton's had become *the* place to eat in St. Cloud. It was filling up. Tony, the Anton of Anton's, had also struggled for many years. One of Matt's favorite stories to tell was when, in the early years, he had ordered a Windsor charge and the bar had just run out; Tony had to send his son to the liquor store to buy another bottle—he was on a cash and carry basis. Now it was a different story. Now many nights you couldn't even get a table.

The success was partly due to the decor and ambiance. The original part had been built in log cabin style in the thirties. Additions had been added over the years, attempting to stay faithful to the original design, but they lacked the same character. It sat on the Sauk River and provided scenic dining. The menu offered a nice variety of steak and seafood. Matt figured this was the kind of place Vince would like because it was reminiscent of his own success. The surroundings were unpretentious. You could be relaxed there whether you came on a Harley dressed in jeans and a leather jacket, or in a Lincoln Continental and a three piece pin-striped suit. Matt liked to reminisce about the old days with Tony. One of the bartenders had told Matt one night that Tony had watched his career and took pride in his successes. Like a surrogate father.

Tony continued on, "Have you seen Vince's new wife, Nikki? There's a piece of work. She and Vince have been out several times since all of this stuff has been in the paper. The last time they had one hell of a fight."

"Do you know what it was about?" asked Matt.

"No, but it was 'fuck' this, 'fuck' that. You know how he gets."

Just as Matt was going to query Tony further, he saw Vince's Lincoln pull into the parking lot. He looked at Tony. "I'd like to know more about this sometime."

"There isn't much more I can tell ya," replied Tony. "She ran out, crying."

When Vince came in he greeted Tony with good-natured handshake. Then he and Matt took a table on the patio overlooking the river, as far from any early diners as they could get. Both ordered a drink.

"Vince, I thought it would be good to take a few minutes so I can tell you where your case stands and I wanted to do it without your wife present. I thought this would be a good place to talk."

"Well, talk away," Vince said.

"First, as far as the experts are concerned," Matt continued, "I heard from our gun expert in New York. We wasted a thousand bucks. What he's willing to say doesn't help us at all. He said, basically, he's familiar with the type of shotgun and he started giving me all kinds of technical stuff about its firing pin and milliseconds and when it was all done, he said he didn't believe that gun would misfire without the trigger being cocked. He also said that he did not believe the trigger could be cocked accidentally. He was willing to do some tests on the gun if we wanted to make arrangements to have it delivered to New York and kick in several thousand dollars more. It's not worth it. So I think we're going with Carlson out of Madison. I'm told he's good. He's worked for the State of Wisconsin as a firearms expert, an office like our BCA. I contacted him and he said he would be willing to work with us. Somehow I have to make arrangements with the county attorney's office to get that gun delivered to his lab in Madison."

The waitress delivered their drinks, saying, "These are on Tony."

"Tell him thanks," said Matt, looking at Vince. It didn't appear that he was listening or seemed at all interested in what Matt was telling him.

"Something bothering you?"

"No, no," said Vince, "everything's fine. What else have you got?"

"I did hear from Dr. Evans, the Milwaukee County Medical Examiner. I've made arrangements to meet with him in Milwaukee. He wants me to get copies of the slides of the autopsy. All I had were some of the three-by-five prints. I'm making arrangements to fly to Milwaukee in the next week or so and talk to him personally. I don't want to see anything in writing until we've had a chance to discuss it. His testimony could be crucial.

"Finally, Vince, I want to talk to you about the real reason I got you here tonight. The state has served me with what is called a *Spreigl* notice. A *Spreigl* notice is required when the prosecutor intends to try and offer evidence of prior bad acts or misconduct. In this case, they have served me notice that they want the court to allow them to introduce testimony by your three prior wives regarding what they claim to be your propensity for violence."

Vince's fist hit the table. "Those fuckheads! Those bitches! Not a goddamn one of them was worth the powder to blow 'em to hell! They sucked me as dry as they could and now they wanna cut my balls off."

His voice had risen and the people at the nearest table turned to look.

"Matt," Vince continued in a slightly quieter voice, "I can't imagine the judge would listen to that shit. I was only twenty when I married that first bitch. We had hard times. Things were tough. But that's ancient history."

Matt noticed that Vince hadn't questioned what violence or asked what they were talking about.

"I have the statements the cops got from all three of them," Matt continued. "I'd like to have you look 'em over and we can go over this at a better time and better place. I can tell you though, Vince, it's some terrible stuff they're claiming and if the judge lets it in, it could have a devastating effect on any jury."

Vince stared at Matt. Matt saw the anger swell in his eyes. "Well if that's the way those bitches want to play, two can play that fuckin' game."

Matt figured this was probably a good time to call it a night. He had planned on having dinner, but with Vince's change in disposition, he decided it was just as well to get out of there. Matt had come to the conclusion that he would have to feed Vince all of the bad news a little bit at a time. He still hadn't brought up the fact that sperm was found in Donna's body, or the fact that her blood alcohol concentration was .25. Either Vince had not read the police reports himself or had chosen not to bring it up. In any event, Matt was going to leave well enough alone, for now.

chapter 12

MATT PUT ON his bright red Pendleton jacket and a blaze orange cap. He had his camera under his arm and his gadget bag strapped around his waist.

"I wish you wouldn't go out there," said his son Jeff. "You know how many crazy bastards there are out there this time of year that'll shoot at anything."

"I'll be okay," replied Matt. "I won't leave our property."

Jeff was a third year college student at St. John's University, only a few miles from home. Matt had tried to talk him into living at home, to save some money, but Jeff thought living on campus was an integral part of college life, so Matt reluctantly gave in. Now Jeff was home almost every weekend anyway. He would pop in all the time, unexpectedly.

The house and the forty acres it sat on was the only thing Matt salvaged from the divorce. He and Virginia had bought the land in the early 70's, when land was cheap. When they finished building the house, they had a mortgage for forty-thousand dollars. Now, twenty years later, after putting the kids through college, the mortgage was over a hundred thousand. Matt took the property with the mortgage—he'd had too many good memories to give it up. The woods, the pond, and the wildlife gave him an escape from all the misery he saw practicing law. He knew his kids came home for the same source of solace.

It was November and the opening weekend of deer hunting season. Matt normally went out on that weekend with his camera. Because of the hunting pressure, the deer were on the move and he had more photo opportunities. Jeff had a reason to be concerned, though. A number of years earlier Matt had been out on a beautiful Saturday afternoon. He'd had his Labrador retriever, Brutus, with him. As they walked toward the back of his property through a thick birch grove, Brutus had caught the scent of something and run ahead. A shot crashed through the trees, then another. He saw Brutus running toward him. A third shot and the dog rolled over, at Matt's feet, with a gaping hole in his side. He looked up and died.

Matt could hear a young voice shouting, "I got it! I got it!" He looked at his dog in disbelief. A boy appeared, putting another shell in his shotgun.

"You dumb son-of-a-bitch!" Matt had hollered. "What are you doing on my property? You just shot my dog!"

The boy gazed, speechless, his eyes opened wide, his jaw dropped. He started to back up. Within seconds his dad was with him.

"We thought it was chasing a deer," said the boy.

"Didn't you see me here?" asked Matt.

They were nothing but apologetic.

"We had permission to hunt," the father said. "We must've just crossed the line without knowing it. I'm really sorry."

Matt looked at them. "Get the fuck out of here!"

He walked the quarter mile to his house trying to think of how he could tell the kids. They loved that dog. By the time he got home, the boy and his father were there. He could see they had told Jeff; he was fighting back tears. The only thing Matt could do was bury his dog. He had walked back to the woods and buried him right there on the site, where he had fallen. As he had picked the dog up, he had been surprised how heavy he'd felt dead, compared to when the two of them would roughhouse in the yard.

Matt had become a lot more cautious since then. He stayed within his property lines and his land was well posted: *No Hunting!*

This day, though, it wasn't so much that he was hoping to get good pictures. Vince's case was starting to weigh heavily on him.

Over the years he'd found that he did some of his best thinking while sitting in the woods with nothing to interfere, the only thing to break the silence was the call of a chickadee, the squawk of a blue jay, or the chatter of a squirrel. He could spend hours in the woods analyzing a case he was working on. Many times he would come up with his entire closing argument in a case before the trial even started. That was his plan today. He would try and figure out where the strengths and the weaknesses were. What next?

chapter 13

MATT WAS LEANING back in his office chair reading the investigative reports on a college student who had been charged with criminal sexual conduct in the third degree. It was the new heading for an old crime—statutory rape. His client had been going with this girl for over a year and when she got pregnant her family pressured the prosecutor into filing criminal charges. She was only fifteen at the time. As he read through the girl's statement, Kay walked into the office.

"Matt, Mrs. Fischer is here to see you."

Matt was surprised. He hadn't talked to Nikki since the broomstick video episode at Vince's house.

"Thanks," he said as he got up and walked out to the reception area. To remain formal in front of Kay and Melanie, Matt politely said, "Good morning, Mrs. Fischer."

"Mr. Collins," she said, "I know I didn't call but I would like to talk to you for a few minutes." There was urgency in her voice.

"Sure," said Matt, "come on in."

Matt led her into the office. As she sat down, she slowly looked around.

"Who took the photos?" she asked.

"I did."

"They're nice. What's that bird? I've never seen one like that."

"It's a yellow warbler. I took the picture last spring."

"What a beautiful bird," she said. "The colors are so delicate. I love wildlife. I helped Vince decorate his office, I used some wildlife prints. Have you been there?"

"No," replied Matt.

"I'll have to show you sometime."

This was the first time Matt had seen her in anything but jeans and a sweatshirt. Today it was navy slacks and a matching navy jacket. Under the jacket a low-cut white silk blouse just barely revealed cleavage. Her neck was tan. Her hair, which hung loosely in curls on her shoulders, had the sun streaks of one who spent a lot of time outdoors. She wore a gold choker. When he looked at her face, her blue eyes, he found it difficult to concentrate on anything else.

She turned from looking at the pictures. "I'll only take a minute," she said.

"No problem," replied Matt.

"I'm concerned about Vince. Ever since the meeting you had with him at Anton's several weeks ago, he's been different. You can't talk to him without him blowing up. He's always mumbling about 'those bitches'. He won't tell me what it's all about."

"Have you had a chance to read the police reports?" said Matt.

"No, he still keeps them hidden."

"I don't know if it is my place to tell you or not," said Matt, "but the prosecutor's office has served a *Spreigl* Notice. That's what I discussed with Vince that night. The purpose of the notice is to have a hearing to see if the court will allow the prosecutor to bring in the testimony by Vince's three prior wives regarding some claims of physical abuse. I know you'll hear about it eventually, Nikki, but I would just as soon you hear it from Vince or that he's present when we discuss it."

"What kind of abuse? I don't believe it. I'm living with the guy; I've never seen any violence. He's got a little temper... nothing I can't handle."

"Well, I can tell you, Nikki, but you have to keep one thing in mind: Vince has a different version of what occurred. Thinking it over, there certainly may be some motive for these women to, if not concoct a story, at least embellish it."

Matt related how the first wife claimed there were numerous occasions when she either got home from work late or didn't have dinner ready or, for no apparent reason, Vince would go into a rage.

"She claimed on one occasion he took a .22 rifle and held it to her chest and said, 'I could kill you'. On another occasion he threatened her with a knife. She claimed that when she was separated from Vince, but before the divorce, she was with another man and Vince chased them down with an automobile and was firing a gun at them." As he finished he could see the concern on her face.

"But you have to remember, Nikki, this was over twenty some years ago," he added, but it didn't seem to help. "The next episode relates to his second wife, Val," he continued. "This was about eight years ago. She claims that Vince was having an affair and when she confronted him about it at one of his gas stations, he grabbed her by the hair and literally dragged her out of the station and threw her in her car. There's some other stuff in her report and it's not clear when it was suppose to have happened or where."

Nikki interrupted, "Vince has told me all about his exes, and this sounds like something they would do, especially the last one."

"I was just getting to her, Pamela Dahl. She's the one who wrote the letter to the Sheriff's Office after Donna's death was in the paper. She claims that about four years ago, in the course of an argument, Vince threw her on the floor, had one knee on her chest and his hands around her throat and was squeezing and saying 'I'll kill you, lady.' She believed she was losing consciousness and was gonna die."

Nikki leaned back in the chair. Her shoulders slumped. "This is quite a shock," she said. "I've never heard any of this. I haven't seen it…I don't believe it."

"Of course," said Matt, "Vince has a different version of what occurred. He told me that as far as his first wife, there were some arguments, but you have to remember, they were young, right out of high school. He said he was still just an employee in a gas station. Money was tight. They were struggling. He says she wanted something better out of life and started shacking up with other guys, as he put it. The fights all related to that. He denies he ever held a gun or knife to her. As far as the shooting incident with the boyfriend, he admits there were some shots fired but only after he was threatened by the boyfriend. The shots were fired in the air, according to him. No intention of hitting anybody, just scaring them."

Matt hesitated. He was having trouble concentrating. He didn't know whether it was from the anxiety he saw on her face, or his own fixation on her beauty. He struggled to clear his head. "As to his second wife," he continued, "he claims their marriage was pretty much over. His business was starting to do real well. He said she knew they had drifted apart but she wanted to hold on. Apparently, she'd become a real pain in the ass. She followed him everywhere. That's why he kicked her out of the gas station. He says he didn't pull her hair; he just pushed her out the door.

"By the time he married his third wife, he was, of course, quite wealthy. He made her sign a prenuptial agreement. She was an airline stewardess. Somebody he met on a flight to Chicago. He said she ended up being just a gold digger. He said the night she is talking about was the night he told her she could get out and just take the clothes on her back. That's all she was gonna get. She apparently said she was owed something for the three miserable years she stuck it out with him. He said the divorce was ugly, she never got a dime and she's had a vendetta ever since. So you see, Nikki, things are not quite as bleak as they seem. We won't know until after the hearing and arguments what, if any, of the statements the judge will let in. I had to be honest with Vince, though. I told him if the judge allowed those three women to testify and if their testimony was consistent to their statements, I expect it to have quite an impact on the jury."

"How can they even let those women testify? That stuff happened years ago. What possible relevance does it have to this?"

"You're right," said Matt. "Normally it wouldn't be admissible. But Vince claims the shooting was accidental and the law may allow this testimony to try and rebut that defense."

"It doesn't seem fair," said Nikki. "I now know what's been

bothering him. I can't imagine he wants to face those three women again in any setting, much less a courtroom. I don't believe them. I would've seen that in Vince by now." Nikki stood up. "I really appreciate you taking the time to talk to me, to confide in me."

"I know how much this angers Vince," said Matt. "Anger doesn't do him, or his case, any good. I was hoping you could help him through this. That's why I thought it was important you know. I need a clear-thinking Vince."

"I've noticed a real sensitivity in you, Matt. I think it will help Vince in this case. I just want you to know, all the reservations I had are gone. I know you'll do well by Vince."

"I appreciate it," said Matt. And as he gazed at her, repeating her words in his mind, taking in her smile, he felt his knees weaken. He walked her out to the lobby and they shook hands. Matt's eyes followed her out the door.

"So that's the fabulous Mrs. Vince Fischer I've heard so much about," said Kay. "How come you're so flushed? What did she tell you?"

"You know I can't talk to you about confidential matters," said Matt.

"Yeah," said Kay, "when they're pretty. You don't have any problem telling me what the ugly ones say."

He gave her a sardonic smile and went back to his office.

chapter 14

Matt walked down the corridor after departing from the 747, having just arrived at the Milwaukee County Airport. He had made arrangements to spend the afternoon with Dr. Evans, the medical examiner who had reviewed Dr. Michaels' report. Matt had brought with him the slides of the autopsy and a copy of the broomstick video. He glanced at his watch: 11:33. He had plenty of time. He wasn't supposed to meet Dr. Evans until after 1:00.

While waiting for his baggage, Matt thought of his earlier encounters with Dr. Evans. He had used him on two prior homicide cases. He'd actually gotten Dr. Evans' name from the daughter of a friend of his who was a student in medical school at the University of Wisconsin in Madison. She had taken his class on pathology. The first time Matt had called him, Dr. Evans had been quite eager to take the case. So eager, in fact, Matt had been a little suspicious. But he called one of the district public defenders for Milwaukee County with whom he had a prior case, and received nothing but glowing reports. Matt was told jurors liked Evans, that he looked the part of a medical examiner.

Matt recalled the first time he saw Dr. Evans when he got off the plane in Minneapolis several years earlier to testify in a case involving a knife wound. He was older than Matt expected. Probably in his late sixties. He was tall, broad shouldered. Still in good shape. He had long gray hair, swept to the back with a touch of blonde in the front, giving an indication of what he looked like in his youth. He sported a mustache and a beard. If asked to pick a Hollywood actor to play the part of an expert witness as a medical examiner in a murder trial, any casting director would've given him the part.

Later Evans jokingly told Matt why he was eager to be involved in the case. He liked to travel and get out of Milwaukee. At age sixty-eight, he wanted to remain active, on the road and involved in his profession. He joked that after years of looking at plugged arteries and plugged up hearts, he had changed his life style and was pretty much a salad and fish man. He confessed, though, he did enjoy a good cigar once in a while, but never inhaled. Matt enjoyed talking with him.

Matt walked out of the terminal and hailed down a taxi. He told the driver to take him to the Government Center, then settled back and looked out the window. A little panic set in as the driver sped around the cars on the freeway.

"What do you do?" asked the taxi driver.

"I'm an attorney. From Minnesota."

"What's your business in Milwaukee?"

"I'm here to talk to the Milwaukee County Medical Examiner."

"Dr. Evans," said the cab driver.

"You know him?"

"I don't know him, but I certainly know of him. His name's been in the paper and on T.V. over the years in every killing in the county, and I'll tell ya, there are a lot of 'em."

The cab pulled up to the steps of the Government Center. Although Dr. Evans practiced at the Milwaukee County Hospital, he told Matt he had an office in the Government Center where he kept his records and he would meet him there.

Matt walked in and looked at the directory. He looked for *Medical Examiner*; he looked for *Evans*; he looked for *Charles Evans*. He couldn't find anything. He followed a hall to the main entrance and asked the woman behind the information desk.

"Oh, Dr. Evans," she said. "Let me call his office. He'll send someone up to get you—you'll never find it by yourself."

A few minutes later a young woman approached Matt. "Mr. Collins?"

"Yes."

"Dr. Evans is expecting you."

The receptionist was right. He would've never found the office. They had to be somewhere in the belly of the city. It seemed they walked for miles. He knew it was at the farthest corner from where he'd started out.

"He's right in there," the young woman said.

Matt walked into a room that was probably twenty feet long and ten feet wide. From the floor to the ten-foot ceilings were metal shelves filled with files, papers hanging out in every direction. Dr. Evans was sitting behind an old oak desk that was strewn with papers. He looked as disheveled as his surroundings.

"Matt." He stood up reaching out across the desk. He was several inches taller than Matt. There was something disarming about that. Matt wasn't used to looking up at people. Matt looked at his desk; Dr. Evans had the photos of Donna's body spread out.

"Did you bring the slides?" he asked.

"Yes, I did."

"Very interesting case you have here," said Evans. "Your client says it was an accident."

Matt didn't know if that was a question or an explanation.

"He said the gun discharged accidentally," said Matt.

"What are the firearms people saying?" asked Evans.

"I haven't really been able to find anything out at this point," said Matt. "That's my next trip. Do you know Dave Carlson from Madison?"

"Yes, I do," said Dr. Evans. "I've run into him on a number of cases where he's been called by the prosecutors. He used to work for the Wisconsin Department of Public Safety."

"That's the man," said Matt. "Do you have confidence in him?"

"Oh, yeah," said Dr. Evans.

"The gun is a single shot twelve gauge and according to another gun expert I talked to, the lever has to be cocked for it to fire. It would never misfire without being cocked. At least that's his opinion," said Matt. "We don't know if it was cocked or not. Vince simply doesn't remember."

"That's always convenient," replied Evans. "I suppose somebody's already asked the obvious question, why would you leave a loaded and cocked shotgun sitting around?"

Matt nodded, although it didn't really need an answer.

"Well, Matt, I know what you want me to say and I'm not prepared to say it at this time. I want to look at the slides; I want to go over Dr. Michaels' grand jury testimony again. I read his report and I can picture exactly what he is saying. The gun was close enough so that the shell and the wad entered the wound and produced the track within the body that you can follow. Combine that with the powder and there is an obvious direction that it follows. The problem occurs in all shotgun deaths at this range, or even a little further away. The pellets have a billiard ball effect. You've played billiards, Matt, the balls are sitting nicely in a bunch and you apply some force with the cue ball and they all go flying in different directions. That's what happened here. The shots all entered her body right out of the shot cup but as it hit her body, the body acted like the cue ball and the shots all scattered. I'm sure you read the report, Matt. It literally tore her to pieces inside. So there's a track to follow and there isn't a track to follow, if you understand what I mean. As you can see in the photographs here, these little bruises or contusions from her stomach all the way up to her neck, are B.B. pellets that hit from the inside but didn't have enough force to break the skin. Her sternum, as you know, was shattered. It was mush. Her heart and lungs exploded. She was dead instantly."

"What's been curious to me, Doctor," said Matt, "is that there was no blood on the deck. There are no pictures of the deck. According to the investigator, Weineke, they were out there the next morning and shot several rolls of film but he claims they did something wrong and the film was all blank. I have no idea what might've happened. But in any event, from the reports of the paramedics at the scene and the deputy sheriff's comments, there was no blood on the deck. With that type of a wound to the back and the fact she was lying on her back, how could that be?"

"She didn't land on her back, Matt. This type of force would have lifted her right off her feet and she would have been lying face down. I would be real surprised if she had been on her back. Somebody turned her over. That wouldn't be unexpected. But the blast caused so much injury inside and the death was so instantaneous that she didn't bleed. Her heart stopped pumping and the blood had plenty of places to go in the chest cavity."

They continued talking for maybe half an hour or so. Dr. Evans went through the autopsy report showing Matt on an anatomy chart what Dr. Michaels was describing. The whole thing was getting pretty gruesome. Even though Matt had been through this before, he was getting a little woozy. A combination of the airplane food and the pictures, he thought.

As Matt was leaving, Dr. Evans said, "Give me a couple of weeks. I have some tests to correct, and then the holidays are coming up, of course. Once I get a chance to go over everything again, I'll give you a call."

chapter 15

MATT LEANED BACK in his seat. The flight from Milwaukee to Minneapolis International was less than an hour. Not knowing how long his meeting with Dr. Evans would take, he'd set his return flight for 3:45. It was closer to five before the plane took off. Word was that it had been snowing in Minnesota and landing was slow at the airport. It never fails, Matt thought, I start out and it's sunny and thirty-eight degrees and by the time I'm coming home, I'm in the middle of a blizzard. He thought about his conversation with Dr. Evans. It was not what he hoped for, but, on the other hand, it wasn't a failure. Dr. Evans hadn't said he *couldn't* help him. He didn't tell him that he agreed with Dr. Michaels, that the gun had to be at Vince's shoulder. In fact, there was a hint in Dr. Evans' comments that he felt Dr. Michaels may have made too quick a judgment and then had to stick by it. Matt knew victories were made a little bit at a time. The trip hadn't been a waste.

By the time they crossed the Minnesota border, it was snowing heavily. Through the dim lights on the end of the wing, Matt could see the snow flying. He could feel the descent, his ears started to plug. The captain's voice came over the intercom, telling the passengers to expect some turbulence and a delay in landing due to the weather. Minneapolis had gotten nine inches of snow and they were expecting another three to four. The temperature had fallen to five degrees above zero.

Matt was not a seasoned flyer. He liked to fly but had limited opportunity to do so. In situations like this, he always looked around the airplane for the person he thought was the most seasoned flyer and he would watch him or her. If that person didn't seem concerned, Matt would try not to be. He picked one out. Obviously a traveling salesman. He was leaning back in his seat reading a Milwaukee newspaper, seemingly oblivious to everything. The plane bounced around; Matt thought they must be going up and down at least a hundred feet. They did this for forty-five minutes, the same amount of time it had taken to get from Milwaukee to Minneapolis. It seemed they had circled the city a dozen times. Throughout the ordeal, he just kept watching his salesman. The guy never took his eyes off the paper.

"Ladies and gentlemen," said the captain, "we've been cleared to land. Flight attendants, please make landing preparation."

Matt settled back, looked out the window and watched for lights below. As they broke through the clouds, the wind was whipping and the plane started to rock, the wings tipping from one end to the other; it was like a giant was sitting on each wing tip, using the plane as a teeter-totter. It was snowing so heavily that Matt couldn't make out the lights. There was just a bright haze as the airport appeared. Suddenly there was a loud thump and the sound of engines reversing. There was a collective sigh of relief and the passengers started to clap. Matt realized he wasn't the only one who had been petrified.

The drive home was white-knuckled: the kind where you don't dare take your eyes off the road or your hands off the wheel. The seventy miles to St. Cloud was on an interstate that the snowplows must have decided to abandon hours earlier. The only people dumb enough to be on the highway were Matt and semi-truck drivers who insisted on passing him at fifty or sixty miles an hour and leaving him in a cloud of snow, grinding his teeth, waiting for an abrupt stop against one of the overpass abutments. Matt loved Minnesota in the winter.

chapter 16

VINCE WAS ANXIOUS to find out what Matt had learned from Dr. Evans. He was disappointed to hear that the doctor wasn't going to say the gun had been under his arm. Matt told him not to despair, that he was very happy with the way things had gone. Vince seemed a little puzzled with that, as though he were starting to wonder whether Matt really knew what he was doing.

Matt had asked the court to give him some additional time to work on Vince's case because he had to complete another case in Stearns County. The matter was coming up for trial on Christmas week. He was representing a young woman charged with attempted first degree murder. It, too, was an interesting case. She had lived with this dirt bag boyfriend for several years before he was sent to prison for a number of petty burglaries and possession of drugs. Once he was in prison, the woman's daughter told her that she had been sexually abused by him on many occasions. She went to the prison, confronted him, and he didn't deny it. The mother didn't want to report it to the police. She had sent him a letter telling him what kind of a scumbag he was and telling him never to come around her home again. She called the parole office and asked that when he was to be released from prison, they should let her know. They forgot.

On a Saturday afternoon she was sitting in one of the local bars when he walked in, sat on the other side of the bar and told the bartender he would buy her a drink. The bartender said she got up, walked over, they got into an argument and he overheard her say something like, "I'll kill you." Her daughter was with friends that night and she went to her small home on the south side of town, got out a gun, loaded it and sat down on the couch. Her story was that she had fallen asleep and she woke up to hear some noise in the kitchen. The street light cast enough brightness into the house to show the shadow of a man coming toward her. She held up the pistol and emptied it. He was hit three times and three went into the ceiling. The prosecutor's office thought she had set him up intentionally.

Christmas was on Sunday. Jury selection for her trial started the prior Monday. The case actually went to the jury late Friday, the night of the office Christmas party. In the trial, over the objection of the prosecutor, the judge ruled that he would allow Matt to question the shooting victim regarding his sexual abuse of the defendant's daughter. He came in to testify and made a rather pathetic figure. The bullet to his head had caused some brain damage and he was partially paralyzed. He walked with a cane. Because he had never been charged with the sexual abuse, the judge felt he should have his own attorney and appointed a public defender to sit with him during direct and cross-examination. When Matt asked him whether he ever had any sexual contact with the defendant's daughter, he would lean over to his attorney and then respond, "On the advice of my attorney, I refuse to answer that on the grounds that it may tend to incriminate me." Matt went through a series of six or seven questions like this until the prosecutor objected as repetitious. Each one was answered the same by the witness. Matt watched the jurors' faces. He realized this was his case to lose.

The jury took seven hours of deliberation, much longer than Matt expected. They came back with a verdict of "not guilty." He later found out that the original vote was eleven to one for not guilty, the one juror who thought his client was guilty held out for six hours. The biggest surprise was that she was the juror Matt was sure they had on their side. She was a young woman who had obviously had a tough life, just like the defendant, and he was sure she would sympathize with the defendant. Turns out, she thought the defendant should have kicked him out of the house long before he had sexually abused her daughter. Who could figure, he thought. The office Christmas party turned out great, though. The jury was back by seven p.m., in plenty of time to still enjoy oneself and they had a little extra to celebrate. The defendant came to the party with a friend, obviously enamored with her defender.

chapter 17

MATT SPENT THE next day, Saturday, recovering from a hangover. That night, Christmas Eve, he spent alone. It was the first time in twenty-two years, since Natalie was born, that there were no kids at home, no excitement of exchanging gifts. He had no place to go, nor was there anywhere he wished to go. By midnight he was starting to feel a little sorry for himself, but he knew it would be better the next day.

Natalie and Jeff showed up early to spend Christmas day with him. Natalie, the vegetarian, cooked Christmas dinner: a broccoli quiche, steamed asparagus, and, to retain some tradition, cranberries. The afternoon was spent in the woods clearing up some dead trees. It was an overcast day, the temperature just at freezing. It snowed off and on, those big, heavy snow flakes that slowly accumulate, outlining all of the dark shadows of the woods in white. By late afternoon, a dull day became a Currier and Ives Christmas card. They had fun together, allowing themselves to forget about school and murder trials for a day. Matt hadn't thought about his other case, Vince's, for over a week. And in the woods, on Christmas day, there were only a few fleeting thoughts of Nikki.

It all started again Monday morning. When he got to his office, there was a message from Nikki: *I read the article in the paper. Congratulations on your victory. Keep up the good work.* Matt was surprised she had called. He looked at the message; it had been taken just ten minutes before. He reached for the phone, hesitated, then pulled back. It didn't require a response. She was just being nice. Oh, what the hell, he thought, and he reached for the phone again and dialed Vince's home. He smiled when he heard her voice.

"Thanks for the call," he said.

"I had an ulterior motive," she said. "I really need to talk to you. Are you free for lunch? I would just as soon not come to your office."

Matt hesitated. Should he be doing this? What would Vince think? Nikki at the office was one thing. Outside the office was possibly something else. He tried to think of a site that would be neutral, that nobody would question. He told her he would meet her at the Monte Club, which would be midpoint for both of them. As he hung up, Matt pondered the significance of the call. There was obvious concern in her voice. He was also intrigued. It had been some time since he'd had a chance to talk to Nikki, and now a clandestine lunch carried a certain mystique.

Being a little over eager, Matt arrived fifteen minutes early. He had the waitress find him a table in the corner and waited. He saw her pull up in the parking lot in Vince's Lincoln. As she got out, she took off her winter coat and threw it in the back seat. She was a splash of color against a rather dreary winter day. When she walked in the door she immediately spotted Matt and headed to the table. Matt watched her walk across the room, as did several other people. Matt's pulse quickened. She was dressed in black jeans and a red turtleneck sweater. As she sat down, Matt noticed her dangling red earrings were cardinals. Her blonde curls rolled over the turtleneck.

"Thank you for meeting me, Matt," she said.

"My pleasure," he replied.

"I'm not so sure," she said. "I'm really getting concerned about Vince. The last time we met, I told you how he was acting. It's getting progressively worse. All he can think about is this case. All he can talk about is how unfair this whole thing has become. How the bitches, as he calls them, are going to put him in prison. He won't let me help him. He won't let me read any of the reports. I have to pretend I don't really know what he's talking about because I don't want to tell him that you and I had that conversation. It can't go on like this. I have to do something to help him. Is there anything more that I don't know?"

Matt hesitated, concerned he may have already told her too much. But he knew she was right, he had to ally with her to help Vince. Otherwise, by the time they got to trial, he would have a total wreck on his hands.

"Well, I've told you pretty much everything," said Matt. "There are two other matters, but at this time I'm not sure how they're going to affect the case. They found semen in Donna's body. It was over twenty-four hours old. So, she obviously had intercourse with somebody the night before she went to Vince's house. I asked Vince whether they'd had intercourse that day and he said they hadn't."

Nikki waived her hand, anxious to break in. "That's not what he told me. He told me that's the reason they sent Troy out. That she was climbing all over him."

"That's the problem. He's told the authorities they had patched up all of their differences and they were going to get married. The fact she might have shacked up the night before with somebody else is pretty strong circumstantial evidence to the contrary. There's more, though. Donna's blood alcohol concentration; according to the medical examiner, her blood alcohol was .25 at the time of her death. That's over twice the legal limit. The reports that my investigator has been able to get indicate that Donna was quite a drinker. In fact, some of her girlfriends in the apartment complex where she lived told him it was not uncommon for her to go through a six pack of beer or more in an evening. Vince has told me that there were times she would get sloppy drunk. The problem for the case is you put all those circumstances together, you have her there drunk, and depending on what is being said, you have a pretty volatile situation."

"This is all making me ill," said Nikki. "I've got to do something to help him. Can we go on a vacation, just disappear for a week or so?"

"As long as there's no court scheduled and you're not leaving the country," said Matt.

"I was thinking I would take him back to Florida. Have you ever been to Captiva Island, Matt?"

"Not to stay. I just drove there once to take a look at it. I was on Sanibel Island. I went to the Ding Darling Refuge to do some wildlife photography."

"I know it well," she said. "We've walked through there several times. I loved it. Vince thought it was hot and dusty. But I loved the birds. My favorite was the tri-colored heron, or," she hesitated, "maybe the roseate spoonbill. It was before all of this. Even before the video at the house. We went deep sea fishing and the dolphins would leap in front of the boat as we went through the bay. The walks on the beach and the sunsets were just incredible."

Matt stared at her. Her demeanor had changed. Her face was alive as she recalled the sights. He pictured her walking on the beach, at sunset, with the waves gently breaking behind her and the sun silhouetting her body. It was so real he no longer heard her words.

"You've never told me anything about your family, Matt," she said.

It snapped him back from the daydream. "I'm divorced," he said. The thoughts that were running wildly through his mind cleared.

"I have two kids still in school, one at the University of Minnesota and one at St. Johns. I see 'em about every week—at least my son, Jeff. I'm paying for room and board, but every time he gets bored, he comes home."

"What's your daughter studying?"

"Environmental Studies. She doesn't know exactly what she wants to do, maybe something with the DNR, Nature Conservancy, something like that."

"That's wonderful," she replied. "I always wanted to do something like that."

They continued talking for a while. Matt started to realize, at least as far as he was concerned, they had many things in common, things they both liked to do. As she talked, he started to fantasize again, his mind wandering off.

"Is there anything further I can get you?" asked the waitress. Matt returned to reality. "No, just the check," he said. "Nikki, I'm sorry, I have to get back to the office. I think that's a wonderful idea. You take Vince on a vacation."

chapter 18

"Matt," said the receptionist, "Judge Thompson is on line three."

Several weeks had gone by since his meeting with Nikki. Vince had called a few days later. He said he and Nikki were going to Florida for a week. Matt had been in a foul mood after that. Nothing was happening on the case. He had another matter set for trial in February and had written to the judge in Vince's case, asking for a continuance.

"Thank you for calling, Judge."

"Matt, I received your letter requesting a continuance. I discussed it with Scott Larson and he had no objection. But you know, the Supreme Court keeps tabs on us and we have to keep filing these reports indicating why we aren't getting these cases handled quicker, so we have to give them an excuse."

"There are basically two reasons, Judge," said Matt. "First I have another trial in February which is going to take about a week and will affect the amount of time I can put in on Vince's case. Secondly, and probably more importantly, the initial firearms expert we contacted is not going to be available. We've arranged to have a guy in Madison take a look at the gun. It's my understanding that Deputy Weineke has made arrangements to transport the gun to Madison so I can't do anything until they finish their testing."

"Well," said the judge, "lets set a date out far enough that we can make sure everything is going to be done and we won't have to continue it again."

"That's fine," said Matt.

"I'm looking at some time in May. I'll talk to Scott and once we have a firm date, I'll have the clerk contact you. In the meantime, keep this matter going."

"I appreciate it, Your Honor."

For the next several weeks, Matt spent most of his time preparing for his February trial. He had a father who was charged with criminal sexual conduct in the first degree—a statutory euphemism to describe sexual intercourse with his fourteen-year-old daughter. It was an ugly case and he had an ugly defendant.

Matt had done a jury study, sending Tim out to talk to citizens of the county, trying to find out what they would want to know about the case, and particularly, what they would want to know about his defendant. The idea was to get information that could help when picking a jury. The results were pretty bleak. What they needed to know about the defendant in order to acquit him, Matt could never provide. It was one of those matters where you give it your best and hope the jury doesn't understand. That very seldom happens. The jury came back with a "guilty" verdict after only two hours. That included an hour for lunch. The defendant blamed Matt. He told him he had fucked it up.

chapter 19

IT WAS THE last week of February. Matt was boarding a flight to Madison, Wisconsin, to meet with the firearms expert, Dave Carlson. It was a beautiful day: sunny and in the thirties. He made sure he got a window seat. As he leaned back, he tried to assess exactly where he was in Vince's case. He had met Vince and Nikki at their home several days before. They both still had a hint of a tan they had picked up in Florida. Vince raved about what a great time they'd had. Nikki was less committal. Matt could tell she was still struggling. He could also tell she was looking to him for some guidance, that he had apparently become her confidant. As he sat there, he thought about how nice it would have been if he'd had an opportunity to talk to her by herself, to find out exactly what had happened and what was going on. The only thing Vince could say was, "I'm glad you lost the last one. From what I read in the paper, that bastard belongs in prison."

As Matt watched out the window, the snow slowly disappeared. By the time Madison was in sight, the ground was just a dull brown. Dave Carlson and another man met Matt at the airport. Carlson introduced his companion as Dan Kramer, a ballistics expert. Both men were in their fifties. Apparently they had both worked for the Wisconsin Department of Public Safety before entering private practice together. They were partners; Carlson did the firearm testing and Kramer did the ballistics.

It was about a half hour drive to their lab, just a dull green tin building on the outskirts of Madison. Carlson spent the first fifteen minutes giving Matt a lesson in shotguns: how the shells were manufactured, what the grain meant, the number of shots in the shell, the difference between shot cups and wads and what this all meant as far as entry wounds. He then went over the types of tests conducted on the shotgun. He brought out a half dozen targets with measurements on the bottom. He indicated they had performed the same tests that Eugene Bishop had done at the BCA. Apparently a test Bishop hadn't done, and they didn't know why, was to hit the gun on the stock, at the end of the pistol grip, while the gun was on safety. The single action had three positions: with the lever closed; with the lever in a safety position, which was half between closed and fully cocked; and the final, of course, fully cocked. With the lever closed, the gun wouldn't fire; in both the fully cocked and the safety position the gun would fire without pulling the trigger, provided it received a knock with a rubber mallet at the end of the pistol grip. But Carlson admitted it took a pretty good knock before it would discharge. They also tested it for recoil. This involved tying it to a weight, discharging the shell, and seeing how far back the rifle flew. Carlson said that the gun had pretty good recoil.

"You know," he said, "Deputy Weineke was a little upset with us. He thought we had ruined that gun. We did manage to put a little dent in the pistol grip when we hit it with the mallet."

"Was Weineke here the whole time?" asked Matt.

"Yeah, he pretty much stayed out of our way, though. I suppose he was afraid of the chain of custody argument," said Carlson.

Matt proceeded to tell the two of them about his meeting with Dr. Evans, the autopsy report, Dr. Michaels' opinion regarding the angle of entry, and the fact that Dr. Evans had not given any firm opinion. As he sat there he took out a piece of paper and drew a stick figure. He then drew a line and said, "This is the gun. What Dr. Michaels is saying is that this gun is at a fifteen-degree angle to the back of the victim. And he puts the gun at Vince's shoulder rather than under his arm."

"That assumes though," said Carlson, "that the target is perpendicular to the ground—like your illustration. What if she was not? What was her posture like? For example, was she a person who slumped over? Was she a person who stood straight? Was she leaning over to pick something up? The certainty of the angle of entry is only as good as the fix of your target. If your target is mobile and moving, it can certainly affect the degree. In this case, Mr. Collins, the difference between whether the gun was on his shoulder or under his armpit is about five degrees. You change your drawing here from perpendicular to like this," and he changed the angle slightly, "you have your five degrees."

Matt leaned back and closed his eyes. Things started racing through his mind. That's so simple; I can't believe I missed it, he thought. I can't believe Dr. Evans didn't bring it up. That's all I need to neutralize Dr. Michaels' opinion. He tried to recall photos he had seen. He thought he remembered a picture that Vince had of Donna in the same leather jacket she wore the night she was killed. What was her posture?

The three of them drove to the Airport Holiday Inn to have lunch. Matt had made early reservations to get back. He wasn't going to get stuck in any snowstorm in the dark, trying to drive to St. Cloud. As they had lunch, his spirits were up. They talked war stories and Matt asked Carlson how he knew the attorney who had given Matt his name. Carlson talked about some of the cases they'd had together. As Matt said goodbye and boarded the plane, he was excited to get back and start working on the case. Based on their luncheon discussion, Matt had gathered the opinion that Carlson had a long and distinguished history and concluded that he had found his expert witness. Moreover, he liked Carlson. He looked the part of an expert who could easily talk to, and sell himself to, a jury.

Matt got back to the airport early. As he walked across the terminal, he looked through his billfold for Dr. Evans' number. He couldn't wait until he got back to St. Cloud; he wanted to talk to him immediately. Dr. Evans wasn't at the Coroner's Office, and he wasn't at the medical center. Matt thought he would try him at home. It was that important to him. Dr. Evans answered on the second ring. Matt summarized his decision with Carlson.

"I've gone over the whole file, viewed the slides," Evans replied. "I'd have to concur with Mr. Carlson's opinion. Basically, you have to remember, Matt, that you don't have stationary objects, you have two moving objects. You have Vince with the gun and you have the young lady who's walking across the deck. Neither one's static. And, Mr. Carlson is right, you change one or the other, and it can affect the degree of angle to some extent. I don't think Dr. Michaels allows for any leeway in his opinion, he doesn't consider the variables. I would suspect that on cross-examination, he would have to admit that."

That's all Matt had to hear. He thanked the doctor. He told him not to put anything in writing at this point and he would be getting back to him. Then he dialed Vince and Nikki's number and Nikki answered.

"Nikki. Hi. It's Matt. I'm at the airport. I just came back from Wisconsin. I have some very interesting news. I was hoping that you and Vince would be home and I could stop by."

"Vince isn't here right now," said Nikki. "What time is it?"

Matt looked at his watch. "It's quarter to four."

"I don't expect him home until almost six, but I know he would be anxious to hear what you have to say. So am I."

Matt left the airport going over in his mind the day's events, but thoughts of Nikki kept interrupting. It had been weeks since he had seen her, but not a day went by when he didn't think about her.

As Matt drove the forty miles from the airport to Vince's house, he analyzed his feelings. What was he really doing? Since the divorce, he hadn't spent much time thinking about another relationship. There had been a couple of dates, but nothing serious. Sure, there were times he would look at women and fantasize. Sometimes, when he was out with his buddies, particularly the single or divorced ones, they would try and push him into some romantic relationship, maybe a bar pick-up, but it was rather shallow. He was content being unattached. He had too many things going on in his life to complicate it with another woman.

Suddenly Nikki had changed all of that. There were times when she so occupied his thoughts that he was oblivious to his surroundings. As he drove on, this was all going through his mind and he wondered what he'd done to himself. There is no reason why she should give him the time of day. She had what she wanted. If not in Vince, then at least in what he provided her with. She'd made that very clear the first time they'd talked. But he had sensed something changing. She had become, he thought, approachable. She had demonstrated warmth that she meant, he concluded in his fantasy, to be enticing.

The warmer temperatures of the last few days had melted most of the snow, everything that wasn't on a pile. As he drove toward the house he could see the expanse of the estate over the snow piles along the driveway. The lake lay frozen and white, stretching for miles. In the distance, Matt could hear the roar of snowmobiles on the lake, their last bastion before they were relegated to the garage for another season. As he shut off his headlights, he could see the lights go on in the kitchen and Nikki's shadow through the curtains.

When she opened the door, Matt was at a loss for words. She wore jeans and a blue shirt with a deep v-neck. He saw the sparkle of a gold necklace with a design of hummingbirds, and there were little gold hummingbirds dangling from each ear. Her hair was in a ponytail that accented her long, slender neck. Matt inhaled deeply; her perfume was intoxicating. They exchanged greetings, but this time it seemed different. This time Matt sensed she really was glad to see him.

"Vince called a short time ago," said Nikki. "He said he'd try to be here by five or five-thirty."

Matt looked at his watch. That's too soon, he thought, only minutes.

"It should give me enough time, though, to say the things I want to say," said Nikki. "Things haven't gotten any better with Vince. All he told you about the great time we had on the trip to Florida, that's all in his mind. It was miserable. He was miserable. He's incapable of enjoying himself anymore. All he can talk about is how women have ruined his life. How those three bitches are going to testify against him. How ungrateful Donna was after all the things he had done for her. He said she was a welfare bitch and he had made her a respectable lady. Matt, it's just terrible."

She was visibly shaken. Her face flushed as she recalled his words. She looked away to avoid Matt's stare. Matt was unsure what he should do, whether she wanted him to do anything.

She turned slowly toward Matt. "And then I saw what those women were talking about. We came back from a restaurant one night, after we'd actually had one of the few pleasant nights of the whole trip, and I somehow said something to upset him. To be honest with you, Matt, I don't even remember what it was. It was so minor. Then he had me up against the wall with his left hand on my throat and he was making a fist with his right. He said something like, and I'm sorry Matt, 'You fuckin' cunts are all the same! All you want to do is take a guy for everything he's got. You're not happy until you cut his balls off!' Then he threw me on the bed and left. I know he went back to the bar and got stone drunk because the next morning I couldn't get him off the couch. I tell you, Matt, it was one scary experience. Something that I would never want to go through again and I don't know what to do."

Matt had not imagined that their relationship had deteriorated that quickly. Before he had a chance to reply, they heard Vince's car in the driveway.

"We'll have to continue this another time," she said. "I can't do anything now. I can't upset him any more than he already is."

Vince walked in and slammed the door. He looked at Matt and in a drunken slur said, "How the fuck's it going?"

Matt smiled. "Well, it's going great for me and if it's going great for me, it's going great for you."

"What are you, the fuckin' Riddler?" Vince replied.

"Vince, please," said Nikki.

"I'm sorry, Matt," said Vince. "A couple of the shops aren't doing well and I had the managers out after work tonight. They just whine about the goddamn competition and how hard things are and I got pissed off. I don't mean to take it out on you."

"That's okay, Vince, I understand. We all have our bad days."

"What's this great news?" asked Vince.

The tension in the room slowly disappeared. Matt went on to tell them about his meeting with the firearms expert and his follow-up call to Dr. Evans. It didn't seem to have the same exhilarating effect on the two of them that it had on him. Obviously they failed to grasp the significance.

"If you remember," Matt said, "as I told you, the best we could ever hope for was a way to neutralize Dr. Michaels' opinion. You're never going to find anybody who's going to come in and say that he doesn't know what he's talking about. But, if everything I heard today stands up, we've just neutralized Dr. Michaels' testimony." Matt waited. There was still no response.

After minutes of uneasy silence, Vince fixed his gaze on Matt. "You do what you have to. All I know is if the judge lets those three bitches testify, I want you to tear 'em new assholes."

Matt knew this was an issue that had to be faced head on. "That won't happen, Vince. And more importantly, if the judge does let them testify, I suspect that I'm going to have to treat them with kid gloves."

"I don't understand this fuckin' system! You mean they can get up there and lie and that fuckin' judge is gonna let them get away with it?"

"I'm just telling you, Vince, based on my experience in this type of a case, you're not gonna make any points with a jury trying to tear these ladies new assholes. Now there are attorneys who would do that for you, and I can give you their names. You have complete control over this case and anytime you don't think I'm doing it right, you can tell me to get my ass out of here."

Nikki sensed a confrontation. "You know, Vince," she said, "I think we should make a rule. I think we should agree that we're not going to talk about this case anytime that you've been drinking." Vince glared at her.

"That's all I need! Another bitch to tell me how in the fuck I should run my life. Remember what I told you in Florida! Don't fuck with me!"

Matt cringed. Nikki was on the verge of tears but didn't want to give Vince the satisfaction. Matt interceded. "I think I'd better be going. Vince, whether you believe it or not, the information I got today helps us tremendously. We still have a long way to go but you're starting to worry me. I told you that there may come a point that the best I can do is put you in front of a jury and hope they believe you. To be believable, Vince, you have to be likable. Those jurors are going to have to like you and, quite frankly, right now you're not a very likable character."

Vince's face turned to stone. Matt waited for an explosion. Instead Vince smiled. "I'll see what I can do. Maybe I can become as sweet as she is," nodding toward Nikki. Vince turned and walked out.

Nikki led Matt to the door. "I'm terribly sorry," he said. "You know I didn't mean for this to happen. You gonna be all right?"

"Ah, he's drunk. He'll go upstairs and pass out on the bed. I'll sleep down here."

She followed him out of the door and into the breezeway. As he turned back to her, wanting to express concern for her safety, to offer to take her somewhere else, their hands brushed against each other. She slowly wrapped her fingers around his palm and squeezed it. She leaned against him; he could feel her hips on his thigh. She kissed him gently on the check as she said, "Thank you." She turned and walked back into the house.

Matt paused for a moment, wanting to follow her. Then he hesitated. Don't make a fool out of yourself, he thought. Just because she gave you a peck on the cheek doesn't mean she wants you. It's probably nothing more than what it seemed, just a thank you for being there.

chapter 20

WHEN MATT GOT to work the next morning, Tim was waiting for him. Matt had asked him to track down some of Donna's best friends to find out what she may have been saying about the relationship. Judging from Tim's excitement, it must have been interesting information.

"I'll tell ya, Matt," said Tim, "the more I find out about this guy, the more I'm fascinated with him. You know he really had Donna for a while. According to some of her girlfriends, after their first couple of dates, she thought the sun rose and fell on the guy. You have to get the picture. She comes back from Hawaii with her two kids after a real ugly relationship with some drug pushin' dirt bag who beat the shit out of her and the kids. Her dad apparently gave her the money to divorce the asshole and then to come back to the states. That's after he ended up in prison on some bad drug deal. Within a month or so she meets Vince at one of the Super Lube Stations and a couple weeks later, they're dating, hot and heavy."

"Slow down a little," said Matt. "You mean her girlfriends are telling you all of this?"

"Yeah," he replied. "They said she loved talking about it, she loved everything about him. He wanted her to live with him out at his fancy shack but she thought that was moving a little too fast. She did stay out there whenever she could. Then he wanted to move her into a big apartment. Said he'd pay all the bills, but apparently she didn't want to seem like a kept woman. But her girlfriends said it wasn't uncommon for her to have a bundle of hundred dollar bills and they all knew where they came from. Then sometime in March her family had a reunion. She told some of her friends that Vince wanted to come and meet the family, but she didn't want him to because she knew her dad didn't like him. Also, she had a sister out in Connecticut who's married to a Wall Street attorney, and she thought her sister would think that she was just going with Vince for his money. Anyway, Vince shows up at the party and presents her with a twenty-thousand dollar diamond ring. A 'friendship ring' he called it. She goes ballistic. She thinks he's trying to buy himself into the family and the evening quickly turns into a disaster."

"So she's pissed because Vince buys her this expensive ring?" asked Matt.

"That's what they said. That was sort of the beginning of the end. She tried to break it off afterwards, at least off and on. Apparently she did shack up with him a few times after that. She also took some of his money. The car deal is another strange one. She did have a hole in her oil pan that caused a slow leak and, eventually, the motor had to be replaced. One of her girlfriends, Jenny Weber, said that Donna told her that she believed Vince had punctured that hole in the oil pan so that she would have to ask him for some help. She said Donna had taken her car to the Vo-Tech School to have it looked at and one of the mechanics there, one of the teachers, told her there was no way that could've been caused by a rock in the Sears parking lot. It gets worse. She talks to this lady the morning that she's going to take her car and drop it off at Vince's house to get it fixed. And the lady asks her if she's concerned about going out there by herself and she says she's not. If she thinks Vince wrecked her car on purpose to get her out there, why would she go?"

"Let me get this straight," Matt interrupted. "The woman that Donna told she believed Vince had purposely sabotaged her automobile to get her to the house was the same woman she talked to the morning that she was going to go to Vince's house. Is that correct?"

"Yeah," said Tim.

"And this woman, Jenny Weber, didn't seem concerned about that?" asked Matt.

"Apparently not," said Tim. "She also told me that during the winter, in February, when Vince was on a trip, Donna met up with some ski bum up at Lutsen. The guy lives in a log cabin along the North Shore. Donna had been with him for a couple of days right before she died. She'd just returned that morning. Jenny had been taking care of her kids."

"That explains the semen," Matt said.

"That's what I thought. But it was the conclusion of several of her friends that Donna was not adverse to continuing to use Vince when it was to her advantage, when she needed something. And if she had to give him a little to pry it loose...." Tim paused and looked at Matt for a response.

Matt leaned back in his chair. "You know, Tim, I had a suspicion something like that was going on. It may well be that she was telling Vince one thing and telling her girlfriends and family something entirely different. She might've decided Vince wasn't the guy for her but on the other hand it was too much of an easy meal ticket to give up. Did any of them indicate he had ever gotten violent or that Donna had ever said that he'd gotten violent with her?"

"Nothing like that," replied Tim. "The only thing annoying to Donna was Vince wouldn't stop calling her, or stop calling her girlfriends, trying to get them to persuade her to change her mind. Another one of her girlfriends, Josie, said Vince actually started bawling on the phone one night about how much he was hurting without her. I hate to keep saying this, but it sounds to me like this guy was totally obsessed with her and she just took every advantage of it she could. Under those circumstances...who knows what happened out there that day."

The thought had crossed Matt's mind many times. Too many things didn't make sense. Either it happened the way Vince said it happened and it was an accident, or he purposely took that gun and shot her in the back. What would've had to happen to make him mad enough to do it? And if it had happened that way, how should that change how Matt would handle the case?

101

chapter 21

WEEKS BEFORE VINCE'S trial was scheduled to start, Matt spoke with Dr. Evans again. The doctor said he would testify and that he could reasonably render an opinion that the degree of entry from the muzzle of the gun to the body could have been ten degrees or even a little less. That's the most that Matt could hope for. He already had Dave Carlson indicating that given the right force, the gun could misfire in both cocked position and in the safety position. He could well argue that Vince might have had it in the safety position when he leaned it up against the garage.

Nothing further had been done regarding the admissibility of the testimony of the three former wives. The judge had taken the position, pretty much consistent with the case law, that he would wait to see if the prosecutor actually needed that testimony before he would decide whether they could testify or not. What he was doing was just protecting the record. What it really meant, Matt knew, was that if the judge believed the state had proven its case and there was no way the jury was going to find Vince not guilty, then there was no reason to let the evidence in. The only thing admitting the evidence could do at that point was to end up getting the judge reversed. On the other hand, if it looked like Vince might be convincing the jury that it was an accident, then the state needed the testimony of the three women to convict him, and the judge would let it in. An appeal is better than an acquittal. So nobody knew whether the three women were going to be able to testify or not.

Matt had talked to Nikki by phone on several occasions. He purposely tried to put her out of his mind. Trying to figure out where she could possibly fit in his life, given the present circumstances, was way too complicated. But then she called.

"Matt, I really need to talk to you. I can come into the office. But Vince is gone to a convention in Dallas and won't be back until Monday, so, if you prefer, I could prepare a little dinner here at the house."

Matt couldn't believe what he was hearing. An invitation! To Dinner! Alone! What's going on? Trying not to sound over eager, he agreed to be there around 7:00.

As he hung up, he remembered his daughter Natalie had called earlier to say she was coming home for a few days. He had been looking forward to seeing her; she had not been home since Christmas. Now he had a dilemma, but he knew who was going to win. At 6:30 he called home and told Natalie an emergency had come up, he would be home as soon as possible. The lie bothered him; it was out of character.

On the drive to the lake, fantasies rushed through his head. He tried to imagine what might be in store. Then all of a sudden he came back to earth, realizing that all he was doing was going out to talk to a client's wife. A client who was charged with first degree murder.

He looked at his speedometer. He was going seventy-five miles an hour. Twenty miles over the limit. He took his foot off the gas and let the car cruise down to fifty-five, deciding there was no reason to rush. After all, he'd probably be disappointed. She most likely had no interest in him at all.

He could feel his body tense as he turned onto the long driveway to Vince's house. He rolled down the window. The evening was cool and refreshing. He turned on the overhead lights to look in his rear view mirror. He thought he looked presentable; he wasn't a bad looking guy. He wondered if he should've shaved, or would that have been too obvious? Don't be crazy, he thought—this is just to talk over the case.

Nearing the house, he had this mental image of Nikki, what

she would look like when she opened the door. But as she stood in the doorway, he realized his imagination had been lacking. He had to remind himself to breath. She was in a deep pink blouse with buttons down the front, the top three buttons seductively open. The silky blouse clung to her breasts to reveal the curves. Her blue eyes sparkled. Her face was radiant. For a moment, Matt was speechless. He tried to think of something clever to say, and it just came out, "Hi." Instinctively he grabbed her hand and shook it, subconsciously trying to set a professional tone to the visit. As she took his hand and led him in, a soft smile crossed her face.

In the great room a fire blazed in the big stone fireplace. On a large burr oak coffee table with a glass top, he saw a plate of hors d'oeuvres. There was also an open bottle of wine and two glasses.

Matt's steps were hesitant. Nikki sensed it and said, "I did invite you for dinner, remember. I thought we might as well relax as we talk."

She served him a glass of wine and they both took a seat on the couch. The room was dimly lit, and as the fire crackled, it sent dancing shimmers of light through the room that bounced off her golden curls. She looked angelic.

"Are you uncomfortable?" she asked.

"No." answered Matt. "Why?"

"You just seem to be awfully uptight. You don't seem to be your usual relaxed self."

"To tell you the truth, Nikki, this is a little unusual. I don't normally have a candle light dinner with one of my client's wives."

"Well this case has been anything but normal, right?" she asked.

"I suppose you're right," he replied.

They spent the next half an hour talking. The bottle of wine was gone and she retrieved another. She told Matt about her background. She had been married once before. She'd gotten married very young. It was an abusive relationship and her husband was a skirt chaser. But she'd grown up poor, her dad was a lot like her husband, and she felt she was unable to really help herself. Her husband went from one job to another. He'd finally found a job as a local over-the-road trucker which gave him plenty of time to be away from home and chase women. He was quite handsome, she added. Then one night, coming from Minneapolis, he'd been drinking and on the interstate he lost control of the truck, it overturned in the ditch. He was pinned in the cab. The gas tank exploded and he burned to death before they could cut him out. People said he was screaming. "He wanted somebody to put him out of his misery," she said. "That's a terrible way to die, even for him."

As they talked, Nikki made periodic trips to the kitchen. There were wonderful aromas filling the house.

"Maybe it's time to eat," she said and motioned Matt to the dining room.

It was an intimate setting. Two places set, candlelight. She had retrieved a third bottle of wine to go with the dinner. The table was set with sirloin tips with fresh mushroom sauce over a bed of pasta, steamed asparagus with hollandaise sauce, and French bread.

They were both relaxed and ate slowly. Every so often Nikki would catch Matt staring at her and would ask him what he was thinking. He would blush and she would smile. Matt sensed she knew that she had him, that she was just toying with him. But other than being very pleasant, charming and beautiful, she made no overt signs that this was anything other than an evening meal between two friends.

As she stood to clear the table, the phone rang. She answered it somewhat reluctantly.

"Hi, Vince. Oh, I just finished with dinner. I'm going to watch a little television…" She was quiet for a moment and Matt could just barely hear Vince's voice.

"There's no reason to say something like that," she continued, angrily. "You've been drinking. I can tell you're drunk again." Matt could hear Vince yelling, a stream of foul language. He watched Nikki's face. Her expression had quickly turned from angelic to angry and embarrassed.

"Do whatever you want to, I could care less!" She finally said and slammed the receiver down.

She turned to Matt. Matt wasn't sure if he should approach her, offer some sort of solace. To his surprise, she sat down at the table, poured herself another glass of wine, and started laughing.

"He said he was gonna go out and get laid. Of course, that isn't exactly the way he put it. I told you things were bad. That was really an understatement. He hasn't been able to get it up for months, since shortly after this whole indictment thing. He's been impotent, Matt. That's why I laughed. I wonder if he's really gonna try. It could be embarrassing for him.

"But I really don't know what to do," she continued. "He isn't the man I knew and he isn't the man I married. And the more this goes on, the more I see the man they claim he is, and I'm scared."

She reached across the table and took Matt's hand gently. There was so much pain on her face that she looked ten years older than when he walked in.

"I'll do anything I can," Matt said.

She got up, moved around the table and leaned over to kiss him on the cheek. Her blouse hung loosely on her shoulders and Matt was able to gaze down the neckline at her breasts. He thought she had done it on purpose. He was afraid to stand up, embarrassed to reveal the effect she had on him. She gave the slightest tug on his hand, he stood and she leaned against him, brushing her thighs against his leg. She took his hand and put it on her breast. She turned her head slightly. Without a thought, Matt kissed her. His hands slid to her hips and he pulled her close. As she brought her head back to look in his eyes, the pain was gone, the radiance was back. Her gaze melted any hesitation; he knew he wasn't going to leave. She took him by the elbow and, as if there had been a meeting of the minds, they both walked from the dining room, through the great room, up the open staircase to the master bedroom. There was a small lit lamp on the nightstand. Nikki sat Matt down on the edge of the bed. He was totally in her control. She took a candle from the nightstand, lit it and turned off the lamp. She looked at Matt and said, "Why don't you get under the sheets, I'll be right back."

Matt was in a trance. He stared through the glass of the sliding doors, past the gazebo, into the evening. The lake was still frozen but the warm days had caused puddles to form all over. The moon was full on the horizon. It cast its light in each little puddle and the lake reflected like a thousand moons. It gave a beautiful aura to the room. He undressed, stretched back on the pillow, and pulled the sheet over himself.

The bathroom door opened and Nikki walked out. She had washed off her make-up and wrapped herself in a pale blue towel, tucked in just above her breasts. She moved slowly to the edge of the bed, smiled at Matt, and then allowed the towel to slide to the floor. Matt stared, looking at the contours of her body, savoring every intimate detail. She crawled in bed, pulled the sheet over herself and put her head on his shoulder. He put his arm around her, caressing her body. Her muscles were in knots. He leaned over to kiss her. She took his hand and placed it between her thighs. She shivered at his touch. This was his dream. He reveled in her scent and softness as he smothered her body. Time was lost, consumed by their passion. Matt could feel the tension leave both of their bodies.

Afterwards she lay by his side quiet and motionless. Matt didn't know whether he should speak. He leaned over and kissed her on the shoulder and she trembled. Then she slowly got up off the bed, poured herself a glass of wine at the bar and walked to the window. The moonlight silhouetted her body and bounced off her skin. Matt wondered what was going through her mind. He got up and wrapped his arms around her so that they clasped just below her breasts.

The sensation was overwhelming. "I love you, Nikki," he said, surprised at how easy the words came out. He pulled her slightly toward him so that their bodies were like one. In the cool air of the room, her body was a furnace. She turned, put down the wine, put her arms around his neck, and almost effortlessly pulled herself up and wrapped her legs around his waist. She seemed weightless, the move of a ballerina. Matt carried her back to the bed.

***

Matt lifted his head from the pillow and looked at the clock. It was after midnight. What seemed like minutes had been over three hours. He had been lying there dreaming, Nikki at his side, their bodies still wrapped together. He slowly pulled away. He heard her moan in her sleep. Then he remembered his daughter was waiting for him at home. For a second, panic set in. He rushed to get dressed. As he was about finished, Nikki turned over on the bed. He could see her eyes sparkle in the dim light of the room. She wrapped the sheet around herself and got up. She came over slowly, looked at him and said, "I love you, too. Can't you stay?"

Matt hesitated, too long he thought. Finally he said, "I can't. My daughter's here, I told her I would be home by 11:00, she'll wonder…I'd just as soon not have to…"

She put her finger to his lips. "Shhh," she said. "You don't have to explain."

Neither one felt this was a moment to talk. She followed him down the stairs, through the great room and out of the breezeway. He kissed her on the lips. She smiled. The night was cool and damp as he walked toward his car.

***

"You dumb bastard!" The words echoed in his car. He had driven a few miles from Nikki's house to the highway. His accusation repeated itself quietly in his head. It took only moments and distance to realize the gravity of what had happened. A lawyer having sex with the wife of a man he is representing on the charge of first degree murder. He knew he had gone there with a sense of anticipation, with a feeling that she had more in mind than just dining. Now, with the excitement of the encounter and the effects of the wine fading, the folly of the whole episode enveloped his mind and he felt sick. How could he look Vince in the eye? How could he and Nikki talk across a table or meet in the halls of the courthouse without some glance or touch giving them away?

And if anybody finds out, how could he face the other lawyers in town and all of his friends without feeling that he had betrayed everything he stood for. Nobody would understand.

As he stood in the bathroom the next morning, hesitating to shave, he stared at his reflection. He looked terrible. He'd had way too much wine, his head felt thick. Natalie called through the open door, "What time did you get home last night? I waited up until after eleven but couldn't stay awake."

"It was around midnight or so. The meeting took longer than I expected."

"Well, whatever bar you were in last night," she said, "should have a no smoking policy. Your suit reeks of tobacco."

He could picture Nikki lighting a cigarette; how many, he couldn't remember.

He stumbled into the shower hoping he could wash away what he felt.

On the drive to his office the night's events rolled over in his mind. He had never known such passion. With the recall of every intimate detail, the regrets, the pangs of conscience, faded. He was already trying to figure out how he could see her again.

As he walked into the reception area, Kay said, "You look terrible. What happened to you last night?"

"Just a little too much wine," he said. "Thanks for your concern."

"You better call Mrs. Fischer," Melanie said. "She's been on the phone three times already. She won't leave a message, but she sounds anxious."

Both women stared at him as he made his way into his office. He sat down at his desk and reached for the phone, then hesitated. Why would she be anxious? Maybe Vince came home. Maybe he had somebody watching the house. Maybe she's full of remorse. Maybe she wants me off the case. He paused at such thoughts, and then he dialed her number. There was no anxiety in her voice. She was calm and pleasant.

"I just want to thank you for last night. I was on the verge of going crazy. I was desperate, but I didn't have anywhere to turn.

I can't simply pick up and leave, I have no place to go...and now I believe Vince would never let me get away without hurting me some way."

"I think we have to talk, Nikki. I think we have created one hell of a problem. Both of our futures could be on the line here. When is Vince going to be back?" he asked.

"Not until late tonight."

"Can we meet for lunch? Same place, same time?"

"Sure," she said. "I look forward to it."

Matt left for lunch earlier than necessary. He knew some back roads he could take that would give him the time to think. Kay had looked at him suspiciously when he left, reminding him he had to be back for a meeting at 1:30. And why shouldn't she be suspicious? How could he seriously believe he could have an affair with a client's wife, a client charged with murder, shortly before the trial is scheduled to start, and not suffer terrible consequences? The thoughts crowded his mind. If someone found out, how could he possibly talk his way out of it? He'd be disbarred. He laughed to himself—that would be the least of his worries.

chapter 22

"I CAN'T LIVE with him anymore," said Nikki.

They were sitting at the same table in the same corner of the same restaurant.

"Just the thought of him coming home tonight makes me cringe. The idea he would try and hug me or kiss me is revolting. I know you have commitments. I know this whole thing may seem impossible to you. But I felt as deeply last night as I've ever felt in my life. After you left, I looked at the clock. I couldn't believe the time had gone so fast. I have never enjoyed being with any one so much. I would hate to see it end."

By then the waiter had put the food in front of them. Matt looked at his plate, there was no way he could eat. His heart was in his throat. The way she looked at him, the tenor of her words, made him simply forget his concerns. He wanted to make love again. He gazed at her for a long time, wrapped in his thoughts and speechless. She lit a cigarette.

Lost for words and to break the silence, he said, "You know, those things will kill you."

He couldn't believe how ridiculous it sounded, but it had its desired effect. She grinned and for a moment the tension was gone.

"I really need time to think this out, Nikki. I feel the same way you do. Right now I couldn't give a damn about anything. We could get up, walk out and take off and not worry about the consequences. But that would be short-lived and I'm sure we would both regret it. I doubt I can ever let you out of my life but we have to do this right."

She smiled and reached across the table and touched his hand.

"Just remember," he said, "if you ever feel in danger, if Vince ever threatens you, if you have any concerns, you get out of there. You give me a call…give the police a call. If something happens to you it won't matter anymore. I know if Vince has any inkling of something going on between the two of us, your life's in danger. There is a dark side to his heart, Nikki."

Neither of them had touched their food. The waiter noticed and came to the table.

"Is anything wrong?" he asked.

"No," said Matt. "I guess we just weren't hungry."

He looked at his watch. It was already one-fifteen. He had promised Kay he'd be back.

Walking to their cars Matt assured Nikki everything would be all right. He wanted her to call tomorrow and let him know what Vince was like when he got home. He told her to be very careful; it was not beyond Vince to have the phones tapped or to have somebody watching her. Matt was already suspicious Vince might be having her followed. When she drove up before lunch, he watched from the window for the longest time to see if any other cars followed her in. There was nothing. But he wasn't going to take any chances.

***

Vince called Matt the next morning. He was in a good mood. He said he had a great trip to Dallas. He had worked out a joint agreement with somebody that was going to make him a lot of money. Vince said he had talked to Peter that morning and Peter wanted a summary of where the criminal case stood. There was some planning they had to do and he wanted the three of them to meet, preferably today over lunch. Matt said that was fine. They planned to meet at the Radisson at noon.

Matt sat back in his chair and gathered his thoughts. He was analyzing exactly where the case stood. He wanted to make a presentation to Peter Maxwell that basically highlighted the defense tactics without revealing the depth of the state's case. He still wasn't sure whether Vince had read all of the police reports. He had no way of knowing whether Vince had revealed anything to Peter on the *Spreigl* notice and the statements of his prior wives. Matt was pretty sure if Peter and Vince had any discussions regarding the case, Vince's attitude would've been, "Those fuckheads don't have anything to go on." He couldn't let Peter believe that. But on the other hand, he couldn't let Peter know that unless something drastic happened, he believed Vince would be convicted of first degree murder.

Matt liked to be early for appointments. He hated to be kept waiting and it was a thing with him to make sure that other people did not have to wait for him. He got the table and was seated, sipping a glass of water, when Vince and Peter walked in. They exchanged greetings. Vince told him about his trip to Dallas. Peter confirmed the agreement could result in huge profits. After a while, Peter asked Matt for an assessment of the case. Matt, true to his plan, told Peter the strength of the state's case based on the physical evidence. He told him about Dr. Evans. How Dr. Evans could come in and testify that Dr. Michaels had been too firm in his opinion and how Dr. Evans was sure that with the right cross-examination, Dr. Michaels' testimony could be softened considerably. He told him about Carlson, the firearms expert. He finished by summarizing the statements Tim had taken from the women, how gracious, congenial and generous Vince had been, and that several of them were willing to testify as character witnesses if necessary.

Vince took it all in with a grin. So he couldn't be criticized later, Matt said, "There is some *Spreigl* evidence regarding some prior arguments Vince had in his previous marriages. I'm not sure the judge will let any of that in. At least, we're trying to keep it out."

Matt had left an opening for Vince to say something. He didn't. Peter, being a corporate attorney, had never tried a case in his life, probably hadn't been in a courtroom for many years. It didn't appear to Matt that Peter grasped the significance of what he was telling him. That was fine. He didn't need anyone to panic.

"We have some concerns, Matt," said Peter. "Not about the way the case is progressing but something that may be happening on the civil side. Vince has heard through the grapevine that Donna's sister, the one who lives in Connecticut, the one married to the Wall Street attorney, has contacted a law firm in Minneapolis regarding proceeding civilly against Vince on a wrongful death claim. Ironically, it's the Culpepper Firm. The same firm we considered talking to about representing Vince in the criminal matter. It's just a rumor, Matt; we haven't received any papers. Vince heard this from one of Donna's girlfriends. He ran into her out at Anton's. She had obviously been there longer than she should've and was more talkative than I'm sure Donna's family would've liked. Timing may be important though, Matt. You have to keep me updated as far as the court proceedings and when we might expect an end to all this. I told Vince that I have complete confidence in you. While I'm sure he will be found innocent, there's no sense being reckless."

Matt had become so wrapped up in the defense of the criminal charges he hadn't even considered what may be happening on the civil side. He'd forgotten that she had left two children who were dependent upon her for their home and care; that regardless of whether Vince was found guilty of intentional shooting or an accidental shooting, those children would be entitled to be compensated for the fact their mother was taken from them. Matt assured Peter he would keep him apprised of how the case was going. Reading between the lines, Matt realized Peter's plan was to make sure, if he could, that Vince's estate would not be subject to any judgment in a civil court on a wrongful death claim.

They continued to chat as lunch was served. The subject changed from business to what was going on around town. Finally, Peter turned to Vince and said, "By the way, Vince, the Chamber of Commerce is having one of those Chamber After Hours tonight. You know, where they go to a business, a relaxed setting, drinks and hors d'oeuvres, you get a tour. Tonight it's at the Stearns County National Bank. I know they intend to put on quite a spread to impress everybody. Maybe you'd want to come along. It may be good for you to be seen at this time with sort of an unconcerned attitude."

"How long do you think it'll be?" asked Vince.

"Why don't I plan on picking you up about six and I'll have you home by ten or so."

"That's fine."

Peter turned to Matt. "Do you ever go to those things?"

"I try not to," he replied.

As Matt walked back to his office, his mind was racing. It was a warm April day. It was a day it felt great to be alive and now Matt knew Nikki was going to be alone. He didn't wait to get back to his office to call. The first public phone he saw, he dropped in a quarter and called. She was excited. Even though Vince had not gone into any tantrums since his return from Dallas, she still dreaded spending the evenings with him. He was cold and aloof. He had not tried to touch her nor made overtures to solve their problems. She said she'd only had one consuming thought: Matt Collins.

Matt didn't trust going to the house. He thought Vince could pull a fast one and come home at any time. He told Nikki to drive to a truck stop along the highway and he would pick her up. He would be there by six. That would give them at least a couple of hours to themselves.

Matt could've forgotten the rest of the afternoon. He wandered around the office aimlessly. He would pull pages out of Vince's file, try to read them, but to no avail. They were just words. Besides, he knew everything in that file by heart. He looked at the clock. He couldn't believe how slow time was going. He went in to talk to Kay, who was busy putting some documents together. She was getting annoyed with his pacing in and out.

She finally looked at him and said, "I wish I knew what you were up to."

"I bet you do," he said.

chapter 23

FROM A BLOCK away, Matt could see Nikki's white Audi in the parking lot of the truck stop where they had arranged to meet. He pulled up alongside. She burst into a smile and climbed quickly into the front seat.

"Hi there," she said.

"Hi, Nikki," he said and he reached over and put his hand on her knee and she put her hand on top of his. He squeezed her leg gently before he put the car in reverse and drove away.

"How'd this happen?" she asked.

Matt explained the luncheon meeting and the Chamber event that Peter had talked Vince into attending.

"Good ol' Peter," Nikki said with a smile. Her warmth and sexuality filled the car. They had no plans. They had no idea where they were going. Matt just drove and they talked. They talked about what they would do under different circumstances, if they were both just free to do whatever they wanted. It was amazing to him how their wishful thinking seemed to meld. For all the things that she had done to survive, she was a very inquisitive and free spirit. She loved nature. Had she been brought up in a different environment, had she had the opportunity she believed she would've been a marine biologist, or worked for a zoo, or maybe a veterinarian. Something to do with nature and animals. She loved the outdoors. She loved to garden. She talked about how she had spent the summer landscaping, or re-landscaping, Vince's yard. She couldn't believe that he had hired a gardener who had filled all of those beautiful flower beds with nothing but petunias and impatiens. She had replaced them with perennials. She enjoyed talking to Matt so much. She had never been able to express this side of herself to anybody, she said. She was always afraid they would laugh.

Matt reached for her hand. They were driving west into the sunset. The sky was a blaze of colors. Matt told her that he knew a spot in the hills above Avon where you could see for miles, where the view would be spectacular. They were only minutes away.

Matt pulled off the highway onto a dirt road, drove for a couple of miles uphill, and finally stopped near an open field. He helped her out of the car and they walked several hundred feet to the crest. There the whole sky opened up. The sun had dropped behind the hills leaving a horizon of deep rose pink. The fields still had the tan and brown colors of winter and the trees against the sky were dark silhouettes with long dark fingers pointing in every direction. Matt looked at Nikki's face. Her delight was obvious.

He put his arm around her shoulder and pulled her tightly to him. She turned toward him and they kissed, a gentle kiss but still conveying all the feelings they had for each other. She smiled at him and said, "Are we safe here?"

"We're not really safe anywhere," said Matt, returning the smile.

"You know what I mean," she laughed.

"We can see any car coming for at least a half a mile up the road. We're pretty close to my territory. I know some of the farmers up in these hills. If I get caught here in the woods with a beautiful woman, I can imagine how fast that would spread. I'm willing to risk it." He really didn't care. Looking in her eyes, he knew what he was going to do. As far as he was concerned, the world could watch.

She was in a colorful spring dress with buttons down the front, from top to bottom. It was held tightly around her waist by a bright yellow belt. In a deep kiss, he put his hand by her hip and pulled the dress up in folds; he felt nothing but bare skin.

She leaned her head back slightly to break the kiss.

"Surprise," she said.

She unbuttoned the top three buttons of the dress to reveal her breasts. Matt leaned down and kissed one, then the other. She shivered. He was again amazed at how warm her body was against the cool evening air.

"We can't do it out here," she said, "although I'd love to." Matt let the folds of her dress fall. They hurried back down the hill to the car where she motioned him into the back seat. They kissed and petted, like teenagers excited to explore each other's body, rushing to climax.

***

Back in the front seat, Matt turned the key and turned on the lights. The clock on the dash said 8:30. He had to get her home. He decided to get off the country roads and onto the freeway as quickly as possible. On the interstate, he asked, "Has Vince been talking to you about any conversations he's had with Peter Maxwell regarding any civil suit against him?"

"He didn't talk to me, but I heard him this morning having a long phone conversation with Peter. He was in the bedroom and he thought I was still asleep. He had called Peter quite early saying something about a conversation he had heard in a bar the night before and some Minneapolis law firm. I didn't put the whole thing together. I heard your name come up but I couldn't make heads or tails out of it."

"I've been wondering—did you sign a prenuptial agreement before you married Vince?"

"I had already moved in with him and there was some talk of marriage when one night he brought a document home. It had been prepared by Peter. He said that Peter had told him that a man in his position couldn't afford to just get married without taking some precautions. He said Peter had pretty much convinced him he had to have a prenuptial agreement signed. He said if it was up to him, he wouldn't require me to sign one. He knew we were going to be together forever, it wouldn't make any difference. I told him, if it didn't make any difference, why should I sign it. To be honest with you, Matt, I knew I had him. I knew he was going to marry me, prenuptial agreement or not. But I decided, what the heck, I don't want anything out of him anyway."

Matt listened, his mind working overtime; he wasn't paying attention to his driving. Looking down, he noticed he was going way over the speed limit. All he needed was to have a local sheriff or highway cop pull him over and say, "Well, Mr. Collins, fancy meeting you here. And who is that in the car with you?"

He slowed down and put the car in cruise.

chapter 24

IT WAS NOW down to three weeks until the beginning of the trial. Everything was in place. Dr. Evans was on call; he knew approximately when he would be expected to be in Minnesota. The same with Carlson. They had not set a date for any hearing on the *Spreigl* evidence. At the request of the prosecutor, the judge had decided to hold the *Spreigl* hearing during jury selection because the state was still trying to get the first wife to appear voluntarily before they served her with a subpoena. Although she had given one of the deputies a statement a long time ago by telephone, she didn't want to come back to Minnesota and she certainly didn't want to have to testify about Vince Fischer.

Matt had objected to the delay, indicating it would cause problems with his preparation for jury selection and the questions that would be asked, but the judge felt the county's request was reasonable.

Matt had not seen Nikki for over a week, since their trip into the hills of Avon. Vince was sticking close to home and it was too dangerous. They talked by phone at every opportunity. Matt knew Kay and Melanie were getting suspicious about all of the long telephone conversations he was having, even though they didn't know who was on the other end. The fact that he couldn't see Nikki, be close to her, kiss her, was tearing him up inside. He'd become irritable and short tempered. He blamed it on the pressure of the upcoming murder trial. Matt and Nikki had to be content talking about how things were going to be different some day.

Matt had thought about that "someday," laying in bed many nights, into the early hours, thinking of how he was totally committed to her and how they could possibly have a future together. What if Vince was found guilty? What would happen? Nikki would have two options. She could either divorce him, in which event she would walk away with nothing; or she could stay in the marriage, with Vince in prison, and they could carry on the way they were now. But Matt knew he couldn't live with that. On the other hand, what if Vince wasn't found guilty? She had the same options. She could divorce him and walk away with nothing, or she could continue living with him, which Matt thought she would never do. Under either scenario, he had to wonder where he would fit in. If she walked away from the marriage, whether Vince was convicted or not, and the two of them were seen together, his career would be over. Who would ever hire an attorney who stole his client's wife in the middle of a murder trial? The thought was too ridiculous. Maybe they'd have to start a whole new life. But with what? Matt hadn't saved a dime. He could barely put his children through college. It was all irrational. How could he have screwed up his life so badly? But then it always came down to Nikki. She was worth anything he had to do to keep her. He laughed at his predicament. He wouldn't be the first man to make an ass out of himself over a woman.

"Melanie," said Matt over the intercom, "would you call Mrs. Fischer and see if she has some time to come in this afternoon? I have to talk to her." He made it sound official. Several minutes later, Melanie came back on the intercom. "Mrs. Fischer is on line two, Matt."

"Can't we meet someplace else?" Nikki said. "I really want to be close to you."

"No," he said, "not now. We have to be careful. But I do have to talk to you. We can do it here in my office. This is as safe as any place. No one would suspect anything."

She agreed to be there in an hour.

Matt closed his door. He picked his most comfortable chair. He needed to script his meeting with Nikki. His meeting with

Peter Maxwell had given him an idea. He believed he knew Vince's character well enough to know that he would not want to give up a dime to Donna's family. Vince didn't have any children and to Matt's knowledge, the only relative left was a brother who ran a gas station somewhere out of town and because of Vince's success, hated him for it. They hadn't talked for years. Nikki would be the natural recipient of his fortune, Matt thought. Now he had to convince Nikki that she should be the dutiful wife; she had to get Vince thinking about consequences of the civil lawsuit, what he could do to best protect his fortune, the fortune Nikki would inherit.

When Kay led Nikki into the office, Matt immediately remembered why he had spent all of those sleepless nights. She was a breath of spring in a deep blue skirt and a pale blue blouse. A black leather belt accented her small waist. Every time he saw her, the feelings welled up inside. Matt closed the door. They sat in the back of the office so Matt could be sure nothing would be overheard.

"Nikki," he said, "I can't get you out of my mind. I've created a living hell of my life...you're my only redemption. There's no way I'm gonna let you go."

Nikki's eyes widened. She moved toward Matt, then paused and smiled. "I feel the same way. I feel like I'm in prison in that big house with Vince. I need your help, Matt, I want out of that prison."

Matt gazed at her. He had made a living trying to judge a person's character. He believed she was telling the truth. He hesitated a moment. If he was wrong, he would lose her and everything else.

Matt chose to be as blunt as possible. "Nikki, there is only one way you and I can come out of this doing the things we've talked about, the things we want to do. That is if you get Vince's money and then he goes to prison for life." He held his breath, waiting for her reaction.

Nikki stared at him. Seriousness came over her face. "God, I can't believe it. When did you come up with that?"

Daniel Eller

"It wasn't a matter of coming up with it. It just sort of developed. The more I thought of you and me and our circumstances, the more desperate I became. It was just there."

"How could we possibly do that?" she asked. "I can understand the prison. I know in my own heart that the jury will look at him, they're gonna see the real Vince Fischer and send him to prison. But I've already told you he made me sign that prenuptial agreement. There's no way I would get his money."

"That's why I had to talk to you." said Matt. "I know there is some planning going on. Peter Maxwell brought it up at our meeting several days ago. Donna's family has already hired the Culpepper Office. When they see somebody like Vince on the other side, with his kind of money, they smell blood. They're gonna go after his gonads. Vince told Peter he would never agree to pay anything. I sensed that there was something personal there. It isn't because of her kids; it's something else in the family, something that bothers Vince deeply."

"What do I have to do?" she asked.

"It's what *we* have to do. We have to keep the civil claim on his mind, bring it up enough so that he gets concerned enough to do something quickly, before the trial. But we have to be subtle; he can't suspect something's going on. You're gonna have to play the good wife so that he's willing to consider how he could hide his assets in your name."

"I can do that. Trust me."

They talked on like co-conspirators, excitedly planning how they could make their scheme work. How she would suggest that Matt come out for dinner so they could talk about the trial and jury selection and all the things that Vince had to know. She would try and set that up in the next night or so. To Matt, it appeared she reveled in the plan.

A grin crossed her face. "I have my surprise clothes on today."

She opened her blouse and slowly pulled one side down to expose her breast. With her other hand, she pulled her skirt up above her knees.

"We can't do anything here," he whispered.

"Why not?"

"Somebody could come in at any time."

"Lock the door," she said.

"I never lock the door. If they heard the click, everyone would wonder what the hell's going on. Melanie's desk is right outside, and Kay's office is right next door."

By then he had stood up to move to the door. She took his hand, placed it on her breast. "I think you're growing," she laughed softly.

"Really Nikki, we can't. We've got too much riding on this. It would just be foolish to risk anything at this point."

She smiled as she buttoned her blouse. "I don't think you should be walking me out in your condition. In fact, I think you better sit down behind your desk. I can find my way out." She leaned into him and kissed him on the lips.

chapter 25

TWO DAYS LATER at 6:00 p.m. Matt was on his way to Vince's house. Nikki had done her job. Vince believed it was to discuss trial strategy. Matt was nervous. The whole plan depended on how well he did tonight. Vince had to believe it was his idea. He had to say, "What's wrong with me putting my stock, accounts, and house in Nikki's name? Anything so that conniving family doesn't get their hands on it!" If Vince thought he was being prodded or conned, Matt knew it would never work. It was up to Nikki to set the stage.

Vince shook his hand vigorously, he was happy, elated. He offered Matt a drink. Matt could tell that Vince had the early exuberance of too many drinks. He wanted him to have many more before the night was over. Vince set a Windsor soda in front of Matt.

"Well, I had another telephone call from Peter today. He's really concerned about that civil bullshit. It's been confirmed that the family hired that Culpecker, Culpepper, whatever his name is, from Minneapolis."

Matt couldn't believe it. How opportune, he thought. He let it pass so as not to seem too eager.

"There are several reasons why I wanted to talk to you, Vince," said Matt. "I thought I could give you a final summary of where we're at, and also the prosecutor, Scott, called me a couple days ago and wanted to know if we could sit down and talk in the next week or so. I think he wants to talk about whether we can get this matter resolved without having to go to trial. Some sort of plea bargain."

"What sort of plea bargain?" asked Vince.

"Vince, I don't think it's a good time for us to be talking about a plea. I have no idea what they may offer, if anything. And anything they do offer will involve prison time. Even first degree assault or manslaughter calls for prison time except under unusual circumstances."

"Manslaughter?" said Vince. "What the hell are you talking about, manslaughter?"

"Well you can have a death, an intentional death, without it being murder. It can be manslaughter. In this case it would mean you killed her in the heat of passion."

Vince raised his hands. "Hold it! Every time I talk to you I get a brain freeze! Where do you guys come up with all this shit?"

"Vince, that's why I said it won't do us any good to sit here and speculate what the state may offer. I knew it would just piss you off again."

"Good. Then let's forget it for now."

By then Nikki had walked into the great room from the kitchen. Matt could see that she had been listening to the conversation while she was preparing dinner. Vince had his back to her. Several times she had looked through the door at Matt, smiled and given thumbs up. Matt had struggled to keep a straight face.

"There's one thing I forgot," said Matt. "Several days ago I sent you a copy of a statement by Donna's sister, Susan Portnoy, from Connecticut. The state has added her to its witness list. Did you get a chance to read the statement?" Matt could see the anger cross Vince's face.

"That's the bitch that's behind this whole wrongful death bullshit," he said. "She's married to some fat ass Wall Street attorney and I'm sure he's the asshole who got in touch with Culpecker. She's a snooty goddamn broad."

"Then you read the statement?" asked Matt.

"Damn right I read the statement and it's all bullshit"

"What did she say?" asked Nikki.

"She said that Donna had talked to her on the phone several

times in the months before her death and complained about how Vince was obsessed with her and would not let her alone. She said Donna intended to tell Vince that it was over. She was just waiting for the right time and place," said Matt.

"What she didn't know," said Vince, "is while Donna was complaining to her over the phone on one day, the next day she was out here asking me for money and giving me a blowjob."

"Vince!" Nikki said. "Let's not get into that."

"I know she was the one who was responsible for breaking up our relationship. I only met her once. That was at that family reunion in March and I know she's the reason that Donna didn't want to invite me. She's a stuck-up bitch with a degree from one of those East Coast pussy colleges, married to a Wall Street jack off."

Matt leaned back. Now Matt knew why Vince's feelings ran so deep about giving any money to the kids. After Donna's death, her sister and her husband had filed for guardianship of the children. The children had moved to Connecticut. If the children got any money, she would be handling it for them. Vince blamed her for the fact that Donna broke off the relationship.

Vince continued, "It was obvious to everybody at that party that she thought I wasn't good enough for Donna. I didn't have any big fuckin' college degree. I wasn't refined and sophisticated and well-read. I didn't go to the New York Opera. I wasn't at a Broadway play every week. I couldn't talk about *Cats*. Can you imagine that, Matt? She started talking about *Cats*, a bunch of goddamn faggots dressed like cats running around on the stage and because I didn't know what she was talking about, she thought I was a hick. I asked her if *Cats* was the same as pussy. I told her I'd seen a lot of pussy running around on stage in my time. She wouldn't talk to me after that. Do you know I gave Donna a ring? Goddamn thing cost me twenty thousand dollars. After that argument with her sister, she threw it at me. I'll roast in hell before I'll let that family get a goddamn dime of my money."

To Matt the whole picture was comical. He could see Vince in his blue jeans and leather vest arguing with some Connecticut society matron over *Cats*.

Matt realized he had gotten Vince to the point where he would be willing to talk about his estate. He appeared to have that "don't give a damn" attitude. Matt approached it cautiously.

"You know, Vince, what Peter was saying the other day might be right. It might be worthwhile to make some overtures to settle for a small amount."

"No fuckin' way!" shouted Vince.

"Look at the alternatives," said Matt. "You hear of jury verdicts all the time into the millions of dollars. There was one in the paper the other day, fourteen million dollars." He didn't tell him that it was a medical malpractice suit in which a young child was going to be a vegetable the rest of his life. "You could face the same problem you're gonna face in the criminal trial. If that jury doesn't like you, you never know what to expect."

"Peter and I have talked about it a little," said Vince. "What are your thoughts?"

"The only option you have," said Matt, "is to try and get whatever you own out of your name. You need somebody to be a custodian, somebody you can trust. The other problem you face is Minnesota does have a Fraudulent Transfer Act. I'm not sure of the exact mechanics of it, but if the estate of Donna's children could prove that you transferred your assets to avoid payment on any judgment they may get, the court can set the transfer aside. So it has to be done carefully. Did Peter say anything about doing it in the form of an estate plan? You know, trying to give it to Nikki, for example, in the form of some trust or inheritance."

Vince sat quietly. It was apparent to Matt, though, that the combination of the liquor, the discussion, and the pressure of the whole situation could lead to another explosion. He thought it best to change the subject.

"It's nothing we have to decide right now, Vince. I'm not even sure why I brought it up other than the conversation we had with Peter the other day and the few thoughts I've had about it since then. I think there's a way you can protect it, but we'll leave that up to the business lawyers." Matt steered the conversation away from the pending trial and they went into dinner.

Later, as Matt got up to leave, Vince went into the great room. Nikki followed Matt to the door to let him out.

"He hasn't touched me," she whispered, reassuringly. "He hasn't even tried"

Driving home, Matt mulled over the conversation with Vince. He had planted the seed. Now what could be said to force Vince to make a move? Based on everything he knew about Vince, he couldn't imagine he would easily turn any part of his estate over to Nikki. They had barely known each other for two years. The marriage was only eight months old. Since the indictment, things had deteriorated. Matt thought about how Nikki had played her part tonight. How she hung on every word Vince uttered. She smiled and pampered him. He would leave it alone for a while. There were several weeks to trial. He would let Nikki continue to do her job.

chapter 26

MATT HAD TALKED to the county prosecutor by phone early in the morning. Scott Larson wanted to talk about a possible resolution but he wouldn't be free until after lunch. Scott was one of the few county attorneys left who did not have his office in the Government Center. They agreed to meet at the Sheriff's Office. Driving the thirty miles to the county seat, Matt played a game, tried to guess what the prosecutor would possibly offer. A typical offer would be second degree murder: that Vince shot Donna intentionally, but without premeditation. But that wouldn't do Vince a lot of good. Rather than life, he'd get twenty-five years. For Vince, that would be life. Matt couldn't imagine that the prosecutor would go down to anything less.

When Matt arrived at the Sheriff's Office, the prosecutor was already there with the sheriff and Deputy Bob Lentz. The conversation started casually: "How are things going? What's new in St. Cloud? Who's gonna be the next judge?" Small talk. Finally, Scott Larson's demeanor turned serious. "You know, we wanted to see if Vince would be willing to plead something out."

"I doubt it," replied Matt. "He's adamant that it was an accident. He thinks this whole thing has been concocted by her family for whatever reason. It would take a real special deal before I could even suggest to him to plead to anything."

"You know this has not been an easy case for us," said Scott, "not only because of who he is but because of the circumstances. We struggled with this. Let me tell you how I see this case. I don't have anything to hide and if this helps to get it resolved without going to trial, all the better. It's never made sense to me that anybody would've left a loaded shotgun leaning up against a wall outside a main door of the house, especially when Vince knew a ten-year-old boy was going to be playing out there. In fact, it never made sense to me that Vince would be out shooting squirrels with a shotgun in the morning in the first place. Troy's going to say he saw that shotgun by the gun case in the great room. That it had been there all day."

"I don't remember seeing that in any of his statements." said Matt.

"You're hearing it now," said Scott. "He was afraid to talk about it. It's taken him this long to get over what happened and that's what he's telling us."

"You sure his aunt didn't put him up to it?" asked Matt.

"We'll never know," said Scott. "I even have a suspicion Vince purposely punctured that hole in her oil pan, knowing she was going to have to come to him for help. Her dad said Vince's ego wouldn't take rejection. I think he's right. It looks to us like he's been able to seduce any woman he's wanted, but he's the one who calls it off, not her. He couldn't get Donna to make a commitment to him. His talk about them getting married is just crap. You know, she was shacking up with another guy and had been there the night before. I believe we know what happened. Donna decided to take his help because she didn't have much of a choice. She also thought this was probably a good opportunity to try and straighten matters out with Vince, to convince him it was over and that they could remain friends and nothing more. From talking to her friends, we know she came to his house with that idea. We also know he got her drunk, which wasn't that hard. Her blood alcohol level was .25 when she walked out that door; that was more than a couple beers. We know they argued because Troy said he heard loud voices and then Vince had sent him outside. Troy said he got bored and he wanted to go home. When he came into the kitchen, his mother wasn't there. Vince said she was in the bathroom, that she would be right out, and he would drive them home. He should go wait in the car. That makes more sense to us. The only thing we don't know is exactly what happened between that time and when she was shot. What was actually said. But I suspect they got into an argument, something was said and whatever it was, she walked out. Vince grabbed the gun, followed her out and shot her. I think he might've had that in mind when he got her there. The whole thing was set up to intimidate her into staying, and if she wasn't willing, to kill her."

"Then you're really talking premeditation," said Matt.

Lentz broke in. "You know, Matt, the night we were there, following her death, we all noticed crumpled up hundred dollar bills on the cabinet. It looked as if they had been thrown there. We took pictures the next day, before anything was moved. There were three one-hundred dollar bills. We suspect they were thrown there in anger, during an argument. Unfortunately, as you know, the pictures never got developed. The camera wasn't working."

"There's no other way of looking at it," said Scott. "Now the real reason for asking you here. Ms. Woods' sister has been in contact with us numerous times. I don't know if you know, but her husband's an attorney in New York."

"I knew that," said Matt.

"The children are with them; they're getting adjusted. She doesn't believe it would be in their interest to have to come back to Minnesota, face Vince and go through the ordeal of a trial. They believe Vince should be punished but they don't think he has to spend the rest of his life in prison. I think Donna was the black sheep of the family. She lived on the edge and the family felt that eventually something bad was going to happen to her. I'm not sure they're really surprised she ended up this way.

"Then there's a more practical consideration they have. They've told me they've hired an attorney to proceed with a wrongful death claim against Vince. Whether he's guilty of intentionally shooting her or not, he's gonna pay. From the attorney's point of view, they would like to keep it accidental so they can first look at his insurance. If there isn't enough there, they would go after him personally. If he gets convicted of an intentional homicide, the insurance company will deny any coverage. So indirectly, the aunt has been trying to persuade me to come up with a deal that will accomplish both purposes. The bottom line is, Matt, I'd be willing to let him plead to second degree unintentional felony murder."

"How would that work?" asked Matt, trying to hide his astonishment.

"If we both agree, you and I both know the judge will take it. He doesn't have any desire to sit in trial for several weeks either. The basis would be that Vince intended to assault her, which is the underlying felony, but he didn't intend to kill her, that was accidental. I'm not sure how that helps out the civil attorneys, but it's the best deal we can give them. It's also the best deal Vince is gonna get. If he takes it, he's looking at ninety-seven months in prison of which he'll do two-thirds. He'll be out in a little over five years. Still young enough to enjoy himself and spend all that dough. If he doesn't and the jury convicts him, he'll never see the light of day."

Matt couldn't make a commitment for Vince. He thanked them for their time and consideration and he told them he'd have to talk to Vince and get back to them. He left in shock—he couldn't believe they would make an offer like that. Either he had misjudged what he thought was the strength of their case and the prosecutor didn't see it as he did, which he doubted, or Donna's sister had leaned on the prosecutor quite heavily. Matt suspected the latter. He couldn't believe his luck; providence was on his side. What he had been looking for was something to piss Vince off to the point where he would panic, where he would want to get his property out of his name. It had just been laid in his lap. The sister, the dreadful sister that Vince despised, had pressured the prosecutor to make Vince an offer to plead guilty. An offer that would not only require him to serve five years in prison, but would also allow her to go after both him and his insurance. He knew this was going to gall Vince.

Matt had made arrangements with Vince to stop at his house following the meeting with the county attorney. Vince was anxious to know what it was all about. When Matt got there, it was still warm out. Vince and his friend, John, the one who had been there the morning of the day Donna was shot, were sitting on an open deck enjoying the sunshine. The leaves were budding and there was the slight tint of green through the trees, and new blades of grass were slowly poking up through the dull brown remains.

Matt had told Nikki not to be there. He wanted to talk to Vince alone. She'd made an excuse to go shopping. He wasn't sure what effect John would have on their conversation. Vince offered him a beer and he accepted. It was obvious they had been sitting, drinking beer for some time. John, from what Nikki had said, was a hanger-on. He worked at a local factory. He was a tough two-fisted drinker Vince had met in one of the local bars. Vince had him do some work on one of his cars and now he felt comfortable enough to use Vince's place as a hangout whenever he had nothing else to do. As Matt settled into the chair with his beer, Vince looked at him and said, "Well, what did the old bastard have to say?"

"It was actually very interesting and quite surprising. He wants you to plead guilty, but not to what we talked about. He's willing to go down to second degree unintentional felony murder. It means that you intended to assault Donna but you didn't intend to kill her. The killing was accidental. Under the guidelines, it calls for ninety-seven months of which you would do two-thirds, so you would be out in a little over five years."

Vince stared off toward the lake. Matt wasn't sure what his silence meant. For a moment he was sorry he had told him. It never dawned on him that Vince would ever consider taking any plea bargain. If he did, the plan was gone.

"So they want me to plead guilty and do five years?" asked Vince in a rather calm voice.

"That's how it would work out," replied Matt.

More silence. Matt wasn't sure what he could say. If this was any other person, under any other circumstances, he would tell him to take the offer, that he'd be crazy not to. He couldn't say that to Vince. If he did, and Vince took the offer, everything he and Nikki had talked about and planned for would be gone.

Vince turned to John. "What do you think, John?"

"To me, Vince, it's real simple. If I didn't do it, why would I plead guilty? Why would I spend five fuckin' years in prison for something I didn't do?"

"That's the same fuckin' way I look at it," said Vince.

That's how the conversation continued between them, each feeding on the other's machismo. Thank God for John, thought Matt.

Now was the time to strike. "You know why they made that offer?" asked Matt. "Because of some pressure they're getting from Ms Portnoy and her attorney husband. What the deal does for them is to keep Donna's kids from coming to Minnesota to see you again and it keeps your insurance company in the civil wrongful death case." Matt went on to explain how the plea would leave an argument open that the death was accidental. As he explained it to Vince, Matt could see the veins on the side of his temples bulge. The blood was rushing to his head. His face turned bright red and Matt waited for the explosion.

"That dirty fuckin' bitch! She's gonna get even with me for calling her out at that party. I told her she was a dried up cunt and I meant it."

Matt decided he didn't need to hear anymore. It was an opportune time for him to leave and allow Vince and John to continue drinking and commiserate about how he was getting taken to the cleaners. Walking to his car he was giddy, he knew he had Vince right where he and Nikki wanted him.

chapter 27

THE NEXT MORNING Matt waited anxiously for a call. He knew he would hear from Nikki, Vince, or Peter. Unless it had just been the booze talking, he thought, Vince had to make some move. Nikki finally called at about 10:30.

"What the hell happened last night?" she asked.

"Why?" asked Matt.

"When I got home, Vince and John were drunker than skunks and Vince was ranting and raving about Donna's sister. I mean, there was such a string of vulgarity—I couldn't imagine what he was talking about. Something about money, and castration, and the same old stuff he's been rambling on about for days. You must've told him something. He was on the phone with Peter first thing this morning. He's there now. When he left, he looked at me and he calmly said, 'I better be able to trust you. If I can't trust you, I can't trust anybody. If this turns out right, I'll make it worth your while. If it turns out wrong, you'll be one of the richest ladies around.' Is he gonna do what I think he's gonna do?" she asked.

"God, I hope Peter doesn't talk him out of it," replied Matt. "To be honest with you, Nikki, I'm not sure what they can do. The quickest thing is to just put your name on everything, get it out of his name, call it some sort of an estate plan or whatever they wanna call it. The most that Donna's relatives can do is attack it in court and Peter's office can keep 'em tied up for years. It's a calculated risk, but Vince doesn't have any choice. At least in his state of mind he doesn't think he has any other choice. We've done everything we can do, Nikki, we just have to wait."

"Matt, I can't believe we're doing this. I have just been on such a high ever since we started planning it. I can't wait to get him out of here. I can't wait until you and I are together."

"Remember Nikki, if he smells anything, we're dead."

***

Matt couldn't believe how things were working out. He had rationalized it all out in his own mind. It wasn't a matter of selling out a client. Vince was guilty. He did murder Donna. He was crude and crass, a womanizer and a batterer. If he wasn't rich, nobody would give him the time of day. All he had to do, Matt thought, was give him exactly what he was being paid for—the best defense possible and then the jury was going to find him guilty. What he and Nikki had planned did not change that.

Days went by. Matt had not heard anything from Vince or Peter. Nikki said that Vince had met with Peter on several occasions but he had never brought home any papers for her to sign or ever talked about what had been done. Matt couldn't take it any longer; he had to talk to Vince. Vince was always too busy to come over to his office during the day, at least that's what he told Matt. He made arrangements to meet Vince that night at Anton's. Matt hesitated about agreeing to meet at Anton's. He knew what he wanted to discuss and he knew that if Vince had a few drinks and got upset again, he could get out of hand. Matt had decided long ago that he was going to hand feed everything to Vince, bit by bit. He still hadn't talked to him about the semen or the blood alcohol concentration. It was time to do that. But before he even got a chance to leave, Vince called: he wanted Matt to come to his office.

Vince had his own office building on the East Side, close to his first station. It was three stories high, built on the Mississippi River. He occupied the entire top floor and leased out the first and second. As Matt got off the elevator, he was surprised to see how tastefully decorated it was. It had a professional touch. The receptionist led him into Vince's office. It covered the entire corner of the third floor. On the left, toward the river, were dark green plush chairs and a coffee table. The windows, which filled the entire wall, came just a foot above the floor so that as you sat by the coffee table, you could take in the entire view of the river and the park. Vince's desk was solid oak. His leather desk chair was tall, much taller than the chairs on the other side, so that Vince would be sure of looking down on whoever he was talking to. The colors of the room were deep mahogany and forest green. The walls were covered with wildlife prints. Matt recognized Redlin, Bateman, the Hauptmann Brothers, Kouba. Behind his desk were pictures of Vince with various notables, receiving some recognition for a donation or a gift made. In the middle of them all was an original lithograph of the first federal duck stamp by J.N. "Ding" Darling. Priceless, Matt thought. Somebody had picked all of his art well. Against the opposite wall was a bar and sound system. The television screen was big enough to be in a theater.

Vince was pouring himself a drink, and when he looked up Matt was puzzled by the expression on his face.

"You care for a drink?"

"Sure. I'll have the same."

"I saw you looking at the pictures. Nikki picked them out. She's into all this wildlife shit. I just let her do whatever she wanted. That duck stamp thing cost a few bucks; she picked it up in Florida."

"I didn't know you could get your hands on one of those," replied Matt.

"Leave it to her. She usually gets anything she wants just by wigglin' that ass and showin' a little cleavage, and she isn't afraid to do it, either. Within limits, of course," Vince laughed crudely. Matt looked out the window to avoid meeting his eyes and sharing the joke.

"Well, Matt," Vince continued. "I thought it was time to cut through all the bullshit. You've been awful quiet about some things. I don't know what you make of me. Moreover, I don't give a shit. But I don't wanna be taken for an idiot. I've read all of the reports you dropped off, I know what people are saying. I wondered why you never asked me how much she had to drink. I wondered why you never brought up the fact that she had semen in her cunt. I suspect I scare the shit out of ya, don't I, Matt?"

Matt looked at him. It was a Vince he had never seen before. He was choosing his words carefully, as if he had thought out exactly what he was going to say.

"There may be a little bit of that," Matt replied, "but that's not the reason I didn't bring those matters up. I wanted to go over things with you one-by-one. Quite frankly, that's what I intended to discuss with you tonight, the reason for our meeting. I know what this case is all about, Vince. I know what I have to do, I just wonder if you're prepared."

"You don't know fuck," he replied. "Matt, I was really tempted to take that offer they made but I could never get up in front of anybody and admit that I did it. You told me one time that nobody really knows what happened there except me. I'm gonna tell you what happened."

Matt jumped up. "Vince, you've already told me what happened, that it was an accident, that's what our defense is, that's what we're going to trial with. If you're gonna lay something else on me at this point, I'm getting the hell out of here."

"You're not going anywhere, you piss ant," said Vince. "I know what you're thinking. You think I give a shit about your ethics? You lawyers are all the same. 'Don't tell me the truth because then we're stuck with it.' I've heard that before, but you're going to know the truth. I have to tell somebody and you're the only one who can't blab. Isn't that right, Matt? I think you would abide by that oath, wouldn't you?" He didn't wait for an answer.

"I really did love that girl, Matt. It's hard to explain. She had spent so much time covering up for her husband and hiding drugs and hiding from cops in Hawaii that when I showed her a little attention, she just went crazy. She was a wild person. Regardless of what she was telling anybody, when she walked into a place on my arm, she was as proud as a peacock. She had Vince Fischer. In the beginning, to her, that was really something. She could drive fancy cars; she loved to take my Corvette. She could eat anywhere, dress in anything she wanted, spend money. It was nothing for her to ask for five hundred dollars and then spend it in one afternoon on clothes. She loved to travel: San Francisco,

Miami, New York, Las Vegas, and when we'd go, all she'd want to do is party and fuck. That's the one thing she knew how to do well. She was a horseshit mother. Her kids were always in her way, 'fuckin' brats' this, 'fuckin' brats' that. She would leave them with somebody else at the drop of a hat. We went on like that. And we were talking about getting married. And then that stupid ass family reunion that her old man had to put together; he just had to bring that snooty bitch from Connecticut. Donna didn't want me to come. She wouldn't tell my why, but I knew what it was. I wasn't in her family's class. Can you believe that? I could buy and sell all of them. Her dad never liked me, would never give me the time of day. He wouldn't say 'shit' if he had a mouthful. Anyway, I did a dumb thing. I didn't think it was dumb at the time. I thought I could impress everybody and Donna would be happy. I knew where they were having the party; it was at the Persian Club. Weeks before I had the jeweler find me a special ring, a diamond friendship ring. It set me back twenty grand. I went to the party. She tried to act as if she was glad I was there but I could tell she wasn't; things went from bad to worse. Then I had that confrontation with her bitch of a sister. It was ugly. Things were never the same again. Oh, she would come over and she would ask to borrow money but we both knew she never intended to give it back. But it was different from before. It wasn't, 'Vince, let me have it.' It was, 'Vince, I'll pay you back.' A few times she came over on a Friday or Saturday night, shacked up with me. She must've just been horny; I don't think there was anything more to it." Vince paused momentarily. He could tell he was shocking Matt; it brought on a slight smile.

He took a swig of his drink. "But there was always more to it for me, Matt. I loved every moment she was with me. I didn't care if she was using me or not. I didn't care how much it cost me. If she wanted to shack up for a night, just to relieve an itch, to me it was pure love. When it stopped, I couldn't take it. I tried everything. I sent her money. I talked to her friends. Sent her letters and called. I couldn't get her to come back. Then one of her girlfriends told me that she had met some asshole from the

Daniel Eller

North Shore. A guy like her first husband. One of those good-looking jack offs who isn't worth the pot he pisses in."

Matt sat there entranced. Vince was making a true confession.

"I followed her up north one weekend. She didn't know it. I got his name and got some information on him. He's some asshole college dropout, a ski bum who considers himself an artist. Carvings and pottery, that kind of shit. He tries selling 'em at those craft shops up and down the North Shore. I could never understand how Donna could go from this to that. She just loved money too much. She came to the house after I found out about the asshole. In fact, she borrowed money. I figured she probably ran up there and took the asshole out to dinner. But I was happy with anything. The slightest attention and I thought there was still a chance. I thought she'd get tired of him pretty quick, get tired of not having money again."

Vince had been sitting by the table. He got up, walked to the window, looking toward the river. He was deep in thought. He turned around and slowly walked to his desk, sat down and leaned back, his drink in his hand. Matt knew it wasn't time to open his mouth. Vince expected him to listen.

"Then I came up with a goddamn brainstorm," he continued. "You know I bought the car she was driving. She could've had anything. She picked that piece of trash. I went over to her apartment one day, she wasn't there. I parked next to her car. Nobody was around. I took a hammer and nail and I punctured a hole in her oil pan. Jesus Christ, the oil ran out faster than I expected. I thought for sure she would notice it right away. Not her. The engine overheated, just about shot. I called her one evening. I was pleasant. I just told her I'd like to talk. I understood her feelings. I could live with that. She brought up the car and the quotes she had received to have it fixed. I told her, 'Why waste your money, just bring it out here, I'll have the mechanic fix it, replace the motor if necessary, would be like new, won't cost you a dime.' She said she couldn't do that. She would talk to her dad. I knew that was bullshit. A week or so later she called me. I could tell she was getting desperate. She was tired of having to rely on

146

people for rides. She didn't trust driving the car. She was short of money, she said. This was on a Wednesday, I believe. So we made arrangements for her to come over on Saturday. Then you know what she does? She borrows Jenny's car so that she can go visit that fuckin' artist on Friday night. She was gonna come back Saturday morning. Somebody else was gonna scratch her itch. The truth is, though, I would've taken her under any circumstances. So when she came on Saturday, I thought I still had a chance. I thought I could charm her over. I didn't know she was going to bring Troy. He just got in the way.

"Matt, I didn't have that gun out on the deck by the breezeway. It was leaning against the gun cabinet. John was heading up north, he was gonna take it along. They planned to go for some walks off the highway. He thought he might have an opportunity to plink a sharp-tailed grouse or two while he was at it. He just left in such a hurry, he forgot it.

"When she came, she said she could only stay for a few minutes. I persuaded her to sit and have a beer. That was always her weakness. She could guzzle more beer than any broad I ever met. And then, one beer turned to two and then two to three and pretty soon she was happier than hell. We started reminiscing and talking about the good times and the trips we took. She even talked to her dad in the afternoon. He had called looking for her. I'm sure he was worried when he found out she came out to my place. She told him everything was fine. She was having a good ol' time, she'd be leaving shortly.

"Troy was in the great room watching television or reading, I'm not even sure. I had the television on; I turned it up loud so that he wouldn't hear what his mother and I were talking about. I told her she couldn't do this to me, that she couldn't come into my life and take what she wanted and then just drop me cold. I told her it was all because of her fuckin' sister. That got her pissed. She stood up. She said, 'I'm getting the fuck out of here!' But she had been drinking beer all afternoon and she had to go to the bathroom. Troy heard the loud voices and came into the kitchen. I told him to go out and sit in the Corvette, that we were leaving shortly, that his mother was in the bathroom and that we'd be right out. He was eager to do it. Then she came out and I tried kissing her. She slapped me away. I could see rage in her eyes. She said something like, 'I don't know where in the fuck you get off. You know it was fun at first, Vince. It was exciting; I didn't know how much fun you could have just spending money, hitting bars, having a good time, playing the big shot. You're right; my sister told me you're nothing but a low life jerk, somebody who just fell into some money with a stupid idea. That you couldn't make a silk purse out of a sow's ear.' Then she said her dad was right: that I'm just a crude bastard. That she should have realized all along they were all right about me. I was so angry, Matt. Here's a bitch who's been taking my money and who's been in my bed whenever she felt like it, and she was gonna do it one more time, she was gonna let me fix *my* car for her. I said, 'If you're so goddamn proud of that stupid fuckin' family of yours, why aren't they here to fix your goddamn car? Here you are again; you're going to suck another four or five hundred dollars out of me.' With that, she reached into her purse, she brought out some hundred dollar bills, crushed them up and threw 'em on the cabinet. She said, 'You want your fuckin' money? Here's your fuckin' money, you miserable son-of-a-bitch!' And Matt, it *was* my money; I know it was my money. Then she glared at me and she said, 'You think I need you? I don't need you. I've got somebody who's a better fuck than you've ever been. You never were any good.' She turned around to storm out.

"I don't even know what happened, Matt. It all swelled up inside. The anger was so overwhelming. She had taken every fuckin' thing I could give her and then she spit in my face. As she reached the kitchen door, she turned around and with all the disgust she could muster, in a final gesture, she gave me the finger and said, 'fuck you!' I saw the shotgun leaning against the cabinet, went and grabbed it, and flew out the door. I got to her just as she was in the middle of the deck. Matt, I've tried to recall that instant many times since that night. I'll tell ya, not one thought crossed my mind that I can recall from the time I picked up the gun until I saw her lying on the deck. Every time it goes through my mind, it's like I'm watching it from a distance; like I'm floating over the top and it's instant replay. The blast was tremendous. She flew off her feet and hit the deck with a thump. I rolled her over. There was just a blank stare on her face. I couldn't believe what had happened. I remembered Troy. I ran out to the car, he was hiding in the front seat. He must've heard the shot. I ran back to where she was lying. My mind started racing. I had to come up with a story. I had laid the gun by her side. I did notice it had gotten damp while it was lying there and that's when I came up with the story of the accident. I went over it in my mind until the first paramedics got there."

There was long silence, neither said a word. To Matt, the silence was deafening. He had just heard a man coolly and calmly confess to a murder. Vince had told his story in such a fashion, moreover, that when it was all over, Matt actually felt sorry for him. If somebody he loved deeply had done that to him, would he have been capable of the same thing?

Finally Vince got up and started to mix himself another drink. "You care for another?"

"I might as well," replied Matt.

"Matt, I don't think I can get you to understand how much I really loved that woman. I mean she couldn't walk in the room without givin' me a hard on.

"You know, Matt, I've seen you look at Nikki. She's a classy, beautiful woman. All men look at her like that. But, she's no Donna. Do you like cats, Matt? Not the Broadway show, but the animal," he said with a smile.

"My kids have had them around the house for years," said Matt.

"My third wife had a Siamese," said Vince. "Nikki is a Siamese—classy, sleek, beautiful. Donna was an alley cat. I'm more at home with an alley cat, Matt. Nikki and I really don't have anything anymore, but I think I can trust her and I need her, for a while at least. You look speechless, Matt. I don't think I've ever seen an attorney speechless." He laughed.

Matt *was* speechless. He sat in disbelief. This couldn't become any more complicated, he thought. All he had to do was clean this guy's act up, put him on the stand, let him tell that story to the jury, and he could probably sell manslaughter. What would Vince get? Four or five years in prison, if that. What would that do to him and Nikki? Our plans are shot. On the other hand, if it had really happened that way, it wasn't first degree murder. There was no premeditation. It was done, as they say, in the heat of passion: *before the blood could cool.* There was no willful, malicious planning. Any other defendant and Matt would have been all over him to tell his story. What was he going to do with Vince?

"The old wheels are turning, aren't they, Matt?"

"Well, Vince, you're gonna have to testify. You're gonna have to get in front of a jury and tell them just what you told me. If they believe you, and there's no reason why they shouldn't, they could find you guilty of manslaughter instead of murder."

"No fuckin' way," said Vince. "I told you that once before. There's no way I will go into a courtroom in front of all those people, newspaper reporters, T.V. guys and say that I was so fucked up over this lady that I couldn't control myself. No fuckin' way! No fuckin' way! You hear me?"

It was clear to Matt that Vince had had enough to drink. The possibility that the discussion could continue on any sort of civil basis was slowly fading. It was time for him to get out of there anyway. He needed some time to think, to talk to Nikki, to try and figure out what had just happened, what he was going to do.

"You know, Vince, you've just given me a real ethical dilemma. If you're not going to tell it the way it really happened, I can't put you on the stand knowing you're gonna commit perjury."

Vince looked at him. With a snarl he said, "I told you before, Matt, you fuckin' attorneys have your own way of doing things and I have mine. If you're not gonna put me on the stand and let me tell that jury how it was an accident, I'll find somebody who will. Criminal attorneys are a fuckin' dime a dozen."

Trying to preserve whatever self respect he had left, Matt said, "Well, you may have to do that."

chapter 28

MATT HAD TO talk to Nikki. Now that he knew for sure the extent of what Vince was capable of in anger, he knew she was in danger. He had to tell her, but he knew he couldn't frighten her; they had to continue working together. But it's better she knows, he concluded. She could handle it; she just had to be careful.

Matt stopped at the first telephone booth he saw. She answered after the first ring. She knew he was meeting with Vince.

"Nikki," said Matt. "I can see the bridge over the Mississippi River from here. I think I'm just gonna take a big leap."

"What happened?" she asked anxiously.

"He just confessed to me. He told me how he killed Donna. It was after a big argument. She gives him the finger, tells him to get screwed and, Nikki, he shoots her. He told it in such a way that, I don't know, Nikki, I actually felt sorry for the guy. I can see how it could've happened. I know it sounds crazy, but you had to be there. You know the guy isn't that dumb. He's not the animal he likes to portray. I think he enjoys carrying on like that just to shock people."

"Matt, what are you trying to say?" asked Nikki.

"I'm just telling you, if he's willing to testify and tell his story just like he told me, I can see a jury finding him not guilty of first degree murder. I'm talking manslaughter, Nikki. At least I'd have a much better case arguing manslaughter. In fact, I bet Vince could go to the prosecutor right now, contrite as hell, and tell them, 'This is the way it really happened. I'm sorry I lied, but I panicked. I made the whole accident thing up. I did shoot her, I couldn't help myself. Here's why. She got me to the point where I didn't know what I was doing.' Given his present disposition, the prosecutor may well be willing to take a plea to first degree manslaughter. If that happens, our plans are out the door. I have no idea what Vince and Peter have done as far as transferring his property. But you know damn well we wouldn't see a dime of it. He gets a few years in prison, if that."

"Where does that leave us?"

"Well, he said he would never admit it was intentional and not accidental. He said there's no way in hell he would go in and tell a jury that. Right now I believe him. But what'll I do? You know I have an obligation to represent the best interest of my client. Now I have to walk away from that one more time. I'm starting to wonder how much I can take."

"If that's all our future means to you."

"Don't do that to me! You know better than that. I'll work it out; I always have. I'm just gonna prepare for trial at this point like nothing happened. We'll just have to keep in touch by phone; it's still too dangerous to meet…unless something unusual happens."

"I have to see you," said Nikki.

"Just stay calm," said Matt. "We'll work it out. How about you, though, are you safe there? Now we know for sure what he's capable of doing, you're gonna have to be real careful."

"You and I both knew that there was something more to it than what he was telling us—that it could've been murder. At least that's been in the back of my mind. So I'll keep doing what I've been doing, acting as the dutiful wife."

That's what he wanted to hear. "Remember," he said, "any hint of a problem and you get out of there."

"I love you," she said.

"I love you, too. Just be smart."

chapter 29

THE TRIAL WAS scheduled to start in a week. Matt had worked on his *voir dire*, the questions he would ask prospective jurors. Because the case was one of first degree murder, Minnesota Rules provided that the jurors would be questioned individually without the other prospective jurors being in the courtroom. The defense got to ask questions first and then the prosecution. If both parties kept the juror on, as soon as they had the required twelve, plus the agreed upon alternates, the trial would actually start and the evidence would be introduced.

Both sides expected jury selection to take a week or so. Matt was a firm believer that jury selection could be one of the most important parts of the trial, if not the most important. He believed that if you had a jury that was willing to look the defendant in the eye, seemed to be open, willing to listen, nonjudgmental, the defendant may have a chance, regardless of how strong the state's case was. He believed that in first degree murder cases, it took a very tough jury to send a person to prison for life. He had done everything he could to be prepared for the trial. To lose it, he thought, was now just a matter of waiting.

Discussions with Nikki were fleeting. They didn't trust using their home phones so the only calls made were when she might be shopping or at the grocery store. The calls were always to his office and always short. The only thing she knew for sure was that Peter had prepared some documents which Vince had signed to protect his assets. She had no way of knowing what those documents might have been. Nikki told Matt that Peter Maxwell had asked to be kept updated on trial preparation. Matt thought that this was a good time to give Peter a call. He set up a time to meet at lunch again.

***

"How's it going, Matt?" asked Peter.

Peter sat down at the table. Matt had gotten to the Radisson early again. He was sipping a Windsor soda. He'd asked the waiter to make it stiff.

"Things must be getting tough when you have to have a drink at lunch," said Peter.

"My afternoon's open," said Matt. "I just finalized some of my thoughts in Vince's case."

Matt gave him a short summary of where he was with the case. Nothing important, nothing new.

"How you getting along with Vince?" asked Peter.

"He can be damn difficult," said Matt.

"Tell me about it," said Peter. "I've been putting up with that bullshit from him for over twenty years. Sometimes I just want to tell him to kiss my ass and walk out. But then I think better of it."

"He's hard enough to take when he's sober," said Matt, "and then when he's drunk…"

To change the subject, Matt brought up the judicial appointment coming up. An attorney in Peter's office was interested. Matt thought that would be a good topic to take their minds off Vince Fischer. They discussed the judicial appointment for a few minutes. When Matt thought it was an opportune time, he asked, "By the way, what have you heard as far as the civil matter?"

Peter was quiet for a moment. "This is strictly confidential, of course, but we worked out a plan to get everything out of his name. How long it stays out of his name depends on what happens in your case."

Matt had no idea what they may have done. "I assume Nikki's involved?" he asked.

"Well, that was the logical choice." said Peter. "Vince still places a lot of trust in her. She's that kind of a lady."

Matt didn't feel he could press it further.

"So, if this manslaughter thing comes out and..." Peter stopped in mid-sentence, as if he caught himself in a mistake. He quickly added, "What do you think Vince's chances are, Matt?"

Matt had no idea what had just happened. His pulse quickened, his eyes searched Peter's face. Peter turned his head. Matt sensed it was to avoid eye contact. He wondered who would have brought up anything about manslaughter with Peter Maxwell. Certainly not Nikki. If not, it had to have been Vince. Maybe Vince had told Peter his story as well. Maybe Peter knew Matt was going to allow Vince to commit perjury. Matt didn't have the guts to bring it up, to ask Peter point blank who had said anything about manslaughter. He was probably better off not knowing, anyway. But it bothered him. It bothered him a lot. If something was going on behind his back, something that would affect how he was going to handle the trial, he wanted to know.

By the time Matt got back to the office, Tim was waiting for him. Tim had been to the county seat to pick up subpoenas for some of the young women that Vince had dated and some of Donna's friends that Matt thought he may call as witnesses. At least he had put their names on the witness list.

Matt had to talk to somebody. "This has taken the strangest twist," he said. "You know, Vince did kill Donna, just the way we speculated it happened. She got him so angry and he lost it—he shot her in the heat of passion.

Matt told the whole story to Tim, just the way Vince had laid it out to him. "Now he won't let me try it on the basis of manslaughter," said Matt. "He's gonna go in and lie. He wants to stick to that accident story. I know at least one other person knows the truth as well. But I'm presented with one damn dilemma after another."

Tim looked puzzled. "What damn dilemma are you talking about?"

Matt wasn't going to tell him everything. "You know there are rules, Tim; rules that are meant to prevent me from putting a client on the stand who I know is gonna commit perjury. Several years ago at one of those criminal justice seminars it was the main topic of discussion. The prosecutors and judges claimed that it was a breach of ethics for a defense attorney to allow his client to testify falsely. The defense attorneys, of course, including the one talking at the seminar, said that was just bullshit. He said a defense attorney should use any means at his disposal to defend his client."

Tim looked at him. "That's certainly no revelation, that you might have a defendant that's gonna get on the stand and lie. We've had all kinds of those."

"The difference is," said Matt, "that they haven't told me in advance that's what they intend to do. We all know they're lying, the judge knows they're lying and in ninety-nine point nine percent of the cases, the jurors know they're lying. But I didn't put the defendant on the stand and allow him to testify to a story that was different from what he'd already told me. I'm supposed to make a record of it, get the court reporter aside and make a record in case it ever comes up in post conviction hearings or in the appeal process."

"With the judge there?" said Tim.

"No, the judge isn't supposed to be there. Just the court reporter."

"A lot of good that'll do," said Tim. "Can you imagine? The reporter goes back to the judge's chambers, the judge asks, 'What was that all about?' You think the reporter's gonna say, 'Oh, nothing.'…Give me a break!"

They both laughed. That's what Matt needed, a little comic relief. Tim had helped him put it in perspective. He had already—or was about to—breach every legal cannon he could. Why should putting his client on the stand and letting him lie bother him now?

chapter 30

As the trial date approached, Matt was getting irritable. Everybody noticed. He had always gotten a little uptight before a big trial, but this was different. One day Kay simply asked, "What is *wrong* with you? You've been marching around here like a storm trooper. You've got the personality of Jack the Ripper. I think you better go hang one on or something."

"You know," Matt answered, "as long as I pay your salary, I'll ask you when I want your advice. Right now I don't care for it." By her stare he could tell she was mad. This was totally out of character for him.

As he went back into his office he knew what was wrong. He was struggling with everything. For what? For a woman he loved deeply, but who he hadn't seen, or touched, or kissed, or...well, anything, for weeks. He wasn't even sure she was still with him. He decided to call the house to talk to Vince, hoping she would answer. She did.

"I have to talk to you, Nikki. I have to talk to you before this trial starts.

"Vince's outside," she said. "He and John are trying to put the dock and boat in. I've got an idea. Don't leave your office tonight. No matter how late it gets, just wait for me to call."

He agreed.

Everybody was gone by 5:30. Matt leaned back in his chair, now a little more relaxed. He had a habit of trying to create his closing argument to the jury even before the trial started, on what he expected the testimony to be. The argument could be modified later based on what happened at the trial. To keep his mind off Nikki, he looked at his notes, what he expected to tell the jury. He believed the evidence would show that Vince had been deeply in love with Donna and that at first, as far as the world was concerned at least, Donna was in love with him. Everybody who knew them or saw them said the same thing. She loved to be in his company. She loved what the two of them did together. Vince provided her a security she'd never had before. That at some point in the relationship, after that family reunion, there were two Donna Woodses; the one who told everybody her relationship with Vince was off, who no longer loved him, no longer wanted to be with him; and the other Donna Woods, the one who continued to rely on Vince, who continued to come to his home, who continued to accept his generosity. That was the Donna Woods who came to Vince's house on that Saturday morning. She was not afraid of Vince. Her fear was a fiction, something she made up to tell her friends. His argument would be that anyone who loved her as deeply as Vince did could not possibly murder her.

As he came across a new thought, he would jot it down. He looked at his watch; an hour and a half had gone by. It was already dark and he was getting hungry. What the hell was Nikki talking about? Another half an hour passed before the phone rang. "Hi," she said. "It's safe, come on out."

"What do you mean?" he asked.

"Vince's bombed. He's already passed out in bed. He and John were drinking all day. I knew it was just a matter of time. The sun and the wind, the work and the beer, just got to be too much for him. John took off over an hour ago. Don't drive in though, Matt. I'll be at the end of the driveway about nine. Park the car down the road and meet me there."

Matt couldn't keep the smile off his face. He missed her so much. He was excited now about how she set this whole thing up. A clandestine meeting on a dark road was risky, but he knew it would be worth it.

Matt hadn't been outside since after lunch. He hadn't realized what a nice day it must have been. The spring night was

158

warm; the sky was clear and full of stars. Not a whisper of wind. He raced to Vince's house. He didn't worry about speed limits, cruised through stop signs. There was little traffic. He parked his car at the edge of the tar road at the public landing. It was a short walk down a small tar path to Vince's driveway. He felt giddy with anticipation. He couldn't believe Nikki would do this for him. As he neared the entryway, he could see her silhouette in the light of the moon and stars. She wore blue jeans and a sweatshirt. She carried something under her arm. As he got closer, he noticed it was a blanket. He ran the last few steps, grabbed her in a bear hug, squeezed her as hard he could, kissed her on the neck. He lifted her up off her feet. "God, I've missed you," he said.

She landed back on her feet and they kissed deeply. "Come on," she said, grabbing him by the hand. "I know a place where we can go."

She took him to the farthest edge of the property, down by the lake beneath the sumac and maples that were already in spring growth. She spread the blanket, grabbed his hand, tugged on it, pulling him down. They rolled over in an embrace. He kissed her, put his hand on her waist and felt her bare skin. He slowly moved his hand up under the sweatshirt, over her bare breasts. He pulled the sweatshirt up, kissed them gently. They kissed and felt each other for a long time. She reached down and opened the button on her jeans, slowly sliding them off her hips. Her body was white in the pale light. Matt knelt between her legs and unzipped his pants. She reached up and pulled on his shirt, pulling him down on top of her. Her skin was cool from the evening air but he could feel her burning up.

***

They both giggled like kids as the put their clothes back on. Matt knew he looked ridiculous. He still had on a white shirt and a tie, hanging loose around his neck. She pulled on it. "This could've gotten you in trouble," she said.

They stretched out on the blanket looking at the stars. "I've always wanted to study the stars," she said, "but I've never had anybody who wanted to sit out with me. Will you sit out with me?"

"I don't know why not," he said. "As long as you always bring a blanket and don't wear panties."

She looked at him and winked. "My pleasure," she said. It was a magical evening. They talked and laughed as if Vince didn't exist, as if the trial wasn't next week. Matt needed this, this assurance. As he lay there with her head on his shoulder, staring into the expanse of the universe, he was sure he was doing the right thing. He would do anything for her.

Hours passed, time and surroundings of no consequence. It was after midnight when they got up and started to walk back to the driveway, staying clear of any view from the house. She was sure Vince couldn't raise his head off the pillow, but there was no reason to take any chances. "Is everything going okay?" she asked.

"Now it is," he said. "I was concerned. I had lost sight of what this was all about, how I got into this and where we were going." He put his arm around her. "How has Vince been?"

"Oh, he's been frightful. But I'm doing what you told me to. I'm as nice as I can be."

As they reached the end of the driveway, he tugged her toward him and put his hands on her hips. She looked up at him and they kissed. "That will have to hold you," she said, smiling.

"You know I'm gonna pick you up Monday morning?" said Matt.

"Yes, Vince mentioned that we would ride to the courthouse together."

"It'll give us a chance to talk in the morning and again on the way home as to how the day progressed and what the next day may bring. As long as it's on the way for me, it just makes sense. If it gets uncomfortable, just let me know and we'll change the routine."

He kissed her again and walked back to his car. He had no doubts.

chapter 31

MATT, VINCE, AND Nikki walked into the Government Center a little before nine on Monday morning. It was the first day of jury selection. Matt found a conference room outside the courtroom, had Vince and Nikki take a seat, and went looking for coffee. Vince was dressed in a suit, like a businessman. He could have been at a board meeting. Nikki also wore a suit, a pale blue suit, modest and appropriate for the occasion. She had to look like the dutiful wife: a wife not afraid of her husband, a woman who would never live with anyone capable of murder.

The coffee shop was on the lower level. As Matt walked in, he could tell there were people there who were not a normal part of the court system. They sat around looking anxious, drinking coffee. He knew they were prospective jurors waiting to be called into the courtroom. He always watched for first reactions, how friendly and open the look, how quick the response. Three women at a table all smiled and said, "Good morning." He acknowledged them and grabbed three cups of coffee and went back to the conference room. It was just a matter of waiting to be called by the clerk.

The three of them sat in the conference room, sipping vending machine coffee from paper cups, their faces blank. Matt tried to ease the tension. "Jury selection can be a boring task," he said. "The first day or so may be interesting, but after that, it loses its charm real fast. You have to ask the same questions over and over, then you never know whether the jurors are telling you the truth or not. You want people who will be open and fair minded.

You always have to worry about the juror who tells you what they think you want to hear just to get selected. People intrigued with the idea of sitting through a murder case."

The clerk finally arrived. "Judge Thompson wants to see both attorneys in chambers," she said.

"I'll be right back," said Matt.

Matt walked into the judge's chambers. He said, "Good morning, Your Honor."

"Matt, good morning. Scott and I were just going over some scheduling matters here. As you know, I normally try to start at 9:00 in the morning, take a morning recess, recess for lunch at noon, start back at 1:30 or so, go until maybe 4:30 or so, with another afternoon recess. Right now, I'm hoping we'll get the jury picked this week so we can start the testimony next Monday morning."

Matt had no problem with Judge Thompson presiding over Vince's case. The judge was a gentleman. He didn't interfere with the attorneys and how they tried their case. He wasn't particularly a stickler as far as whether you started right on time, or if you needed a few extra minutes to prepare. Some judges were on the bench at nine and if you weren't there, they started without you. This judge would never do that.

***

Jury selection went as expected. Matt had prepared a series of questions trying to get to any biases or prejudices, any feelings that a perspective juror may have that would make him or her unsuitable for the case. Did they own a firearm? Had they ever used a firearm? If not, did they have strong feelings against a person who may own or use a firearm? Had they ever had one go off accidentally? Were they familiar with any case where a firearm may have gone off accidentally? Had anybody in their family been hurt by a firearm? The questions to which a defense attorney needs answers.

It took Matt around an hour to question each person. He and Vince had worked out a system where they would each rate a prospective juror on a rating of one to five, one being the worst, strike 'em, and number five being the best, keep 'em. In Matt's experience most jurors ended up being a two or three. If it appeared that a juror may be good for either side, chances are he or she would be gone. One of the jurors, for example, had been putting his shotgun away, leaning it up against the wall in the closet when it discharged, blowing a hole in the ceiling. He said he knew a gun could go off without pulling the trigger. Matt and Vince gave him a five, Scott Larson, the county attorney, must have given him a one, striking him. Another prospective juror, a young lady, had a sister who was in an abusive relationship and charged her husband with domestic abuse. She wasn't the kind of person Matt could leave on the jury. He struck her. That's what made the process so interesting, thought Matt. You want to have jurors with a lot of life experiences. But if those experiences resemble the evidence in the case too closely, one or the other side gets rid of them.

This went on for two and a half days. They had seven jurors. They had agreed on two alternates so they had seven more to go. It became obvious during the questioning that both sides were getting tired. Matt was trying to keep elderly women. He believed that he had a good rapport with them. He watched for a warm smile. If they had a warm smile, he thought they were less judgmental and more likely to overlook or forgive human frailty.

In this case he wasn't sure what he wanted. Was he looking for a jury who could likely find Vince not guilty, or was he looking for a hanging jury? He knew it had to appear he was looking for a jury that would acquit. He couldn't fumble around, looking stupid. He didn't want Vince getting a new trial based on incompetent counsel.

At the end of the third day, the judge asked both attorneys into his chambers. Jury selection was going a little slow, he thought. He told the attorneys to move along a little faster. He wanted to start the trial Monday morning. He decided that since they were getting close to starting the trial, he would have the *Spreigl* hearing the following afternoon. The state should have the three ex-wives ready to testify.

Matt pondered how to break it to Vince. He planned for an ugly drive home. When he got out in the hall, Nikki was standing by herself. Vince was in the men's room. Matt gazed at Nikki. She reached out and touched his fingers. He raised his eyebrows, "The ex-wives are going to testify tomorrow afternoon."

She shrugged her shoulders. By then Vince was there. On the way to the car, Matt told Vince the plan. Vince was surprisingly quiet. "I like the way things are going, Matt. You're doing a good job picking jurors. I think we have seven people who are willing to listen. If we can get the rest as reasonable, we should be all right."

He had become the businessman again. Serious and calculating. Vince knew this was no more bullshit, this was serious business. Maybe he had decided he was going to be the likable guy I said I wanted the jury to see, thought Matt.

The next morning they picked one more juror. It took until noon. At lunch, Matt found himself behind the stacks in the law library reviewing the statements of the ex-wives. He'd read them so many times he had them memorized. In reality, he didn't want to go to lunch with Vince and Nikki. He felt Vince needed some time alone to think. To let Nikki calm him down. It would be a difficult afternoon for him. Above all, Matt knew he had to keep control of his case, which meant keeping control of his client.

The afternoon session started promptly at 1:30 with the *Spriegl* hearing, which they would complete before finishing jury selection. Judge Thompson sat down, everybody settled in and the prosecutor looked at the bailiff and said, "Call Marilyn Fischer."

Marilyn Fischer had been married to Vince over twenty years ago and had never changed her name. The only picture Matt had seen of her was a wedding picture. Standing next to Vince in the photo, it was obvious she had been quite a catch. Now, though, she was no longer a beauty. The years had not been kind. Her testimony didn't change; it was right off of her statement. She went through the litany of abuse by Vince and the times she thought she was about to be killed. Vince fixed an icy stare on her, which she ignored. Matt's cross-examination was unable to bring out anything new. She admitted to the arguments, to her few affairs with other men, but it was obvious she had been a victim.

The second wife, Val Feia, was called. She had been divorced from Vince eight years earlier. She was still quite attractive. During her entire testimony she never looked at Vince. She turned to the prosecutor when he was asking questions; she looked at Matt when he was asking questions. Vince had told Matt earlier that his divorce attorneys had abused her in the process, that there was still some real resentment because she hadn't been able to take him to the cleaners. Matt could tell that Vince had lightened up a bit since she had taken the stand. Probably still relishing somewhat in her defeat, he thought. She did well on the stand, told her story just as she had told the deputy sheriff. In response to Matt's questions, she acknowledged the marriage was over when she had argued with Vince. She admitted that she should not have confronted him at his business. That was all Matt was going to get out of her.

The prosecution left the best for last. Pamela Dahl was Vince's third wife. She was the one who wrote the letter to the Sheriff's Office after Donna's death saying it was no accident, that Vince had murdered Donna. The bitterness she still felt was written on her face. When she glanced at Vince daggers crossed the courtroom. She was there, as Vince had aptly put it, to castrate him. She finished her testimony dramatically. In tears, she told the judge how Vince had her on the floor, his hands around her throat, and his knee on her chest. She was losing consciousness, she was sure she would die. Her testimony was credible. She sat trembling after she was done speaking. The judge called a recess.

After the break, Matt sat alone at his table in the courtroom. He was concerned. The third wife was explosive. He had to handle her carefully. The wrong question could cause more harm. As he was looking at his notes, preparing to cross examine her, the assistant prosecutor walked in and dropped a document on the table. Matt scanned it quickly and realized it was Weineke's report of his trip to Madison with the shotgun. This was over two months ago, thought Matt. Why in the hell am I getting this now? As he went down the page, he saw Weineke's description of the tests being conducted by Carlson. One of them was the recoil test.

The words leapt off the page. Weineke quoted Carlson as saying, "If this guy's saying that gun was under his arm when it went off, he's full of shit. This gun has so much recoil that if it wasn't against his shoulder when fired, it would have flown four or five feet. It would have ended up off the deck."

Matt couldn't believe it. The prosecutor had been sitting on a report that either nullified his expert witness or at least seriously affected his credibility. The ramifications were flying through Matt's head, his anger rising. Finally, he looked across the room at the prosecutor's table. He could see that they were pleased by the bomb they'd just dropped on him.

By then the judge had come in and sat down. Matt was supposed to start his cross-examination but he had lost his train of thought, any aggressive edge he may have had. He asked a few questions and rested. As the witness was excused, Matt asked the judge for a short recess. He rushed out of the courtroom; he had to find a quiet place to think. Every instinct said: You have to raise hell about this. It is unconscionable. What did the prosecutor think he could gain by sitting on this report? It's a basis for a mistrial.

In the hallway, both Vince and Nikki realized something had happened.

"What the hell is it, Matt?" asked Vince.

"They just handed me some new information. I need some time to think. Why don't you two have a cup of coffee? I'll be in the law library. I'll meet you out here in about ten minutes."

As he stared out the window in the library he asked himself what he was supposed to do. He'd have to make a motion for a continuance. He had to get a new expert. Or maybe a motion for a mistrial. But if the judge granted a new trial, who knew what would happen. It could really screw everything up. But he couldn't ignore it. If Vince was convicted, that could be a basis for an appeal and a reversal. If Matt didn't make some motion, that would be tantamount to ineffective assistance of counsel. Any attorney, even one right out of law school, would know enough to do it. Within minutes, his panic had settled some. Matt was thinking clearer. This judge wasn't going to grant any continuance or a mistrial, he thought. Matt would make the motion to protect the record and hope that he had gauged this judge correctly. It was the only thing he could do.

In the hall he explained to Vince and Nikki what had happened. He had decided he would make a motion for a continuance or for a mistrial. Vince's reply was that it was a further proof that the system was totally fucked up and that Weineke was out to get him.

***

"Your Honor," said Matt, when they were back in session, "just before my cross examination of Ms. Dahl, the prosecutor presented me with some additional discovery."

Matt told Judge Thompson the substance of the report. "Your Honor, if this is true, there is no reason why this report was not disclosed to me months ago, right after Deputy Weineke came back from Madison. The case law is quite clear, both of the parties are required to follow the rules of discovery and the sanctions have to be commensurate with the violation. This is probably as serious a violation of the rule as I've ever seen. I'm asking the court for a mistrial.

"Short of that, as an alternative, we are asking that this matter be continued for the purpose of allowing the defense to contact Dave Carlson and get the substance of what occurred. We've been put in a terrible position: either it happened the way Deputy Weineke reported it, in which event we're entitled to hire a new expert, or we're going to battle over the credibility of our expert. We should not be in that position. In either event, Your Honor, the only way Mr. Fischer will get a fair trial is if this court declares a mistrial."

In his response, Scott Larson rambled on about how the report was with Deputy Weineke and he, for some unknown reason, never delivered it to the prosecutor's office until just the day before. There was no sinister motive involved, just a simple mistake.

167

Bullshit, thought Matt.

"Moreover," he argued, "there is certainly no prejudice to the defendant. It is an accurate report of what occurred. It was, after all, somebody that the defense had hired. There has been too much time and expense already expended to grant any motion for mistrial or continuance."

The judge denied the motion for the mistrial summarily. As for the continuance, he indicated he would take that under advisement until such time as the defense called the expert witness. If it appeared that something had been sabotaged, he would consider a continuance at that time.

In the hall Matt shook his head. "That's a terrible ruling."

Vince glared back. "Don't give me that shit. How did you fuck up on our expert?"

"I don't believe it. He came with the highest credentials. He never said anything like that to me. Weineke could be making the whole damn thing up. I'll find out."

"You bet your ass you better find out. We paid that fuckhead a lot of money for that kind of horseshit."

"Vince, I want to tell you something. You never know when there's gonna be jurors walking through the halls. Watch your tongue!"

"Kiss it," Vince responded.

chapter 32

ON MONDAY THEY resumed jury selection, and by late afternoon they had the entire jury panel—twelve jurors and two alternates. The trial would start Tuesday morning.

On the way home from court, Nikki had decided it was good time for the three of them to talk. Now that jury selection was over and the trial was about to start, she said they should try and relax, gather their thoughts. Vince agreed, but he didn't want to go home; he preferred to stop where he could have a few drinks and a good steak. As the waiter seated them at the table, Matt glanced at Nikki. The week had worn on her. She had dressed conservatively every day, stayed at Vince's side, smiled at the jurors and the judge, even smiled at the bailiffs. A picture of sweetness.

Matt actually wanted to keep the conversation off the trial and off the evidence. There was nothing that could be accomplished tonight. He'd prepared a short opening statement and would make it the next morning. He pretty much knew what the prosecutor would say and he knew the first day's testimony would probably be rather anticlimactic: the dispatcher, the paramedics, the first deputies. Nothing surprising.

After their drinks were served, Vince turned to Matt. "I see in the paper that Tom Moore from Peter's office has been nominated to be a judge. What do you think of that?"

"I think he should be all right," replied Matt. "He's got a lot of experience."

"Peter said he can be a pain in the butt," said Nikki.

The comment startled Matt. He stared at Nikki. She looked away.

"Yeah, I've had a couple of cases with him when he's been that way," said Matt. He looked away, deep in thought. When had she talked to Peter…and why would the subject of a judgeship come up?

He glanced Nikki's way, she had her eyes on the menu. "I'm glad you mentioned Peter," said Matt, turning toward Vince. "Have you talked to him recently?"

"No. It's been a week or more. He called me shortly before the trial started to wish me good luck and see if I needed any help or had any concerns. Nothing important."

Matt decided to let Nikki's comment slide. It was one of those things you put in your memory bank for later withdrawal.

It was a congenial meal. They were like three old friends. Anybody who saw them would have no reason to believe that they were in the middle of a trial for first degree murder. Matt saw that a few of the patrons must have recognized somebody at their table. He noticed a quick glance and a whisper. They parted company early and Matt went back to his office.

It was a little after nine when Matt walked into his office. It was dark, no one was there. He hadn't planned to stop, but the comment Nikki had made about Peter weighed on his mind. There was something he wanted to check. The press was covering the trial and he had told Kay to save all of the newspapers. Many times he believed he could get an idea of what the jury might be thinking based on a reporter's slant of the trial. But now he was looking for an article on the judgeship. He remembered seeing it, but it wasn't a week ago; it was recently. He found it in Saturday's paper, reporting a news release by the nominating committee from the day before, nominating Tom Moore for the judgeship. He was right. If Vince hadn't talked to Peter for over a week, and if Peter said something to Nikki about the nomination, it would have had to have been in the last day or so. Either Vince was lying, but there certainly would be no reason for that, thought Matt, or Nikki had talked to Peter very recently and hadn't told him about it. He wondered why Nikki would be talking to Peter. It had to be about Vince's estate. Maybe she had to meet with him to sign some documents or to switch some accounts. Matt was sure that it had to do with Vince's money and Nikki hadn't wanted to concern him about it with the trial and everything. That made sense, he thought.

chapter 33

OPENING STATEMENTS WENT as Matt expected. Both parties took a cautious approach, not trying to promise more than they could deliver. The jury was engaged. Matt knew they would be. Talk of murder, guilt or innocence, had a way of grabbing you by the throat. They were about to embark on a journey they would never forget.

The prosecutor started his case as Matt expected: the dispatcher, the paramedics first on the scene, Dr. Charles Olson, the local coroner, all of the deputy sheriffs. They testified to the statements that Vince had made regarding how it was an accident. By early afternoon, it was Deputy Bob Lentz who told the jury how he found a frightened little ten-year-old boy sitting in the red Corvette and took him to the neighbor. He related his discussion with Vince and how he told him what happened. He told the jury about the crumpled up hundred dollar bills on the curio cabinet.

It had been Matt's experience that in almost every case a police officer may testify slightly differently in court than what he had written in his report. The defense attorney would then try to make a big deal out of it. Matt did that to Deputy Lentz, in good spirit. Defense attorneys know that normally it doesn't amount to much. Deputy Lentz took it seriously, though. He turned red each time Matt caught him in the smallest discrepancy.

In the hall Vince walked up to Matt and said, "You really made some points in there. You left poor Lentz looking like a dumbass."

Daniel Eller

"Those are little victories, Vince. In the outcome of this trial, they won't make any difference at all."

Vince appeared upset about being so quickly deflated. Matt ignored it.

Entering the courtroom, Matt wasn't sure who the prosecutor would call as his next witness. As he walked by Scott, he asked, "Who do you have on next?"

Scott looked at him calmly and replied, "Troy."

Matt hadn't expected Troy until the following morning. He wasn't quite sure he was ready for him. As he worked his way up to the table, he could see that the courtroom was packed. There were maybe a half dozen reporters. Many friends of the Woods family. Donna's parents and siblings were sitting through the trial. Many of Vince's friends and neighbors were there. The rest were general curiosity seekers, people who have nothing better to do than sit through a good murder trial.

"The state calls Troy Woods," said the prosecutor.

It took a few minutes for the boy to enter the courtroom. Matt could tell everyone was curious to see what he looked like. Matt had only seen pictures of him. As he walked in the door, there were "ahs" from the spectators. He was much taller and mature looking than Matt expected. By now he was twelve years old. It had been close to two years since his mother's death. He had sandy blonde hair. Peach complexion. Blue eyes. He could have been a choir singer. He could have been an angel. The prosecutor directed him to the bailiff and he took the oath and said, "Yes ma'am, yes I do." He slowly took the stand, sat down and pulled the microphone toward himself. Matt looked at him and thought: God, he's not a kid at all, way too poised. Could this have been rehearsed?

Answering the questions of the prosecutor, Troy told the jury and the filled courtroom he was now twelve years old and in junior high school in Connecticut. Since the death of his mother he and his sister had moved in with his aunt, Donna's sister, and he was very happy there. Scott asked him if he remembered the events of October 7, 1994. He said he did. He told the jury about how, at the last minute on that Saturday morning, his mother asked him if he would go along to Vince's house. He'd been out there many times. He liked going to Vince's house. He liked being at the lake, going on boat rides, the other things they did. But that day, he really hadn't wanted to go, he said, because he had other things to do and the boat was already put away for the winter. He told the jury how he'd kept himself busy running around the yard, playing by the lake, doing a lot of pretending, being a little boy by himself. He said when he'd come into the house Vince and his mother were sitting at the kitchen table drinking beer, talking. He hadn't paid any attention to what they were saying. They were having a good time, he thought. Then he told the jurors how later in the afternoon he'd been getting bored and he had wanted his mother to go and she was getting a little mad at him. He'd gone into the great room and they'd put a movie in the VCR for him. He didn't remember exactly what it was, something about race cars.

"Do you know what a shotgun looks like?" asked Scott.

"Sure."

"Does Mr. Fischer have any guns, Troy?"

"Yes, he does," he said. "He has a whole bunch of 'em in a cabinet right there in that big room."

"You mean in the great room with the fireplace?"

"Yes," said Troy.

"Did you see the guns there that day?"

"Well sure," said Troy. "There was a cabinet full of guns and then there was one gun leaning up against it that wasn't in the cabinet."

"Did you try to play with that gun, Troy?"

"No, sir, I wouldn't do that. I was told I could never play with guns."

"When you were outside, Troy, did you play around the deck at all?"

"Yes."

"Did you come in the back door, through the breezeway?"

"Sure I did."

"Did you ever notice a shotgun leaning up against the wall there, by the garage?" asked Scott.

"No, sir."

"You were telling us about how you were getting bored and you wanted to go home."

"I could hear my mother and Vince arguing. The voices were getting loud. There were some swear words. I tried not to listen."

"Let me stop you for a moment there," said Scott. "You heard them argue?"

"Yes, sir."

"Do you remember what the argument was about?"

"I heard only bits of it. Vince used some bad words…then my mother used the same words back. It got really loud. I was embarrassed. I tried not to listen."

"Do you remember anything Vince may have said?"

"Just a little. He used the "f" word when he talked about my aunt. Then my mom's voice got really loud. Then she used the "f" word and screamed that she was getting out of there. Then Vince hollered some more, but I don't remember everything."

"What did you do then, Troy?"

"The movie was over. I went into the kitchen, Vince was standing there. I asked him where my mother was and he said she was in the bathroom. His face was bright red. I'd never seen him like that. He was walking around the kitchen real fast. He looked at me for a long time. I could tell he was kinda mad…didn't say anything. Then he screamed at me to get out to the car, he was gonna drive us home."

"What did you do?"

"I did that. I went out to the car and I sat in there and I pretended I was in a race and I was the driver."

"What happened after that?"

"I heard a loud bang and I got scared. I thought somebody was shooting at me. I think I crawled onto the floor. I didn't do anything."

"Did you see Vince at all?" asked Scott.

"Yes, he ran out by the car. He looked at me and I could tell

176

he was really scared."

"Then what happened, Troy?"

"Nothing. Nothing. I just sat in there until this sheriff came and told me my mother was hurt and took me over to this house."

"Did the deputy sheriff talk to you that night, Troy?"

"He asked me a few questions but I was really scared."

"Troy," said Scott, "when the deputy sheriff talked to you that night, did you tell him you heard your mother and Vince arguing?"

"No." he said.

"Why not?"

"Because he never asked me."

"Troy, when the deputy talked to you that night, did you tell him that you had seen the shotgun leaning on the cabinet in the great room?"

"No." he said.

"Why not?"

"He never asked me."

"Troy, one last question. When the deputy talked to you that evening, did you tell him that Vince had sent you out to the car to wait for your mother?"

"No." he said.

"Why not?"

"Because he never asked me."

"Thank you, Troy," said Scott. He turned and looked at Matt. "Your witness."

Matt hesitated. How should he approach this? Troy's testimony was devastating. This little angelic boy had every one of those grandmothers Matt had left on the jury in the palm of his hand. They all looked at his face, listened to his soft, innocent voice, and wanted to take him home. Matt knew he wouldn't make any points by giving Troy a hard time.

What he did was the only thing he could do. He tried to create the impression that Troy was testifying honestly, but not to what he saw but to what he had heard or was told.

"Troy, were you over at your grandfather's the day after your mother died?" asked Matt.

"Yes, I was."

"And were there a lot of people there?"

"Yes, sir."

"And they were talking about the shooting?"

"Yes, sir."

"And were they mad at Vince?"

"Yes, sir."

"And did your grandfather say he didn't believe it was an accident?"

"Yes, sir."

"And you stayed at your grandfather's house for a long time?"

"Yes, sir."

"And other relatives and people came to the house, is that right?"

"Yes, sir."

"And they all talked about what had happened and how your mother was killed?"

"Yes, sir."

"And they talked about how they thought it happened?"

"Yes, sir."

"And you overheard all this, Troy, is that right?"

"Yes, sir."

"And that was all in October of 1994?"

"Yes, sir."

"And then a month later, in November of 1994, you moved to Connecticut with your aunt?"

"Yes, sir."

"And Troy, from the night your mother was killed, October 7th, until you moved to Connecticut with your aunt in November, nobody from the Sheriff's Department tried to talk to you, to get a statement from you as to what you remembered about that night, isn't that right?"

"Yes, sir."

"And I have a copy of a statement you gave several months ago to a deputy from the Sherburne County Sheriff's Office. Do you remember talking to him, Troy?"

"Yes, sir."

"And that's the first time you said anything about the gun being in the great room? Isn't that true, Troy?"

"Yes, sir."

"And that's the first time you said anything about Vince and your mother arguing? Isn't that true, Troy?"

"Yes, sir."

"And that's the first time you said anything about Vince telling you to get into the car? Isn't that true, Troy?"

"Yes, sir."

"And Troy, between November of 1994 and the date you gave this statement just a few months ago, how many times do you think you talked to your aunt about your mother's death? About what happened that night?"

"Oh, lots of times."

Taking a calculated chance, Matt finally asked, "Troy, have you ever been in this courtroom before?"

"Yes, sir."

"And that was last night? Right, Troy?"

"Yes, sir."

"Was it after dark?"

"Yes, sir."

"And who brought you here?"

"I came with my aunt and with Scott."

"Scott Larson, the prosecutor?"

"Yes, sir."

"And what did you do, Troy?"

"Well, he put me up here and he told me this was where I was going to be sitting and he asked me some questions, like he did today."

"Thank you, Troy," said Matt, giving him a friendly smile.

Troy smiled back. Matt was pleased. He had done as well as he could've under the circumstances. He took a chance and glanced at the jury. It didn't appear that he had engendered their anger in his handling of Troy.

chapter 34

THE THREE OF them left the courthouse in Matt's car. Nikki was sitting in the back seat. She tapped Matt on the shoulder and said, "You did a beautiful job with Troy. When the prosecutor was done with him, I tried to think of what I would ask him, I couldn't come up with one question. I could see the jury liked him. I had no idea how you were going to be able to handle his testimony."

"After that bitch had him for the last two years," said Vince, "I wouldn't be surprised at anything he said. I'm sure she's fed him full of her bullshit."

The comment angered Matt, but he let it pass. Vince had shot the boy's mother, almost in front of him, and now he had the gall to complain that Troy's testimony was bullshit.

"Tomorrow morning I have to go to my office before court," said Matt, "so I might be a little late. It's probably just as well if we drive separately."

That was a lie. Matt was starting to feel uncomfortable; there was too much tension in the car. He was getting upset too often with Vince. He wanted to say things to Nikki but he would have to bite his tongue. To be with her all that time but not to be able to say anything, not to be able to talk about how she felt and how things were going, was just too difficult. Matt felt he needed to get away from that, to keep his sanity, to keep himself focused.

***

The state started the next morning with Eugene Bishop, the firearms expert from the Bureau of Criminal Apprehension. He was shown the gun. He agreed it was the shotgun he had received for testing, but he acknowledged it was not in the same condition as when he received it. It hadn't had an indentation or dent on the pistol grip when he'd gotten it. Scott asked him if he knew how that had happened. Bishop said it was his understanding that it had been done in Madison, Wisconsin, during another test. He told the jury how he had examined the gun, the tests he had put it through, and that he could not get the gun to misfire. With that, the state turned him over to Matt.

Matt had only a few questions. He'd noticed in Bishop's report he had done a recoil test. The prosecutor had conveniently failed to bring that up in his direct examination. Matt asked him about the test. Bishop told the jury he had done a recoil test and the result.

Matt continued, "Mr. Bishop, what did you observe regarding the gun's recoil?"

"That it had normal recoil for that type of gun."

"And so, if I were to hold the gun like this, Mr. Bishop," and Matt indicated putting it under his arm, "and it were to discharge accidentally, would the recoil be enough so that it would fly out of my hand?"

"I don't believe so," said Mr. Bishop. "Not based on my tests."

"And have you been advised, Mr. Bishop, that the defense has had that gun tested as well?"

"I have."

"I noticed in your reports, Mr. Bishop, that there's no indication that you tried to get the gun to misfire when it was in the safety position, that is half cocked, by hitting the gun on the pistol grip."

"No, I didn't perform such a test."

"Do you know, Mr. Bishop, is that a standard test?"

"I don't know if you would call it standard," said Bishop. "One could certainly use that test."

"You understand that the dent on the grip resulted from

such a test?"

"Yes, I do."

"Do you understand that the gun misfired doing such a test?"

"I understand that's what the report says."

"And Mr. Bishop," asked Matt, "did you also receive, at your lab, a bag said to contain the clothes Mr. Fischer was wearing when the gun was said to discharge?"

"We did receive a bag of clothes, Mr. Collins. Yes."

"And looking at your report, Mr. Bishop, what did that bag include?"

"It included the boots he was wearing, the blue jeans, the leather vest and the sweatshirt," he paused, "and, oh, I'm sorry, and his underwear."

"Did you conduct any tests on those clothes to determine the presence of gunshot powder?"

"No, we did not," he said, rather defiantly.

And Matt rested.

Matt knew that whether the test was done or not made little difference. Everybody knew the gun was held by Vince when it went off. There was no way for the test to conclusively show the gun was either under his arm or at his shoulder when it fired. But the fact the tests hadn't been done could be something Matt could use in his closing argument to the jury. He hoped the prosecutor ignored it. Scott looked at the witness and said, "I have nothing further. Thank you."

Matt was relieved.

The prosecutor got up and apologized. He told the judge he had made arrangements for Dr. Michaels to be the next witness but things had gone faster than he expected. Dr. Michaels probably wouldn't be there for another half an hour or forty-five minutes. With the indulgence of the court, he would like to take a recess. The judge obliged.

Once in the hall, Vince said he was going to go outside and have a cigarette. As he walked away Nikki approached Matt. "He's really upset over this Carlson episode, Matt. He's blaming you. He thinks you hired some hack that's screwing up the case."

"Listen, Nikki," replied Matt, "I talked to Carlson. I faxed him a copy of Weineke's report. He said it's all bullshit. He said no way in hell he ever said anything like that. But you guys must not have been listening. The state's own witness, Bishop, said there's no unusual recoil to that shotgun. Didn't you just hear 'em? We may not even have to call Carlson. Everything he was gonna say, I got in through Bishop. It's something we have to talk about. Wait and see how Michaels does."

"Vince worries me, Matt," she said. "You've been saying all along that if he smells something rotten about this, watch out. These little things are starting to weigh on him, I can tell."

"Nikki, hang in there. We'll get through this."

She smiled. "I hope so. For our sake."

chapter 35

"THE STATE CALLS Dr. Owen Michaels."

Dr. Michaels was the consummate expert witness. He was the state's best known forensic pathologist. An expert on the cause of death, he was always willing to give an opinion within a courtroom setting. Tall, thin, studious looking, and handsome. He had dark hair with just enough gray to give him the credibility of age. Michaels also knew how to play to a jury. He would look at his interrogator with an intense stare and then, as he answered, he would look to the jury, as if he was lecturing to a small class at medical school, and reply with a short, concise, and humorless response. He was just what the jurors would expect a forensic pathologist to be. Matt always agreed that he was qualified as an expert but the prosecutor would run him through his credentials anyway, as an additional point to impress the jury.

The prosecutor took him through the entire autopsy procedure. Dr. Michaels testified just as he had written his autopsy report, without putting any significance to any particular finding. Then the lights were turned off, Dr. Michaels brought out the slides and proceeded to show the jury what he had just described. The slides had been picked by both sides with the approval of the court, all being relatively discreet in an attempt to show respect for the victim and consideration for those in her family who would be watching.

The first slide showed a young woman lying on her stomach on a table; her colorless face was turned to the side. There was an ugly gaping hole in her back. As the picture hit the screen, gasps and moans were heard throughout the courtroom. This was always difficult for Matt. He tried to imagine what a mother, a father, loved ones, would feel when they first saw the object of their affection on a cold, steel table.

Dr. Michaels went through all of the slides slowly, calmly describing the wound, the powder burns, and contusions visible on her chest. When he was done, the lights went back on. The prosecutor returned to his seat. "Dr. Michaels," he said, "you described the entry wound as eccentric. Is there some significance to that?"

"There is. I used the term 'ring of abrasion'. The abrasion ring results from the bullet rubbing raw the edges of the hole as it pierces the skin, the bullet abrades the skin. The abrasion ring can be concentric or eccentric, depending on the angle between the bullet and the skin. A bullet from a gun that is perpendicular to the skin would normally produce a concentric abrasion. The extent that the bullet penetrates at an angle, the ring of abrasion in the skin will be eccentric, with the ring wider on the side from which the bullet comes. So in this case, based on the eccentric nature of the entry wound, the gun had to be at an angle to the decedent."

"And Doctor, do you have an opinion as to whether that angle was from down to up or up to down?"

"In this case, the collar of abrasion I described was at seven o'clock to two o'clock, so it was from up to down, meaning that the gun was pointing in a downward direction at the decedent."

"And Doctor, based on your examination, do you have an opinion as to the degree of the angle; that is, if perpendicular is zero, do you have an opinion as to the degree that the gun had to be pointing down to produce that type of wound?"

"Yes, I do."

"What is that opinion, Doctor?"

"It is my opinion that the angle would be approximately fifteen degrees."

With that, the county attorney stood up. He looked at the judge. "With the court's indulgence, I would like to have Deputy

Weineke give me some help."

The deputy came from the side of the courtroom and went up in front and turned around a large cork bulletin board. He had with him a ruler and a tape measure.

Scott continued, "Dr. Michaels, did you take some measurements of Ms. Woods' body?"

"Yes, I did."

"And what was her height?"

"She was exactly five foot, three inches."

"And did you measure where that wound was in relation to the bottom of her feet?"

"Yes, I did."

"And what was that, Doctor?"

"Forty-four and a half inches to the bottom of the wound and forty-six inches to the center of the wound."

"Now, did Ms. Woods have shoes on that would affect her height?"

"Yes, she did."

"Did you have access to those shoes?"

"Yes, I did."

"What kind of shoes were they?"

"Boots. I have them here in the bag if necessary."

"Maybe you should take the shoes out and show them to the jury."

Dr. Michaels opened the bag at his feet and took out a pair of brown leather low-heeled cowboy boots.

"What would they add to her height, Doctor?"

"One-half inch," he said.

"And so if we added that to the measurement from the bottom of her feet to the center of the wound, we would have forty-six and one-half inches. Is that correct, Doctor?"

"Yes, that's correct."

"Okay." continued Scott, "then I'm going to ask Deputy Weineke to measure from the floor to the bulletin board exactly forty-six and one-half inches, which represents from the bottom of her feet with her shoes on to the center of the entry wound. Is that correct, Doctor?"

"Yes, it is."

"And then I would ask Deputy Weineke to place a pin there, representing the exact location."

Weineke placed a colored pin directly at the spot on the bulletin board. He turned and looked at the prosecutor.

"Deputy, please bring the exhibit in," said Scott.

Weineke went into the hall and walked back carrying a white cardboard silhouette of a woman that was obviously intended to be Donna Woods. He took the silhouette to the bulletin board and pinned it so that the spot that had been marked as the measurement for the center of the entry wound corresponded with the spot on the silhouette's back.

With that, Matt stood up. "Your Honor, I object to this. I've never seen this before. There was never any disclosure that the state intended to use a cardboard cut-out of the victim."

The prosecutor broke in, "Your Honor, it's simply for illustrative purposes. If Mr. Collins has any reservations regarding whether it actually depicts the body of Ms. Woods, he certainly has a right to question that in cross-examination. That has nothing to do with our right to use this to demonstrate to the jury what the doctor is testifying to."

The judge looked at the cork board with the white silhouette pinned to it. "Objection overruled."

"Doctor, prior to today, have you had an opportunity to review the cardboard cut-out silhouette that Deputy Weineke has just pinned to the bulletin board?"

"Yes, I have."

"And to your knowledge, is that cut-out silhouette the same height as Ms. Woods wearing her boots?"

"Yes, it is."

"What is that height again?"

"Five feet three and one-half inches."

"Now, Doctor, we have already drawn lines on that bulletin board horizontal and vertical to the spot depicting the center of the wound. If we wanted to try and picture the angle you believe the trajectory of the shot followed, we would have to do what?"

"You would have to find the line that is fifteen degrees above the horizontal line that is perpendicular to the body."

"Maybe you could do that for us, Doctor. Deputy Weineke has a protractor."

Dr. Michaels walked to the bulletin board, picked up the protractor and put his finger where fifteen degrees would be.

The prosecutor continued, "Now Doctor, you will notice we've already penciled in a line that should correspond to the fifteen degrees. Do you see that?"

"Yes, I do."

"Doctor, Deputy Weineke has some yellow tape. I would like you to take a piece of that yellow tape and put it along the line showing the fifteen degrees from the point on the silhouette's back."

Dr. Michaels proceeded to take approximately five feet of the yellow tape, placed one edge against the silhouette of the body and strung it out along the fifteen-degree angle and pinned the other edge at the far edge of the bulletin board. There it stood; a picture of a young woman with what everybody knew was supposed to be the barrel of a gun pointing down at her back. There was total silence. The demonstration had engulfed everyone. Dr. Michaels returned to the witness stand. The jurors squirmed restlessly in their chair.

"Now Doctor," said Scott, "you've also conducted some tests on the gun itself, is that correct?"

"Yes, it is."

"And maybe you can tell the jury what sort of tests you conducted and the purpose for them."

Dr. Michaels told the jury how they had taken the gun to a firing range, the purpose to determine the distance from the edge of the muzzle to the body. They knew it was close but not a contact wound. He had the targets they used and he showed them to the jury to demonstrate the damage done at one inch, two inches, three inches and so on.

"Based on those tests," said Scott, "do you have an opinion

as far as what distance the end of the muzzle of the gun was from Ms. Woods when it was fired?"

"I do."

"And what is that opinion?"

"That it was from one foot to two feet."

"So the muzzle of the shotgun could've been as close as one foot and no further than two feet from her body. Is that your opinion, Doctor?"

"Yes, it is."

"Doctor, please move that tape back to the minimum you believe the muzzle of the gun was."

Dr. Michaels went to the bulletin board, removed the yellow tape from the spot against the body and moved it back one foot.

"Doctor," continued Scott, "I have just a couple more questions. First, the shotgun you tested is the same gun entered into evidence as Exhibit Number 6, is that correct?"

"Yes, it is."

"And Doctor, I'm going to have Deputy Weineke provide you with another exhibit, again for illustrative purposes. If you please, Deputy."

Deputy Weineke reached behind the bulletin board and produced a white cardboard cut-out of a shotgun and handed it to Dr. Michaels.

"Now Doctor, have you had an opportunity to compare this cut-out with the actual shotgun, Exhibit Number 6?"

"Yes, I have."

"And are they identical?"

"Yes, they are."

"Again Doctor, with your indulgence, I would ask that you take that to the bulletin board, and pin it to the board along the line produced by the yellow tape. Deputy Weineke will help."

Dr. Michaels took the white cardboard shotgun to the board, pinned the muzzle at the one foot mark, and laid it up along the line fifteen degrees to the female silhouette's back, and pinned the stock to the board. It was a rather surreal site.

"I have nothing further, Doctor. Thank you." And the

prosecutor sat down.

They don't teach you in law school how to try cases; you don't learn many trial skills. At least for Matt, when he had graduated from Georgetown twenty years earlier, they hadn't prepared him to try a first degree murder case. He had learned those skills through experience. All of the books he had read on cross-examination preached two cardinal rules: First, don't ask a question if you don't know what the answer is going to be; and second, unless you consider yourself an equal in the particular specialty to which the expert witness is testifying, don't get into a pissing contest with him on his turf. Matt had lived by those cardinal rules whenever possible and he intended to follow them in his cross-examination of Dr. Michaels.

He started cautiously, getting the doctor to repeat answers already given regarding the autopsy exam on his direct examination. When he got to the part of the examination on the internal tract of the wound, he questioned Dr. Michaels about the billiard ball effect of the pellets. Dr. Michaels' testimony had been almost identical to the explanation given to Matt by Dr. Evans.

"Now, Dr. Michaels, would it be fair to say that when you are called upon to examine a wound inflicted by a single projectile bullet, for example a thirty-two caliber, through soft tissue, you can follow the track or path of the bullet quite easily?"

"That would be fair to say."

"And I'm sure you've had to do that many times in the past. Is that right, Doctor?"

"Hundreds of times," he said.

"Now, in this situation, where you have a shotgun blast from a relatively close distance, it is my understanding that you have different projectiles entering the body. You can have the pellet."

"That's correct."

"You can have the shot cap that's holding the pellets."

"That's correct."

"You can have some of the powder, both exploded and unexploded."

"That's correct."

"And you can have the wad, the material holding the shot in the cup."

"That's correct."

"And all of these can enter the wound."

"That's correct."

"And once they're in the body, as you testified, you have a billiard ball effect, where the shot spreads in every direction. Is that correct, Doctor?"

"That's correct."

"And I would assume, Doctor, that the energy released by the shot shell in this billiard ball effect could also affect the track of at least two of the other items, the wad and the shot shell."

"That may be possible," said Dr. Michaels,

"So unlike a single projectile bullet, Doctor, with a shot shell at this distance, you're creating a wound that spreads throughout the soft body cavity. Is that correct?"

"Yes."

"And even though you believe that you can trace the track of the shell based on the interior damage, would it be fair to say that it is not as accurate as it would have been had it been a single projectile bullet?"

"That is true," he replied.

Matt was satisfied with that. He quickly changed the subject. "Now if you look at the bulletin board, Doctor, which is being used for illustrative purposes, if I understand correctly, the determination of the degree of entry is based on two things. One is the eccentric nature of the entry wound." He waited for Dr. Michael's reply.

"That's correct."

"And the second is the path of the wound inside the body cavity."

"That's correct."

"Now for illustrative purposes here, Doctor, you have the fifteen degrees calculated on the basis that the target was perpendicular. That is, straight up and down vertically. Is that correct?"

"Based on that illustration, that is correct."

"So this is based on two static points. One being the end of the muzzle of the gun and the other being the back of Ms. Woods. Is that correct?"

"I guess I would say that's correct."

"Would it be fair to say, Doctor, that you could create that eccentric wound in a target by not only moving the gun from perpendicular, but also by moving the target from perpendicular?" Matt asked, demonstrating with his hands.

"That would be true, I believe."

"So if Donna Woods was not standing straight or perfectly perpendicular to the gun at the time it discharged, that could affect the degree. Is that correct, Doctor?"

"To some extent, yes."

"Have you looked at any photographs of Ms. Woods while she was alive to see what her posture was?"

"No, I have not."

"Doctor, I notice on the silhouette used to portray Ms. Woods you do have her back at a slight slant, an inward slant from the top of her shoulder to her waist. Do you believe that to be anatomically correct?"

"It should be pretty close."

"If her back is at a slant to the gun when fired, that could help produce the eccentric nature of the entry wound, isn't that correct?"

"That is correct."

"So, Doctor, if her posture was something different from what is portrayed in your illustration, that could affect the eccentric nature of the entry wound, isn't that correct?"

"Yes, it is."

"Would you have any way of knowing whether she was turning around, bending down, leaning back, or in any posture other than perpendicular at the time she was struck?"

"Well, I know she wasn't turning around. She was hit quite square in the back. But other than that, you're right."

"I'm sorry, Doctor, that wasn't a trick question. So, Doctor, would it be fair to say that in attempting to determine the exact degree of entry, or the angle of entry, one would have to keep in mind that you do not have two static figures but rather two dynamic figures, figures that are moving the whole time and could affect, to some extent, the degree of the angle of entry."

"That would be fair to say."

That was all Matt needed to have. With that he quit.

Matt knew his cross-examination hadn't really damaged the prosecutor's case; it just gave him some room to argue. He was really trying to set the stage for Dr. Evans' testimony that Dr. Michaels could be five degrees or more off. He didn't want to ask Dr. Michaels if that could be correct, because he would be stuck with the answer. It was apparent after the redirect by the prosecutor, Scott didn't know what the answer to that question would be either.

By the time they were done, it was mid-afternoon; the judge took the afternoon recess. Before excusing the court, the prosecutor asked to talk to the judge at the bench. As they leaned over the front, he again apologized. The testimony was going much faster than he expected, he had not arranged to have any more witnesses today and would it be possible to simply recess until tomorrow morning. Judge Thompson was happy to oblige.

Later, as Matt, Vince, and Nikki talked in the hallway, it was obvious to Matt that Vince was satisfied with the way things were progressing. There was the initial impact of Dr. Michaels' testimony but, after the cross-examination, it seemed to soften. The defense had not alienated the jury. They could still look at Matt and Vince. At the end of the day, when the judge announced the recess, the jury could still smile as they nodded and walked out. Over the years Matt had spent many hours watching juror's faces. He believed he could almost pin point to an exact minute in a case when the jurors turned against his client. If they had not done so by closing argument, the defendant still had a chance. His instinct had been uncannily accurate.

Matt thought as long as they had a little extra time, this would be a good opportunity to stop on the way home and discuss whether Vince was going to testify or not. Vince had already made it perfectly clear that he wasn't going to change his testimony. It was an accident and that's what he was going to tell the jury. Under the circumstances, Matt had no choice but to go with that. But Matt knew the next stage of the trial was going to be the most difficult for Vince. The list of witnesses for the state included Donna's girlfriend and neighbors, her relatives, her father, her sister from Connecticut. People who were going to testify to Vince's obsession with her and her decision to terminate the relationship. That, Matt figured, could get ugly.

***

"You know, Vince," said Matt, "if this was a normal case, with the way things have gone through today, and if they did not get any worse, I'd probably suggest you didn't testify. I know that sounds strange, but you're going to open yourself up to a lot of questions by the prosecutor that could be difficult to answer."

"I'm not afraid of him." said Vince. "He hasn't shown me anything."

"So far he's been a sleeping giant," said Matt. "I'm not sure we ought to wake him."

At that point, Vince waved his hand. They were at a small bar near the courthouse rehashing the day's events and Vince had seen somebody he knew across the room. He told Matt and Nikki he'd be right back. Nikki turned to Matt. "What's going on here?" she asked.

"This trial is going better than I expected," said Matt. "You've been in there. If it doesn't get any worse than this and he takes the stand, if he sells the jury on that accident story, or even creates a reasonable doubt, we've just pissed away one good plan."

"I don't think it's going as well as you think," said Nikki. "You're busy; I get to watch those jurors' faces. There's a tremendous amount of sympathy for that little boy and for what happened. I think they want to blame somebody."

"That could change," said Matt. "If that jury ends up not liking Donna, they could well blame her. I've seen it happen."

"What do we do?" she asked.

Daniel Eller

"Maybe you're right. Maybe I'm just panicking. I'm so wrapped up in this; I don't always see what the jury sees. We just have to give it some time."

Nikki fixed her eyes on Matt. "I wish we were on that blanket again. I want you really bad," she said. She reached under the table and brushed his lap. "It seems you miss me," she said with a wink. Matt blushed.

chapter 36

THE FOLLOWING MORNING the first witness called by the state was Deputy Kurt Weineke. After going through his credentials and his years of service, Weineke testified that he was the chief investigator in this homicide case. He had been present at the Sherburne County Law Enforcement Center on October 8th when Vince Fischer had come to give a statement regarding the events of the prior day and night. The prosecutor showed him a thirty-three page document.

"Is that the transcribed statement given by Mr. Fischer?" he asked.

"Yes, it is."

"And this is exactly what he told you the day after the event?"

"Yes, it is."

The statement was introduced into evidence. "As part of that interview, Deputy, did you ask Mr. Fischer if you could measure his height?"

"Yes, I did."

"Did he voluntarily agree to do that?"

"Yes, he did."

"Did you measure his height?"

"Yes, I did?"

"Did you take any other measurements?"

"Yes, I did. One to his shoulder and one to his armpit."

"Do you have those measurements with you?"

"Yes, I do."

"Would you tell us what they are, please?"

"Well, I measured Mr. Fischer standing on a tile floor. The measurement from the floor to the top of his head was five foot six and one-half inches, or sixty-six and one-half inches. The measurement from the floor to a location on the right shoulder, midpoint to where a person would hold a gun for firing if he had it at his shoulder, was fifty-five inches. And the measurement from the floor to the underside of his armpit was fifty-two and one-quarter inches."

"Deputy Weineke, on the night of Ms. Woods' death, did the Sheriff's Office take custody of the clothing Mr. Fischer was wearing?"

"That's correct."

"And Mr. Bishop from the BCA was here yesterday. He brought that bag of clothes along."

"Well," replied Deputy Weineke, "I wasn't here yesterday but I know he brought that bag of clothes along."

"Do you know where they are right now?"

"Yes, they're in the evidence room."

"Could you get those, please?"

Weineke left for the evidence room and there were a few moments of complete silence in the courtroom. He returned carrying a brown paper bag.

"I believe there's a pair of boots in there, Deputy," the prosecutor continued. "Would you get those out please and place 'em on the bench?" The deputy reached into the bag, shuffled around a little bit and pulled out a pair of black motorcycle boots.

"Deputy, when Mr. Fischer came in on October 8th to give that statement, do you recall what he was wearing?"

"Yes, I do. He was in a suit."

"Do you recall what he was wearing for shoes?"

"They were just regular shoes, dress shoes, I believe."

"And the measurement you have on the bulletin board here is the measurement you took that day?"

"That's correct."

"And did he have his shoes on or off?"

"We made him take them off."

198

"The measurements that you have given us, Deputy, are those measurements with the boots on or off?"

"Those are Mr. Fischer's measurements shoeless. They do not consider the height of the boot."

"You have the boot there, Deputy. Did you make a determination as to what height, if any, that boot would add to Mr. Fischer?"

"Yes, I did. If you look at the boot, you will notice that the heel is an inch and something. In fact, it's a little bit more than an inch, but I added on an inch."

"So would I be correct in saying to get Mr. Fischer's exact height, the night of the death of Donna Woods, we would have to take the height according to your measurements and then add one inch for the height provided by the boot, is that correct?"

"Yes, that's correct."

"Deputy Weineke, did you bring with you another cardboard silhouette today?"

"Yes, I did."

"Would you get that please?"

Deputy Weineke went into the hall and brought another figure, a white cardboard cut-out depicting the silhouette of a man.

"Deputy, what is the height of that silhouette?

"Five foot seven and a half inches. The height measurement I took of Mr. Fischer and adding the one inch for the heel of the boots.

"Would you place that against the board?" asked the prosecutor.

Deputy Weineke pinned the figure to the board. The courtroom was dead quiet—everyone awaiting the results—there it was, a white cardboard shotgun at the shoulder pointing down, fifteen degrees, to the midpoint of the entry wound.

"Thank you, Deputy. I have nothing further."

Matt looked at the white figures clinging precariously to the bulletin board with a couple of colored pins in their shoulders. Something seemed wrong. He apologized to the judge for the delay, told the court he had to find something in his file and started to shuffle through the papers. The courtroom remained silent. The judge kept his gaze on the board.

Matt turned the pages of his notes, then stared at the bulletin board with the two white figures for a long time. There was something wrong, but what? It appeared to Matt that they had made a mistake in Vince's measurement. But how could they have possibly done that? Unable to find the exact location of the pertinent notes, he could feel the tension building; beads of sweat formed on his forehead. Matt looked at Thompson, he wasn't sure whether Weineke had it figured out by now or not. He looked at the judge again. "Your Honor, I'm not sure, have those clothes and boots been introduced as an exhibit? Are they in evidence?"

The judge turned to the clerk.

"Yes they are, Your Honor," the clerk said. "They're exhibit fourteen."

"I have nothing further. Thank you, Deputy."

The prosecutor stood up and said, "Your Honor, I'd like to have a brief recess."

As people stood up to walk out of the courtroom, Matt put his hand on Vince to have him stay behind. When the courtroom had mostly cleared, Matt whispered to Vince, "Do they have your measurements right?"

"I don't know," said Vince. "I didn't pay a whole lot of attention to what they had written down that day when I was in the Sheriff's Office. It looks to me like they're right; at least that's what it says on my license."

Matt looked at him and said, "Don't go standing around that bulletin board for the time being. At least not when anybody can see you."

Matt and Vince got up and walked out to the hallway. Nikki was waiting. Vince went and stood next to her.

"Nikki," asked Matt, "what is your height?"

"Almost five foot seven, why?"

"I'm just curious," replied Matt.

He looked down, Nikki had on flat shoes and Vince wore his business shoes. Both appeared about the same height. Matt hadn't thought about it before, but he had never seen Nikki in anything but flats. Now the reason was obvious, if she wore heels, she would be taller than Vince. Vince would never have that.

As Matt drove home that night, his mind was mush. He was trying to analyze where he was in the case but he couldn't put things together. There had been some high points, the sort of high you get when you've done a good job and you know it. But that was fleeting. As the highway pounded beneath him, he was in a trance. He wanted to lose the case. He had to lose the case. But every time there was a weakness in the state's case, an opening he could take advantage of, his instincts kicked in and he pounced on it. He knew up to this point they were all little victories, nothing to turn the case. But as he thought about the rest of the case, what he expected, and how Vince may testify, he wondered how much difference those little victories would make.

chapter 37

"THE STATE CALLS Susan Portnoy."

Court had started promptly at nine a.m. the next morning, which was a little out of the ordinary. Matt was surprised the prosecutor called Donna's sister first. He expected him to call some of her local girlfriends. Scott must have a reason, he thought. As she came down the aisle, past the counsel table up to the clerk, Matt was even more surprised. She was not what he expected at all. She was tall, thin, very attractive, conservatively dressed in a suit. As she took the oath and then strolled to the witness stand, she carried herself with style and class that was disarming. Matt knew now why she and Vince could never have gotten along.

As the prosecutor proceeded through his questioning, she answered everything slowly and deliberately, never missing a beat. To Matt, it was obvious she had gone over this testimony in her head hundreds of times. She had been waiting for this moment to get even with the person who had killed her little sister. She told the jury about her special relationship with Donna, how Donna relied on her and no matter what trouble Donna got in, she was always willing to listen, to take her older sister's advice.

"Did Donna ever mention the name Vince Fischer?" asked the prosecutor.

"Not by name—not at first."

"Did you know that your sister was seeing him?"

"It was rather strange," she said. "I knew she was seeing somebody, she talked about the house he owned and the money he had and the trips they took, how he got along with the kids, but she never put a name to him."

"When was the first time you met Mr. Fischer?" asked Scott.

"Dad had put together a family reunion at the Persian Club in March of 1994. March the 13th, to be exact. For some reason, Donna had not invited Mr. Fischer. I gathered from things she said that morning, this man and my dad did not get along. We were at the Persian Club that evening. We had our own little room and were having a good time. Then about 8:00 this man walked in. This wasn't a fancy party; everybody was nicely dressed, however. But this man was definitely out of place. He had on blue jeans, big boots, a sweatshirt and a leather vest. Let me put it this way: he just stood out in the crowd. You could tell Donna was upset but she was going to make the best of it, I think. She started to introduce him but I didn't need any introductions. I thought I recognized him when he walked in, just twenty years older. It was Vince Fischer. I knew him in high school. That is, I knew him by his reputation."

It wasn't just the word reputation, it was the way she said it and how it rang through the courtroom, dripping with all the animosity her voice was capable of projecting.

Matt leapt to his feet. "Objection, Your Honor."

"Sustained," said the judge. "That last comment will be stricken."

"I'm sorry," she said.

But she knew what she'd done. She'd probably planned it all along, thought Matt.

On his legal pad, Matt scribbled out, "Do you remember her?"

Vince looked at him and wrote, "No."

The prosecutor continued, "Ms Portnoy, why don't you tell us what happened after that?"

Matt jumped up again. "Your Honor, may we have a conference at the bench?"

As the judge leaned forward, Matt said, "Your Honor, you've already ruled that you're going to allow in testimony that may go to Ms. Woods' state of mind—things that she may have said— but it's obvious to me that this witness has some real animosity against my client. The prosecutor should not be asking open-ended questions which allow her to get in cheap shots before I can object."

The judge turned to Scott. "I have to agree. You have to ask her questions that require a specific answer. Give Matt a chance to object if it's improper."

As they returned to their seats, the prosecutor looked at the witness. He continued, "Ms Portnoy, did you have a conversation with Mr. Fischer that night?"

"You could hardly call it a conversation. I was having a discussion with some friends regarding the Broadway musical my husband and I had seen. Mr. Fischer broke in and turned it a little vulgar."

"Objection, Your Honor."

"Sustained."

"Ms Portnoy, did Mr. Fischer present your sister with a gift that night?"

"Yes, it was outrageous."

"Objection."

"Sustained." The judge looked at Susan Portnoy. "Just answer the question without editorializing."

"Fine, Your Honor," she said. "Yes, he did give her a gift, or what he intended to be a gift. It was a friendship ring. Donna was actually stunned, she had no idea."

"Did she talk to you about it?"

"Yes, she did."

"What did you say?" asked Scott.

"I told her that she couldn't take it, that he was just trying to buy her, playing the big shot in front of the family. I told her she was too young, too beautiful, she had too much going for her to get involved with a person like him. I believe that despite his money..."

Matt stood again. "Objection, Your Honor."

"Your Honor, she's only testifying to what she told her sister. We believe it goes to her sister's state of mind after that party."

"I'll let it in, but go on to something else."

"Continue, Ms Portnoy," said Scott.

"I simply told my sister that despite his money, he hadn't changed at all. A leopard can't change its spots. Don't waste your life on him."

She couldn't have said it with more venom, thought Matt.

She went on to tell the jury the numerous conversations she'd had with her sister. Donna had complained to her that Vince would not let her break off the relationship, that he had continued to harass her, beg her, plead and cry over the phone. He had wanted to marry her. She told the jury Donna had given the ring back to Vince. Within a month or so after the family reunion, it was her understanding that Donna had broken it off entirely. She was no longer seeing Vince at all.

The prosecutor thanked her, looked at Matt, obviously pleased, and said, "Your witness."

Matt gazed at Susan Portnoy for a long time. She was so explosive, so willing to say almost anything, whether it was a response to a question or not, he had to be extremely careful. He also thought the jury liked her. Particularly the women on the jury. He knew they would sympathize with her, feel for her and the obvious void she felt because of the loss of a sister, especially under such circumstances. Matt knew already his cross-examination was going to be short and cautious.

"Ms Portnoy," he stated, "it is my understanding that the family reunion was on March 13, 1994, is that correct?"

"Yes."

"And I believe you testified that it was your understanding from your conversations with your sister, the relationship she had with Vince had been terminated or ended approximately a month after that, is that correct?"

"Yes, it is."

"If I understand correctly, from your conversations with your sister then, you believe that from the middle of April or so of 1994, she had no further contact with Mr. Fischer, is that correct?"

"If you're asking me if that's the way I understood it, from my conversations with my sister, yes, that is correct."

Matt knew that was not in fact the case. If the state's witnesses wouldn't acknowledge it, he could bring in witnesses who would put Vince and Donna together many times after that. Matt was sure that Donna had kept many things from her sister. He looked at his notes, looked at her. That's the most you're going to accomplish with this witness, he thought. He thanked her, excused her, and quickly jotted down some notes for his closing argument.

As she left the witness stand, she took her last opportunity to get even with Vince. Walking past the jury box, she looked at some of the female jurors and smiled. They smiled back. Her walk and look was defiant. She was in Vince's face and she knew that she was tearing him up inside.

After her testimony, Matt knew this was going to be dump on Vince Fischer day. The prosecutor proceeded to call his list of Donna's friends. Each of them echoed the theme that following the family party in March, Donna's feelings toward Vince had changed drastically. Several admitted she still took his money, but they added that was just Donna, you had to know her to understand how she could do such a thing.

As Matt listened to the testimony of the young women, he sensed a theme. Even though they considered themselves friends of Donna, he did not sense any fondness in these friendships. These were all women who had families with children; they lived in apartment complexes with husbands who had jobs from eight to five. They lived, he suspected, rather mundane lives. To them, keeping up with Donna's life and escapades was like watching a soap opera. Somebody who was footloose and fancy free, having affairs with men, going on trips, leading a fantasy life.

The last one the state called considered herself Donna's best friend, Jenny Weber. She was the one available to take her children anytime something exciting came up, something that Donna just couldn't forego. Matt suspected that was quite often, but he didn't believe it was necessary to make a point of it. He thought the jury had already concluded the same. She told the jury that she knew that Donna had a new man in her life, a guy she called Smokey, some artist who lived along the North Shore of Lake Superior. In fact, she had loaned Donna her car to visit him two days before her death. She had just returned that morning. Troy and his sister had stayed with her while Donna was visiting her friend. She told the jury how she had talked to Donna that morning. Donna told her that she was going to take her car out to Vince's, and that Vince was going to get a new engine and have the mechanic install it. She had decided to take Troy along. That was the last time she talked to Donna. She told the jury they did have a small get together following the wake, and that Vince had stopped over. He told everyone about what a great day he and Donna had had, how they had patched up their differences and were planning on getting married. She said they all talked about it after he left, all wondering how he could have made up such a story.

As Matt listened to her testimony, jotting a note here and there, he was again struck by the inconsistency of her being so concerned for Donna but yet letting her go there that Saturday, by herself, expressing no concern. He was also curious why the prosecution never solicited any testimony from the young women regarding Donna's drinking habits. He knew from his own investigation that they all admitted that she drank quite heavily. Matt wondered whether the prosecutor was staying away from that for some reason.

Donna's blood alcohol concentration at the time of her death, the .25, had always bothered Matt. He knew that if Vince testified, the prosecutor would make him explain his comment that they'd only had a couple of drinks. He knew the prosecutor believed Vince had purposely gotten her drunk with the intention of getting her loose, maybe to get her into bed. But Matt believed it had another side as well, one he could use. He could argue it showed she was carefree. He could argue she came that day because she really enjoyed Vince's company, that they were in fact reminiscing about old times. Her drinking substantiated Vince's version of what had occurred. Matt wondered whether Jenny Weber would be a good witness with whom to approach the subject. After he watched her for a while, he thought better of it, he would let it rest for the time being.

As the prosecutor concluded his questions, Matt hesitated at first whether to ask her anything. She had not really hurt Vince's case, but he was still curious about her attitude that morning. He felt he wanted to know. "Ms. Weber," he said, "if I understand correctly, you talked to Ms. Woods minutes before she left for Vince Fischer's home that Saturday morning."

"Yes, I did."

"And, sometime earlier Ms. Woods had confided in you that she believed Mr. Fischer was somehow responsible for the automobile problems she had encountered, is that correct?"

"Yes, she had told me that weeks before. She told me she thought Vince had punctured her oil pan or something like that."

"And it was your understanding, Ms. Weber, that she believed Mr. Fischer had done that for the sole purpose of getting her out to his home, is that correct?"

She looked at him, knowing where he was going and reluctantly said, "Yes."

"And that Saturday morning, Ms. Weber, when Ms. Woods told you she was in fact going out to Vince's house to make arrangements to have her automobile fixed, did Ms. Woods bring that assumption up? Did she talk about it?"

"No, she did not."

"Did you bring it up with her?"

"No, I did not."

Matt looked down at his note pad. Remember, he told himself, don't ask a question when you don't know the answer. But then again, what the hell…. "Why didn't you bring that up that morning?"

She looked at him, thought for a while and said, "To be completely honest with you, I never knew if what Donna was telling me was the truth or not. I thought, at times, that she had a tendency to exaggerate to make a good story, to add a little excitement to it, if you know what I mean. I always thought it was a carryover from her marriage. It sounded as if her life then was in a constant uproar, and maybe things were too quiet for her here."

It wasn't what Matt expected. It caught him totally by surprise. In one sentence, this woman had summed up Donna's life, at least her life for the months before her death. The answer was good for Vince Fischer, but it was not what Matt wanted to hear.

***

Driving home that night he recounted the day's events. His head was pounding. When he took this case, it was to win; he wanted that jury to find Mr. Fischer not guilty. Then as he learned more about the case, he was convinced that the jury would never come in with a not guilty. At most, what he really had was a case for first degree manslaughter. Then Nikki came along and the plans changed again. Now he had to lose. Vince had to go to prison for life. But as the case was progressing, it became more apparent to Matt he could make one hell of an argument for first degree manslaughter. Particularly if Vince did not testify. He started to wonder what the judge was thinking. Whether the judge would consider instructing the jury on manslaughter even if the defense did not ask for that instruction. At that point, he felt he had very little control over where this case was going. He couldn't purposely lose it, it would be too obvious. If Vince didn't catch on, the prosecutor and judge certainly would. If Vince got a new trial because he screwed up, he hadn't accomplished a thing. By the time he reached home, it had become pretty clear—Vince had to testify and the prosecutor had to, how had Vince put it? *Tear him a new asshole.*

Following the testimony of Jenny Weber, the prosecution had advised the judge she was his last witness, the state was ready to rest. The only matter left to resolve was whether the court would allow the *Spreigl* evidence, the testimony of the three ex-wives, as part of the state's case in chief. The judge indicated that with the weekend recess, he would further consider the matter and he would let the attorneys know on Monday morning. He told the prosecutor he should have the three women available to testify, just in case.

***

Matt went into the office on Saturday morning. It had been close to three weeks since he had spent any time there. He wanted to check to see whether his practice was falling apart in his absence. It looked like Kay had things under control; there were no huge piles on his desk.

Matt was rummaging through the notes when the phone rang. He hesitated. Saturday calls normally mean nothing but trouble, somebody's in jail, somebody needs immediate help. Whatever it was, he felt he had neither the time nor the inclination to deal with it. It was always in the back of his mind, however, that it could be Nikki. He took the chance and answered. He was right.

"Hi," she said.

He could tell from her voice she felt good, she had been able to put away the stress of the trial and was more relaxed.

"How can you call?" he asked.

"Vince's gone, he left last night. I think he went to Minneapolis. Anyway, he said he wouldn't be back until Sunday morning."

"You sure he's not trying to set you up?" asked Matt.

"Why would he try to do that?"

"There's no reason why he should disappear now over the weekend when we have to decide whether he's going to testify next week or not."

"I don't think he's gonna testify," said Nikki. "I think you've convinced him that based on how the case is going so far, he doesn't have to. He thinks you're doing a tremendous job. He thinks they're gonna find him not guilty. Actually, I think he went out to celebrate."

"I can't believe this," said Matt. "What kind of a nut am I dealing with?"

"He believes the jury thinks she was a tramp. He said you told him one time, Matt, if the jury didn't like her, it could make quite a difference. That's what he thinks is happening."

"Now it only depends on what the judge does Monday morning," said Matt. "If he lets those three women testify, it'll change the whole picture. Whatever that jury is thinking now, it won't be the same if they hear the testimony of those ex-wives, particularly Pamela Dahl."

As the sentence trailed off, Matt remembered Nikki's first comment. "Nikki, if Vince was gone last night, why didn't you call me?"

There was a long pause. "I thought about it, really I did, and then I thought we all needed some rest."

"When did you say Vince was going to be back?" asked Matt.

"I'm not sure," said Nikki. "He might be back tonight."

"Well, when he gets home, have him call me."

They talked for a few minutes before hanging up. As Matt put the receiver down, he had an uneasy feeling. Nothing he could grasp. She seemed distant; too distant, he thought, for what they had been through.

chapter 38

VINCE DID CALL Matt on Sunday evening. He sounded in good spirits. He said he'd decided to take a couple days off, get away from everybody. He'd gone to a favorite spot of his in Minneapolis and returned just hours ago. Matt wasn't sure how to bring up the question of Vince testifying. He approached it cautiously. "The judge is gonna let us know first thing tomorrow morning whether the ex-wives can testify," Matt told him.

"No way he's gonna let them testify. He can't! Not the way things have been going."

"It's precisely the way things have been going, Vince, that may make the testimony admissible. I told you before, one of the basis for its admission is to the prove lack of accident. If this judge thinks the prosecutor's case has weakened to the point the state needs the testimony or you'll walk, he'll let it in. Then we have to decide how we confront it. Then you're going to have to testify."

There was a long silence.

"Right now I have no intention of testifying. I don't think I need to. You know I can't take this bullshit anymore, that's why I took a couple days off. Every time I manage to get my head straight, you manage to fuck it up. I've had enough of this shit!" Vince slammed the phone down in Matt's ear.

Matt leaned back in his chair; that uneasy feeling persisted. He couldn't put his finger on it. He thought about his discussion with Vince. It was totally calculated to get Vince to testify and the only reason for that was to make sure that the jury would convict him...for Nikki's sake. As he continued to ponder what he was doing, a sick feeling set in.

chapter 39

ON MONDAY MORNING Matt had gotten to the courthouse early. Things had started to weigh so heavily he couldn't sleep. Sipping more vending machine coffee, he was unable to concentrate on anything. What happened now all hinged on what the judge decided to do.

During the course of the trial he had seen a few of the jurors in the coffee shop. They didn't appear as friendly as the first day, before the trial started, but he knew from experience that jurors became more cautious in their expressions as the case progressed. He always thought it was because they didn't want to act in a manner that may telltale their feelings. Matt noticed that they weren't as talkative, not as excited and animated as they had been when they were still just prospective jurors. His experience was that once the jurors started to hear the evidence, saw the pictures of the victim, finally realized the enormous chore ahead of them—to decide somebody's fate—their demeanors changed. The smiles slowly disappeared, replaced with stares. There was still a "good morning," but it was hesitant, as though they didn't want to get caught acknowledging him. Matt felt he had not lost the jury yet, but he could certainly tell they were deep in thought.

Ten minutes before court was scheduled to start, Vince and Nikki walked in. Vince wore the appropriate serious face. Dressed in a very expensive three-piece suit, he looked every bit the successful businessman. Nikki was radiant in the same blue colored suit that highlighted her blue eyes and blonde curls. She held Vince's arm. Just as they were about to exchange good mornings, the judge's clerk came out and indicated Judge Thompson wished to talk to both attorneys in chambers.

The judge told the attorneys he had made a decision on the *Spreigl* evidence. He had not had an opportunity to put it in writing so he wanted the parties to go into the courtroom and without the jury present, he would issue his ruling. Matt didn't need to hear it. He could tell by the judge's words and manner he had decided to let the women testify. He wasn't gonna tell Vince that, though; he would leave that up to the judge.

Reaching the counsel table, Matt noticed there was a rustling in the courtroom. The case had picked up new spectators every day and the courtroom was packed. One of the bailiffs had to save seats for Nikki and for Donna's family. The judge came in, looking very somber, sat down and shuffled through some of his papers.

"As everybody is aware," he started, "the court has taken under advisement the state's motion to produce certain witnesses, who we call *Spreigl* witnesses, who would testify regarding prior misconduct by the defendant. There are certain conditions imposed on the court as to when to allow the admission of such testimony. The rules provide that one of the bases for its admission is when the defense is one of accident. As in this case, if the defense claims what occurred was accidental and not intentional, the state can ask that testimony of prior occurrences of a similar nature be admissible to prove the lack of accident, or, in other words, that what occurred was not an accident. That is what the state has asked me to do in this case.

"When I first heard the testimony of the state's witnesses, I had some reservations. Those reservations related to the length of time between the alleged acts of misbehavior and the death of Ms. Woods. Under the rule, I also have the right to wait until I see whether the state will need the testimony as part of its case. I gave this considerable thought over the weekend and I'm going to issue an order allowing the state to call the three witnesses.

"My basis for allowing the testimony is twofold: First, if there had been no allegations of physical abuse by Mr. Fischer from the time of his first marriage until his third marriage, I would agree that the testimony of Marilyn Fischer is too remote in time, and so likely to be too prejudicial, that I would not have allowed it in. But the testimony that there was another physical assault, albeit not as serious, on the second wife, only eight years ago, which I believe is not too remote in time, establishes a pattern which I believe makes Ms Marilyn Fischer's testimony admissible. Secondly, Mr. Fischer has indicated in the statement admitted into evidence that the death of Ms. Woods was an accident. I believe the testimony goes to that question. I do not believe that any prejudice to the defendant by my admission of this testimony outweighs the probative value. I will, moreover, certainly give the jury the precautionary instruction. We will proceed in a few minutes."

He closed his file, got up, and walked out.

Vince turned to Matt, his face bright red, anger boiling over. Matt thought Vince might have a few choice words for the judge, right there, and he quickly got him out of the courtroom.

In the hall Vince was muttering, "I can't believe this fuckin' system. I can't believe that fuckin' judge. I can't believe this is fuckin' happening to me. He's gonna let those bitches get up and lie through their fuckin' teeth."

Matt had had enough. "Vince, just shut up! You're not gonna be happy until you can't get that damn foot out of your mouth anymore."

Vince fixed his gaze on Matt. "Don't start fuckin' around with me. You know what they say, 'Don't get into a pissing contest with a skunk.'"

He turned and walked away. Nikki watched the whole episode, stunned. She looked at Matt. "What do you think this means?"

"It means he's gonna get on the stand and fuck up his whole case."

"You're getting as foul-mouthed as he is," she said.

The comment took Matt by surprise. "God, I hope not. I'm sorry."

Daniel Eller

She smiled. "Never mind."

"Everything's going pretty much the way I expected. We wanted to force Vince into testifying. The judge has just done that for us."

"I always had confidence in you," she replied.

The judge's decision to allow all three wives to testify did surprise Matt. He had not been able to find any cases, at least Minnesota cases, where the court had allowed testimony that was so remote in time. The judge had taken a gutsy position and Matt knew why. He was pretty sure that the judge had already decided that Vince had shot Donna intentionally. He might not believe it was premeditated, but Matt was sure he did not believe it was accidental. So the judge was concerned that the jury could find Vince not guilty. A real miscarriage of justice. Because the judge had seen these three women testify at the previous hearing, he also knew how devastating their testimony would be, the effect they would have on the jurors. To Matt, it was clear that the judge's decision was calculated to get Vince convicted.

Matt could feel the tension when he went back into the courtroom. The family and spectators had heard the judge's explanation, now there was the anticipation of what it all meant. None of them had heard the testimony at the previous hearing. Matt noticed a well-dressed and attractive middle-aged woman at the front of the courtroom talking to one of the bailiffs. Matt looked at her more closely and realized it was Marilyn Fischer. The prosecution must have bought her new clothes and sent her to the hair salon. Matt realized Scott was more concerned than he had thought. He was pulling out all the stops.

Matt had already decided there was nothing to be gained by trying to give the ex-wives a hard time. Vince didn't agree with him. Matt simply told him that was too bad, if the women came across the way he expected, the way he saw them in the previous hearing, any attempt to simply badger them would further alienate the jury. He just wasn't going to do it. Vince had no choice.

After her name was called, Marilyn Fischer took the stand. She had a more confident walk and attitude than at the previous

218

hearing. She had obviously gotten over the fear of her first encounter with Vince, and now she looked as though she planned to pound a few nails in his coffin. Matt didn't have to listen to her testimony, he knew it by heart. He just watched the face of the female jurors as the prosecutor ran her through her statement. When it came to the part where she told the jury how Vince had wrapped a towel around her neck and had pulled tightly, that she had been gasping for air, he could actually see some of the jurors taking a deep breath, living her experience. Tears came to her eyes at the appropriate time, her hands shaking. She, too, is on a mission, thought Matt. It was as if she has spent twenty years thinking about the day she was going to get even. Today was that day.

The testimony of Val Feia, Vince's second wife, was actually a relief. It went easily and, compared to the testimony of Marilyn, it was nothing. Matt now knew that the only reason the judge let it in was to justify his bootstrapping of Marilyn's testimony, to argue the continuity. Vince had grabbed her by the hair and pulled her out of his shop. There weren't even any tears.

The judge asked whether the attorneys wished to take the morning recess. Scott quickly jumped up and said, "I only have the one witness left and that shouldn't take long, I would prefer to keep going."

Matt knew what Scott was doing. The prosecutor had the momentum going for his case. Everybody could tell that the jurors were glued to the testimony of the witnesses. His best was yet to come. A recess at this time could break the spell. Any other case, Matt would have pushed for the recess. In this case, he let it pass.

Ms. Dahl walked in, exuding confidence. She walked to the bench and said her "I do" loudly in response to the clerk's recitation of the oath. Matt knew she was tough. He could tell it in her statements, in her letters to the sheriff, from her testimony at the previous hearing. It was apparent she was afraid of no one. Matt thought she was dressed rather seductively in a tight short skirt with dark nylons accenting very shapely legs. A white silk blouse clung very tightly to her breasts, revealing cleavage. She had long black hair and beautiful dark eyes. As she sat down and looked around the packed courtroom, she carefully avoided any eye contact with Vince. She's here as well, thought Matt, to cut him off above the knees.

As the prosecutor took her through the episodes with Vince, she was even more animated than she had been in the previous hearing. Everything was acted out. Vince didn't just slap her, she would swing her hand forcefully through the air, trying to convince the jury that this wasn't just a love tap, that he really meant to hurt her. By the time she got to the last episode, she had the jury mesmerized. They were hanging on every word. She was in tears, almost hysterical when she described Vince putting his hands around her throat, kneeling on her chest, and her belief that she was about to die. The jurors could see her lying there, panic on her face, looking up at Vince.

Then she told the jury, "We were eye-to-eye. I thought this is the last thing I'm ever going to see…his face. It was bright red. Anger filled his eyes and the veins on his temples bulged like they were ready to pop."

With that, every juror looked at Vince's face. Matt snuck a glance. There it was, the same expression, the veins on the sides of his face popping out. There was no way he could hide it. Pamela Dahl slowly slumped in the chair as if exhausted by her ordeal. You could've heard a pin drop. The prosecutor asked her if she needed a break, if she needed a drink of water. She replied, "No, I'm all right. I just wanna get this over with."

"What happened after that?" asked the prosecutor.

"Within no time, it was like it never happened. Vince was bouncing around the house like it never happened. There was no apology, nothing. Hours later he said he was gonna run some errands. While he was gone I packed my things and got out."

"Thank you," said Scott, "Your witness."

There was nothing Matt could do. He could run her through her testimony again hoping for a slight discrepancy, but why repeat it? He could try and get her to admit that Vince might have had some provocation but nobody in that courtroom would ever believe she had provoked him enough for that response. All he could do is take the attitude in front of a jury that this wasn't even important enough to talk about. It was so insignificant; he didn't even have any questions for her. As all of this was going through his mind, the judge on the bench said, "Mr. Collins?"

"I'm sorry, Your Honor. I have no questions. Thank you."

The prosecutor stood. "The state rests."

Matt rose. "Your Honor, I believe I've already explained our situation to you. We intend to start with Dr. Evans, the Medical Examiner, and possibly another witness from out of state. They will be here tonight so we won't be able to start our case until tomorrow morning."

The judge turned to jury. "Well, you've heard our situation. It's a nice day today. I'm sure none of you will regret having the afternoon off. We'll start promptly tomorrow morning at 9:00. We expect that the case will probably be submitted to you by Thursday. Thank you for your continued patience."

Matt always waited for the jurors to leave the jury box and the courtroom before he exited. He felt it showed the jurors some respect. He also felt he could get some feeling as to where they stood by watching them leave. Whether they looked uptight, relaxed, whatever. As the jurors stood up, Matt stood up and looked squarely at them. Only a few dared look at him and then only for a split second.

Matt made Vince sit at the counsel bench with his back to the spectators until the courtroom had cleared out. Vince needed a chance to regain his composure. He wanted to give him time to bring his blood pressure down so the veins on his temples stopped pounding. He knew the jury had seen it; he didn't want Donna's family to see it as well.

By the time they got into the hall, everybody had cleared out. Nikki excused herself to go to the ladies' room.

Matt and Vince stood in the middle of the hallway in front of the courtroom. "That was a fuckin' disaster," said Vince. "I never want to go through something like that again. I'm just glad that's over with. I never have to face those bitches again. I think you were probably right, Matt. There was no reason to prolong the agony by asking them any questions. They would just continue to lie through their fuckin' teeth. I think the jury could see that."

Matt looked at Vince and realized he had no grasp of reality. He was living in his own little world. He had just been castrated and he didn't feel a thing. The thought brought a smile to his face.

"I didn't think it was funny," said Vince.

"I'm sorry. I had my mind somewhere else," said Matt.

"That's your fuckin' problem."

Matt looked at Vince. "This is neither the time nor the place for that kind of bullshit."

"You're the bullshit," said Vince.

chapter 40

MATT HAD MADE arrangements to pick up the firearms expert, Dave Carlson, at the airport that evening at 5:30 and drop him off at the Radisson. Vince wanted to be there when they talked to get firsthand what happened with Weineke when he had brought the gun to Madison. They'd made arrangements to meet at 7:30 for dinner.

As the two of them left the airport parking lot, Carlson was nothing but apologetic. "I don't know how in the hell we got into this, Matt. I certainly didn't say anything like that to Deputy Weineke. I've tried to remember exactly how the testing went, I'm not even sure he was there when we did the recoil testing."

"He had to be there," said Matt, "he describes it in detail. He wouldn't let that gun out of his sight. Look, we're going to have to go over this whole thing with Vince this evening. I would just as soon put it off till then. I've had a long day. I'm beat up. Let's talk about something else."

"Fine," Carlson agreed.

The rest of the trip they talked about cases that Carlson had had with Matt's friend in the Milwaukee County Public Defender's Office.

Matt and Carlson were already seated at the table when Vince walked into the Radisson dining room. Matt had warned Carlson to be prepared for a tirade. Vince was surprisingly calm.

After he took a sip from his drink, he looked at Carlson and said, "Tell me how this thing got fucked up."

Carlson went through the explanation one more time. He

never said anything comparable to what Weineke had written in the report; there was no way he could've said anything that stupid. He told Vince both he and his partner were surprised at the amount of recoil the gun produced and yes, if he was asked, he would have to admit that. But in his opinion, to testify that the gun would fly out of a person's hand if he were holding it to his side would be pure speculation. He would never agree it would *have* to fly out.

Matt listened like a spectator. He started to realize he could never put Carlson on the stand. He was doing more side stepping than a square dancer. He was wondering how this guy had made it as far as he had without screwing up.

By the time Carlson had finished explaining to Vince all the tests and what had happened, he had pretty much convinced him that it had been a conspiracy on the part of the prosecutor's office and Deputy Weineke to manipulate the evidence to get him convicted. Based on the conversation, it sounded as if Vince was convinced that Carlson could explain this all to the jury. Matt knew, however, that was exactly the problem—that he *had to* explain to the jury. They shouldn't have been in a position to have to explain anything to the jury. Carlson was there for one reason, to tell the jury how he got the gun to misfire when it was in the safety position. To give the jury an alternative to consider. If Matt put him on the stand to testify to that, the prosecutor would be cross-examining him regarding the alleged statement to Weineke. If Carlson admitted that he'd made it, the state had the gun flying out of Vince's hand, which Vince never mentioned. If he denied that he made the statement, then the prosecutor would put Deputy Weineke back on the stand and he'd tell the jury that he had made the statement and his credibility would be shot. Either way, it didn't help Vince's case and everybody was going to wonder why he'd bothered to put Carlson on the stand in the first place. As Matt thought of all the possibilities, he decided he wasn't going to mention any of this to Vince or Carlson that night. He didn't need to get into a screaming argument with Vince in the Radisson dining room.

***

Matt walked out of the judge's chambers the following morning a little after 9:00. He had been there early to set up a meeting with the judge and the prosecutor to let them know he had encountered some problems in his case. He told the judge that he needed some time to go over Dave Carlson's testimony with him and he still wasn't sure whether he was going to call him. The second problem was that Dr. Evans had been unable to make it the prior evening and would not be getting in until 5:50 that day. So, he would not be able to put him on the witness stand until the following morning. If Matt didn't call Carlson, that left him with several of Donna's friends, some the state did not call, who would testify about the relationship between Vince and Donna. And then he had to decide whether Vince was going to testify. He had to drag it out long enough that if Vince was going to take the stand, it would not be until after lunch. He needed that additional time to go over his testimony with him. The judge and the prosecutor were both understanding. Matt knew it wasn't a question of being understanding, really. It was more that they were both starting to feel sorry for him. They started to see the steel gates closing on Mr. Fischer and they both knew there was little Matt could do to stop it. Neither one wanted to kick him when he was down.

As Matt walked back into the hallway, Vince and Nikki were pacing the hall, looking for him, apprehensively. They had no idea what was going on. He had already had Carlson sitting in one of the attorney conference rooms and he motioned Vince and Nikki to follow him.

In the conference room he turned to Vince and said, "I don't think we should have Carlson testify."

Vince looked across the table. "What the fuck are you talking about?"

"Just what I said," he replied. "There's no reason to have Mr. Carlson testify. All he can do is hurt your case."

Nikki said nothing. She had no idea what Matt was doing. Carlson sat there quietly. He knew what a difficult position it would put Matt in if he took the stand. Even if Weineke was lying, they could never convince the jury of that.

Matt continued. "The only thing Mr. Carlson can testify to is the fact the gun misfired when he hit it on the pistol grip with a mallet when it was in the safety position. That is basically already on the record. Bishop, in cross examination, acknowledged it could happen. He said he didn't conduct any tests similar to that but he understood that the test had been done. I can already argue to the jury that, contrary to Bishop's direct testimony, we know the gun will misfire under certain circumstances. If that's the case, there may be other circumstances under which the gun could misfire in either the cocked or uncocked position. We're still free to argue about that.

"More importantly though, Vince, if you remember, Bishop testified the gun had normal recoil. If we put Carlson on the stand, he's going to have to admit that in his opinion, the gun had more than normal recoil. The test is in his report. Scott can cross-examine him about it and then Scott is going to smugly ask him the question, 'Didn't you tell Deputy Weineke that if Vince said this gun was under his arm when it went off, he's full of shit. The gun would have flown all the way across the deck.' Carlson's going to say, 'No, I never said that.' And Scott's gonna say, 'So if Deputy Weineke has that in his report, the report he made the day after he watched you conduct those tests, you're telling this jury he was lying.' And Mr. Carlson will have to say, 'yes.' And then in rebuttal, Scott's gonna call Deputy Weineke, who will tell us that's exactly what Mr. Carlson said. Who do you think the jury's gonna believe? You just made a major issue out of a point we've already won. Why in the hell would we want to do that?"

Nikki looked at Vince. "It makes absolute sense. Matt's right, I've sat back and listened to everything, it's just the way he said. There's no reason why this man should go on the stand."

Matt glanced at her, not knowing whether she really understood or was simply trying to urge his position.

Carlson finally gathered enough nerve to look at Vince. "It makes no difference to me, Mr. Fischer. Again, I apologize for what happened. But if that's what Bishop testified to, then he conducted a different test than I did because I certainly wouldn't concur with that opinion. You're better off that the recoil of the shotgun is not an issue."

"Why?" asked Vince.

"It's very simple," replied Matt. "The gun was lying by Donna's side, according to everyone there. If the recoil was such that it would fly from your hand, you would've had to go back, pick it up, and place it by her body. If the gun was at your shoulder, you only had to put it down."

Vince looked at them all, shrugged his shoulders and said, "What the fuck."

Matt knew that with the matter explained this way, Vince had no choice. Matt had made arrangements with Tim to be at the courthouse to whisk Mr. Carlson away before the state had any bright ideas of talking to him again. The only thing Carlson wanted was to be reimbursed for his airline ticket. Vince wrote him a check. Matt could tell that Vince was fuming. It wasn't a good time to bring up whether Vince should be their first witness.

Matt knew the rest of the morning was going to be just filler. He had subpoenaed three of Donna's friends. All of them had had numerous conversations with Donna and she had never brought up anything about breaking up with Vince or any suspicions Vince had somehow sabotaged her car. They told the jury how Donna had admired Vince for what he had accomplished, because of how generous he had been with her and the children. Donna had talked to them about all the good times she'd had with Vince. They also had experienced Donna's capacity to drink beer— the amount of which amazed them all. Even though they all considered themselves Donna's good friends, having talked on a regular basis, Donna never said anything to them that even came close to criticizing Vince or his behavior. Matt could never figure out why Donna must have decided to confide in some and not in the others. The problem was that there was no way of knowing to which group she was telling the truth. That, at least, is what he intended to tell the jury.

The prosecutor asked each of them only a few questions. It was apparent to Matt that Scott had concluded that these were nice women who were testifying truthfully. They weren't hurting his case, so why give them a hard time? By the time the last one was done, it was 11:30. Matt asked the court for an early luncheon recess.

***

Matt asked Nikki and Vince to join him for lunch. He wanted to find a quiet restaurant where they wouldn't see anyone from the trial. Matt knew he was never going to be able to eat, but he didn't want to sit around the courthouse for an hour and a half, pacing the floor, telegraphing his doubts to any who saw him, including jurors. During the drive from the courthouse to the diner he had selected, not a word was exchanged. It was as if they all anticipated what the next few hours would bring.

After they ordered, Matt said, "Vince, we have no choice, you have to go on the stand first thing this afternoon."

Vince knew it was coming. The waitress put a cup of coffee in front of him. He took a sip. "I can do it. I'm not concerned, Matt. I can do it."

No emotion, no cussing, Matt couldn't believe it. Vince had once again reverted to the businessman. Calm, cool, collected, totally in charge of his emotions. After a moment of reflection, Matt asked. "But what are you gonna say, Vince?"

Glancing first at Nikki, Vince turned to give Matt a cold stare. "Don't you worry about that, counsel."

Nikki knew exactly what was going on but she couldn't say a word. She sat quietly, watching the body language, watching these two men try to measure the other's resolve. Matt knew he had Vince where he wanted him. "Is there anything you feel we should go over before we go back?" asked Matt.

Vince continued to sip his cup of coffee while he stared at Matt for a few seconds. "I don't think so. If I'm not ready now, I'll never be."

It was a different Vince than Matt had ever experienced.

The waitress brought their meals. Matt picked at his food,

his stomach turned, afraid anything he swallowed would come up right in the middle of some question. Vince had no problem. Matt thought he was actually jovial. Vince took a bite and with a mouthful said, "You know, Matt, that Julie who testified the other day, she's really a good gal. We had a lot of good times. You couldn't tell the way she was dressed, but she really has a nice pair of...." He glanced at Nikki, and said, "Sorry, Nikki. She just has a nice pair."

It was Vince's new image, thought Matt.

"Anyway it was a Christmas party out at Anton's. She was there; some of our other friends were out there. Donna and I were there. Julie got a little tanked. All night long she would walk around the guys, total strangers, and ask them if they wanted to see her 'Christmas presents.' Then she'd pull open her blouse and stick them right out. She had this bright red bra on with a little bow on the front of each cup, right over the nipple. Some of these guys damn near died. Some guy ended up following her around. I think his wife finally dragged him out by the ear. Donna just cracked up every time she saw it. It was all in good fun. Julie was pretty embarrassed the next time we saw her."

Matt listened to the story, grinning at the proper moments. But he couldn't believe how Vince was telling the story as if he didn't have a care in the world—just a casual conversation among old friends. Vince continued on like that during the entire lunch, one story after another about all the good times he and Donna had had with some of the young women who had testified. It was as if he was preparing himself to take the witness stand, he was putting himself in the congenial mode to convince the jury he really wasn't such a bad guy, that he was actually the likeable guy Matt told him the jury had to see.

chapter 41

JUDGE THOMPSON LOOKED down from the bench. "Mr. Collins."

"Thank you, Your Honor. The defense calls Vince Fischer."

Vince got up, exuding confidence, turned, smiled at Nikki and walked to the bench to take his oath—the oath he was about to break. Matt thought he knew almost every word Vince was going to say in direct examination. He had rehearsed the questions in his head many times. He believed Vince would do a credible job and the prosecutor would eat him up on cross examination. At least, that's the way he had it pictured. He led Vince through his background, his early years, his family, where he grew up, where he went to school, how he got started in business. Vince was beaming as he told the jury how he opened his first Super Lube and how the business grew. Matt asked him about his first marriage. Vince admitted they were terrible years. He and his first wife, Marilyn, had been high school sweethearts. They had gotten married way too young. They lived in a little trailer house on the east side of town. He told the jury how they were constantly arguing over everything, some terrible arguments, and a couple of times they lead to wrestling matches. He had never put a towel around her neck to choke her, though. He had never brought a knife toward her; he hadn't even owned the kind of knife she had described. As far as the other guy she'd been seeing towards the end, Vince admitted he had shot a pistol but it had been pointed in the air and it was only intended to scare the guy. He had really been acting in self-defense, he thought.

As the questions continued, Matt realized that Vince had

indeed transformed himself into the respectable businessman. His answers were quick, responsive, and delivered in such a fashion he was looking quite credible. Val Feia, his second wife, he told the jury, simply left out a few things in her testimony. He had asked her to stop coming to the station many times. They were in the middle of a divorce and the attorneys had told her to stay away. But she was angry because she felt she wasn't getting the financial settlement she thought she was entitled to. And Vince said, "I had nothing to do with that. I was simply taking the advice of my attorneys. That was between the attorneys. I was willing to give her whatever she wanted."

Matt looked at him, incredulous. He had never heard any of this before.

He had politely asked her to leave many times, Vince continued. She wouldn't stop screaming at him, disrupting business, embarrassing the employees. He had no choice but to carry her out. He didn't pull her by the hair. If her hair was pulled, it could have been by one of his employees who was assisting him in removing her.

By the time Vince got to testifying about his third wife, Pamela Dahl, he was really in the swing of things. He told the jury she was an airline stewardess. They met on a business trip, fell in love and got married. He wanted her to quit her job. He thought there was no reason why she should continue working for the airlines, being gone so often. There were plenty of positions in his company and she was qualified for many of them. He would have been happy to have her working with him side by side. But she wouldn't do it. Then, he told the jury, he started to wonder why she wanted to be away from home so often. So, even though he knew it wasn't right, he hired a private detective, somebody to follow her when she was out of town to see what was going on. Unfortunately, he was right. She had a boyfriend in Seattle. A guy who worked for the airline. She would see him every other week. The detective brought back some photos of them dining and dancing together. Vince couldn't understand why she had done this to him. He told the jury he didn't bring it up right away.

He thought maybe it was somebody she had been seeing before they got married and it was difficult for her to break it off. Or else they might just be friends, nothing sexual to it.

Matt had no choice but to just go with it. He knew where Vince was going and he was going to get there whether Matt led him or not. It was a performance worthy of an Oscar, thought Matt. Vince told the jury how heartbroken he was, how he couldn't understand why his wife would do that to him. He had tried to provide her with everything. If this was a lover, why had she bothered marrying him in the first place? Then he said he finally couldn't take it anymore.

One night when she came back from Seattle, he confronted her about it, showed her some of the pictures. She exploded, he said, she called him every name in the book, some he'd never heard of. How dare he have the audacity to have somebody follow her, who did he think he was with all of his stinkin' money to do something like that. And she swung at him as hard as she could, catching him across the side of the face. He brought up his arm with such force, he told the jury, he caught her under the armpit and she fell backwards and he fell on top of her. His knee landed on her chest and his elbow on her throat and she started spitting and coughing and he rolled off. She called him a bunch of names that he didn't want to repeat. She left that night, he said. She filed for divorce and tried to get some money out of him but she had signed a prenuptial agreement, and again, he had let the lawyers handle it. He had been willing to give her something, but they had told him he didn't have to.

This was the same Vince Matt had seen in his office that night when he confessed to him how he had really killed Donna. He has to be on something, thought Matt. He's coming up with this stuff way too fast. Matt could only wonder what the prosecutor was planning. He had to be stewing in his juices over there. He had to be ready to leap across the table.

Vince went on to tell the jury about the first time he saw Donna, when he was visiting one of his stations and she brought in her car. He told them about seeing her kids in the car—a busted down old car that was probably only going to make it another few miles. He said he went out and talked to her. He discreetly asked why her husband hadn't brought the car in. She told him she didn't have a husband; she was divorced. He told the jury how he called her for a date, never expecting her to say yes. How, if he could have, he would've done cartwheels when she said okay. It was corny, but Matt thought he heard some jurors giggle. He went on to portray to the jury a warm, loving relationship. He said he loved Donna's children and tried to include them in everything they did. The days they spent leisurely at his house, lying in the sun, buzzing around the lake on their jet skis, taking the children water skiing. He couldn't believe he had found this lady. He wanted to spend the rest of his life with her.

He still didn't know what had happened, he told the jury. But following the family reunion, things changed. He knew now that buying her that expensive ring was the wrong thing to do. He regretted that. He knew now, he told them, that he should have never gotten into that argument with her sister. But after all, he was proud of what he had accomplished and he didn't think it was fair for her sister to put him down so badly. So when Donna told him she needed some space, some time to think, that he was getting too serious, he told the jury he understood and told her he would just wait for her to make up her mind.

As Matt asked questions, Vince looked to the jury box as he responded. He would pick a different juror each time. It was as if he was talking to each juror individually. This was no longer a court setting to Vince. He had the juror across a table, in a casual conversation. He was slowly laying out his life for each one to inspect. He came across as if he had nothing to hide; he was just a vulnerable soul.

He admitted to the jury he had been totally in love with Donna. He hadn't been able to get her or the children off of his mind. He wanted to do whatever he could to help all of them. Even if she no longer wanted to have a relationship with him, that would have been fine, but he hadn't wanted to be cut off from her and the children entirely. He had wanted to know what she was doing, not like a spy, but like a good concerned friend. He knew she had become dependent on gifts he had made her, the money he had given her over the months they were together. It had not been uncommon for her to ask for four or five hundred dollars a week, he said. He couldn't imagine how she had been getting along without that. So when she had asked for a loan or a favor, or she had a friend of hers ask for a favor, Vince said he had been happy to oblige. He had kept hoping that eventually she would come around. Given a little time and distance from the things he knew her sister had told her, he had believed she would realize she still had feelings for him and they would get back together. He'd told the jury of his excitement when she had agreed to bring her car out that Saturday morning, when she had been willing to let him help her. And he had thought this was her way of saying everything's okay, I'm back, without him being able to say, "See, I told you so."

He calmly went through the whole day. The shooting of the squirrels, his forgetting the gun by the breezeway next to the garage, the joy he'd felt when she and Troy walked in, the hours they'd spent at the kitchen table reminiscing. He said she had been happy that they were back together. She had talked to her father over the phone and then giggled about what a worrier he was after she hung up. Vince told the jury he had leaned over and kissed her and how she had responded and he had known at that instant that she was back in his life. They'd made plans to have dinner that night at Anton's and she would drop Troy off at Jenny's and spend the night with Vince.

"Troy was watching the movie in the great room," he continued. "I kissed Donna but she was afraid that Troy would see. When Troy came in the kitchen, Donna sent him out to the car to wait. Troy was all excited about being able to sit in the Corvette by himself. We kissed again, passionately this time. I was gonna walk her to the car."

Vince sat up straight in the witness box and put his hands on the railing. He hesitated for a moment, gathering his thoughts, anticipating where he was going, to give his most dramatic presentation. He started calmly, telling the jury what had happened as they reached the deck. He went through every detail. The pain of recall was on his face as he told the jury the shock of seeing her lying there on the deck. The tears slowly came down his cheeks. He talked about his shock and his panic and his loss. He told them he had gone over those moments in his mind thousands of times and still couldn't believe that it happened. He would do anything to take it all back. As he finished, he slumped in his chair, portraying a man spent and crushed.

The judge stood up. "This is a good time to take recess."

Vince sat in the chair, his head down, as the jurors filed out and the courtroom emptied. Matt walked from the counsel table to the witness stand. "You can look up now," he whispered.

Vince was obviously pleased with himself. Matt just mumbled to himself, "You son of a bitch," and turned around and walked out. There was no way he could talk to Vince.

Nikki was in the hall. As Matt approached her, she said, "Quite a performance."

"The guy's amazing," said Matt. "I've never heard any of that. I don't know if he's making it up as he goes, or if he's had it planned all along."

"Knowing him," she said, "he had this planned all along. Can't the prosecutor call those women back to testify, to call him a liar?"

"Sure he can. But would they come back? Why would he want to make that the biggest issue in the case? I don't think he'd want to do that. For all we know, Marilyn's probably back in South Dakota and Dahl's probably flying back to her boyfriend in Seattle. I'm sure Scott never expected this. I don't imagine he told them to stick around just in case he needed them. I think what he can't do in cross-examination he's going to just forget."

"What does that do to your case?" asked Nikki.

"You tell me, you were watching his performance, and you were watching the jurors. What were they thinking?"

"They were listening; they never took their eyes off him." said Nikki.

"He can do that when he wants to," said Matt.

As Vince approached the two of them, Matt turned around and walked away. He heard Vince ask, "What the hell's the matter with him?" But he didn't hear Nikki's reply.

***

When Matt entered the courtroom after the recess, he went quickly to the counsel table. Vince came in and walked right past him to the witness stand without saying a word. Everybody sat quietly, waiting for the judge.

The judge entered the courtroom, sat behind the bench and waited until everything was nice and quiet. He turned to Vince, "Mr. Fischer, I'm sure you understand that you're still *under oath.*"

The last words echoed through the quiet courtroom. It was the judge's way of making a comment on Vince's testimony that was obvious to the jury, but would never quite reflect the same significance on the transcript if read by an appellate court.

Matt stood. "I have nothing further, Your Honor. State's witness."

Matt expected a thunderous beginning to the prosecutor's cross-examination. Instead, there was complete silence for the longest time. When Scott started, it was in a slow hushed voice. "Mr. Fischer, what you want this court and jury to believe is that what happened to Donna Woods October 7th, 1994, at your house, was completely accidental, isn't that true?"

"Because it was an accident," replied Vince.

"And what you want this court and jury to believe is that a man of your obvious intelligence would leave a loaded shotgun leaning against the wall on the deck where a ten-year-old boy would be playing, isn't that true?"

"It's true, it happened that way. Yes," said Vince.

"And what you want this court and jury to believe is that because it had been misting out, you decided at that point and time to pick up the shotgun and take it back into the house with you. Is that what you want us to believe, sir?"

"Yes, it is. That's the way it happened."

"And, Mr. Fischer, what you want this court and jury to

believe is that as you placed that shotgun under your arm to take it back into the house, as you sit here today, you have no idea whether that gun was fully cocked, on safety, or uncocked. Is that what you want us to believe?"

"That's the truth."

"Mr. Fischer, you further want this court and jury to believe that without touching that trigger, the gun discharged and just happened to strike Ms. Woods in the middle of the back?"

Vince looked at the prosecutor and with all the sincerity in his voice he could muster, he quietly said, "Yes, sir. Yes, sir. That's what happened."

You could see the pain on his face again, as if he was recalling the picture of the explosion and the love of his life falling to the deck. The prosecutor knew it was time to move on to something else. "Mr. Fischer, you heard the testimony of your first wife. Is that correct?"

"Yes, I did."

"You have told this jury a little different version of what occurred. You want this jury to believe that Marilyn Fischer was lying?"

"Mr. Larson," replied Vince, "I don't believe she was intentionally lying. I think that's the way she remembers it, but she's wrong. I told you we had fights and there was some mutual combat, but I never tried to choke her or stab her."

Scott continued, "Mr. Fischer, you heard your second wife testify, did you not?"

"Yes, I did."

And you want this jury to believe that when she said you bodily threw her out of the station, pulled her by the hair, she was lying, is that right?"

"That's not what I said," replied Vince. "I did escort her out of the station, but if her hair was pulled, I did not do it. It was one of the employees and then it must have been inadvertent."

Matt could tell that Scott was getting upset. This wasn't how he expected his cross-examination to go. Matt figured that the prosecutor wasn't sure how he was going to get it back on the right track.

"Mr. Fischer, you were here when your third wife testified and you heard her testimony regarding the incident where she thought she was going to die at your hands."

"I heard that testimony," said Vince.

"And you want this jury to believe that she was lying as well?"

"I didn't say she was lying," replied Vince. "I said we swung at each other and we ended up on the floor. I can see how she could've thought I'd done it intentionally, but it wasn't intentional, and as soon as I realized what had happened, I rolled off."

"Mr. Fischer, you were here when Troy Woods testified, isn't that true?"

"Yes, I was."

"You heard Troy Woods testify that he saw the shotgun leaning against the gun cabinet in the great room, did you not?"

"Yes, Mr. Larson. That's what I heard him testify to."

"And you want this jury to believe that Troy was lying?"

"Well, I know he didn't see the gun in the great room because it wasn't there. Whether he overheard people talking about…"

"That isn't what I asked you," interrupted Scott.

"I'm sorry," said Vince. "What did you ask?"

"Mr. Fischer, you heard Troy testify that you and his mother were arguing that afternoon, voices were raised, the two of you were swearing, did you not?"

"I heard that testimony, yes."

"And you want the jury to believe that Troy was lying about that as well?"

"I'm not sure how you expect me to answer that, Mr. Larson. He wasn't lying, but he wasn't telling you what he actually overheard because it never happened. I don't know where he…."

And again Scott interrupted, "That's okay Mr. Fischer, there's no question to be answered. You heard Troy testify that you were the one who told him to go wait in the car, not his mother, is that correct?"

"If you're asking me if I heard him testify to that, yes, I did. It certainly isn't correct."

"You mean you never told Troy to go sit in the car?" asked Scott.

"No, I did not."

"Is it your statement that Troy was in fact lying when he said that?"

"You don't understand," said Vince, "this is a young boy."

"Just answer the question. Yes or no?"

"No," said Vince, "I don't believe he was lying in the sense that he knew what he was saying was wrong."

Scott looked at Judge Thompson. "I ask that the last part of that sentence be stricken as non-responsive."

"So ordered," said the judge.

The scene continued like this for another forty-five minutes. The prosecutor slowly and methodically went through all of the state's witnesses: Had Donna's sister been lying when she'd testified Donna had told her there was no way she was going to marry Vince? Had Donna's friends been lying when they had testified she'd told them that her relationship with Vince was over, that she no longer had any feelings for Vince? Had her neighbor, Jenny, been lying when she'd said Donna had expressed concern that Vince had intentionally damaged her car, hoping she would need his help?

Vince handled each question without hesitation, responding calmly by giving his own slant to what had occurred. He hadn't known what Donna was telling other people, he told the jury, but he knew she wasn't telling *him* anything like that. As far as he'd known, she had just wanted a little time. If that wasn't true, he said, why would she have continued to spend a weekend with him, here and there, and why would she have continued to take his gifts and money?

To the relief of the prosecutor, they finally reached recess time. As Vince walked past Matt, he smirked and whispered, "Sleeping giant, my ass." When he reached Nikki near the back of the courtroom, Matt heard him ask her how she thought he was doing. At that point, Matt finally realized why the prosecutor was not going to get anywhere with Vince. He couldn't successfully cross-examine a person who didn't know what the truth was, who could make up the truth, as he saw it, as he went along. You couldn't catch him in a lie because everything he said was a lie. Matt thought the prosecutor had finally figured that out as well.

**

Vince took the witness stand following the recess, beaming with confidence. Waiting for the prosecutor to continue his questioning, he looked about the courtroom, glancing at the jurors, flashing them the slightest smile, not enough to make them uncomfortable.

Scott finally stood up at the counsel table, looked at Vince and said, "Mr. Fischer, I have just a few more questions. You were in court last week when Dr. Michaels testified, isn't that correct?"

"Yes, I was, sir."

"And you heard him testify regarding the blood alcohol concentration of Ms. Woods?"

"Yes, I did."

"And you heard him testify that her blood alcohol concentration was .25, two and a half times higher than the state of Minnesota considers as being under the influence?"

"Yes, I heard that testimony."

"In your statements that night following her death, and in the written statement the next day, you indicated to authorities she had only had a couple of beers, isn't that what you told them?

"Yes, it is."

"And you heard Dr. Michaels testify that for a woman her size and weight, she would've had at least twelve beers from the time she arrived at your house until she died. Isn't that what he testified to?"

"That is what he said, yes."

"Mr. Fischer, do you want this jury to believe that Dr. Michaels is lying about the amount of alcohol Ms. Woods would have had to consume at your home that afternoon?"

"I don't believe he's lying," responded Vince. "I said I only saw her have a couple of drinks."

"She didn't bring any beer with her? Yes or no?"

"No."

"And so the only beer she would have been able to consume would have been at your home? Yes or no?"

"Yes."

And the whole time she was there, she was never out of your sight for more than a couple of minutes. Yes or no?"

"No, she wasn't."

"And so if she had to consume twelve beers, more or less, she consumed those in your presence? Yes or no?"

"Yes, she did."

Matt watched, his heart racing. It appeared the prosecutor had finally caught Vince in a web of deceit from which his glib tongue would not be able to free him. Matt waited for the next question with anticipation.

Scott continued, "So when you told the police officers that she'd only had a couple of beers, and when you told that to the jury just a few moments ago, you were lying?"

"Yes, I was," said Vince. "I was lying to protect Donna."

Scott had the choice of letting the answer slip by and going on to something else. He made the mistake of asking Vince, "How did a lie protect Ms. Woods?"

Vince gazed at the prosecutor, hesitated for a second. "Everybody was concerned about Donna's drinking. I know her dad was concerned. It was nothing for her to go through a couple six packs of beer at a sitting. She loved to drink beer. After the telephone call from her dad that afternoon, she'd told me she felt bad. You see, she had told him, she had told everybody, she was gonna stop. I didn't think about any blood tests when they asked me the question. The only thing I had in my mind was to protect that last image of Donna. I know it may sound like a lie to you now, but at the time, it made absolute sense to me."

Scott knew he had made a mistake, asked one question too many. He hoped to recover. "Isn't it true that Donna had no intention of getting back together with you; the only reason you were giving her beer all afternoon was to get her drunk, hoping that she would lose her resolve, hoping that you could take advantage of the situation. Isn't that what really happened?"

"If you think that's what really happened, then you didn't know Donna. She could drink a twelve pack at a sitting without batting an eye. To tell you the truth, I don't think I ever saw her drunk, at least what I would consider drunk. And you certainly wouldn't be able to take advantage of her. The more she drank, the more obstinate she became. In that state, she would've taken your head off before she would let you do anything to her—unless she wanted ya to. So I certainly wouldn't have used alcohol to try and pry her loose, if that's what you're intimating."

"You loved Donna?" asked Scott, a hint of anger.

"Yes, I did."

"So much so that you would be concerned for her safety?"

"Yes."

"I believe you already testified how fond you were of Troy."

"Yes, I was. I loved him, too."

"As fond as you were of the two of them, you were willing to let her take your car, drive home, with a blood alcohol reading two and half times above the legal limit. Is that what you want us to believe?"

"If I'd had any concerns, I would never have let her get behind that wheel. But I had seen her drink that much many times before and she never had a problem driving. I'm telling ya, I've been a passenger and I can't remember a time I was ever worried. I don't know how to explain it—she was just one of those people who never showed it. That's what I mean, if I'd have thought she'd had too much to drink, I would've never let her drive."

Matt sat in wonderment. *Where is this guy coming up with this stuff?*

Scott continued, "Mr. Fischer, it is your testimony that you and Ms. Woods talked of marriage that afternoon, and, that at least as far as you're concerned, the two of you had mended your differences. Is that correct?"

"Yes, it is."

"You told Deputy Lentz that you and she had not had sexual

intercourse that afternoon. Is that correct?"

"No, we hadn't."

"You heard Dr. Michaels testimony that the autopsy revealed that Ms. Woods had semen in her vaginal cavity, did you not?"

"I heard him say that."

"You already told us that you had not seen her for weeks before October 7th, 1994, so we would be correct in assuming that was not your semen. Isn't that correct?"

It was obvious to everyone, including Vince, where Scott was going. Vince hesitated with his answer, obviously upset. He put his head down for a second, and then fixed his gaze on Scott. "Why don't you just ask me whether I knew she was having an affair with somebody else? Why are you pussy footin' around? I can tell you...."

Scott tried to interrupt, stop the flow. He had no way of knowing what would follow. "Just a second, Mr. Fischer, there's no question...."

Vince continued, over Scott's objection, "I can tell you that when I read those reports, that was the cruelest cut of all. I couldn't believe it. With what she told me that day, what her feelings were for me, and then to find out that just hours before, she was in somebody else's bed."

Vince rushed to get the words out, his voice straining. His face was flushed and tears came to his eyes. Judge Thompson banged his gavel on the bench.

"Mr. Fischer, I've been very tolerant up to this point. I'm only going to tell you once, when Mr. Larson objects, I expect you to cease testifying until I have ruled on his objection. You understand that?"

Vince turned toward the bench. "I'm sorry, Your Honor. I have nothing but respect for this court. It was just in the heat of the exchange, it won't happen again."

The prosecutor sat there, a spectator along with everyone else. It was evident to Matt that Scott was upset with the court's admonition, that the judge had given Vince another opportunity to play martyr before the jury. Vince slumped in his chair, looking every bit the poor soul again.

Scott had to just keep plodding along. "You were in court when Deputy Bob Lentz testified, isn't that correct?"

"Yes."

"And you heard Deputy Lentz testify that when he came into your kitchen area that night after Ms. Woods' death, to talk to you, he noticed crushed up bills on a cabinet in the kitchen. You heard him testify to that, is that correct?

"Yes, I heard him testify."

"And he further testified that the following morning when they went back to take pictures that the money was still on the cabinet, still lying there crushed and it consisted of three one hundred dollar bills. Do you recall that testimony?"

"Yes, I do."

"And isn't it true the two of you were arguing over the money you say you were always giving to her, that you were upset because you got nothing in return, and she took those three one hundred dollar bills from her purse and crushed them and threw them on the cabinet in anger. Isn't that what happened, Mr. Fischer?"

"Well, they were thrown on the cabinet but not by her and not in anger."

"Are you telling us you threw the money on the cabinet?"

"Yes, I am."

"Why would you do that?"

"Well, she told me I had been way too generous with her and she felt a little guilty about continuing to take my money without some commitment. She wanted to pay me for buying the motor for her car and she laid the three one hundred dollar bills on the kitchen table. I took them, crushed them and threw them on the cabinet and said, 'That's all that money means to me.' She just laughed. She was going to retrieve the bills but we got a little involved and she must've forgotten."

Undaunted, the county attorney tried one more tactic. "You heard Dr. Michaels testify about the tests he performed on the gun."

"Yes, I did," said Vince.

"In your statement to the deputy sheriff, you indicated you and Donna had walked through the breezeway, onto the deck that ran the length of the house and the attached garage, when you noticed the gun on the deck, leaning against the outside wall of the garage, and you were concerned it was getting wet from the mist in the air. Do you recall that statement?"

"Yes, I do."

"And is that the way you recall it now, today?"

"Yes, it is."

"You further told them Donna was going to use your Corvette to drive Troy home and you were going to meet her later in the evening. Is that correct?"

"Yes, it is."

"And she was walking toward that Corvette which was parked on the far side of the deck as you picked up the gun. Is that correct?"

"Yes, it is."

"And she continued walking toward the car as you picked the gun up. Is that correct?"

"Yes, it is."

"When you first noticed the gun, how far away was it from the door to the breezeway you had just come through?"

"A few feet—just out of reach."

"You would have had to take a step or two to pick it up?"

"Yes, I did."

"And as you picked the gun up and put it under your arm, it discharged, hitting Ms. Woods in the back. Is that your testimony?"

"Yes, it is."

"Mr. Fischer, why don't you stand up for a second."

Vince stood up in the witness box. "I don't want you to use the gun, but why don't you just show the jury how you tucked that gun under your arm when you picked it up."

Vince looked to his right, as if he had spotted the gun, took a half step over, turned and picked up the imaginary shotgun and tucked it under his armpit, nice and high under his armpit with his hand over the pistol grip.

"Is that exactly how you did it, Mr. Fischer?"

"I believe so, yes."

"It seems a little awkward to me," said Scott. "Seems to me that you would hold it a little lower than that."

"This is what I think I did," said Vince. "I could be wrong, but this is how I normally would've picked it up to carry it away."

There was no fear or doubt in his voice. He wasn't stumbling for words or pausing to collect his thoughts. As Matt watched Vince put on his demonstration and listened to the words, it was as if they were actually there on the deck. That's how Vince's voice and demeanor had captivated the courtroom.

Scott continued, "Going back to Dr. Michaels' testimony, you heard him testify that in his opinion, the muzzle of that gun was at a minimum of one foot and a maximum of two feet from Ms. Woods when that shot was fired. Do you recall that testimony?"

"Yes, I do."

"And based on your statement to the deputy sheriff, and your little demonstration here, Ms. Woods would have been well beyond two feet from the end of that gun by the time you had it under your armpit."

"Is that a question?" asked Vince.

"How would you explain that, Mr. Fischer?"

"I guess I can't explain it. I'm not sure I have to explain it. I wasn't paying attention to her movements for a split second, maybe she stopped. I know when I turned around with the gun, she was right there. It all happened so fast and I'll never get it out of my mind. I'll never forget that sound; I'll never forget the instant pain I felt. I can't explain it, Mr. Larson. I must've been wrong, she must've been that close."

As far as Matt could determine, the prosecutor had not been able to hurt Vince at all. It was like two boxers sparring, throwing punches and every time you thought the prosecutor was going to throw a knockout punch, it glanced off, harmlessly.

"Mr. Fischer, you were here when Dr. Michaels' testified regarding the wound he found on the body of Donna Woods, isn't that correct?"

"Yes, I was."

"And you heard him testify that based on his autopsy, it was his opinion the track of the wound was slightly from right to left and slightly up to down?"

"Yes, I did."

"And you heard his testimony that in his opinion, the degree of up and down from perpendicular was fifteen degrees, placing the gun at a fifteen degree angle?"

"Yes, I did."

"And you were here when we set up this display, this exhibit, for illustrative purposes."

The prosecutor pointed at the bulletin board with the two white cardboard silhouettes and the line drawn between them.

"Yes, I was here when that was put together."

"And you obviously understand, Mr. Fischer, that the male figure that we have placed on that board is intended to be you."

"I figured that out. Yes," he said with a slight smile.

"If you would be so kind as to step over to the board and stand by the male cut-out, Mr. Fischer."

"I would be willing to do that, sir."

Vince left the witness stand and started toward the bulletin board. Scott interrupted, "Before you do, Mr. Fischer, would you be so kind as to put these boots on?" Scott pushed the pair of boots across the table toward Vince.

"I have no problem with that," replied Vince.

He grabbed the boots and sat on a bench in front of the jury. The room was dead quiet while he put the boots on. When he finished he got up from the bench, walked across the courtroom and stood by the white male silhouette. Murmurs quickly ran through the courtroom, it was obvious to everybody that Vince was at least an inch taller than the cut-out depicted. The prosecutor wasn't quite sure how to proceed. The judge stood up and said, "I think this is a good time to take a recess. I'll see counsel in chambers."

Matt looked at Vince. Vince was trying to keep a straight face, to keep the proper demeanor before the jury and spectators, but

Matt could tell he was biting his lip in the process. He had known all along, though, that they had screwed up his measurements, but he never said a word, waiting for just the right time to spring it on everybody.

Walking to Judge Thompson's chambers Matt wondered how the judge was going to handle this. The prosecutor was already seated at the table in front of the judge's desk when Matt walked in. It was apparent to Matt that the judge had been having a little fun with the prosecutor. The judge looked at Matt. "He tells me he doesn't know how in the hell this could've happened. I was telling him, that's about as bad as Chris Darden asking O.J. to put on the gloves. Scott, I have no idea what the hell you were doing. You certainly didn't need it. The question is what do we do to straighten this whole thing out?"

Matt said nothing. The whole spectacle was a little overwhelming. "What do you want me to say, Judge?" he asked. "They screwed up."

The judge broke in, "I suspect that Mr. Fischer figured it out as well. That's probably why he was so willing to walk up to that bulletin board and stand there with that shit-eating grin on his face."

The prosecutor had been sitting quietly. "All I know is I want to have Mr. Fischer brought in here and we're going to take an official measurement. I'll get Deputy Weineke in here; I wanna get this record straightened out." He was angry, convinced that Vince had set him up.

Judge Thompson turned to Matt. "I think that's the way to approach it. I'm no mathematician; I can't tell you how that will affect Dr. Michaels' testimony, whether it's twenty degrees or fifteen degrees, or ten degrees. We'll leave that for you guys to argue and the jury to figure out. I just know I'm not gonna send that jury into deliberation without knowing what Vince's actual height is. I suggest you get your client in here, Matt."

Matt discretely brought Vince in from the side door so no one saw. Deputy Weineke, Judge Thompson, the prosecutor and the court reporter were in the room. Weineke had his tape measure out. It went quickly. Vince took his shoes off and stood on the tile floor. Weineke ran the measurements and recorded them for the court record. When it was over, the judge looked at the parties and said, "I'm simply going to indicate on the record that the parties have stipulated that Mr. Fischer's correct height is five foot seven and one-half inches. We won't make a big deal of it."

The parties agreed and went back into the courtroom. As everybody settled in, the judge looked at the jury and said, "Ladies and gentlemen of the jury, it appears that there may have been a mistake made in the initial measurement of the height of Mr. Fischer. Pursuant to the agreement of the parties, we have taken Mr. Fischer's measurement and the parties have agreed and stipulated for the record that he is five foot seven and a half inches in his stocking feet. Is that correct, counsel?"

Both Matt and the prosecutor said that was their understanding. The judge looked at Scott, "You can continue."

Scott glanced down at his note pad, scribbled a couple of words and then looked at Vince with derision. "I have nothing more for this witness."

The move caught Matt totally by surprise. He had counted on the prosecutor having at least another hour of cross-examination, after which the court would recess until he would have Dr. Evans there the following morning. He had no other witnesses lined up. There was no sense in him asking Vince any questions; it was time to leave well enough alone.

Matt rose. "Your Honor, I have to apologize again, I expected Mr. Fischer's cross-examination to take most of the afternoon. As the court is aware, I don't have Dr. Evans coming until tomorrow morning. I have no choice but to ask the court to recess until then."

"That's no problem, Mr. Collins, things happen. Ladies and gentlemen of the jury, it looks like we'll have an early afternoon again. I want to admonish you one more time to keep everything you've heard here to yourself, do not discuss it at home or with other jurors and we'll see you back here tomorrow morning at 9:00."

It was 3:45 when Matt walked out of the courtroom. He was scheduled to pick up Dr. Evans at the airport at 5:50. He wanted to spend some time with Nikki, to get her impression of Vince's performance, but he knew he couldn't put up with listening to Vince gloat. As he turned around, she was standing directly behind him. Vince had snuck out to have a quick cigarette. "What do you think?" he asked.

"Matt, whoever that was on the stand today, I've never seen that guy before. I've heard other people talk about how smooth he can be in business deals. Peter raves about him all the time but I've never seen it. You were right, he's a split personality. I watched the jurors, Matt, they were listening. I thought some of them might actually feel sorry for him. It's just what you said on the phone that night."

"We aren't going to have to wait long," said Matt. "I'll have Dr. Evans tomorrow morning. The state may have a little rebuttal and then we're done. Then I suspect the judge will want to have us make closing arguments the following day. At least I'm gonna ask for some time to prepare the closing argument and this could well go to the jury by sometime on Thursday. We'll probably know Vince's fate by the end of the week."

"You mean our fate," she said.

"You're right. It's our fate as well," replied Matt.

Nikki's eyes softened, and with a heart stopping smile, she said, "It'll be all right. Everything's going fine. You'll see."

She reached out and touched his hand gently. "It will be all over soon and we can get on with our lives."

Matt wanted to just pick her up, carry her off and say to hell with everything. As he was going to put his hand on her shoulder, he saw Vince reach the top step at the end of the hallway. "Here comes Mr. Personality," he said.

Nikki quickly lost the smile. As Vince reached the two of them, he said, "Well, counsel, I told you I was ready."

"Well, Vince, that was an Oscar-worthy performance."

"Don't pull that shit on me," snapped Vince. "You're the one who said I had to testify. I told ya all along what happened that night, just what I said today. I just embellished it a little."

Matt didn't respond. He glared at Vince, ready to explode.

Nikki tried to break the tension. "Where do we go from here?"

"I'm picking up Dr. Evans at 6:00 or so," said Matt. "I'm gonna take him to the motel and we'll have a chance to discuss the testimony of Dr. Michaels and what he thinks he can do to help us. I expect his testimony could take a couple of hours and then we're basically done. I would expect the prosecutor to possibly call some rebuttal witnesses; he may even have Dr. Michaels here. That's still the guts of their case, where that gun was."

"Well you better get it right this time," said Vince. "I watched those jurors, they listened to me. I think they believe me. It's your case to lose, Matt."

Matt snapped, "What the fuck are you talking about?" It was the first time he had sworn at Vince. He quickly knew better. "I'm sorry," he said. "It's been a long day."

Vince straightened up, surprised. "Counselor, I think you're losing your fuckin' wheels."

Nikki again became the peacemaker. "Guys, guys, Matt's right, it's been a long day; you're both wound up. Let's take a time out. Matt, you have things to do. Vince, let's go home."

chapter 42

ON THE DRIVE to the airport to pick up Dr. Evans, Matt thought about the day's events. He could feel his animosity toward Vince growing. Was it going to affect his ability to finish this case? At least finish it in a professional manner.... It was too late in the game to screw it up now. The plan had been to get Vince to testify, to let him tighten the noose around his own neck. On the face of it, at least, it hadn't worked that way. Nobody knew what the jury had actually thought of his testimony. But it wasn't just what he'd said, it was the way he had said it. He had put on a show trying to convince the jury he wasn't that bad of a guy, he could be trusted. Peter had been right. Vince was a good communicator when he wanted to be.

Matt knew that Dr. Evans would simply give him enough leeway so that he could reasonably argue the gun was where Vince said it was when it discharged. That was the sole purpose of his testimony. If the jury believed Vince, they would find him not guilty. If they didn't believe him, they would find him guilty of murder. If they believed Troy, that the gun was in the great room and that Vince had to pick it up and walk through the breezeway and onto the deck before he shot Donna, that's sufficient time for premeditation, that's first degree murder. If they felt sorry for him, they could find him guilty of second degree murder. If they felt *really* sorry for him, or they just didn't like Donna, they could find him guilty of manslaughter. That's where Matt thought the case was going—manslaughter. He couldn't see a jury letting Vince off completely. After all, a young woman was killed, two children left motherless. And then there was the testimony of the three ex-wives. He could tell that the jurors would've hung Vince at that point in the trial.

Matt wondered whether the judge would give the jury an instruction for manslaughter. The jury couldn't find him guilty of manslaughter if they weren't given that choice. If the only choices they had were first or second degree murder, the jury had to return a murder verdict or let him walk. But he had to ask for a manslaughter instruction. However, it wasn't his decision, it was up to Vince. If Vince didn't want an instruction on manslaughter, the judge probably wouldn't give it. Matt figured this judge believed Vince was guilty of murder and wanted the jury to find him so.

Matt paced the hallway in front of gate number fifty-four at the Metropolitan Airport. Dr. Evans' flight would be a little late. No reason was given. Any other time, Matt wouldn't have minded waiting at the airport. He always enjoyed watching people scurrying about, coming and going, wondering what sort of adventure they were off to. It was fun to watch the faces of the people waiting for the passengers to depart from the plane, then seeing the excitement when they recognized their loved ones.

Today, though, he had other things on his mind. Matt always believed he could judge where he was with a particular jury as the case was winding down. Especially if he was going to lose. If the jury was going to find the defendant guilty, he, and probably all of the other court personnel, could sense it. Except on a rare occasion or two, he'd been absolutely right. But in Vince's case, he had no idea what that jury was thinking. It bothered him.

Deep in thought, Matt didn't realize the passengers had come off the plane. There was a tap on his shoulder and he turned around to see Dr. Evans. He looked a little disheveled— his coat thrown over his left shoulder, his travel bag over his right shoulder, the top button of his shirt open, his tie slightly undone. He looked more like an egghead than Matt remembered. The jury ought to love him, he thought.

As they pulled onto the highway, Dr. Evans asked him how

the trial was going. Matt didn't want to give him a blow-by-blow account. He summarized the testimony of Dr. Michaels and Mr. Bishop, then he told him about the bulletin board, the cut-out silhouettes and the measurements, how they had simply made a mistake in Vince's measurements and their diagram was close to an inch off.

"That's interesting," said Dr. Evans. "You know I didn't diagram it out, I was going on Dr. Michaels's report. That inch is obviously going to make a difference in the angle of entry and maybe you don't even need my testimony."

"I tried to figure it out," said Matt. "I'm not sure they're even off. The measurement to the shoulder may be correct. A slight difference doesn't take it all the way off the shoulder anyway, it might tuck it way under the armpit. Not a normal position to be carrying a gun. I know that's what the prosecutor will argue."

"You know the nature of the entry wound," said Dr. Evans. "You have some room to argue there. Then the next issue is the internal track of the wound. I'll have to go over that again tonight. I can try and firm that up before you leave."

Matt had always liked Dr. Evans. The man was bright, personable and easy to talk to. As they drove along, Matt turned to the question of Donna's blood alcohol concentration.

"Dr. Michaels testified that her BAC was .25, but the prosecutor didn't make a big issue of it. I suspect the reason is they didn't want to draw attention to her drinking habits. But the question that hurt was when the prosecutor asked Vince how he could let somebody he loved who had that blood alcohol concentration drive his Corvette. Vince basically told him he had seen her consume that much alcohol many times and it never seemed to affect her abilities, including her ability to drive. You know, Doctor, I can understand that to some extent because I've had the same experiences. I've had guys I've represented on a drunken driving charge with a blood alcohol concentration of .30 who still appeared to function fine. In fact, I had a guy stopped one time at .32. The officer's observations were that he was moderately under the influence, his eyes a little red, his speech was okay but a little slow, his walk wasn't that bad. Of course, the officer wrote this all down before he knew what the blood test was gonna come back at. We actually won that case by convincing a jury that with those observations, the blood alcohol tests obviously had to be wrong. How could a person with a .32 function that well?"

"There are so many variables in that," said Evans. "You take a young lady like Ms. Woods, a .25 is awfully high. She did have to consume quite a bit of alcohol, but that doesn't mean she had to react the same way somebody else would have at .25. The body assimilates the alcohol the same way whether you're a first time drinker or whether you're a real boozer. The difference is the boozer's body has become acclimated to the alcohol. So you can have an inexperienced drinker who's had three, four drinks and can appear totally intoxicated. On the other hand, the experienced drinker may need two or three times that much to have the same reaction."

"I know," replied Matt. "I've had calls at night from people who've been picked up and want to know if they should take the test or not. I listen to the words, I try to see if I can detect whether they have slurred speech, the things you'd normally listen for. I don't know how many times I've been surprised. The guy I tell, 'You know, you don't sound bad', will come out .18 or .22 or whatever it is, and the other guy who sounds drunker than a skunk may come out to a .11. When I meet them and look at their history, I realize why that happens. I know I have some clients who are .20 or above every day, who couldn't function unless they had at least that much alcohol in their system. I would suspect after a heavy bout, they could be well over .30 or even higher."

"Then you know what I'm talking about." said Dr. Evans. "A first time drinker, I've had them in an alcoholic coma and near death with the same BAC as Ms. Woods."

"What is the highest reading you've ever seen?" asked Matt.

"Several years ago I did an autopsy on a sailor from the Milwaukee port. He'd been on the Great Lakes for several months, came into town intending to just hang one on. He started drinking straight shots at some bar. He started chug-a-luggin' from a bottle. After about an hour and a half of that, his friends thought he had fallen asleep, they put him in a corner to sleep it off. Actually, he had already gone into an alcoholic coma. Had somebody gotten him help right away, they might've saved him. My tests showed that he was a .56."

"How in the hell could he get it so high without anybody noticing the symptoms?"

"You have to remember, the body takes a while to assimilate the alcohol. If he's drinking straight booze that quickly, the alcohol just overcomes him before he even knows what happened."

"I imagine you've seen a lot of that," said Matt.

"Actually, straight alcohol deaths are rather rare. What's probably more common is the guy who doesn't know enough to get out of the cold and freezes to death. Or the guy who throws up in a drunken stupor and chokes to death, those kinds of things."

"Whatever made you get into forensic pathology?" asked Matt.

"Oh, I just like it, and the patients don't talk back. It's been so long, I don't remember exactly what my thought processes were that took me this way."

"How many autopsies do you think you've done?"

"Into the tens of thousands. I'll tell you one nice thing about it," he said. "My malpractice insurance runs only six hundred dollars a year. I've never had a cadaver threaten to sue me."

Matt decided to stop and have dinner on the way back. They had a pleasant time, each of them purposely staying away from the case. They exchanged war stories about other cases they were involved in, or interesting things that happened in the course of a trial. If you were into blood and gore, Dr. Evans could keep you entertained for hours.

Matt had made reservations for him at the Radisson. He followed the doctor up to his room. He wanted to go over Dr. Michaels' reports one last time so he wouldn't have to worry about it the next morning. It was a strange situation for Matt. When he first talked to Dr. Evans months earlier in Milwaukee, he was going under the theory Vince was telling the truth, that the gun was under his arm. Now he knew better. He knew the gun was at Vince's shoulder and Dr. Michaels had pretty much hit it on the head. Knowing the truth, Matt wondered what Dr. Evans could do to soften Dr. Michaels' testimony. They already had the fact that the measurement was close to an inch off, but that may not get them all the way home.

Dr. Evans took the autopsy report, sat in one of the easy chairs and started reading. Matt sat on the edge of the bed and watched Dr. Evans' face. As the doctor got to the page where the internal injuries were being described, he started to say a few of the words out loud. Matt could see on his face that the doctor was creating a mental image and that that image was bothering him. When he was done, he paused for a second and looked at Matt.

"You know, Matt, every time I read this, I can tell exactly what he's talking about. There's definitely a downward angle to that track. We're still talking fifteen degrees, right?"

"Yes."

The doctor let out a big sigh and said, "That's close. I agree with you that if we had a single projectile it would be easier, but if he's off, it isn't by much."

Matt thought for a moment. "Look, Doctor, I don't expect you to make anything up for me. We've been through this before; you know I'm not trying to buy an opinion. Whatever you think you can reasonably live with is what I'm asking for."

"That's fine." said Dr. Evans. "I told you before, I thought the doctor was being just a little too stringent in his opinion. I could reasonably testify the track is anywhere between ten and fifteen degrees. I think that's fair."

"Well," said Matt, "if that's what we've got, that's what we've got. We're just going to hit two high points with your testimony. The first being the fact that just because the entry wound is eccentric, that doesn't give you an exact degree of entry because you don't have a static target. The second one being, based on your review of the autopsy and the internal injuries described by Dr. Michaels, it is your opinion the angle could be anywhere from ten to fifteen degrees. Is that a fair summary?"

"That's as good as we can do, Matt."

"That's all I expected."

***

Matt spotted the pay phone in the hotel lobby on his way out. He'd wanted to talk to Nikki ever since they had left court that afternoon. There were things he had to discuss with her before he talked to the judge, before they submitted proposed jury instructions. He wanted to know what Vince was thinking, what Nikki was thinking. Most of all he wanted to just hear her voice in a conversation that didn't involve Vince and Donna and talk about mortal wounds. He was sick of it all. Without hesitation, he sat down, put in his credit card and dialed Vince's number. He breathed a sigh of relief when Nikki answered.

"Hi," he said. "What's happening?"

"Hi there," she said. "Where are you?"

He could tell by her voice that Vince wasn't nearby.

"I've just tucked Dr. Evans into bed. I'm on my way home to work on my closing argument. Where's Vince?"

"He's with Peter."

"What's he doing with him?" asked Matt.

"I don't know. When we got home he called him and made arrangements to meet with him and he said he'd be back by ten."

Matt looked at his watch; it was a little after nine. "We've got to talk." he said. "Does Vince ever say anything about manslaughter?"

"You know what he says. I can't even repeat the words. I don't even talk to him anymore. You know I don't want to get him mad. I'm not gonna end up like Donna, lying on the deck with a big hole in my back."

"Have you worried about that?" asked Matt.

"Not really worried but every once in a while it crosses my mind, I think about that poor girl. Sometimes I just want to scream, 'you murdering S.O.B!' But I don't. I know what that would do to our plans. I can't wait for this to be over so we can be together again."

"You sure this phone is safe?" asked Matt.

259

"Yes, there's nothing on this phone. If there was, I would've been in trouble a long time ago."

"You know I have another problem," said Matt. "The judge has asked for any proposed jury instructions by tomorrow afternoon. I've seen what the judge is proposing. They're all the basic instructions. I know what he's looking for—to see if I'll ask for an instruction on first degree manslaughter. If I don't request it, the judge will ask me why. If I tell him Vince doesn't want the instruction, there's a good possibility he'll bring Vince into chambers and ask him if he understands what he's doing. It is his case after all."

"I don't know what I can tell you," said Nikki. "You know it's all Greek to me. That's what you're supposed to do. You're supposed to figure this all out. I'm placing my trust in you, you know."

"That's fine, but it has to be done in such a way that neither the prosecutor nor the judge has any reason to question anything. The plan hasn't changed, Nikki. Vince has to go to prison for life. It doesn't do us any good if I'm up in front of another judge or an ethics committee investigating why I screwed up this case so badly. So far I think everything's fine, this is going to be the last hurdle."

"Matt," said Nikki, "I've always told you, I have complete faith in you. I'm in this with you one hundred percent. I believe everything we're going through will be worth it. All I want is to love you, to be with you. I wish you were here now. I miss your touch so much. I love you."

As Matt was going to respond, she said, "Oh, oh, I think I just heard Vince's car door."

"I have to talk to him," said Matt, "but I don't think I could tonight. But I do have to talk to him before I talk to the judge. Get him to court a little early...."

Suddenly she said, "I love you, Matt," and she hung up.

Matt had always worried whether she was in danger. She knew what Vince was capable of doing in a fit of anger. He was sure if Vince ever found out anything about him and Nikki, one or the other, or both, would be dead. Nikki always said, though, that as long as she knew what Vince was capable of doing, she would make sure she never got him to that point. That's fine, as long as he's in the dark, thought Matt. But if he ever gets some idea. He didn't like to think about it.

chapter 43

"THE DEFENSE CALLS Dr. Charles Evans."

The bailiff led Dr. Evans through the courtroom door. With everybody else seated, Evans cut an imposing figure. Even his answer to the oath seemed dramatic. He took the stand and neatly arranged all of his documents in front of him. Matt first took him through his credentials, his education, his training, his years of experience with the Milwaukee County Coroner's Office, his teaching position at the University of Wisconsin Medical School, the number of autopsies, the number of times he's been called in to testify in court, how many by the prosecutor, how many by the defense, how many civil cases he has been called in as an expert witness. As he relayed all the information, he looked at the jury. Matt thought his assessments had been right, the jury did like him.

He next took Dr. Evans through the entire autopsy. Not because he was questioning anything in it, but to allow the doctor to become at ease, to establish a rapport with his questioner and with the jury.

"Dr. Evans," he said, "you've had an opportunity to look at the photographs and the slides depicting the entry wound in the back of Ms. Woods."

"Yes, I have."

"And Dr. Michaels classified the wound as an eccentric wound and he explained that to the court and the jury. What is your understanding of an eccentric wound?"

"Well, I'm sure it is the same as Dr. Michaels'," he replied.

"To some extent you can tell at what angle the gun may have been to the target based on the entry wound. As I'm sure he said, if the wound is concentric, meaning exactly circular, you would expect the barrel of the gun to be perpendicular or square to the target. To the extent the wound starts to become eccentric, the barrel of the gun is becoming tilted."

"Can you tell us, Dr. Evans, based on the nature of the entry wound in this case, what the degree of the gun may have been to the target?"

"Well, I have to agree again with Dr. Michaels that it's clear that the gun was at an angle, a slightly up to down angle, to the target. I think it is difficult, though, to give it an exact degree because you don't have two fixed points, you have other dynamics at work here. For example, what was the decedent's posture at the time of entry? What effect did the intermediate target, in this case the jacket with its pile lining, the sweater, and a small part of her bra, have on the angle of entry? I think those all have to be taken into consideration. So I couldn't be so precise to say it had to be fifteen degrees or twelve degrees or seventeen degrees. Now, when you look at the internal track of that wound, that might be of a little bit more importance."

"Stop there for a second, Doctor," said Matt. "Let's talk about that. You read the autopsy report of Dr. Michaels and how he described the internal wound, is that correct?"

"Yes, I did."

"And he testified that based on those internal wounds, you could also make a determination as to the angle of entry. Would you agree with that, Doctor?"

"Yes, I would."

"And based on his examination, Dr. Michaels told this jury it was his opinion that the angle of entry was approximately fifteen degrees to perpendicular, if you understand what I mean."

"I certainly do, Mr. Collins, and I also agree with Dr. Michaels that the track of the wound will give you an indication of the angle of entry. Where I have to differ with him slightly, though, is how precise it actually is. A shotgun shell has such a different way of reacting when it hits the body compared to a single projectile bullet. The shotgun shell has such tremendous kinetic energy and when the shot enters the body, it expends all that energy inside. It simply explodes and that accounts for all of the internal injuries that one sees in a typical shotgun death. The billiard ball effect which he described is typical of this type of wound. So again, depending on the distance from the body when the shot is fired, some of the powder, the cap and the wad may enter the body and give you a track to follow, but it's not always clean, it's not always precise."

"Dr. Evans, based on your education, training and experience, and based upon all of the reports, documents and autopsy papers that you have had a chance to review in this case, have you formed an opinion as to the angle of entry?"

"Yes, I have."

"And, Doctor, what is that opinion?"

"I believe that Dr. Michaels is probably at the top of that angle at the fifteen degrees. I believe it could go down as low as ten degrees or anywhere in between."

"Thank you, Doctor," said Matt. "I have just a couple more questions. Based on your review of the autopsy and accompanying documents, what is your understanding of the blood alcohol concentration of Ms. Woods at the time of her death?"

"According to the autopsy report, the toxicology, she was a .25."

"In your position as coroner for Milwaukee County, have you had to do studies on the effects of alcohol on the human body?"

"I'm not a forensic toxicologist if that's what you mean, but I have had courses in toxicology and it is a typical part of every autopsy."

"Well, have you had to render an opinion before any court regarding the effects of alcohol on the body?"

"Yes, I have."

"How many times do you think that has occurred?"

"Oh, probably into the hundreds."

"And your opinion has been accepted as an expert opinion?"

"Yes, it has."

"Well let's talk for a moment about that," said Matt. "How would you normally expect a person who had a blood alcohol concentration of .25 to react?"

"There is the typical reaction which everybody pretty much expects. At about .10, there's euphoria, decreased inhibition, diminished judgment and attention. As you go higher on the scale, between that and .20, the person starts to experience impaired sensory response and muscular coordination, their eyes become dilated, their face flushed, they seem to have a thick tongue. That's the typical picture of the person under the influence. And from .20 to .30, they start to lose coordination, have very slurred speech, they can be staggering, they can be disoriented, they may even get sick and vomit. Those are the ones you consider really drunk. Then after .30, they start to go into a stupor or they may just fall asleep. Very decreased response. Than at .40 and above, they can actually be totally unconscious, go into a coma which could eventually lead to death. At .25 a person would fall probably in what you would typically think to be getting close to grossly impaired, but you notice I said, 'typically'. If a person is an accomplished drinker and has been doing it for a long time, he or she may have a quite markedly different response. I have had situations, for example, where people have been in an automobile accident, their BAC has been in excess of .30, but according to everybody who talked to them prior to the accident, their observable symptoms were rather minimal. People who saw them would have never guessed that they'd had that much to drink. I'm sure if you went into the history in those cases, as I did in several of them, you would find that they had a long history of alcohol abuse."

"There has been testimony, Doctor, from some of Ms. Woods' friends that she could drink a considerable amount of beer. For example, one neighbor testified that she could drink twelve bottles of beer at a sitting."

"If that's the case," said Dr. Evans, "it would appear to me that she'd developed a tolerance to the alcohol."

"Doctor, one final set of questions. You saw Dr. Michaels' report regarding the distance from the body the muzzle of the gun had to be at the time of discharge?

"Yes, I did."

"And it was his testimony that the gun had to be at a minimum of one foot and at a maximum of two feet from Ms. Woods' back when the gun was discharged."

"I remember that, yes," said Dr. Evans.

"Based on your own experience, do you have an opinion as far as the distance of the muzzle of the gun from the body?"

"Again, I have to rely on Dr. Michaels' opinion to some extent because he conducted the testing. Typically, you would judge distance from the type of entry wound. Dr. Michaels notes that there is scalloping of the wound but there's no individual B.B. or pellet holes surrounding the wound. With a shotgun shell wound, Mr. Collins, as you get further from the body, the shot starts to separate, and so normally after two feet, and definitely after three feet, you will see individual pellet marks around the entry wound, which gives you some indication of distance. So I would tend to agree with Dr. Michaels. But again, I would think that it could have been further away than two feet. It could have been close to three feet."

Matt looked at his watch, the doctor had been on the stand for close to an hour and forty-five minutes. He quickly looked at all of his notes. Was there anything he had missed? If there was anything he needed to get in, now was the time to do it. A little panic set in. He wondered what he could have forgotten. He looked at all of the highlighted areas on the pages, flashed through the doctor's testimony in his head and finally said, "Thank you, Dr. Evans, I have nothing further."

The judge took the morning recess.

Matt waited for Dr. Evans to get off the stand and led him out into the hall. Both Nikki and Vince were there waiting to greet Dr. Evans. Vince shook his hand, congratulated him on an excellent job. Vince was finally pleased with something other than his own performance.

"Doctor," he said, "I appreciate what you've done here. I didn't murder Donna. I know your testimony will help convince the jurors of that."

"I hope I've been of some help," replied Dr. Evans.

If he only knew the truth, Matt thought. He suspected the doctor would probably tell both of them to go to hell.

Matt turned to Dr. Evans. "You did an excellent job, Doctor. I'm not sure what the prosecutor could possibly ask that would change anything."

"Don't worry about him, Doctor," said Vince. "He's a pussy cat."

Matt quickly grabbed the doctor by the arm and walked him down the hall. It appeared to him that the two personalities were about to clash—the doctor didn't appear to care for Vince.

"I really can't imagine what he's gonna ask you," said Matt. "Is there anything you want to talk about? Any questions you have?"

Dr. Evans thought for a second or two and said, "No, I'm fine."

***

The cross-examination actually went as Matt expected. It was apparent that the prosecutor lived by the same cardinal rules of cross-examination as Matt. Moreover, thought Matt, Dr. Evans really hadn't hurt the state's case. Both sides were still free to argue for their point of view without having to be embarrassed that they sounded ridiculous. Matt knew all along that this case was going to be decided on the credibility of Vince Fischer. The prospect was a little frightening.

The prosecutor took Dr. Evans over his testimony, getting him to reiterate his opinion regarding the angle of entry and what he believed to be the degree of that angle. Dr. Evans didn't waver from what he had already told the jury. The prosecution was done with him at quarter to twelve. Matt didn't have any additional questions. As Dr. Evans left the stand, Matt stood up and said, "The defense rests, Your Honor."

The prosecutor stood. "Your Honor, we may have some rebuttal witnesses. We called Dr. Michaels; he said he can be here by one thirty. I would ask the court to recess until then."

The judge turned to the jury. "We'll break for lunch, why don't you plan on being back about one fifteen or so. I can tell you that we will not finish this up this afternoon. I expect that we will be doing closing arguments tomorrow morning and you should have this case sometime by noon. Counsel, I would like to see you in chambers."

Matt turned to Dr. Evans and asked him to wait for him in the hall. He had made arrangements for Tim to drive him back to the airport. As he walked back to the judge's chambers, he knew what the judge's question was going to be: Do you have any specific requests regarding jury instructions? Matt would beg off until after lunch. He intended to talk to Vince over lunch regarding the manslaughter issue. After talking to Nikki the night before, he hadn't been able to sleep. Everything had kept flashing through his mind. What would happen if he could argue manslaughter? What would the jury do? If the jury found Vince guilty of manslaughter, what would that do to his and Nikki's plans? He could no longer think clearly. As he came to one conclusion, it changed as quickly as he could come up with another problem. He knew his future with Nikki depended on Vince being convicted of murder and that meant not giving the jury the option of anything less.

The judge had the jury instructions on his desk. "Matt, I was wondering if you've had a chance to go over the proposed jury instructions."

"Yes, I have."

"Is there anything either of you wish to add or any changes you'd like to make?"

Matt spoke up first. "No, Judge, I think it pretty much includes everything we would expect to have the jury consider. I noticed you did not have an instruction on first degree manslaughter and my client and I have had some discussions about that. I intend to talk to him again over lunch and we can make that determination before we recess today. If that's not a problem."

"Well, Matt," said the judge, "based on the way the evidence has come in, I can see where the jury could consider manslaughter. Even though Mr. Fischer's testimony remains that it was totally accidental. You talk to him and let us know. Scott, how about you, do you have any other suggestions?"

The prosecutor was upset. "Judge, I can't agree with that. You sat through Mr. Fischer's testimony. You heard him tell that jury, in a rather shameful performance, I might add, how this whole thing was accidental—no anger, no arguments, no exchange of words. He's telling us she walked out of the house happy, giddy, in fact. Where is the heat of passion? How can we justify giving that to the jury based on his performance? He murdered her, plain and simple, now he wants us to give him a cheap out. He doesn't deserve it."

Scott's voice was rising with each word. Matt knew Vince had gotten to him, he hadn't realized how badly.

The judge seemed shocked. It was an uncharacteristic performance for Scott.

"But Scott, you opened the door. You went into some detail with her son, Troy. It didn't appear to me that he wanted to tell us the blow-by-blow of what happened, but there was obviously a confrontation—a heated exchange of words. It got me thinking. But we don't have to make these decisions right now," he said. "We'll meet back at 1:30."

Matt said his farewells to Dr. Evans. For lunch, he, Vince, and Nikki went to the same diner for lunch they had visited prior to Vince's testimony. Matt just picked at his food, his stomach turning. He kept the conversation away from the real reason he'd gotten Vince there until it appeared Vince had relaxed. Then he said, "Vince, the question we have to decide before we get back to the courthouse is what additional jury instructions we should ask the judge to give."

"What instructions are you talking about?" asked Vince.

"After the attorneys have made their closing arguments, the judge will give the jury what he considers the law, the law they have to follow in applying the facts as they heard them. He also gives them the elements of the offenses charged. In this case, for example, first degree murder requires that you had to premeditate the killing of Donna and then you intentionally shot her. The judge will tell the jury how the law defines premeditation and intentional. Or the other instruction is second degree murder, which is without premeditation but with the intention to kill. We have a right to ask him to submit what they call lesser included offenses. We've talked about it before, Vince. I'm talking about first degree manslaughter, meaning you killed her in the heat of passion, provoked by something she said or did. It means your blood got so hot that before you had a chance to think about it, to contemplate what you were doing, before your blood had a chance to cool, you killed her. That's manslaughter."

"I told you before, many times, forget about manslaughter. There's no way I'm gonna let people think that this bitch got to me."

That was the answer Matt was waiting for. He was pleased with himself for correctly gauging his client. He figured from everything Vince had told him before that manslaughter wasn't an option, now he simply had to keep Vince believing he had made the right decision.

"We don't have to argue manslaughter," said Matt. "The judge can give the instruction, but I can still argue it was an accident."

"What good does that do?" asked Vince.

"Well," said Matt, "it's actually a double-edge sword."

"God, I hate when you do that," said Vince. "Can't you speak in fuckin' English?"

"Vince," said Nikki, "not in here!"

"What the hell do they teach these guys in law school?" Vince replied.

Matt figured he had Vince upset enough where he wasn't thinking very clearly.

"What I mean is this," he continued, "if there are some people on the jury that don't want to convict you of first degree or second degree murder, but they don't want to find you not guilty, the manslaughter verdict gives them an out. It allows them to salve their conscience by punishing you for killing Donna but not calling it murder. That's one edge of the sword. The other edge, however, is that if there are enough people who feel you are not guilty and who are willing to vote not guilty, they can be talked into a compromise verdict of manslaughter. That way, they can salve their conscience by not finding you guilty of murder. If the judge doesn't give the manslaughter instruction and the jury believes the state has not proved you guilty beyond a reasonable doubt, than the prosecutor has not proved the killing was murder...then the jury has no choice but to find you not guilty. If the manslaughter instruction is included, however, they can find you guilty of manslaughter. It's a gutsy decision with a lot of risk involved. It's up to you."

Matt knew that's all he had to say. He just had to tell Vince it took guts to make the decision and Vince would do it.

"Well, I know where that jury is," he said, "and they're no way near finding me guilty of murder. So why would I give them an opportunity of letting 'em find me guilty of manslaughter? No fuckin' way."

Nikki glanced around again, nervously, making sure nobody heard the last comment. She looked at Vince.

"Vince, this is all very confusing. It's your life, you have to make the decision, but I agree with you, I think the jury's gonna find you not guilty. I don't think you should take the chance."

Good old Nikki, thought Matt, an accessory to the end.

chapter 44

MATT REACHED THE top of the steps of the hall leading to the courtroom. As he took a right hand turn down the hall, he saw Dr. Michaels talking to Deputy Weineke. Matt assumed Weineke was filling him in on Dr. Evans' testimony and the missing inch. Matt looked around for other faces, particularly any of the ex-wives. The prosecutor indicated he had rebuttal witnesses. Matt assumed he had managed to bring one or more of the wives back, but he only saw Dr. Michaels.

They were all seated again by 1:30. The prosecutor put Dr. Michaels on the stand, to go over again the distance from the gun Ms. Woods would have had to have been when the shot was fired. Dr. Michaels testified that his first impression was that it was quite close, within six inches or so. However, that was changed based on the testing he had done. Based on the tests, he had refined his opinion: it was a minimum of one foot and a maximum of two feet. How could he be so sure about that, the prosecutor asked.

"Because after two feet, the pellets start to separate and the wound becomes very jagged, much more so than the wound in the back of Ms. Woods."

The answer was a little surprising to Matt. The doctor had used the term, "first impression." He admitted that his first impression was wrong. That was unusual. That was something Matt believed he could use in his closing argument.

"Dr. Michaels," the prosecutor continued, "you have been advised that we have amended the record to correct the measurements for the height of Mr. Fischer, is that correct?"

"I understand that. Apparently, our illustration of the male figure was one inch short," he looked at the jury with a smile. Several jurors smiled back.

"Dr. Michaels, with the court's indulgence, I need you to consider a change to our illustration. Deputy Weineke will help. Doctor, what we've done is we've gotten a piece of wood exactly one inch thick which we will put on the floor to raise the male cut-out exactly one inch, which would be the correct measurement for Mr. Fischer with the boots he had on that night. Deputy Weineke, will you do that?"

Deputy Weineke went to the bulletin board, removed the pins holding the male cut-out to the board, placed the piece of wood on the floor, and placed the cut-out back on the bulletin board, pinning it as before. Now the white cardboard shotgun that ran to the shoulder of the male cut-out was an inch lower than it had been previously.

"Dr. Michaels, you testified in your direct examination regarding your opinion as to the angle of the gun to the body of Ms. Woods when fired. Do you recall your testimony?"

"Yes, I do."

"And it was your opinion, based on the nature of the entry wound and the track of the internal injuries, that the gun was approximately fifteen degrees up to down to the wound. Was that your opinion?"

"Yes, it was."

"Now you have seen what we've done to our illustration, the one inch difference, does that change your opinion, Doctor?"

The doctor looked at the cut-out silhouettes and the white cardboard shotgun. It appeared to Matt that he was taking time to give the jury an impression that he was seriously considering the question. Matt knew, though, that Deputy Weineke had already laid it out for him long before he took the stand, so he knew exactly what he was going to say, but the jury had to believe he was deep in thought.

"You have to remember," he said, "my opinion was based on an estimation, an estimation taking into consideration all of the different factors. When I said fifteen degrees, that doesn't mean it couldn't have been thirteen degrees or seventeen degrees. When you look at our illustration, the inch difference does make a slight change but not enough to change my opinion. I still believe it was approximately in the area of fifteen degrees."

He did it again, thought Matt. This time the doctor admitted that his original opinion was based on estimation, and for the first time he used the word approximate. It was approximately fifteen degrees. Another good argument laid in my lap, thought Matt.

The prosecutor was done with Dr. Michaels. He looked at Matt.

"Your witness."

"I have no questions," said Matt, knowing there was nothing to be gained by asking the doctor anything else.

Scott turned to face the judge. "The state rests."

The judge looked at the jury and said, "Ladies and gentlemen of the jury, we'll start tomorrow morning at 9:00 for closing arguments. I will then give you the instructions, which is the law that applies to this case, and you will begin your deliberation. Once you begin, you will be sequestered, which means you won't be free to go home until you have reached a decision. So each of you should bring a suitcase with any essentials you believe you need because the state's going to put you in a nice motel at its expense until this matter is decided. Remember—don't talk to anybody about this case."

Everybody stood and waited until the jury left. Matt watched their faces, there appeared to be little joy. They knew the day of reckoning was finally upon them.

Both attorneys walked into the judge's chambers at the same time.

"Your Honor," said Matt, "I had a chance to talk with my client regarding the manslaughter instruction and it is his request that we do not give it."

"Why would he want that?" asked the judge.

"Well, because he's not guilty, he thinks the jury's gonna find him not guilty."

"I'm sure you've told him the ramifications?" asked the judge.

"We spent the last hour talking about it."

The prosecutor broke in, "Your Honor, I want to renew my objection to the manslaughter instruction in any event. It would be a travesty of justice. After what Mr. Fischer did in this courtroom, to give that jury an opportunity to consider manslaughter is a slap in the face. For once I agree with Mr. Fischer. If he thinks he's got this jury convinced that he's not guilty, let him go with that. Don't give the jury a chance to come up with a half-ass decision by giving them an out with manslaughter."

"Well," said the judge, "if that's where everybody stands, so be it, it won't be given. We'll see you here in the morning at 9:00." With that the judge said, "Good day," and left the two of them sitting there.

As Matt got up to leave, the prosecutor said, "I don't think much of your client. I don't know who was responsible for that performance he put on, but you and I both know it was bullshit. I wanted to tear his heart out. I still do. But I'm a practical man. There are some other interests here, other people to look out for. Moreover, I don't particularly care to spend the rest of the afternoon and tonight trying to put together a closing argument for tomorrow. You know I made you an offer at one time, and I'd be willing to make that offer again. If Mr. Fischer would be willing to plead guilty to second degree unintentional homicide, we could take that plea right now and both you and I could forget about this case."

Matt was caught totally off guard. Was he still being pressured? Whether it was just a matter that Scott really didn't want to waste the rest of the day on his closing argument or whether he thought his case had gone so badly that he might lose, that any plea was better than nothing. "I'll certainly talk it over with my client," Matt said. "If you want to wait here, I'll be right back."

By that time, Vince was outside having a cigarette. It was a warm day. He was leaning up against a retaining wall, blowing puffs of smoke in the air. Matt got him aside. "Vince you're not gonna believe this, but the prosecutor just renewed his offer. He said he's still willing to take a plea to second degree unintentional homicide."

Vince's eyes narrowed. "I told you he was worried. Tell him to get fucked."

Matt didn't argue. He had known Vince would turn the offer down, otherwise he wouldn't have told him about it.

chapter 45

MATT SAT BY himself that night, putting the final touches on his closing argument. He knew exactly what he would say and how he would say it: just enough to convince Vince he was still his advocate. But he was finding it hard to concentrate. His thoughts were more on what would happen after Vince was convicted. His fantasy was that he and Nikki would just disappear, wherever she wanted to go. In his more resolute moments, that was exactly how he saw it happening. After all, he deserved that kind of happiness. He had spent, he felt, over twenty years helping every poor, miserable bastard he could through one crisis or another, until he was miserable himself. There were people on the street who would be sitting in prison right now if it hadn't been for his own hard work. Most of them never even said thank you. It was time to leave that shit behind.

But then there were times in his flights of fantasy when he would pause, when he would ponder—could he really do it? Could he walk away from everything dear in this life, especially his son and daughter? Would they understand, even care to understand, the depths of his feelings for Nikki? He knew they wouldn't. They would see it, as he did in his moments of despair, as a betrayal of everything he had tried to instill in them about what was important in life. He couldn't expect them to understand—or to forgive him.

Then there were moments of total fear. Matt had not told Nikki, but on many nights he had a recurring dream and he would wake up in a cold sweat. In the dream he and Nikki would be lying on a blanket, making love, by the edge of the ocean. It would be a clear, warm night, and the only sounds would be the rhythmic splashing of the waves lapping the shore, and the pleasure they were taking in each other's body. Out of the dark, Matt would hear a "click," the sound he recognized to be the hammer of a gun being cocked. There would be a flash of light and a deafening sound—a shotgun blast. Matt would wake up, shaking, unable to get it out of his mind.

It was two in the morning before he finally went to bed. As he laid his head on the pillow, he smiled. It was funny. In his wildest imagination the thought had never crossed his mind that he would be in this predicament. He couldn't believe he was jeopardizing his family, his career, almost everything, for this one woman.

***

Matt got to the courthouse early so he'd have a chance to go over his notes for the last time. He was deep in thought when Nikki and Vince walked in. As Nikki approached him, he watched the movement of her body, picturing every inch of it, recalling the feeling of her bare breasts against his skin. As she got closer, he could see she had a restrained smile, appropriate for the circumstances. Vince was in a surprisingly relaxed mood. This guy's really got to be on something, thought Matt.

"Well, I'm as ready as I'm ever going to be," Matt said.

"I know you'll do a wonderful job," answered Nikki.

"Just don't fuck it up," said Vince.

"Thanks for your confidence," replied Matt.

"I mean it," said Vince.

"I'm sure you do."

***

With everybody settled in, the judge turned to the prosecutor and said, "Mr. Larson, you may proceed."

Scott stood up. He stuck out his chest and pushed himself away from the table. A podium had been put before the jury box. His presence filled the courtroom as he strolled to the podium.

He had no notes with him. Nothing. He would do this from the cuff, by heart.

"If it pleases the court, Mr. Collins, ladies and gentlemen of the jury." His voice resonated through the courtroom. The voice of an orator.

"This is a democracy," he continued, "that is why you are here. We don't take a person's freedom without giving him due process of law. We don't take a person's freedom without giving him a chance to be judged by his peers. That's why you are here.

"This has been an extremely difficult case for us. We were called to the home of a prominent business man to find a young woman dead. The businessman tells us it was an accident and nothing you see disputes that. That's the first impression that you get—this was a terrible accident. And then days go by and you start asking yourself questions. Why would Vince Fischer be out shooting squirrels on his property early on a Saturday morning? Why would he leave a loaded shotgun on the deck, leaning against a wall near the entryway to the house, especially once a ten-year-old boy is there? Why would he pick up that gun as he is walking Ms. Woods to the car rather than on the way back, which would seem more natural? Then you start to get reports back from the medical examiner, the autopsy, that cast even greater doubt on that first impression. When Dr. Michaels tells us that the angle of entry is more consistent with that gun being at the shoulder of Mr. Fischer than under his arm; that the distance from the muzzle of the gun to the wound is one to two feet rather than the five to six feet that Mr. Fischer claimed he was behind Ms. Woods; and Mr. Bishop, from the BCA, being unable to get that shotgun to misfire under any reasonable conditions. Then you start to have doubts about what Mr. Fischer told you. It doesn't stop there, though. Ms. Woods' friends and relatives tell you that she had no intention of marrying Mr. Fischer. That, in fact, she had terminated the relationship months earlier, she would never have considered marrying him. And you start to wonder, is he telling the truth? Then you find out she had been drinking all afternoon. She had a blood alcohol concentration of .25, two and a half times the legal limit. Mr. Fischer said she only had a couple beers. We find out the autopsy reveals the presence of semen. Mr. Fischer acknowledges he had not had intercourse with her. Does that sound like a young woman who had made a commitment to marry Mr. Fischer? Then you know your first impression was the wrong impression. This wasn't an accident. But was it murder?"

The prosecutor went on for over an hour outlining every point of the state's case, the testimony of every witness. He emphasized what he obviously believed to be his most important witness.

"Ladies and gentlemen of the jury, you saw Troy Woods testify. You heard him say he did not see a shotgun on the deck near the breezeway door, leaning against the outside wall of the attached garage. He saw that shotgun leaning up against the gun cabinet, outside the cabinet, in the great room. You heard him testify he heard his mother and Vince arguing, they were angry, he said cuss words were being exchanged. You heard him testify it was Vince who told him to go sit in the Corvette; Vince was going to drive Troy and his mother home. There was no kissing, there was no talk of reconciliation, there was no talk of going out to dinner, there was no talk of Donna coming back and spending the night. There is nothing the defense can say to you that can discredit the testimony of that young boy.

"What the defense will ask you to believe is the testimony of Mr. Fischer. After all, he was the only one there. You saw his performance. Glib. Smug. He thinks he can con you people into believing his story. And that's what it is, a story. Think about it, ladies and gentlemen, think about that young mother lying there on the deck, the last seconds of her life. And after shooting her, what does Mr. Fischer do? He runs out to the Corvette to see if Troy had seen anything." The prosecutor turned to Vince, his voice had been slowly rising; he fixed his gaze on Vince.

"Judge his testimony against the evidence. It doesn't stand up. His testimony is a fiction, concocted in his head after he shot that young woman and saw her lifeless body lying there on the deck. The judge will give you an instruction on premeditation. It doesn't take long to premeditate a murder. Just long enough to form the plan in your mind and then carry it out. Just seconds. As she walked out his kitchen door, Mr. Fischer went over to the gun cabinet, grabbed that gun, followed her out the back door, through the breezeway, onto the deck, raised that gun to his shoulder and pulled the trigger. That, ladies and gentlemen, is premeditation. If you believe Troy Woods' testimony, that's how it had to happen. If you believe that's how it happened, then the question is answered—it was murder!"

In the dead quiet of the courtroom, the last three words, *it was murder*, rolled over the audience like a shock wave. The prosecutor had the jury spellbound. It was one of the best performances Matt had seen. Everyone in the courtroom was mesmerized. They stared directly at the prosecutor, hanging on every word. Matt was wondering whether Vince was still thinking *sleeping giant, my ass.*

The prosecutor closed his argument sympathizing with the jury on the serious task they had ahead of them. They had been chosen because the attorneys knew they would take that obligation seriously. The prosecutor knew that when they were through reviewing all of the evidence and discussing it, coolly and calmly, dispassionately among themselves, they would come back with the right verdict, the only verdict—Mr. Fischer is guilty of murder in the first degree. The argument was close to two hours. The judge took a recess.

***

Vince, Matt and Nikki stood, rather somberly, in the hallway.

"That's gonna be one hell of an act to follow," said Matt.

"You can do it," said Nikki.

Vince was quiet. The prosecutor had handled his testimony the best way he could. What he'd told the jury was to not listen to the words but to look at the source. Was there any way they could believe this guy, given everything else that has been said? The prosecutor didn't try to dissect Vince's testimony, go over it, lie for lie. Rather, with one broad brush, he'd simply cast massive doubt on Vince's character and left it at that.

Now Matt had to appear to try and convince the jury they should listen to Vince. That wasn't going to be easy.

***

Matt stood at the podium. Unlike Scott, he put his notes before him. He had learned years earlier, in one embarrassing moment, that he should never again do a closing argument without having something in front of him to reference his thoughts. That had become another cardinal rule he lived by. His mouth was dry; he was nervous. He looked at the jury, all fourteen of them. They returned his look, straight in the eye. It was always a frightening experience. He could tell five or ten minutes into his closing argument whether he was going to be any good. Then the dryness left, the trembling stopped and the words came pouring freely. He always looked for some level of rapport building between himself and the jurors. If it was obvious to him that he had lost some jurors, then he would focus on the ones who still appeared to be listening.

Matt thanked the jury for their attention throughout the trial. They had taken on a solemn obligation and he had watched their faces through the course of the trial and knew they took that obligation seriously.

"The only thing left to do," he said, "is to go into the jury room and fulfill that obligation by following the law. The law that states Mr. Fischer is presumed innocent. He came into this courtroom an innocent man and you all agreed to give him the benefit of that presumption of innocence. The law imposes a burden on the state to convince each one of you Vince was guilty beyond a reasonable doubt, to a moral certainty. These concepts are the cornerstones of the criminal justice system. You cannot take them lightly. Once you have reviewed all of the evidence and held it to that type of scrutiny, you will have a reasonable doubt and must, therefore, find Mr. Fischer not guilty."

That was boiler plate. Matt used it in every case. It gave him a chance to ease up, to relax, and to see whether the jury was listening to him. It was a warm-up. Looking over the jury panel, he could tell several of the men had already formed an opinion;

284

others seemed to be listening.

"This case was indeed about first impressions and how first impressions can be wrong. Dr. Michaels agreed he had a first impression and then proved himself wrong. Your first impression here is that Donna Woods had decided to have nothing further to do with Mr. Fischer. But look at the testimony, wasn't she telling her friends and family one thing and doing something quite different? How do you explain the fact she continued to go out with Vince, to take his money; that she continued to sleep with him? How do you explain the fact that she went to his home that morning with no apparent concern for her safety or her son's safety? How do you explain the fact that she talked to her father over the phone that afternoon and expressed no concern, in fact was in a light-hearted mood? Don't rely on first impressions... think it through.

"What about the testimony of Mr. Fischer? The prosecutor wants you to simply ignore it, slough it off. Consider its source, he says, that it was all a fiction. The judge will tell you it is your job to decide the credibility of the witnesses. And in doing so, you apply your own common sense, your own life experiences. We're required to do that every day of our lives. Somebody tells you something, something that's important to a decision in your life and you have to judge whether you're going to believe that person or not. How do you do that? You ask yourself, does it make sense? Does it ring true? What was his demeanor? How did he say it? Do you trust him or not? It's a gut reaction. It's the same here. Mr. Fischer didn't have to testify, but he got on the stand, he looked you squarely in the eye and he said this is the way it happened. And he said it with such sincerity and with such honesty that you have to believe him. No one who loved a person as much as Mr. Fischer loved Donna Woods could consider killing her. Could he, in cold blood, grab that gun, point it at her and pull the trigger with her a foot or two in front of him? No way! It would never happen."

Matt next turned to the testimony of the doctors and of Bishop.

"The most revealing part of Dr. Michaels' testimony was in his rebuttal, where he first used the word *estimation*, that the angle of entry was estimation. That's exactly what Dr. Evans told you. With this type of wound you can't be so doctrinaire as to say this is the only way it happened or this is exactly the way it happened. If you're going to be honest with the jury, you're going to say, 'Based on my education, training and experience, I have an opinion, and that opinion considers some estimates, some approximations.' That's what Dr. Evans told you and that's what Dr. Michaels had to agree with. So you can't decide this case based on physical evidence alone. It's not precise.

"We want precision in our decision, and, if need be, we look for something to help us. An airplane pilot, for example, has a whole panel of electronic instruments in front of him, so precise that they can help him land an airplane in fog so thick that he can't even see the landing strip. A doctor has instruments so precise that they can enter the brain and isolate the smallest amount of tissue. Even the carpenter has precise instruments to make sure he's staying square. What's precise about what the state has given you in this case? Nothing.

"The truth is, ladies and gentlemen, the expert testimony in this case does not give you a precise answer. If you look at the testimony of all of the experts, what do you have? You have estimations, approximations, could have been this, could have been that. The prosecutor went through elaborate preparation to give us an illustration of how they believed this happened, where the gun was at Vince's shoulder when the shot was fired. Dr. Michaels, in fact, testified based on that illustration. Then we find out, late in the case, that somebody made a mistake, that the deputy did not have the correct measurements. The prosecutor has to correct his illustration. When Dr. Michaels is called back he says, 'Well it really doesn't change anything. My original opinion was based on estimation, an approximation'. That's what they're trying to get you to decide this case on.

"The truth is that it could've happened exactly the way the prosecutor wants you to believe it happened. And the truth is that it also could've happened exactly the way Vince Fischer said it happened. The physical evidence supports both of those conclusions. So what do you rely on for your decision? You rely on the testimony of the only person who was there, the only person who can come in this courtroom and tell you what happened. That's Vince Fischer. And he told you exactly the way it happened. He told it to you in such a way you can have no doubt that he's telling the truth."

Matt glanced at his watch; it had been over an hour and a half. The jurors had been locked in those chairs for close to four hours with just a short break. He could tell some of them were getting restless. He didn't know if he was losing them or if they just needed a break. He turned to the bench, "Your Honor, if we can take a short recess."

"Sure, Mr. Collins, that would be fine. We'll take fifteen minutes."

Matt went into the hall and quickly got a drink of water. Vince came up to him.

"You're doing a great job, Counsel. You almost got me believing it," he grinned.

"God, you can be so cold," said Matt.

"Not cold," said Vince, "just practical. Keep up the good work. It may be worth a few extra bucks." He turned and walked away. It was a time for a cigarette.

"I'm glad you asked for a recess. I was about to wet my pants," said Nikki.

Not exactly the greeting Matt expected.

"And I'm happy to see you too, Mrs. Fischer."

"With what you've got, you're doing a great job. Which side are you on anyway? We want this jury to convict. You're actually making me feel sorry for him," she whispered.

"I don't think we have to worry, Nikki," he whispered back, looking around to make sure no one was listening.

"If I'm any judge of reading faces, there are some men in there who already have him convicted. I don't know if they really believe he did it, or if they just hate his guts for all of his money and women, but it doesn't make any difference. There are a few women, though, that are really listening. They scare me. It may depend on who is the most dominating once they get into the jury room. That I can't tell you right now."

She smiled. "Don't do too good of a job."

"I have to, Nikki. It would be too obvious if I didn't."

***

Matt finished his closing argument by talking about Troy and first impressions again.

"The first impression is that he was a fine young man who was telling the absolute truth as far as what he saw and heard. But first impressions, again, may be wrong. If what he testified to was the truth, what really happened, why didn't he tell that to Deputy Lentz or the sheriff that night? More importantly, why didn't he tell that to the grand jury? Why did it come up the first time just months before the trial? Was it what he really heard and saw or was it what everybody had told him they thought happened? How did it influence him to be in that house for days after his mother's death with everybody talking about how it must've happened? What influence was it on him to live with his aunt for two years? You could tell her feelings about Vince. Take all that into consideration.

"You know, ladies and gentlemen of the jury, this has been a very difficult case. An attorney assumes a tremendous burden when he takes a case like this. You want to make sure that you've done the best job you can for your client. You want to make sure that you've done the best you can to convince the jury that your cause is just and that your client is innocent.

"We bring ordinary people into these surroundings; we provide them with a very sterile atmosphere, cold courtrooms with marble and oak. We have a judge sitting behind a bench with a black robe, we stand up when he walks in, we follow very strict rules. It's a very formal and cold setting. I believe we may have a tendency to forget that we're dealing with a person's life. But there's really nothing cold about it at all. This is really high drama. These are important issues, not to be decided lightly. This may be the only time you're ever called to serve on a jury. This may be the only time you're even in this courthouse. But it isn't going to be the only time you ever think about this case. Days, weeks, months, maybe years from now, you may drive past this courthouse again, or you may see a young boy that reminds you of Troy, or you may see somebody who looks like Vince, and you're going to remember this case. And you're going to wonder if you did the right thing. If you made the right decision. You're going to want to feel good about what you did. We believe the right decision here is 'not guilty.' With that, I place the future of Mr. Fischer in your hands. Do the right thing. Do not take your duty lightly. Thank you."

Matt took his notes and walked slowly from the podium and sat next to Vince. Vince reached over and touched him on the shoulder, a sign of confidence. There was always such tremendous relief when it was over, when the last word was said and Matt could sit. In the pit of his stomach, though, he knew he had held back... this wasn't his best, and he knew why.

The judge turned to the jury.

"Ladies and gentlemen of the jury, you've heard the arguments of counsel, now it is my duty to give you the law that applies in this case."

With that, he spent twenty-five minutes laying out the jury instructions, the rules they were required to follow, the charges they were required to decide. At the end, he told them they had to pick a foreman, they would retire to deliberate and their verdict had to be unanimous.

Now he had to excuse the alternate jurors. As the judge told the two they should remain behind, the disappointment on their faces was obvious. The judge thanked them for their service, apologized that he had to dismiss them. The two walked out, neither one looked at Matt or Vince. Normally, Matt would consider that a bad sign. Today it was different. It was a good sign.

***

In the hallway, Nikki asked, "What do we do now?"

"We wait," replied Matt.

"For how long?" asked Vince.

"Until they reach a verdict."

"How long could that be?"

"Could be a matter of a couple of hours, could be a couple of days." said Matt. "I don't know how late the judge will let them go this evening. Typically, if they haven't reached a verdict by eight or nine o'clock, he'll let the jurors decide whether they want to stay longer and see if they can reach a verdict, or would they rather take the night off. In that event, he'll put them up in a hotel, then they'll start tomorrow morning again."

"What's the longest you've ever had to wait?" asked Nikki.

"Four days," replied Matt, "and then they came back and found the defendant guilty. The vote at the end of the first day was eleven to one for guilty. It took the eleven three days to talk the other one into voting guilty."

"What happens if they can't agree?" asked Vince.

"Then you end up with a hung jury and the prosecutor decides whether he's going to start it all over with a different jury."

"How can they do that?" asked Vince.

"Well, it's just the way it is."

"This fuckin' system just keeps amazing me," said Vince.

"You might as well take it easy," said Matt. "I think it'll take a while. The judge doesn't want us to go anywhere this afternoon where we can't be back in a couple of minutes. I think the first thing the jury will do is have lunch. We may as well do the same."

Even though Matt was relieved to have the actual trial over, the tension he felt was suffocating. So many things could still happen to spoil their plans. He had this lingering thought that if Vince was found guilty of first degree murder, Vince would have to appeal. What would the appellate attorney think of Matt's performance? What was obvious? What did he miss? What did he screw up?

When the outcome was in doubt, waiting for a jury to return was the most unbearable part of any trial. Even though in a majority of cases the defense attorney knows the jury will come back with a "guilty" verdict, it was still agonizing to wait. But when there is some doubt as to what the jury would do, it was constantly on your mind. When your whole future may rest on what the jury decides...well, you suffer. Matt had watched the jurors as the judge read the instructions, he could tell the wheels were turning. What did that portend?

***

The three of them sat at the same table with the same waitress, ordering almost the same lunch. There was no unnecessary talk, there was no animation; they sat in a daze.

Vince finally broke the silence.

"For what it's worth," he said, "the other evening I had a meeting with Peter. We pretty much have all the plans in effect. He's confident the bitch from Connecticut won't see a dime."

Matt didn't want to talk about it. Vince turned to Nikki.

"Whatever happens, babe, you're gonna have to stick with me."

"Don't worry, dear, I'm with you to the bitter end."

They finished picking at their food and drove back to the courthouse. It was late in the afternoon. By then Matt felt he had spent as much time with Vince as he could take, and he told them he needed to do some work in the law library. On his way, he walked past the judge's chambers. The court reporter was sitting in the empty room finishing up a transcript of a previous trial. He invited Matt in.

"Matt," he said, "you did a hell of a job, but I don't think you gave them enough. They want to find him guilty of something." Matt considered court reporters a pretty good sounding board as to how the trial went, and they always felt a little freer to talk about their thoughts on the trial than the judges did. Over the years, Matt had estimated that the court reporters had predicted correctly what the jury would do in over ninety percent of the cases. Every once in a while they were surprised as well. This time he thought the court reporter was right. At least he hoped he was.

With any other case, Matt probably would've argued his cause. Now he was tired of arguing. He was tired of being beat up. He was looking for a place to hide out from Vince and this was as good as anywhere. They spent an hour or more talking about the case, the different witnesses, and the court reporter's assessment of them. It was surprising to Matt how well he had actually figured some of them out.

"You know, Matt," he said, "her sister, Ms Portnoy, was probably one of the most chilling witnesses I've ever seen. She had ice in her veins. You could certainly tell she had a vendetta. I don't think your client ever recovered with some of the jurors after she testified. You were smart just letting her go. She was a time bomb."

When Matt finally made his way to the law library, he picked up a newspaper and sat down, but he couldn't get himself to concentrate. The comment made by the court reporter, "Matt you did a hell of a job," was gnawing at the little piece of pride he still had. Only two people knew what a fraud he had just perpetrated on the court and his client, he and Nikki. It had all seemed so simple, now he knew better. Also the realization was setting in that even if Vince was convicted, there would be motions for a new trial, motions for post conviction relief, an appeal to the Supreme Court. The appellate attorneys would have a transcript of this trial; everything that he had done would be under a microscope. He couldn't escape it. He knew Vince would hire a new attorney to handle an appeal, and that attorney would have questions, a million questions. Was it all still worth it? Could he stand up to what he knew he would face? Would Nikki stand by him? He shook his head, disgusted by his recriminations. It was too late, anyway. As his mother had said to him many times, "You made your bed, now lie in it."

At 6:30, the judge called the attorneys into his chambers. He told them he was going to ask the bailiff to give the jury foreman a note to see whether they wanted to continue or take the evening off. The bailiff came back in a few minutes and said the jurors wished to go to dinner and then to the hotel. Matt was relieved, he wanted to get out of there. He shook Vince and Nikki's hands as he left and said, "Just hang in there."

On the drive home his mind was numb, incapable of holding the slightest thought. He stared ahead. It was a warm, windy spring evening. The potato farmers were in their fields planting, creating clouds of dust as their tractors crawled across the dry soil. In spots, the dust was so thick he had to slow down to see the road. Things must be terribly dry, he thought. He couldn't even remember what the weather had been for the last several weeks. The sun was just starting to set on the horizon, the dust filtered the rays and it hung like a huge orange ball. The beauty of the sunset gave him respite from his thoughts.

chapter 46

WHEN MATT PULLED into the courthouse parking lot the next morning, Vince's Lincoln was already there. Vince and Nikki were sitting in the coffee room. Matt knew they had picked that spot because it was the closest exit for running outside to have a cigarette. Vince was to the point of chain smoking. Nikki wasn't far behind. Matt had quit years earlier. He figured if he hadn't smoked through all of this, he wasn't about to start now. There was nothing to talk about. They read the paper. The reporters had given the highlights of the closing argument and the fact that the jury was out and had not reached a verdict. Matt thought the reporting had been fair. It was apparent, though, that the trial, particularly the testimony from the former wives, had caused quite a stir in the community. All the women that Vince had snubbed over the years, all those "artsy fartsy" women that Vince disdained so, could now say, "See, I told you he was a woman hater."

Noon came. The bailiff told the attorneys that the jury would have lunch brought in. Matt, Vince, and Nikki decided to have lunch together again, but they wanted a different spot, a place where they could get something harder than coffee. They found a small bar and grill several blocks from the courthouse. Matt ordered a rum and Coke. They were in no hurry and he was just starting to wind down. He'd always meant to talk to Vince about his business. If he and Nikki ended up with it after all, he might have to know how to dispose of it. And Vince loved to talk about it.

Vince boasted about how he had set the whole thing up. What controls he had, professionals he had picked up to do the day to day operation. It was quite a feat, thought Matt, something very few could accomplish.

"I've always thought that this world is made up of the movers and shakers," Matt said. "The people who can take an idea and run with it and make it a success, like you did, and then the rest of us who just settle on a path and go to work every day." Vince looked at him, beaming. It wasn't intended to be a compliment to Vince, though; it was something Matt had thought about many times over the years.

"It's true," he continued. "They always talk about everyone's chance to succeed, to fulfill the American dream, but you also have to have the grunts, the people willing to do the dirty work every day. Take your business, Vince. All the guys you have working in the pits, going home greasy every night. At what, a few bucks over minimum wage? The world needs the grunts, though; life couldn't go on without 'em. Who would do all the dirty work for the rich? I'm a grunt. I might be a little better educated, I might make a few more bucks, but I still just handle other people's dirty work."

Nikki looked at him. "You're sounding awful sorry for yourself. I have the impression that you have some regrets about what you're doing."

Matt wasn't sure if that was a double entendre. He let it pass.

"If that's how you feel, Matt," said Vince, "I'd be glad to pay you the same dough I pay one of the grease monkeys."

They all laughed. The liquor had eased the tension. They sat there like that, exchanging barbs, until about 2:30. Matt finally said, "I think it's time to get back, we don't want to miss the jury."

"I wouldn't mind," said Vince.

***

When Matt walked into the courtroom hall, the clerk was waiting for him. "The judge wants to see you in chambers."

"Have they reached a verdict?" asked Matt.

"No, they haven't. But the bailiff says they have questions."

Matt sat down in Judge Thompson's chambers.

"The foreman told the bailiff they have a question or two

for the court," the judge said. "I told them we would wait until you got back and have them put it in writing. He should be in any minute."

The bailiff came back with a sealed envelope. Inside was a note from the jury foreman, John Pearce. Judge Thompson read it: *We would like to know if we could have a transcript of the testimony of Troy Woods. If we can't have a transcript, could we have someone read his testimony to us again? Some of the jurors want to know why we didn't receive anything on manslaughter. They want to know if we can consider manslaughter.*

Matt sunk in his chair. The judge looked at the attorneys.

"Who in the hell would've come up with that?" he asked. "Can you imagine that, they're asking us why we didn't give them a manslaughter instruction? Somebody's been watching too much television, *L. A. Law* and all that crap. Question is: What do we do?"

Matt took the opportunity immediately. "I don't think we can do anything, Judge. The case law is pretty clear; you can't start providing them with transcripts of certain testimony and not all the testimony. You can't give emphasis to one over the other. As far as the jury instructions, they have the law of the case. I would think if you gave them a manslaughter instruction now, it would be an automatic reversal."

The prosecutor responded, "I knew we were gonna screw this up. He's right, Judge. I think you just have to tell them they have all the instructions they're gonna get. They just have to do the best with what they've got. Based on the question, Vince's B.S. must have some takers. I certainly don't want to try this case over again, though."

That was the agreement. The judge called the jury into the courtroom. Matt watched their faces as they sat down. Several of the women looked at him and Vince. The men didn't. Matt tried to figure out who the foreman was. John Pearce. John Pearce, he thought, that's the third one from the left. The stern looking guy. Vince is really in trouble, he thought.

Judge Thompson asked the foreman to rise. Mr. Pearce got up.

"Mr. Foreman," the judge said, "you've sent in a note with some requests."

"Yes, we have."

"Well, I have to tell you, ladies and gentlemen, that the law does not allow me to respond to your request. All I can tell you is that you have all of the instructions and all of the evidence we believe you need to decide this case. I can give you nothing further. We hope you are able to resolve it based on what you have. Thank you."

The jurors were obviously disappointed. The jurors whom Matt thought were still on Vince's side looked at him as they walked out.

Matt followed Vince and Nikki out. They were going to have another cigarette.

"What the hell do you think that means?" asked Vince.

"It's what we talked about," Matt said. "I knew there were some women on that jury who would consider manslaughter. They want to know why they don't have that opportunity. Now the question is, if they can't vote for manslaughter, will they vote for not guilty? You have to hope they do."

"Jesus Christ!" said Vince. "I can't believe that after all this, my life is in the hands of some more pussy."

Matt still felt enough lingering effect from the liquor to be a little sarcastic. He looked at him. "Vince, you're really a sensitive kinda guy, aren't you?"

Vince glared at him. "Fuck you."

chapter 47

TIME CRAWLED. MATT had read every word of the morning newspaper, even the want ads. He was forty miles from his office. The judge would never let him go back to work. Even if he did, he wouldn't be able to concentrate. He talked to the clerk for a while; then he talked to the court reporter. Everyone was bored. The only people who knew what was going on were the bailiffs. Jury deliberations were supposed to be secret, but Matt had never found a courthouse where the jury room was sound proof. The bailiffs, stationed right outside the door, could normally tell what was going on. They always pretended they didn't know, but everybody knew better. The only one they would keep current would be the judge. It was now 6:30 and they still weren't back. Judge Thompson sent the bailiff in again to ask them if they wanted to continue deliberations. The foreman told the bailiff it was no use, they wouldn't finish up tonight; they might as well start fresh in the morning.

Vince and Nikki left quickly. The day had really worn on Vince and he wanted to get out of there. Matt could tell Nikki wanted to talk to him but there was no opportunity. There was nothing they could have talked about anyway. Matt was dying to make love to her. He thought about that often. He wanted to feel her close. He knew it wasn't possible.

He stopped at his office. Things were piling up, but it was no use trying to sort through the messages and the mail. His mind failed to focus on anything, so he sat for a long time, staring into space like a zombie. He finally decided to just go home. His hesitation was his kids; he was afraid one of them would call and he didn't want to talk to them about the case. It wasn't like other cases where he could give them a daily update on his day in court, how he handled this witness and that witness, what he expected the outcome to be, what his client was really like. Now he had to be so careful about everything he said. He had to keep up the deception. He was starting to hate himself for it.

***

It was 10:48 a.m. Saturday morning. Vince, Nikki and Matt were sitting in a conference room at the courthouse. Nothing was being said. The morning paper had been passed around; different sections were strewn around the room. When the bailiff knocked on the door, they all jumped. He stuck his head in.

"They've reached a verdict. We've called Judge Thompson; he'll be here in fifteen to twenty minutes."

The next half an hour or so, thought Matt, would be the longest half an hour in their lives. Unless you've been through it, you could never imagine what it's like to know that twelve people have decided the fate of another person, whether that person will be tagged a "murderer" or not, and it remains a secret. There is nothing you can do but wait for the answer. Vince looked at Matt.

"What do you think?"

"I have no idea." he replied. "The book on it is the longer the jury's out the better it is for the defendant. If they're going to find the guy guilty, they can normally do it rather quickly...but I've had it go both ways."

Vince sighed. "I think it's gonna be second degree murder."

The comment took Matt by surprise. He thought it was a realization by Vince that he was guilty and he couldn't believe a jury was going to let him walk free. It was his way of compromising.

Matt turned to Nikki. She had not said a word. He could tell by the look on her face that she was frozen in time. There was no way of telling what was going through her mind. Vince put his arm around her.

"Well, honey, we're gonna find out what your future is today, too."

She looked at him and snapped, "Vince, don't say that, you know you're gonna be coming home."

Matt knew he had to prepare Vince for the worst.

"Vince, if it's guilty, the judge will probably require that you be taken into custody."

"What about the bond?" asked Vince.

"If they find you guilty of murder, Vince, the judge doesn't have any choice; he has to send you to prison. The prosecutor will argue you're a threat to abscond. With your money, you could disappear and they'd never find you."

"That's bullshit, and he knows it."

"There's no sense arguing about it now," said Matt. "If it's guilty, you'll have to appeal. You can renew your request for a bond at that point."

Matt expected a blast from Vince. It didn't come. Vince remained stoic, as if he anticipated his fate and now was going to take it like the gentlemen he tried to portray.

The bailiff knocked on the door. "Judge Thompson is back and he wants everybody in the courtroom."

Nikki gave Vince a hug. Matt shook his hand and said, "Good luck."

Spectators were rushing to fill the courtroom. Matt and Vince had to elbow their way through. Matt glanced around. There was the press, Donna's family, some of Vince's friends and, to his surprise, one of the excused alternate jurors. A middle aged lady, one of the last ones called, one Matt had liked. The prosecutor and his assistant were already seated. Matt and Vince sat at the counsel table to wait for the judge.

The tension in the courtroom was palpable. To Matt, waiting for the judge and the jury to enter those last few minutes was like waiting to go to hell. Every muscle ached; his brain was incapable of focusing on any one thought. He stared ahead, wanting to get it over with.

Finally, the bailiff said, "All rise." The judge walked in, took his seat and told the bailiff to bring in the jury. The bailiff opened the door to the jury room. Matt could hear talking and nervous laughter. At that instant, he knew their verdict.

The jury walked in, one by one, their faces giving them away; either they looked to the back of the courtroom or down at their feet. Not one of them would look at Vince or Matt.

The phenomenon never failed to amaze Matt. Twelve people who, after days of deliberation, finally conclude that the defendant is a murderer, have enough guts to write that on a verdict form and sign it, and they know they will have to walk into an open courtroom and tell the defendant they think he's guilty, but when they walk in the courtroom, they can't face him or his attorney. They never make eye contact. The exception may be the lone juror, or two, who had been on the defendant's side throughout the process. That juror will look at the defendant and his attorney—the glance that says, "I tried." That's what happened here. As the jurors finally all sat down, two of the women in the front row, the ones to whom Matt had addressed his closing argument, glanced toward the counsel table, they looked at Matt, then Vince. They gave them both that "we're sorry" look, and then turned to the judge.

"Ladies and gentlemen of the jury, have you reached a verdict?"

Mr. Pearce stood up. "Yes, we have, Your Honor."

"Will you hand it to the bailiff?"

The bailiff took the verdict form, brought it to the bench and handed it to the judge. Judge Thompson opened it slowly, read it, and handed it to the clerk. They both had read it, expressionless. No one in the court could tell what the verdict was based on their reaction. The clerk stood up.

"We the jury impaneled in the case of *The State of Minnesota v. Vince Fischer,* on the count of Murder in the First Degree, we find the defendant, *guilty.*" There was a murmur through the courtroom. Donna's family cheered. Vince's friends sat in disbelief. The spectators took it all in. Reporters got up and quickly rushed out the back door. The clerk continued, "To the second count of the indictment, Murder in the Second Degree, we find the defendant, *guilty.*"

Vince and Matt had been standing. Neither one moved a muscle. Neither one changed their expression. Not a word was said. The prosecutor and his assistant shook hands.

"Your Honor, I would like the jury polled," said Matt.

The judge went down the list of the jurors, called each one by name.

"Is that your verdict," he asked.

"Yes, it is," they all said without hesitation.

The judge looked at Mr. Fischer.

"The jury has found you guilty of both counts of murder. I am gonna ask the bailiff to take you into custody. I'll order a pre-sentence investigation."

Matt had no idea why the judge had ordered a PSI. Under the statute, life in prison was mandatory. It must've taken him by surprise as well. Matt turned to Vince and said, "I'm sorry. I'll be down to see you in a minute."

Vince said nothing. Nikki came from behind the bench and hugged Vince. The bailiff separated them gently, took Vince by the arm, and walked him through the back door of the courtroom. Vince had lost some of his stature; he looked whipped. The judge thanked the jury and told them they were excused. As they were leaving, the alternate juror ran to one of the female jurors in the front row.

"Gayle", she said, "I can't believe it! I can't believe you could've found him guilty of murder. Seems to me there would've had to have been more evidence for a verdict like that."

Gayle acknowledged her but didn't respond. Instead she motioned her outside. The alternate juror turned around, shaking her head, continuing to comment, "I can't believe it. I can't believe it."

Matt followed the jury out. Nikki was leaning against the wall, her face buried in her hands, her body shaking, sobbing. Some of Vince's friends were trying to comfort her. Matt took her by the arm and led her into the conference room. As the door closed she said, "Matt, I'm sorry, I can't help it. I know this is what we wanted but as he walked away, as that jailer took him through that door, it was such a pathetic sight, I just broke down. I'll be all right."

She reached out and put her arms around Matt. They hugged tightly. "Love you," she said. "I love you for what you did. I know you did it for me. I'll never forget it."

Matt could feel tears welling up in his eyes. He couldn't help it. It had been so long, the tension so high, that physically and emotionally he was ready to collapse. Now, as he felt her body in his arms, he wanted to wrap himself around her, stay close, until everything passed.

After minutes she leaned back, looked at him and asked, "What do we do now?"

"I hate to keep having to say this, Nikki, but we wait. I have to go to the jail and talk to Vince. He'll wanna appeal. I should call Peter, let him know what happened. You and I have to talk. There's still so much we have to do before we can feel safe. You know Vince's gonna be paranoid. He'll worry about what you're doing, especially what you're doing with his business and his money. I know he'll be second guessing everything I did at trial, talking to other attorneys, to Peter. We have to be extremely careful. Remember, he hired a private investigator to follow Pamela Dahl. I have no doubt he would do the same to you. Everything we do has to be strictly business."

"You have to stay with me, Matt. I need you. I can't do this by myself. There's no way I can survive, there's no way I can make it through this thing without you."

"You go home," he said. "I'll be there. I'll talk to Vince and then I'll be there."

chapter 48

MATT WALKED UP to the glass window and waved to the guard.

"I want to see Vince Fischer."

"Just a second," she said. She picked up the phone. "Vince Fischer. His attorney's here." Then she motioned to Matt. "You can go through that door."

Matt could hear the electric lock open. He walked in, the door clanged behind him and the electric lock squeaked closed. One of the deputies directed him to a holding cell with a small table and two chairs. Matt paced the floor, too anxious to sit down. The deputy brought Vince in. He was the same as when he walked through that door of the courtroom, completely calm, taking small steps, stooped over. He sat down by the table.

"Vince," said Matt, "this is the most difficult part. I don't know what I can say. I thought we had given 'em everything we could. I thought they believed you."

"Don't blame yourself," said Vince. "We knew that there was a risk. You did a good job. It was the judge who fucked us over. Those women should've never been allowed to testify. He shouldn't have let Weineke lie through his teeth. How do we handle this, trying to get me out of here?"

"You have to appeal," said Matt.

"Who's gonna do that?" Vince asked.

"Maybe you oughta talk to Peter, Vince. He's got connections; he'll find somebody."

"You can't do it?"

"No, I can't," replied Matt. "I can help whoever he hires, but

I've never handled an appeal to the Supreme Court by myself. You have to understand, it all takes time. The judge has to first sentence; he has no choice but to give you life in prison. Then it's a matter of filing a motion for a new trial, whatever the appellate attorney feels is necessary. You're gonna have to sit tight. I'm really sorry. I'll get a hold of Peter; we'll get right on this." Matt could tell, for the moment at least, that Vince was continuing to put his entire trust in him.

***

Matt drove up Vince's driveway and parked in front of the deck, next to the Lincoln. It was about 2:00 p.m. The beautiful spring day was bright and sunny, making him feel guilty about Vince in his gloomy, windowless cell.

Matt stood on the deck, almost in the spot where Donna's body had fallen, looking at the manicured yard and garden. Despite the trial, he thought, Nikki had spent some time doing what she loved. The grass was bright green and the red splendor crab apples were in full bloom, the rays of sun were hitting the petals, flashing a deep pink against the blue sky. Matt stood there for several minutes; he was like a lost child. As he approached the door to the breezeway, he could hear music inside. He didn't bother knocking. The music came from the master bedroom above the stairway of the great room. Nikki called down the steps, "Lock the door."

He went back to the door leading to the breezeway and flipped the lock. His hands trembled, his mouth dry. Entering the master bedroom he saw Nikki sitting at the table in front of the sliding glass doors overlooking the front yard of the estate and the lake. She was dressed in a silky slip, transparent against the sunlight flowing through the windows. The bottle of wine on the table was almost gone. As he approached her she stood and the sun silhouetted her naked body. Without a word she reached for Matt, grabbed his suit coat and slipped it off. She then took his tie, loosened the knot and threw it on the chair. She started to unbutton his shirt. Matt froze, completely in her control. As she opened his belt and slid his pants down, he kicked his shoes off.

He grabbed her, picked her up, carried her to the bed and they fell in a deep kiss. They remained like that, each immersed in the other's body. The climax was the culmination of weeks of tension, anxiety, fear. Fear that their plan would fail. Nothing was said. Nothing had to be said. It was pure passion. Totally exhausted, they fell asleep.

Matt woke at dusk. He couldn't believe it. Hours had passed. How could that have happened? Nikki was lying by his side, sound asleep. He pulled his arm out from under her head and she opened her eyes.

"That's what I needed," she said.

"I guess we both did," he replied. They lay quietly for a few minutes before Matt brought them back to reality. "Nikki we have to talk about this all. Vince wants to start the appeal process. I have to talk to Peter."

"I've already talked to him," said Nikki. "I called him as soon as I got home. He had to know what had happened. He said he expects you to call him; he'll take care of everything."

"Why would you call him?" asked Matt.

"I thought he should know. He has a lot of things he has to take care of now, things that he has to protect. I just thought he should know."

"I would just as soon you let me talk to him, Nikki. I don't want him to become suspicious of anything."

"It's okay, Matt. He doesn't suspect anything."

"This may be the last time we're together for a while," said Matt. "We can't take any risks."

"That's why I waited for you," said Nikki. "I knew that. We can meet at your office, can't we? You know, on a business basis? Or with Peter? There are things we have to do, things that shouldn't cast any suspicion, right?"

Nikki saw the flashing red light on the phone. She had turned her phone down so she couldn't hear the ring. She picked it up. "Hello...hi, Vince," she said. "I've been just sitting here miserable, worrying about you."

Matt shuttered. It was like Vince actually catching him in

Daniel Eller

the bedroom with Nikki. As Nikki talked, he gathered his clothes from around the room and got dressed. He tried not to listen to the conversation. It bothered him to hear Nikki playing the part of the grieving wife.

Nikki hung up and turned to Matt.

"They only gave him a couple minutes. He sounds miserable, Matt. It sounded like he was almost crying."

"What do you want me to do about it?" Matt snapped, guilt surfacing again.

"I don't expect anything!" she said. "We're in this together, don't pull that 'poor me' crap."

"I'm sorry, Nikki," he said. "I'm standing here in the bedroom of the man I just helped get convicted of first degree murder, after making love to his wife. It's a rather strange sensation—don't ya think?"

Nikki kissed him to silence him. Matt could feel her warm body under the silky negligee. What the hell, he thought. She's right. I'm a big boy; I knew what I was getting into. You wanted Nikki, now you've got her. Now, how are you going to keep her?

chapter 49

MATT WALKED INTO the offices of the Maxwell Firm first thing Monday morning. He was ushered directly into Peter's office. Peter stood up. "Matt, what the hell happened?"

"Peter, you know what happened. We all knew there was a possibility of Vince being convicted. I told you from the very beginning—Scott Larson is a good prosecutor and not somebody who should be taken lightly. Vince never agreed with that assessment. The prosecutor made an offer that he should've taken. Vince's comment was, 'Tell him to get fucked.'"

"That was the unintentional homicide?" asked Peter.

Matt paused. He didn't remember discussing that with Peter. Matt never wanted Vince to consider it seriously, that would've ruined the plans. Vince must've discussed it with Peter.

If he'd accepted that offer, Peter, he would've done about five years in prison. But you know he wouldn't do it...just like he wouldn't let me argue for manslaughter."

"Well, that was his mistake," said Peter. "I met with Vince yesterday. He was in such a panic over the phone that I drove out there in the afternoon, had a hell of a time getting in. Nobody there knew I was his attorney. They all knew you, but nobody knew who I was. I finally convinced them. He was a wreck. I could tell he hadn't slept all night. They had him in prison clothes. He looked pretty ridiculous after the three piece suits. He wants me to get the best appellate attorney money can buy. I know there's nobody in town who will do it. I have a couple of ideas. Do you have anybody in mind?"

"Yes, several guys I know in Minneapolis specialize in appellate practice. A couple of them used to be with the State Public Defender's Office. Any one of them would do a good job. I'll get you their names and numbers and you can talk to them yourself."

Peter looked at Matt. "You know, there were some plans put into place regarding Vince's estate to protect it from the civil suit, plans that have some timelines that have to be followed. Realistically, what do you see happening as far as when this may actually be over?"

"Peter, you know as well as I do, once it gets to the Supreme Court, a number of different things can happen. As far as time, it's gonna take awhile."

"What is your realistic opinion, Matt?" asked Peter.

"As far as what, the outcome?"

"Yes."

"I don't think the Supreme Court has reversed a first degree murder case for years. The only real legal issue the court can look at relates to the judge allowing the three wives to testify. I believe that's one hell of an issue. And maybe Weineke's interfering with the firearms testing. Once a jury has convicted, though, it's real difficult for the Supreme Court to reverse. If the judges believe he's guilty, which I believe the trial court judge did, they'll skirt the legal issues. They're not going to let him out or give him a new trial. It doesn't happen."

chapter 50

WEEKS TURNED INTO months. As required, Judge Thompson had sentenced Vince to life in prison. Notice of appeal was filed and a transcript was ordered. The trial transcript took six weeks to prepare. Vince had decided on an attorney from Minneapolis to handle the appeal. One who had considerable appellate experience, including arguing first degree murder cases. He had the trial transcripts and Matt was expecting a call from him any day.

Matt's contact with Nikki was limited to brief conversations over the phone or in Peter's office when Nikki was there to work on Vince's estate matters. Matt never knew how they had set it up and Nikki always claimed she never knew exactly how it worked, that Vince and Peter had purposely kept her in the dark. Matt could understand that.

Matt had been retained in another homicide case. This one was a young boy who had been involved in an argument with a family friend and had shot him. The boy's mother had hired him. She's obviously had not read the papers, thought Matt. But it gave him a chance to keep his mind off Vince and, more importantly, off Nikki. He was reading part of the file in his office when Kay told him Mrs. Fischer was on line two. Kay was still in the room when he picked up the phone and said, "Hello."

He looked at Kay and motioned her out. Matt always felt she was somehow suspicious and this time was trying to see his reaction to Nikki's voice. Kay gave him a dirty look and walked out. As she left, he said, "Shut the door behind you." He heard it slam.

Daniel Eller

"Hi." he said. "I had to get rid of somebody. Where are you?"

"I'm at our favorite restaurant," she said. "I don't suppose you could come for lunch?"

"Nikki," he said, "you know better than that."

"I know," she said. "I just miss you so much. We've got to somehow get away. Maybe we can go down to Minneapolis, find a place where we're safe."

"Nikki, listen to me. It's not worth it. We know too many people, too many people know us. Vince could have you followed. I can see us in some motel room, some thug walks in, blows us both away. He's capable of it, Nikki: you know he is."

"I don't think so," said Nikki. "You haven't seen him lately. I visit him. He's a broken man."

"Revenge has a way of mending broken men, Nikki. Especially a broken man who is in prison while his wife is shacking up with his attorney whose job it was to keep him out of prison in the first place."

"That's a terrible way of putting it," she said.

"I'm just telling you the way he would look at it. Nikki, there are people out there who would cut your throat for a couple of bucks. Vince's got an unlimited source of funds. Who do you think he could hire?"

"You're starting to sound scared," she said.

"I'm not scared. I'm just being realistic."

"Is that what it's going to be like?" she asked. "Are we going to have to be running scared the rest of our lives?"

"No, Nikki. No. Once this appeal is over, once it's settled that Vince sits in prison for the rest of his life, we'll have his money and we can just disappear. We'll figure out a way that he will never find us."

"I hope you're right," she said. "I'm counting on it."

"I am, and you can count on it."

And as far as he was concerned, she *could* count on it. He had rationalized everything in his own mind: As far as his career, who needed it once he had her? As far as his children, they would just have to understand. He thought the bonds were strong enough

312

that he could make them understand. He had spent his life being an advocate for others, a mouth piece; he could certainly convince his own children that he had the right to love this woman. They would never have to know about his betrayal.

chapter 51

"MATT," SAID KAY, "there's a Chris Koerber on the phone for you. It's regarding Mr. Fischer."

Matt had been expecting this call. Koerber was the attorney selected by Vince and Peter to handle the appeal to the Supreme Court. The trial transcript had been completed. Matt was sure that he wanted to talk to him about what he had read.

"Mr. Koerber. This is Matt Collins."

"Matt, I would like to meet with you within the next couple days, if that's possible. I've had a chance to do a cursory review of the transcript; I hope to be able to have it completely read by this weekend. How about some day next week?"

Matt looked at his calendar; they picked Wednesday at one.

***

At the appointed time the following Wednesday, Chris Koerber walked into Matt's office. He was several years older than Matt. Very well dressed, very formal, with an aura of confidence about him that made Matt feel ill at ease. Matt was nervous that he may be too good, could somehow decipher what had really happened. He knew Koerber had to be smart, otherwise Vince would've never hired him. Matt had way too much to hide to be at ease with anyone who was going to judge his performance.

"Matt," he said, "I've gone over the transcript. This case is really difficult. There are some great legal issues to be raised, but it appears to me that the trial judge was aware of that; he tried to cover his ass as much as possible. The strongest argument, of course, is going to be that he erred by allowing the ex-wives to testify. But you know as well as I do, if those justices believe that Vince is guilty, they'll come up with some reason to justify that trial court's decision."

Koerber's attitude caught Matt completely by surprise. He was expecting to be grilled: Why didn't you do this? Why didn't you do that? How come you did this? How come you did that? The assessment Koerber made of the case was the same assessment Matt had made months ago. He was relieved. Apparently there was nothing he saw that was a glaring mistake.

"You know I have one question, though," continued Koerber. "Why didn't you request the judge to give an instruction on first degree manslaughter?"

Matt hesitated. Maybe he had been a little premature in his judgment; Koerber was just now getting to the probing questions.

"It wasn't my decision," he said. "I told Vince that I figured the judge would give the manslaughter instruction if we requested it and I told him I thought some jurors would consider it. Vince wouldn't hear of it. He was sure he'd be found not guilty of the murder charge. It turns out I was right. I talked to some of those jurors. The reason it took three days to reach a decision was because several of the women jurors thought it was manslaughter. We'll never know what effect it would've had if the instruction actually had been given. We might've been able to convince the rest; it might've ended up in a hung jury. Who knows?"

"That will be a part of our appeal as well; the judge should've given the instruction whether it was requested or not."

There was silence for several moments, then Koerber continued, "I've talked to Vince several times; he's not blaming you, at least not yet. That will probably still come. There are some things he doesn't understand. He doesn't understand how Carlson, for example, could've, as he put it, 'fucked up his testing.' And he doesn't understand how Weineke could've screwed things up and got away with it. But you and I know, Matt, that in the course of a trial, shit happens. Shit happens that you don't have any control over. In your closing argument, Matt, you had the right assessment. If the jury wanted to believe Vince, it went one way, if they didn't, it went another. What we're arguing here now are technicalities and whether the system gave him a fair trial. I think the judge screwed up, but I don't know if we can convince the Supreme Court of that."

They continued to talk for more than an hour. As the discussion went on, Matt felt more and more comfortable with Koerber. It was obvious to Matt that he was very practical and at this point, at least, he hadn't detected anything in Matt's performance that would affect his judgment. He sensed that Koerber respected him for what he had done, the effort he had put into the case. However, his comments kick-started that gnawing at Matt's conscience again. If he really knew what a damn fraud I am, thought Matt, he'd have my ass in front of the Supreme Court, he'd have me disbarred and Vince would have his new trial so fast it would make my head spin.

After Koerber left, Matt shut his door. He wanted some quiet time, time to think. It had been months since he had made love to Nikki. It had been weeks since he had even been able to talk to her. He had no idea where she was, what she was doing. He thought that Koerber had given him a good opportunity, or at least an excuse, to call her. She answered.

"Hi," Matt said. "How are you doing?"

"God, I'm glad to hear from you," she said, "it's been way too long. I've been in hell wondering what's going on."

"How do you know you can talk, Nikki?" he asked.

"Oh, I can talk. I've had this phone checked over, it's not bugged. I'm positive."

"How can you be so sure, Nikki?"

"I'm just sure, don't worry about it. I really want to see you," she said, "I can't stay away any longer."

"What are our possibilities?" he asked.

"Why don't you just come here? It's safe here."

"I can't do that," said Matt. "I don't have your confidence. I know damn well that Vince's got somebody watching you."

"You're sounding a little paranoid," she said.

"Well somebody has to be."

"Why don't we meet at the truck stop?"

Matt thought for a moment.

"You take the interstate, I'll park at the off ramp and I'll watch to make sure that nobody's following you. Once I'm sure it's safe, I'll drive up."

***

He was parked at the off ramp. At the time they had picked, Matt saw Nikki's Audi exit the interstate and take a right turn into the truck stop. Nobody was behind her. He waited another fifteen minutes or so. The only vehicles exiting were semis and delivery trucks, or family cars filled with people. Nobody that concerned him. He drove into the truck stop. Nikki had parked at the farthest location. As he pulled up next to her, she jumped out of the Audi and into his car. Her face had a glow. It had been so long he had forgotten how beautiful she really was. Everything they had been through started to come back. Even before they had left the parking lot, he reached over and ran his hand down her thigh. She giggled. "Miss me?"

"What do you think?" he said.

He grabbed her hand, put it on his lap. She squeezed, he flinched. "You did miss me," she said.

"Nikki," he said, "you know, we can't be seen; we have to be really careful. Even if we had an accident, nobody would understand why the two of us were in the same car this time of night, out in the country."

"You're a worry wart," she said. "Just get us somewhere off the road. Anywhere."

He turned onto the first country road. As he started to slow down, she moved over, opened his zipper. He reached down to pull up her skirt and felt skin. He pulled off to the side of the road and stopped. He slid over from behind the steering wheel; she flipped a leg over him to straddle his lap. Spread-eagled, she fumbled with her left hand to help him enter, while with her right she opened her blouse and brushed her breast across his face.

318

Matt could feel the heat of her body as she started to move on him. In the distance he could see the headlights of another car.

"Nikki," he said, "there's a car coming."

She paid no attention.

"Nikki," he repeated louder, "there's a car coming!" She moved faster. All Matt could do was succumb to the excitement, and wonder how fast the headlights would be there, whether the car would stop. Within seconds, their bodies trembled, it was over, and she dropped her head to his shoulder.

"We have to get out of here," he said.

She raised her right leg off of him and fell back. Matt had the car in gear and his foot on the gas before he slid behind the wheel. The oncoming car slowed; its headlights passed within feet. Matt glanced at Nikki. She smiled, wide-eyed.

"God, you're gonna get us in trouble one of these days," he said.

"What's the matter?" she asked. "Don't you like to live dangerously?"

He thought about it. He hadn't until he met her. He had never experienced anything like that…nothing even close. She displayed no inhibitions in her passion. If this was living dangerously, bring it on.

He forced his thoughts to turn to business. Matt wasn't sure how he could approach Nikki to ask her what was happening with Vince's estate. He didn't even know whether she knew anything more, whether anything had actually been done. He started with a little fib.

"I talked to Peter the other day; he said you'd been working on trying to finalize some of Vince's papers."

"I don't want to talk about that stuff," she said. "Why is it that every time you or Peter get me alone, all you want to talk about is Vince's money?"

Matt was surprised. "Nikki, what are you talking about?" he asked.

"That's how we got into this in the first place. If it wasn't for his money, we would've been out of here a long time ago.

We wouldn't have just gone through all this crap…the trial and everything else."

She went silent. Matt reached over and grabbed her hand.

"Well, I can tell you," she continued, with a glance, "everything that's important is in my name. Some sort of trust. Vince can change that for a short period yet and then it's my understanding that it has to stay in my name. I'm the beneficiary. At least that's what they've told me."

Matt's mind raced. How had they set it up? Beneficiary would mean some sort of a trust. Would a trust protect his estate from claims by Donna's children? He wasn't sure. But what the two of them had set out to do had been accomplished. Now they just had to wait for Vince's appeal to be completed, for his conviction to be affirmed.

"Matt," she said, "you can't imagine how lonely it's been at that big house all by myself. I've only been able to stay there a few nights. There are sounds all night long. The wind coming off the lake, whistling through the trees. I feel it's full of ghosts. Donna's ghost is there. Vince's ghost is there."

"Oh yeah? Where do you stay when you can't stay at the house?"

"Oh you know, at a hotel," she said vaguely.

"What hotel?" Matt asked.

"Why are you grilling me?" she demanded.

"Sorry, I didn't mean to. This is just all so…stressful."

"Anyway, I want just the good memories of that house. Sometimes I can picture you and me that first night with the moonlight coming through the doors. I dream about that."

"I dream about us, too, Nikki, but it has a different ending," Matt said.

"What kind of ending?"

"It's not important, Nikki. It's my nightmare."

"That's what I mean. You've got to get this over with; we've got to get on with our lives. When can we?" she asked.

"I wish I could tell you," he said. "The appellate briefs have been filed. The only thing they're waiting for is the court to set oral argument and then the judges have time to file an opinion. If they affirm the conviction, if they believe he's guilty, it's all over for him. There are some other avenues he can use but it'll never make any difference. He'll be in prison for the rest of his life... and we go ahead with our plans. We start living."

"That's what I don't understand," she said. "There's something that has to happen before I can get my hands on Vince's money. That's probably what it is. If he would have another chance, there's no way he would let me get my hands on his estate."

"Peter doesn't tell you anything?" he asked.

"No, he's very secretive. Will Vince get a new trial?" she asked.

"Koerber thinks there's a slim possibility. If the judges don't think the trial judge should've allowed the ex-wives to testify... or if the judge should've given the manslaughter instruction, then maybe. But the chances are really slim. They don't like to let murderers off on technicalities. There's nothing fair about the system at all; it's a fiction to make people feel good. The system is really set up to convict. And when a jury decides that a person is guilty of first degree murder, why would anybody give him another chance? The typical response would be that there might've been some errors committed in the trial but the evidence of guilt was so overwhelming that the errors were harmless. If I had any money, Nikki, I would certainly bet against a new trial."

He weaved his fingers through hers. She squeezed his hand, took it and put it high on her thigh. "You wanna go again?" she asked.

"You're gonna get us killed," he said.

"But we'll go happy," she replied.

Matt had already started to head back to the truck stop. He thought she was in a strange mood, but he couldn't put his finger on it. She was relaxed. She was more at ease. Something had happened. Her responses were actually more flippant. Matt couldn't decide whether that was good or bad. They pulled into the truck stop; she gave him a kiss.

"I miss you," she said. "Let's do this again."

"Why not?" he said, "but bring Vince's car next time. It's got a bigger front seat than yours or mine."

Watching her leave, Matt knew it wasn't going to happen for a long time. At least not until the Supreme Court sealed Vince's fate. In the back of his mind was always the thought that if he and Nikki were caught, he saw the flash of the gun, both of them would be dead. Especially if Vince thought he would never again see the light of day. What's two more lives. They would be freebies. He would certainly get more sympathy for these killings than he had for the first. But he didn't want to be a statistic for recidivism by murderers. His plans were to get Nikki and disappear. They didn't have to live extravagantly. They could live a nice comfortable lifestyle doing things they talked about. They would have the money to do it. He often fantasized about the two of them walking the beach on some island in the South Seas, the sun setting across blue water, warm breezes, and the sound of the surf. It was the fantasies that kept him committed.

Within days, Peter Maxwell called. He wanted to know if Matt could come to his office for a few minutes. He had some questions about the progress of the appeal. Matt put everything aside and walked across the street. He was anxious to know what was going on, details only Peter could tell him.

"Matt," he said, "I went to see Vince a couple days ago in prison. He looks like shit. He's literally wasting away. This thing is on his mind day and night. The appeal is dragging. Nobody's giving him any assurances. He's convinced he's gonna rot there."

"He may be right," said Matt. "Have you talked to Koerber on the appeal? He doesn't hold out much hope."

"Yes, I have, and that's what he's telling me as well. You follow this stuff, what's your feeling?"

"On a scale of zero to a hundred, with a hundred being the best, I guess I'd give him a two or three, maybe a five."

"That bad?" asked Peter.

"This was a jury verdict, Peter. The court has to really stretch to overturn a jury verdict. They don't do it lightly—they never have. And if they don't like Vince, and there's not a lot to like in that record, the easiest thing is for them to just say, 'Sorry.'".

"The reason I'm concerned," said Peter, "is that we did some planning, as you know, regarding his estate and we started shortly before the trial started. We were doing some estimating at that time as far as how long we expected the trial to last and if the worst came out, if he was convicted, how long the appeal process would take. We received some estimates and made plans based on that. Our time is just about up, so some things have to be finalized. If there's a possibility of a new trial, we do one thing; if there isn't, we do something different. So you're telling me we shouldn't count on a new trial?"

"I certainly wouldn't bet on it."

"That's what I needed to know," said Peter. "Thanks for your time and candor. Most of all, thank you for your help through this. I know Nikki relied on you." Peter stood up to indicate the meeting was over.

The next day Matt received a letter from Koerber, the Supreme Court had set the date for oral arguments. Matt put it on his calendar, set it aside, decided to call Nikki to see if she knew. She didn't want to talk about Vince. She said she wanted to talk about the two of them, what they were going to do when this was all over. She said she was anticipating the end, that Peter had told her things would be finalized shortly.

chapter 52

WEDNESDAY MORNING MATT walked into the Minnesota Supreme Court Building to attend the oral arguments. Vince's case was set for 9:30; he was a little early. He picked up a copy of the court's calendar and was about to walk into the back of the courtroom when he noticed the prosecutor, Scott Larson. They shook hands like old friends. He had not seen Scott since Vince had been sentenced to life in prison. Neither one brought up the case. They made small talk and then Matt said, "Good luck," and walked through the big oak doors.

The court was in session. It was an impressive sight. A huge ornate courtroom, the judges sitting behind a semi-circular bench, the chief justice in the middle, elevated sufficiently so that everybody had to look up. There were two podiums centered in front of the bench. Matt took a seat in the back row and looked at the court's calendar. The matter before Vince's case was entitled *Disciplinary Proceedings against Roger Olson*. He knew Roger Olson; he'd had several cases with Roger in Douglas County. The speaker was the director of the Lawyer's Board of Professional Responsibility. He was going through a litany of complaints against this attorney: Failure to return calls, failure to complete files, misrepresentation on work done. He was giving specific examples, one after another. When he was finished, he said the board recommended that Roger's license be suspended. Nobody was there to speak for Roger. A chill ran down Matt's spine. This could be his future. If anyone knew what he had done, what he still planned to do, his name would be before the Supreme Court.

Certainly no one would speak for him.

The appellate process is the opportunity for the reviewing court to correct any reversible errors that may have occurred in the trial of the defendant. Vince's attorney, Koerber, was here to convince the court that such errors had been committed, that he had been wrongfully convicted and he was entitled to a new trial. In the course of a long murder trial, errors can be many things. They can be things that were said or things that were not said; things that were done or things that were not done. Trial attorneys and the judge are required to make decisions in seconds. Appellate judges have the luxury of weeks, sometimes months, to calmly read transcripts, cogitate, and then, with all due deliberation, decide whether somebody made a mistake that warranted their intervention. In criminal cases, Matt knew they liked to blame mistakes on defense attorneys and seldom believed any recourse for the defendant was required.

Scott Larson started first. Unlike his argument to the jury during Vince's trial, he was quiet and totally dispassionate. He told the judges the trial court was correct in allowing the ex-wives to testify, that this was precisely the kind of evidence that was always admissible when accident was claimed. The continuing course of conduct by Vince made the oldest testimony admissible. He told the judges that Deputy Weineke had every right to be present during the testing in Madison, Wisconsin. He certainly could not let that shotgun out of his sight. All he reported was what he heard. Under the circumstances, the trial court was correct in denying the defense motions.

For the defendant to now argue that he had a right to an instruction on manslaughter was ludicrous. There was nothing in Mr. Fischer's testimony that would give the jury the right to consider manslaughter. Moreover, the judge had given the defense counsel two opportunities to request the instruction. That's the most any trial judge should be required to do. Finally, it was for the jury to decide who they were going to believe. If they believed Mr. Fischer, they had the right to find him not guilty. If they believed Troy Woods, then they had to believe that Vince

Fischer picked that gun up in the house, followed the victim outside and killed her. That is premeditated murder. The judges had very few questions. Matt could tell they respected Scott.

When Koerber's turn came, Matt figured he was going to give a more passionate plea. But he never got a chance. Every time Koerber got into an issue and it was obvious that he was about to make a point, one of the judges interrupted with a questions: *If Mr. Collins was concerned about Deputy Weineke interfering with the independent testing, why didn't he accompany the shotgun to Madison? Why shouldn't a trial judge be allowed to let a jury hear evidence of misconduct by the defendant even if it is fifteen, twenty years old, if there's been a continuing course of misconduct? Why should we consider the court's failure to give an instruction on manslaughter reversible error when defense counsel never requested it?*

The questions continued, one after another. Koerber handled them all but he never got a chance to establish any pace to his argument. Matt sat back and cringed as the questions started to center on what he, as Vince's defense attorney, had or hadn't done. Vince didn't have a chance with this court.

The chief justice noted that the appeal was under advisement. As Matt got up to walk out, his agony finally over, he noticed, for the first time, Peter Maxwell sitting across the courtroom. He had entered by a different door. Matt met him in the hall.

"Well, it sounded like they wanted to give you a hard time," said Peter.

"I knew that would happen," Matt replied. "But it was a little bit more than I expected."

"I don't hold out much hope for Vince," said Peter.

By then Koerber had joined them. Both of them congratulated him on handling a very difficult situation professionally.

"I just hate it when they do that," he said. "Every once in a while they do that just to keep you off guard. You never get to establish any sort of rapport, any sort of rhythm to your argument. Based on their questions, I don't think we're gonna get anywhere on the *Spreigl* evidence." He hesitated. "I should know better than to speculate, let's just leave it at that."

Daniel Eller

Matt and Peter talked for a few minutes. Peter told Matt there were some things he had to talk to him about and they made arrangements to meet within a couple of days.

chapter 53

WHEN MATT WALKED into Peter Maxwell's office, the receptionist said, "Good morning, Mr. Collins. They've been waiting for you."

Matt was surprised at the word *they*. He had expected to meet only Peter. The receptionist led him to the large conference room and opened the door. Peter and Nikki were standing shoulder to shoulder looking out the window. They turned as he walked in. Nikki wore a sleeveless blue dress, her favorite color. Her skin had the golden hue of days spent in the garden or lounging by the lake. She's beautiful and she's mine, he thought. But she looked away with no greeting.

"What's the matter?" Matt asked.

Neither one said anything for a few moments, as if each was waiting for the other to speak. Finally, Peter said, "This isn't the way I wanted to do it, Matt. If it was up to me, Nikki and I would be long gone. I don't care where; we'd just be far away from here. But she didn't want to do that to you."

Matt's mind was racing. What the hell? What's this 'Nikki and I' crap? Why doesn't she say something? He looked at Nikki. She wouldn't meet his eyes.

"Nikki, what the hell's he talking about?"

"Matt, I'm sorry," she replied. "Peter and I started long before you came along."

Matt fixed his gaze on her. This has to be a joke, he thought. They've conjured this up; they'll both break out laughing any second. But why Peter? Why would he be involved? The look on her face told him she was serious.

"What do you mean, long before me?"

"Just that," replied Peter. "Nikki and I have this thing, it started before you became a necessity; it started when we first met. It's rather ironic—it was when she came in to sign the prenuptial agreement. I knew right away I had to have her. It took me a little while to convince her that she felt the same, though."

Matt's knees weakened.

"I don't believe it! Nikki, how could you have…I mean, what we did? And Peter, how in the hell could you have let her? What the fuck's going on here?"

Peter returned his glare. "Don't pull this 'holier than thou' crap on us, Matt. We had to be practical, just like you had to be practical; there's no sense running away with his wife without his money. If this murder thing hadn't come along, it would've been one thing, but once the grand jury returned the indictment, it was quite something else—then we saw the opportunities. I knew Vince could've murdered that woman just the way they said he did. I've been with him long enough to see him pissed, fly into a rage. I knew that's how it happened—he didn't have to spell it out for me like he did you. There are only four people in this world who really know what happened that night. Three of them are in this room. The other one's gonna rot in prison for the rest of his life, where he belongs."

Matt stood in stunned disbelief. The magnitude of their deception and the sense of betrayal settled on him and anger surged.

"Nikki! Look at me! Tell me that all this bullshit isn't true!"

But she wouldn't look at him, instead turning to Peter—her spokesman.

"Matt," he said, "I can understand why you're pissed, but don't just blame her, you're as culpable in this thing as she is. She seduced you and you were willing to be seduced."

"You mean this whole goddamn thing was an act, Nikki? You're telling me this whole thing was an act? You start out with this whole poor Vince bullshit, all this crap about how I have to help him. Then all of a sudden you act like I'm your knight in shining armor; I have to protect you from this woman batterer. It was all a con? All of our plans and all of our passion—the passion, Nikki, that was just acting? I don't believe it."

"She never told me about the passion, Matt. I knew baiting you was a necessary part of the plan, but I never wanted to know the details." Peter threw a dark look at Nikki. She stared back at him, defiantly.

"We have our own thing," he continued. "To me, you were a necessary evil. If I'd known she was going to…enjoy herself so much…I may have thought better of it."

There was silence again.

"You know, Peter," said Matt, "I thought I was the scum of the earth over this thing, but fuck, you take the cake."

"Take it out on me if you want to, Matt, I don't give a shit. I've got thick skin. You know I've been putting up with Vince's bullshit for twenty years: do this, do that, kiss my ass and I'll pay you. Every time I told the other partners I wanted to dump him, that I couldn't take the bullshit anymore, they begged me to hang in there for the firm's sake. He brought in too much money. Too much money, Matt. You know when that asshole came to me he had nothing but this idea. I got it off the ground for him. I'm the reason he's rich. Now he doles it out to me, a little bit here and a little bit there, and I should kiss his ass every time he writes a check. Then Nikki came along. You can understand that, Matt. Like you, I'd do anything for her. And so I did…we just needed you to help us."

"You mean even my being hired as Vince's attorney was part of your plan?"

"I wanted somebody local so I could keep track of what was going on. Then, once you started, we realized that hey, this guy—you—may actually be able to win this case, at least that was a possibility. We couldn't have that; that's how Nikki got involved. God knows I didn't want to do it, especially her involvement with you. She convinced me that we didn't have a whole lot of choice. She said she thought you were vulnerable. From what I could see, she was right."

Matt looked to Nikki, then at Peter and said, "You're a bigger asshole than I thought."

"Maybe so," replied Peter, "but we've got the money, we've got the airline tickets, and we're out of here."

Matt couldn't believe he'd been taken. Seduced by this beautiful woman, and all she had to do was simply spread her legs at the right time. How could he have been so damn stupid? How could they expect to get away with it? He'd never let them get away with it. They couldn't make a sucker out of him any more than they could out of Vince…and think they could walk away.

"How are you gonna get away from Vince? He'll never let you go."

"You took care of that. He's in prison. He's there for the rest of his life," replied Peter.

"You don't know that! The Supreme Court could reverse that conviction, give him a new trial."

"Matt, don't try to snow the snowman," replied Peter. "You've told me what his chances are. Koerber told me what his chances are. I was at the oral argument, those judges believe he's guilty, there's no way they'll give him a new trial. Don't try and scare us with that crap. It wouldn't make any difference anyway. The money isn't in his name anymore—it's in Nikki's name. Anything of any value, other than a few small accounts, is in Nikki's name or an offshore bank. They're never gonna touch it. Vince can't touch it. The kids' aunt can't touch it. The only one who can call that bank and get some answers is this lady right here. It was beautiful, Matt, a work of art. You would've been pleased at how we set it up. You know I have some of the smartest financial planners right here in the office. I didn't even have to pay for it. Vince was writing out all of these big checks for legal services, they were going in my pocket. Then he became paranoid about Nikki. He wanted me to hire a private dick to follow her. I told him it would be at least a grand a week. He didn't care. Well, I never hired anyone, but I told him I had. Told him Nikki was being a perfect angel. More dough in our pockets. Nikki and I needed some seed money. We've got way more than we need to get out of here."

"What about me?" asked Matt. "How do you know I'm not going to turn your ass in? How do you know I won't at least tell Vince?"

"Go ahead," said Peter. "What's Vince gonna do from prison? He doesn't have any money left. Even if he does send one of those thugs he calls friends after us—we'll be long gone; our plane leaves this afternoon. As far as going to the authorities, what are you gonna tell 'em? That you and Vince's wife had this plan to get him convicted of first degree murder so you could run off with his money and somehow this other attorney got there before you? Just to say it sounds ridiculous. Can you imagine what they're gonna tell ya? But be my guest, Matt, if you want to ruin what's left of your life, go ahead. As far as anybody knows, you did a great job of defending Vince, you did your best. You still have a practice, as miserable as it may be. Start blabbing around and see what happens. Remember, Matt, without Nikki, you don't have the money to get out of here. Those dreams you talked to her about were always pipe dreams."

Nikki had remained quiet. Finally she turned to Peter. "Peter, give me just a couple of minutes to talk to him, I owe him that."

Peter stared at her. "You don't owe him anything. He's a big boy, he'll survive."

"No, Peter, I want to talk to him alone."

"I'll be right outside. If you need any help, just let me know."

As Peter closed the door, Nikki gazed at Matt. She had the slightest hint of a smile on her face.

"You know, Matt, I did have feelings for you—I still do. To be honest with you, there was a time there, after Vince went to prison, when I struggled with whether to tell Peter. I know you think I'm a tramp, but I'm not. I'm a victim and I'm tired of being a victim. I want to do something. I have to get away from Vince but I can't do it with you. I realized that you have too much baggage. Too many people depending on you…your daughter, your son, your ex-wife. I know what your feelings are. Before long, you would've been feeling guilty, you would've made yourself miserable…made me miserable. Peter doesn't have that. He doesn't understand empathy. He deals with a different clientele. It's all money and power, that's what he understands. He and I can do the things we talked about, the same things you and I talked about, and he'll never tire of them, and he'll never feel guilty about it. I never have to worry about some day waking up to a note on the pillow saying, 'I'm sorry, but I had to go back home.' For what it's worth, Matt, I enjoyed making love to you more." She got up, walked over to Matt, and leaned down and kissed him on the cheek.

"I'm sorry," she said. "I truly am. By the way, you're a very good attorney as well." She walked over to the conference room door and opened it for Peter.

"Matt, you have to admit, she has a lot of class," Peter said, pulling the door shut behind him. "I didn't want to face you—she made me. As far as I'm concerned, right now we'd be in the airport bar waiting for our flight. My partners here don't even know."

Matt stood up and glared at the two of them. His anger hadn't lessened with Nikki's apology. He strained to think of something clever to say, something smart. It wouldn't come. He looked at Nikki and all he could think of was, "God, you're good. You're *really* good."

"Look, Matt," said Peter. "We'd like to give you this, just a little something to lessen the sting. It was Nikki's idea." He held out an envelope. Matt thought about taking it for a split second and then realized it must contain cash—money stolen from Vince.

"Rot in hell," he said, then turned and left the conference room, slamming the heavy walnut door behind him. Everyone in the outer office looked up, but no one was overly surprised—Peter Maxwell had always had his share of volatile associations.

Matt couldn't go back to the office, he was shattered. The woman who had consumed his every waking moment for over a year had just torn out his heart and walked away. All of the fantasies, all of the dreams, everything he had thought about for months and months had vanished in a matter of minutes. He walked around the block, the events of the last hour rushing through his head. As he came around the corner again, he saw Nikki coming out of the office building by herself, getting into Vince's Lincoln. His first reaction was to run to her, to try and talk to her, to convince her she was making a mistake. Then he paused, thinking about how she had been sleeping with both he and Peter at the same time—probably Vince, too—and there was never a hint that she felt any guilt, experienced any pangs of conscience. She wasn't who he thought she was.

Matt realized that if he had any remaining self respect, he would simply allow her to disappear the way she wished. But he still felt like his guts had been ripped out. It was Nikki... *his* Nikki, and she was leaving him. She noticed him as she pulled out of the parking lot, stopping and looking his direction for a moment before driving off. His eyes followed the car until it was out of sight. He didn't know how he could have been such a fool.

***

The following Monday the courthouse was abuzz with talk of how Peter Maxwell had decided to take an early retirement. How, at the age of forty-four, he had left his practice. How he planned to spend some time in Europe, do some traveling. He'd said he needed some time off. He couldn't take the pressures of trying to keep a big law firm operating. Everybody wondered whether it wasn't his health. One of the judges brought it up with Matt. Of course, Matt knew Peter wasn't in Europe; he was probably basking in the sun in the Canary Islands, his beautiful blonde at his side. Matt had spent many hours thinking how he could turn the tables, what he could do to Peter to get even. He always ended with the realization that there was nothing he could do. Peter was long gone and if Matt said anything now, he would only take himself down. Like a wounded dog, he had decided to lick his wounds and go on.

chapter 54

TWO WEEKS LATER Matt got word from Koerber that the Supreme Court would hand down their decision on the coming Friday. It had been quick, less than a month from the oral argument. Koerber assumed that meant the Supreme Court was going to simply affirm the conviction, that's why the opinion would have been so easy to write and be done so quickly.

On Friday morning Matt came into the office late, as he had become his habit in the weeks since Nikki had left. He had become lethargic and didn't feel like giving a damn about much. Kay had brought it up a number of times. He just told her it was the weather, or there were things he had to do at home, things that were keeping him from coming to work. Matt barely got his foot in the door and Kay called to him, "Did you hear the news?"

"What news?"

"You haven't had the radio on?"

"No, I've been playing tapes. Why, what's going on?"

"The Supreme Court gave Vince a new trial, they reversed his conviction. Something about the judge making an error, something about manslaughter; I don't have the whole story. Vince's already been calling. Apparently he can get out. He's wondering what's going on."

Before Matt had a chance to think, the phone rang. The room went quiet as Melanie answered, "Collin's Law Office."

Matt could hear Vince's loud voice, "Get 'im on the phone!"

Matt walked into his office and sat down. Kay followed him in. He looked at her and shrugged his shoulders, picked up the phone and said, "Isn't that tremendous news?"

"It's great news!" hollered Vince, "but get me the fuck outta here. I don't know what's going on. I called Peter. They tell me he's on some sort of extended vacation. I've been trying to call Nikki, but there's no goddamn answer at my house. In fact, they tell me the phone is disconnected. I haven't heard from her for weeks. No calls. No visits. Nothing! I don't know what the fuck's going on. You've gotta help me."

"What do you want?" asked Matt.

"Just get me outta this goddamn prison. I need a ride and I want it fast."

"You're free to leave?" asked Matt, surprised.

"Damn right. My cash bond's still good. Now stop asking stupid questions and get me outta here!"

"Give me a second," Matt said. He knew there was no way he could go pick Vince up and spend several hours alone with him. He may have to face him again eventually but he didn't need that kind of pressure right now.

"Is Tim around?" he asked Kay, putting his hand over the receiver.

"Yeah, he's in his office."

"I'll send Tim for you," he told Vince. "It'll take him at least two hours to get there."

"Give him some money, Matt, I'll pay you back. I wanna stop and get a bottle of Scotch and a big cigar. In fact, Matt, give him enough money to get a goddamn limo. I wanna leave here in style. I'm going home to find that puss of mine. Matt, I've learned something in here. I've got a whole different attitude. I'm just gonna spend my fuckin' money from now on instead of working, trying to earn more."

Tim said he'd be more than happy to pick Vince up, always looking for a way to add some excitement to his day. Matt gave him five one hundred dollar bills he had hidden away. That should get them started, he thought. After Tim left, Matt called Kay back into his office. "You've got to get over to the law library—they've got access to the Supreme Court's pressroom. You can get a copy of that opinion; get it back here as quickly as possible."

Suddenly it was quiet. The first quiet Matt had experienced since he walked in the door. He leaned back in his chair to ponder all of the ramifications. From what Peter had told him, they weren't able to get everything out of Vince's name. He wondered how much money Vince still had. Knowing Vince, he figured he probably had some hidden somewhere. Cash that he had kept away from Uncle Sam.

Matt knew Vince would know in no time. What would he do? Would he try to find them? Jesus, you know better than that, Matt thought. He'll chase 'em to the ends of the earth. He hoped so; Peter had been so damn smug. But would Vince harm Nikki? Matt was ambivalent. He'd been committed to her for so long, heart and soul, that her betrayal had cut him deeply. He believed he would never get over her, never get her out of his mind. The memories of her still haunted him. But now, more often, in a dark mood, the anger would surface. She'd made her choice and taken her chances. Why should he worry about her? But he did, and he was now. The memories would continue to haunt him. He knew they would for a lifetime.

Matt was still deep in thought when Kay walked in and laid the Supreme Court's decision on his desk. He picked it up, eyes galloping over the court's syllabus. There it was. The court had reversed the conviction on the basis of the trial court not giving the instruction on manslaughter. Everything else was okay. He couldn't believe it. The court had written:

> *The mere fact that the defendant's testimony in a murder prosecution repudiated a heat of passion shooting did not preclude the jury from finding facts supporting the conclusions that the shooting death was neither deliberate nor accidental but some lesser degree of homicide, and did not preclude submission of an instruction on first degree manslaughter.*
>
> *From testimony in a murder prosecution as to, inter alia, defendant's arguments with the decedent, a former girlfriend, and from testimony of her family, friends and neighbors, the jury might reasonably have*

inferred that the defendant, frustrated and desperate about the apparently eminent breakup of the relationship, intentionally shot the victim in heat of passion aroused by a bitter argument, and thus such testimony warranted submission of a lesser included offense of first degree manslaughter.

In a murder case tried to a jury, it is preeminently the trial court's duty in the exercise of its discretion to determine what lesser degrees of homicide to submit, and neither the prosecution nor the defense can limit the submission of such lesser degrees as the trial court determines should be submitted. The trial judge has the ultimate responsibility to insure that all essential instructions are given.

The opinion criticized Matt because he should have requested the manslaughter instruction, regardless of whether the defendant wanted it or not. He'd had a duty to his client, they said, to ask for it. The trial judge, however, had the ultimate responsibility of submitting the instruction to the jury. The fact that he hadn't done so required the conviction to be reversed and the defendant granted a new trial. Vince was a free man again.

"Tim's on the phone," Kay said, interrupting Matt's reverie. "He sounds upset and says he only has a second."

"Matt!" Tim hollered when Matt picked up the phone. "He's on his way. He's a fuckin' crazy man!" The line went dead. Matt realized all he could do was wait for the storm to hit.

***

It seemed like mere minutes had passed before Vince came slamming into the office.

"Get outta my way," he snarled as Melanie attempted to intercept him. Matt jumped up to go out and intervene, but before he even made it around his desk, Vince stood before him, his face flushed, the blood vessels in his temples bulging. Matt sat back down and gazed at him, biting his lower lip to keep from grinning. Suddenly Vince slammed his fist down on the desk, sending everything bouncing into disarray.

"Don't tell me that bitch took off with my money!"

Matt said nothing.

"Don't tell me that bitch took my money and took off with that fuckin' weasel, Maxwell!"

Matt had always considered himself a charitable person. Throughout his career as a criminal defense attorney, he had probably dealt with every type of miscreant and every form of human perversion possible. He had never judged people harshly for their human foibles. But as he leaned back, considering the possibilities, he could no longer repress his smile.

ABOUT THE AUTHOR

Daniel Eller graduated from St. John's University in Collegeville, Minnesota, in 1965, and received his law degree from Georgetown University Law Center in 1969. After graduation, he served as law clerk to Federal Judge Miles Lord, Federal District Court for Minnesota. He moved back to St. Cloud, in the fall of 1990, and became District Public Defender in 1977, a position he held until 1990.

As public defender and in his private practice, Eller has tried serious felony cases with state-wide notoriety, including many cases of first-degree murder. He has been recognized by his peers as a Leading Attorney in his field of criminal law and has been selected as a "Super Lawyer" in criminal defense based on research conducted by *Law & Politics.*

Eller continues to practice law in central Minnesota.

By the same Author
Rogues' Gallery
In the Interest of Justice

Watch for these future legal mystery novels
by Daniel Eller

In Search of a Reasonable Doubt
A case of Felony Murder

Breinigsville, PA USA
29 November 2010
250237BV00002B/2/P